Burns yet the candle?

by

Mary Rose Hayfield

Mary Rose Hayfield

I

Published in Great Britain by
Beloved Warwickshire Products

Mary Rose Hayfield,
Maengwyn House,
Maengwyn Street,
Machynlleth,
Powys,
SY20 8EF

ISBN 0 9513501 3 7

Computer set in 11 on 12.5pt
Palatino by
ARIOMA Editorial Services,
Gloucester House, High Street,
BORTH, Dyfed. SY24 5HZ

Printed by
Artist Valley Press,
Birmingham House,
Machynlleth,
Powys,
SY20 8BG

Illustrated by Mary Rose Hayfield.

CHARACTER LIST

BOOK ONE

Janetta
    Captain James

KENT COUNTRYSIDE

Old Jacko

LONDON

Vincent Fallon	Doctor
Michael Brandon	Doctor
Mary Ransome	Housekeeper

BOOK TWO

SECKINGTON PARISH

Seckington Hall
    Lord Ainsley

Lady Isobel Ainsley	His Wife
Jonathon	Eldest Son
David	Second Son
Charlotte	Eldest Daughter
Esme	Youngest Daughter
Jenny Bains	The Maid
William Grave	The Butler

UPPER TELSO VILLAGE

The Park
    Lady Loundes

Elizabeth Loundes	Her Daughter
Mason	The Butler
Mrs.Burns	The Cook
Andrew Tysen	The Gardener
David Oaks	The Stable Boy

Hill Farm
    Tarant Barnes

Marion Barnes	His Wife
Arthur His	Son
Anne His	Daughter

Telso Mill
    Zeb Mysen Miller

Emm Mysen	His crippled Wife

Cross Keys Inn
 George Arms   Innkeeper
 Esther Arms   His Wife
 Daniel   His Son (away at sea)
End Cottage
 James Painter   Lord Ainsley's Groom
 Mathew Painter   His Son (Apprentice to Farrier)
Leanto Cottage
 Evan Sykes   Harness Maker
 Mary-Ann   His Wife

ROCK BOTTOM LANE

Wood Cottage
 Old Albert Dale
 Arthur Dale   Lord Ainsley's Cowman
 Eliza Dale   His Wife
 Ilsa Dale   His Daughter
 Sailor & Simon   Twin Sons
Wychwood Cottage
 John Price   The Farrier
 Betsy   His Sister
Chalfont
 Bernard Bistock
 Jane Bistock   His Wife
 Charles Bistock   Eldest Son
 Rust Bistock   Second Son
 Rachel Bistock   His Daughter

LOWER TELSO VILLAGE

Parsonage
 Rev.Andrew Mallard
 Harriet Mallard   His Wife
 Luke Mallard   His Son
 Maisy Mallard   His Daughter
 Lucy Fulton   Housekeeper
Parson Cottage
 Mabel Dunn   Retired Cook
Churchyard Cottage
 Tom Hart   Sexton
Thatchers Cottage
 Thatcher Gibbs
Glebe Cottage
 George Swift   Lord Ainsley's Shepherds
 Tom Carter
 Jack Acres

IV

Lower Farm House
    Francis Trewis
    Amanda   His Wife
    Ben   First Son
    William   Second Son
    Johnny   Third Son
    Arms   Fourth Son
    Velvet   Daughter
    Hannah   Baby Daughter

LOWER TELSO

Cottage Row
No.1
    John Symes   Ploughman
    Cathy Symes   His Wife
    Peter   His Children
    Kate
    Mary
No.2
    Martin Bones   Estate Worker
    Emmy   His Wife
No.5
    Ben Hastley   Widower
    Flossie   His Daughters
    Pheobe
No.6
    Mother Ross
    Jeannie   Suspected Witches

GYPSY SETTLEMENT

The Romanies
    Black Dyer
    Jewel   His 3rd Wife
    Jason   Eldest Son
    Falcon   Second Son
    Saul   Third Son
    Raven   His Daughter
    Mary   Baby Daughter
Hut in Dumble
    Amos the Poacher

LORD AINSLEY' S KEEPERS

    Keeper Anderson   Head Keeper
    Hendrick   Under Keepers
    Josh Ames
    Davie Heston

V

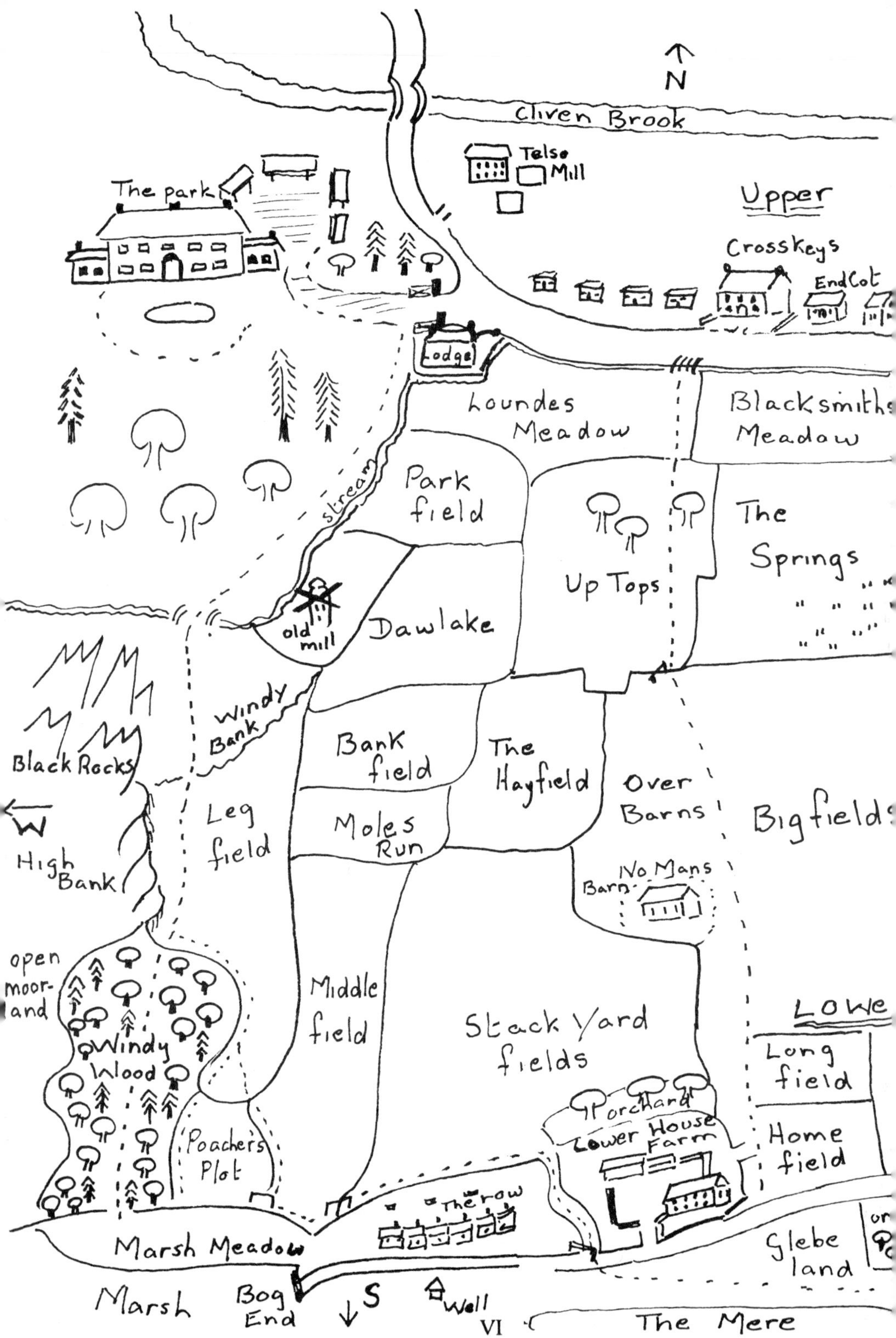

N
Cliven Brook
Telso Mill
Upper
Crosskeys
EndCot
The park
Lodge
Loundes Meadow
Blacksmith Meadow
Park field
stream
The Springs
Up Tops
old mill
Dawlake
Windy Bank
Black Rocks
W
High Bank
Bank field
The Hayfield
Over Barns
Bigfields
Leg field
Moles Run
No Mans Barn
open moor-land
Windy Wood
Middle field
Stack Yard fields
Lowe
Long field
Home field
orchard
Lower House Farm
Poacher's Plot
The row
Glebe land
Marsh Meadow
Marsh
Bog End
S
Well
The Mere

N

To Seckington 1 mile
To Wesper Lane

Chalfont Farm

Cliven Brook

Old Bridge

Telso

Home farm

Hillfarm   Hillfarm Cot

Cliven Brook

Smithy

Chalfont well

Watery Meadows

Fresh water springs

Crab Tree

Seckincham Hall

prings

Pool

Telso Wood

hut

E →

Bigfields

Dumble Wood

Footbridge

Low Wood

stream

stream

TELSO

Cleaners Acre

Wood Cot

Dingle

Rock Bottom Lane

Wych Wood Cot

Wych Wood

Brays Bridge

Church

Parsonage

Quarry Bottom hollow

Open Moor

church Cot

Parsons Cot

Paddock

S

Thatchers Cot

well

Potters

VII

Dole Meadows

Gipsy Camp

Cliven

CONTENTS

Author's Preface

This book is for all those who love the country-side, All those who love village life. My hero, David Ainsley is a Doctor who chose in dangerous times, to use his skills for the country-folk in his own village in the midlands. "Burns Yet the Candle?" is set in the year 1665-6 when death in plague's cloak crept across London and deep into villages all across the country. The villages of Upper and Lower Telso could have been anywhere but the people who lived there are for me the dear, brave, ordinary country-folk who peopled my childhood and girlhood long ago. I would give a special word for the lovely Church of Eyam in Derbyshire and for the long forgotten community there who have become plague's own symbol of selfless courage down the centuries. I wonder did they also follow London's example of setting a lighted candle on the window-sill in every house where plague had struck, to show that there was still life within? In this book I have tried to show that even when great sorrow comes we are upheld by nature's glorious seasons. The snowdrop and the primrose, the woods and fields and moorland, Springtime and Harvest do not fail. In all these things and in every sunrise we are made whole again and can continue to be brave and build our lives anew.

Mary Rose Hayfield

This book is for my Husband Tommy.

BURNS YET THE CANDLE?
BOOK ONE - LONDON
CHAPTER I

BURNS YET THE CANDLE?
BOOK ONE LONDON
CHAPTER I

On the last day of June in the year 1665, the Kent countryside lay quiet and parched in the mist of the early morning sunshine. A man stood upon the rough jetty, his hand shading his eyes to watch the old ship sailing north into the softly shifting mist. Quickly she was lost from his view. The sound of the slight early morning breeze which filled her sails and lapped the boards beneath his feet grew less every moment. He felt bereft. For four long years his world had been between her decks, his companions, her captain and crew. They had crossed vast oceans together, braved storm and tempest, roasted in the hot climes of other lands. Hacked through ice in the arctic waters of the North. And for what? He had asked himself that same question a dozen times during those four years of close confinement. Often he had lacked even the most elementary comforts of life. A hard bunk, shortage of good food and pure water. Sickness and ailments of every kind amongst the crew, and only his own skills to bring them back to health.

Thinking back he recalled how often he had had only the most primitive medicines and remedies at his disposal. Often he had been unsuccessful. Still further back he well remembered how much his family, more particularly his Father, had been set against his going to sea. They had opposed it right from the start. Only his stubborn desire to stand out alone, to prove his manhood, to practice his hard won surgery had spurred him on to defy his Father's wishes.

He had set aside a comfortable secure home. Second son of a peer of the realm. Easy options of a London Practice, bought for him with his Father's wealth. Marriage with Elizabeth - a fine house ..... Elizabeth! How his heart and body had yearned and cried out for Elizabeth during the worst of the black reality of being a ships surgeon. Now at the remembrance of her, his head lifted - he breathed the air deep and turned his back on the sea.

The jetty was but a few boards, whitened with long contact with the salt water. It had until recently fallen into disuse. The rowing boat which two of the crew had used, to ferry him across the shallows from the ship, had scarcely stayed a moment to see him safe landed. He had turned to bid farewell after planting his feet on dry land. The boat had already pushed off. The two oarsmen bent to their rowing, intent upon widening the distance between themselves and the shore, having no backward glance for him. He had shrugged and turned away, well used to the taciturn ways of His Majesty's Navy.

Now he turned his attention to the land before him. England was in the grip of a heat-wave. Here in the flatlands of Kent close to the lower reaches of the Thames, only a few hours after dawn it was already hot. Here there was little to be seen of interest save the marsh grass alive with sea birds, and the great sweep of the Medway far away to his left. A few ancient cottages, no doubt the homes of fisher-folk, broke the uniformity of the flat Kent landscape. A small hill here and there in the distance.

He lifted his leather pack, settling the strap more comfortably upon his shoulders. He then stepped boldly out upon the rough track which Captain James had directed him, South-Westerly towards Rochester. In that town he understood he might take the new regular Stagecoach for London. A tall man, his long legs quickly adjusted to solid ground. He settled into a comfortable easy stride. He was dressed in the fashion of a surgeon of his day. Knee breeches and long hose encased his legs. Stout shoes buckled to his feet. A plain shirt of fine linen and a cravat at his neck. His long coat lay neatly folded in his pack - too warm even at this early hour. Soon he stopped upon a small bridge over one of the many dykes which served as drainage waterways on this flat land. Setting down his pack upon the rough boards he removed and folded his cravat, loosening his shirt for greater freedom and comfort. He took a few sips of wine from his flask resting his arms for a few moments upon the bridge. Then he resettled his burden, long nimble fingers stowing away tidy as was his habit. The skin upon his hands and arms was brown and healthy, as was that upon his face and neck. The even tan lent power to his strong jaw-line, firm lipped mouth and powerful body. His eyes, the most striking feature of his face, were light blue. The lashes short and straight, making dark fringes to the intent alert orbs they sheltered. His dark hair worn with no wig, was cut low about his ears, curling and springing from his narrow head. At nine and twenty in spite of over six years hard training in London, followed by four even harder spent within the confines of an old and worn out ship - he looked strong and fit in health and spirit. When he laughed his mouth softened and revealed strong white teeth. He never indulged himself and took much pride in his healthy body and mental alertness.

David Ainsley was very adaptable by nature. As now, when he quickly began to adjust to his new surroundings. He found the warm scents and summer colours of the countryside exhilarating. Picking up his pack once more he set off again. As he moved further from the sea the grass became a little less burnt up and stunted trees began to appear. In the distance a squat church tower and a cluster of houses came into view. The buildings gradually took form and substance as he came nearer. It was very quiet. He followed the rough road into the hamlet. He saw no one. In an enclosed field nearby two cows grazed placidly. A few fowls pecked and scratched in the dusty street. Half a dozen thatched cottages stood silent beside the track. A door stood wide. A few garments spread to dry upon a hawthorn bush, moved a little in the warm air. Still he could see no one. Perhaps they were at work in the fields. Yet with the country being so flat, it seemed unlikely, since he had seen no one.

Soon he was past the houses and at the church gate. Here he saw his first and only sign of human life in this place. The graveyard was small and enclosed by a low wall. No more than half an acre. At the far end amongst the tombstones he saw a patch of red. He paused at the lych gate. Intently he watched. The red patch moved. He saw it to be a child's gown. She had been kneeling upon the grass - her head deep between her folded arms. She had heard his step. Startled she stood up. Even from here he saw her deep distress. The white tear grubby face, shabby dirt stained clothing, scarcely hiding the thin body and arms. At the sight of him she froze for a moment making no sound. "Good day little miss," he called to her. At the sound of his voice she leapt to activity. Turning away she fled from him and was lost from sight amongst the long grass and memory stones. He looked again where she had been, and found difficulty in believing that his eyes had not played him false. He stood a moment before continuing on his way. He saw nothing else alive in that place and soon came again into open country.

He had hoped to ask in the village for direction to Rochester. Strange to find the place so empty of life. Even in the intense heat, and it was now close on noon, with hot sun and clear blue sky. Surely the farm labourers from the cottages should have been in the fields hereabouts? Their women at their household chores? Their children at play in the lane-way? Perhaps they rested in the mid-day sun, like the Spanish villages in siesta time. His mind turned to his own home village. In Telso and Seckington the farm houses and cottages were always bustling with life and people, about their daily business. How he longed to be back there. He pictured the Midland Shires with their woodlands and undulating fields. Villages with their sprinkling of thatched cottages, streams, copses and ponds. Every stick and stone known and loved since boyhood. Every face, even those belonging to folk he did not like so well, were clear in their very familiarity. Especially now when he felt a little at a loss in this barren area, so empty of people and human contact.

He began to feel weary, best to rest a while until the worst heat of the day was past. A little way ahead lay a small copse of trees, shade and cool grass. Perhaps a small dell where he could sleep without danger of robbery. Always a risk upon these unfrequented tracks. He soon found a place to suit him. No stream to refresh him, but several great oaks with mossy grass beneath. The area surrounded by hawthorn and wild rose thickets. Two hundred paces away from the highway, he felt safe in this small sanctuary.

He threw himself down and made a simple meal of wheaten bread and a wedge of cheese from his pack, washed down by a drink of wine from his flask. He made a pillow of his pack and settled down upon the dry mossy grass. Soon he drifted into deep sleep.

When he woke the sun was sinking in the west, a wide clear sky and no wind. Every sign of the warm weather continuing. He gathered his things together and after relieving himself in the privacy of the copse, once more took to the road. From the sun's course he was heading due west. Perhaps not the route for Rochester. He might well pass by the town and not come in sight of its Coaching Inn. Much refreshed after his sleep, this did not worry him. He was not expected at home on any specific date.

He would take his time to London, rest there a few days, renew old friendships at his old hospital and take the coach up Watling Street for the Midlands. There was plenty of time. He must learn to relax and forget the constant press and movement of life within a ship.

He occupied his mind with thoughts of Elizabeth - dear, beautiful, Elizabeth. They had written little over the four year period of his absence, yet he felt as deep in love with her as ever, her slight aloof dark beauty of face and body had sustained him in every dark place. Thinking of her now, he imagined their reunion. Holding her again in his arms, the warmth of her kiss, to see her every day and soon make her his wife. He planned to settle in Telso or Seckington and look after the health of both rich and poor alike. There was no surgeon within miles since the old doctor had died a year since. This he had heard from his Father's long informative letters. He had not come home empty handed. Surgeons in His Majesty's Navy were not well paid but his needs on board ship had been small. Over the years he had saved four leather bags of gold coins and carried them stitched deep in the lining of his coat. It was comforting thinking that, and the air now cooler, his stride lengthened and he covered many miles without fatigue.

Here was rough land, unfenced and open but more trees than before. A good place for a man to sleep in the open. A sense of adventure entered him, much nicer the pure air after the confines of the ship, than some perhaps unsavoury country Inn. As it grew dusk he again left the track and taking the downward lie of the land, he found a small stream's beginning. It was no more than a pool in the rocks amongst the heather. Two springs bubbled up from deep in the earth, icy cold and pure. He drank deep and splashed his hands and face. He ate again from his pack, but knew his rations ran low. Tomorrow he must find habitation, discover his whereabouts and make for London.

He settled in the heather, lying back to gaze at the wide sky; dark blue now and stars beginning to twinkle, the sky seemed to hold a kind of warmth, so different from the overhead sea skies which had been his experience at night time for so long. It had to do with the uneven line of horizon, also perhaps with the scent of the gorse and heather plants, and the night-time noises of small

7

animals in the undergrowth about him. An owl flew muffle-winged over his head, his eyes closed and he relaxed into peaceful sleep.

He woke at dawn to mist and cool air about him, the sun had not yet risen. He stretched himself and shifted his limbs. Feeling travel stained and sweaty he reached for a clean shirt from his pack. He stripped and washed himself down in the icy spring - gasping at the impact of the cold water. He carried no towel, so dried off with his soiled shirt, hanging it to dry upon a bush of heather afterwards.

The only food he had left was a thick slice of wheaten bread and a slice of salt pork which the ship's cook had wrapped for him in a shred of muslin. The bread had grown stale and the meat salty, nonetheless it tasted very good but left him with a great thirst, he drank water from the spring again to spare the last of his wine for later in the day.

Sun-up found him again on the road - still only a rough track and no sign of a village or township. He set course still to the west, sure in his own mind that he had by-passed Rochester and was headed for London. Somewhere on the right the Thames must be. He pondered as to why Captain James had not made port for Tilbury or Gravesend as had been their usual practice in times past. The Captain had steadfastly refused to sail up the Thames making the excuse that his cargo would sell better up north prior to taking the vessel in for extensive repairs and refitting. Ainsley knew the latter to be true but was certain better prices would have been obtained for her cargo on the London river. It mattered not. He should reach London within a day or so - he might pick up a ship on the Thames and pay his way up river to the city. Time would prove. The sun shone. Life was good in his new freedom.

It was close on mid-day when he sighted another village, he still had no glimpse of the Thames, no scent of the never to be forgotten smell. A few seagulls mewed overhead, that was the only reminder of the sea. The village lay below the road, a string of single story thatched cottages, with a church spire at the centre. One large house he saw close by the churchyard, probably the parson's house. A grass path ran down to the nearest cottage, close cropped by sheep, which were to be seen grazing the common land round about the village.

The bracken brushed his breeches as he passed by. Amongst the hot grass a small snake basked in the sun. The first cottage was built of wattle and daub on a simple rosy brick base beneath a worn grass grown thatch. As he reached it four or five geese waddled into view, hissing at the sight of a stranger. He rounded the corner of the cottage wall and came into the village street. Peaceful and quiet in the hot sunshine. Two great chestnut trees grew together upon the small triangle of grass near the church, twenty paces beyond the cottages. Beyond again, another handful of humble houses strung along the roadside.

He at once saw two people, one a man, sat upon a seat beneath the chestnut trees, the other was a woman, in a simple country-made blue gown, she was walking away from him up the lane. She wore a white sunbonnet and carried a basket on her arm. The man intent upon watching the woman's progress did not notice David Ainsley's approach. Ainsley noticed that they did not speak to one another, and sensing something unusual in this, in so small a community, paused in his stride. He stood still watching the scene before him, enjoying the pretty picture of rural life that it made.

Suddenly the woman seemed to stumble and fall, when she did not rise or make any movement or struggle to get up, David frowned sharply. The man on the seat so close by, made no effort to go to her help. Indeed he seemed to draw back even while keeping his eyes upon her. For a few seconds all was still, only the fruit and eggs from her basket made movement as they rolled in all directions. David found his voice "Is she hurt? May I be of help? I am a surgeon," he could not keep the rebuke out of his voice, directed as it was at the man still seated beneath the trees.

By this time Ainsley had reached the woman and knelt down in the dust beside her, she lay as if dead, her limbs twisted and muddled beneath her. Her bonnet had fallen back, dustied and soiled, revealed a woman of about thirty years with the roughened hands of a working woman. Her boots were worn almost to holes beneath her feet. He turned her over gently, straightening her limbs, he bent and listened at her chest and mouth but could find no sign of life, yet he saw no superficial signs of injury. His Doctor's concentration and inquiry were in his fingertips and keen eyes, he half-turned glancing towards the seat beneath the chestnut trees.

"Here, give a hand, help me get her into her house, where are her family? Is there no friend to help?" His sharp questions were wasted, there was no one on the seat! His angry eyes scanned the small green with its trees and bushes, only the geese could be seen where they had settled upon the sunlit bank, wings spread to catch the heat. Another sound came from behind him, he turned, from the farthest cottage an old black-clad woman and a strong looking rough dressed youth of perhaps seventeen years came forth. They moved slowly, reluctantly towards him saying nothing. "Be dammed to Hell! What is this?" he muttered to himself. They came up to him and stared down at the woman. "Is she your kin? Help me to lift her within - I may be able to help her, I'm a surgeon, can we get her to a bed or couch?" Slowly the two pairs of eyes lifted to his and he saw fear upon their faces for the first time. In the boy it was manifest in the beads of sweat on his brow and the pallor of his cheeks, in the old woman it showed in her trembling lips, hands and body, it was she who spoke.

"Let un bide there, us'll see her right. Mind your own business and let'un us mind our'n." Rough, grating and obstinate her voice came. He was just about to argue with her when the boy settled it quickly. "I'll get 'er," he muttered and suiting action to words, he bent and lifted her in his strong arms and carried her sack fashion, arms falling doll-like, skirts awry, towards the gate. David made to open it for him but the old woman was too quick, half pushing him aside she pressed the young man forward up the short path and over the step. David followed behind intending to go in after her, instead the door was slammed shut in his face and he heard the bolt thrust home. He stood incredulous for a moment, a wooden shutter was slid across inside the window and through it's crack came the harsh voice, "Get you gone, Zur - nowt for you here - we mun care for our own, you means well but us knows best. These times 'tis best you gets along your own ways." She said no more and he heard no further sound from within. He turned and looked up and down the sunlit street, nothing moved, every cottage quiet, every door closed. Had they all been closed so throughout? He could

10

not be sure, his attention had been upon the woman lying on the ground, but he thought not. His earlier impression had been of doors open to the sunshine.

Reluctantly he moved away latching the small wicket behind him, he shrugged in troubled incomprehension, his dark brows drawn together. Best leave it. He was fairly certain the woman had been dead - a sudden heart attack in the heat perhaps. It could easily be near 90º in this low lying valley with the sun blazing down. He moved away down the street adjusting the strap of his pack and setting his sights upon the road ahead. There was no Inn to replenish his rations. Well he'd had enough of this inhospitable place. He did not look back, the incident gave him angry energy and he made no pause until he had put six miles of rough country between himself and that strange village.

As he came over a rocky wooded bluff of hill land, he saw a small farm over to his right; there was a rough track leading to it between high hawthorn hedges. Perhaps here he could ask for water and a pitcher of milk and a fresh loaf, even a meal might be forthcoming, if he offered to pay well. His step quickened and he soon came into a grassy forecourt in front of a small white farmstead. A byre stood at right angles and a low wall completed the making of a neat tidy little place. He could hear hens cackling in the stockyard where a haystack and straw pile were bleached white in the sun. In the corner of the forecourt was a well with a thatched roof above, a winding device and bucket looked to be in daily use. A small damp area where someone had recently filled the bucket steamed a little as the hot sunshine dried the smooth stones. He went to the farmhouse door and knocked, looking round the yard while he waited. No one came, another deserted place?

All England it seemed was unwelcoming to the weary traveller, at least here he could wash and replenish his flask. He moved across to the well and bent his back to wind the windlass, watching the bucket dropping down into the darkness. He heard the splash as it reached water level, and began to rotate the handle back; he reached out to steady the bucket.

"Don' 'ee drink that, Zur. Foul that there may be. All dead they is! Nine we was 'ere only days back, only me left, Zur!" It was a very old man's voice. David turned and saw a nut brown

11

wizened face over the rickyard wall, the ruffled white hair stuck out above the face which was crumpled with suffering and tears. A short built little man, his head and shoulders leaning over the wall pushing towards Ainsley as if to emphasise his words. "My three sons, my old wifey, two daughters by law, and the two babbies," the old voice shook and tears rolled down onto the rheumaticky work worn hands from the unshaven chin. Ainsley was moved at once to pity.

"My friend tell me. You mean all your family dead? An accident? Has something poisoned them? I grieve for you. Is there anything I can do? I'm a surgeon you understand just passing by on the way to London. Recently finished my term of service in His Majesty's Navy. On my way home to my family in the Midlands. I came to ask for food and drink and maybe a night's lodging. Also to get direction for London." He spoke slowly and quietly hoping by his company and gentle manner to soothe the distraught old man. In some measure he was successful, the man answered him more calmly.

"Nay, Zur, 'tis wors'en that, tis the plague bin here, come down the big river it has, run through these villages like fire in the corn it have, reapin' all in front of it. Just a happy little family we was, then young Ben - my son he was - went with pigs to market. Comes back right as could be - then dead in a day. Struck down with shivering and shaking, them 'Tokens' came all over his back. Us couldn't credit. Then one of the babes was taken along o' his Mam. After that the others. The pain and the sickness and crying out in the night, and then no help, no one comes near. In all they villages 'tis the same, Zur. No one dare help his neighbour, no one dares touch another's clothing or go in his house. Don't drink the water here, Zur, all dead they are, all my dear ones gone. In the orchard they lie," He paused and pointed a shaking finger across the stockyard. "My son, he buried the first uns, then he was took and I've had a struggle since then. No one to tek they to the Churchyard you sees. Three mile that be - no one to fetch they home to God's acre. Mind they do be together - and all done decent as I could. Don't know who'll see to me, can't fairly understand why I been let linger, an I don't feel bad. Just the lonely you know, can't rightly settle to tend the farm, none to share you see." The quavering voice faded and weak tears coursed down the wrinkled cheeks again, unheeded, the old fingers clung to the wall. "You best go your ways, Zur, 'tisn't your troubles. Don'ee take'n risk for me - you've your own folk to see right, get you home to them - that's my advice." His voice shook and lapsed. Ainsley smiled at him kindly. "I'm not afraid of illness my friend - I've spent eleven years with sickness and suffering, made it my life's work you might say. Perhaps I can help you more than you know, and perhaps you can help me too. Let us face matters quietly, there's no need for me to come in the house if you prefer not. I shall be glad of a night's rest in the hay, the water as you say, best left. I have seen Plague in Italy and other places - always it attacks suddenly, violently and with terrible suffering. None know its beginnings but in my own mind I incline towards prevention being clean air and keeping away from enclosed places and gatherings of people. Milk is good and eggs. Fresh food, keep out doors. Plenty of rest and sleep." Even as he spoke he knew the hollow emptiness of his words. What was left for this poor old man to survive for? Looking beyond him across the stockyard he could see the fresh turned earth beneath the apple trees. It took little imagination to visualise this frail old man struggling to carry his dead, probably just wrapped in worn sheeting to bury them together in that unhallowed plot. Every day expecting to die himself, and now it seemed that only fear and utter loneliness were left to him.

"Do you have a cow in milk?" Ainsley asked the simple question to draw the old man's mind away from his grief.

"Aye she be over yonder, back of the house. I've been caring for she all along - company like, she have plenty of milk just now."

"And wine - do you have any wine? Safer than water these times, keep to wine, let the well alone for a while. How long since the last of your family died?" Ainsley asked the old man. The lined brow wrinkled even more in confusion, a muddled look settling on his face. "Eight days - nine perhaps, I bin a bit flustered since - not rightly noticing the days and nights passing."

"No matter - but mark it each day that passes now. It's my belief that plague clears in twenty-eight days. Keep your food as clean as you can. Bake fresh bread and throw out all that lies about. Lay a cloth tight about the bread and lift it away from flies and vermin. Open the house windows - all of them. Keep in the fields as much as you can. That's my advice as a physician. When this is over, others will survive as well as you perhaps. Then you must all build your lives again. There will be many left alone like you."

In his minds eye Ainsley saw again the thin little girl in the lonely village churchyard. The old woman and the young man in that other hamlet who had refused him entry to their house. Lifting their own dead and by that very contact putting their own lives at risk.

What of Captain James? Sly old fox that. He must surely have known of the plague epidemic. If it ran wild in London as the old man said, then the Thames would be shunned by every sea captain from Lands End to John O'Groats. He remembered the two sailors rowing, not making any farewell, unable to meet his eyes. All explained now. What a fool he had been - and a Doctor at that! Well all life was a risk in his calling. He would stay a day or two and try to help this poor old man, and at the same time be resting himself.

Then on to London as planned - find his friends and former colleagues and see how they fared.

The old man was slowly digesting his words; after a few minutes he spoke, "There's fresh grain in the earthen jars in the pantry, they'm got lids on top, and we've a small hand grinder. Her's hard graft to work, us usually teks grain to Myton Mill to grind he down. But then - I dare say the hand one'll do for now. There's some kegs of elderflower in the back. Us made un last year. Never's got drunk - bit tart it is on the tongue."

"That's splendid, you fetch some out and bring your pail to get milk. I'll see if there's any eggs - I heard your hens just now. Then you must see if you can grind more flour and bake a loaf or two of fresh bread. I'll leave the windows for you to open the shutters." David's kind smiling face cheered the old man's heart. He went into the house and a few minutes later appeared at an upstairs window as he folded back the shutters. That night, when the heat of the day was past, and the blessed cool of the starlit summer night sky hung over the farm, both men slept outside. David on the open haystack and the old man on the straw.

The moon was at her half and hung in a cloudless sky. By her light Ainsley could see the outline of the house. Windows and doors now wide to the clean air. They had drunk the sharp elder wine and eaten the somewhat solid bread that the old man had managed to bake. Together with fresh eggs and milk they had not fared too badly.

David lay back relaxed thinking of his home in the pure air of the Midland farmlands. It seemed a long way off. London lay like a great black menacing waste a few miles away across the Thames. Who knew what dangers must be faced before he might hope to see his family and Elizabeth again? Sufficient unto the day, he decided, was sound sense enough.

The old man and the surgeon spent two more days together and their companionship grew in warmth and understanding. David watched over old Jacko as though he were a patient. He saw the colour come back to the frail cheeks, noted the improvement in his appetite. Saw the renewal of his ability to think and plan the work of the small farm single-handed. It was an awakening from his grief.

David himself kept out of doors and in fact never went in the house at all. Nonetheless there were many ways in which he was able to help. He chopped wood for the coming winter, and in so doing gave the old man faith in the hope that he would live to see it burning upon the farmhouse hearth. In the sad orchard graveyard they added many barrows of soil to the shallow graves and laid fresh cut turf above each plot. He made a rough lettered cross to mark the place. The old man did not know his letters nor could he write his name. To him the rough cross with the year and the month of June upon it was a fine memorial to his family. He would fence round the plot after Ainsley had gone on his way. Perhaps the best thing David did for him was to write a note to his nephew John who lived twenty miles away at Northfleet. In the letter he explained the old man's plight and asked that if the plague should spare John and his widowed mother, they should come later on and live with old Jacko at the farm and take a share with him in its profits.

It was with this letter in his pocket, and having given the old man his promise to see it safely delivered, that David went on his way. Jacko had directed him to a track which led across country to the Thames. An old road used by the drovers and very few others. An unfrequented tree-lined lane it proved to be a good route. He came to no more villages and saw no one except shepherds and sheep on the partly enclosed land.

Before sundown he reached Northfleet and the river. First he sought out the old man's nephew. He found the cottage easily enough. It stood a little apart from the rest. At the window he saw a woman of middle age shaking her duster. He called to her from outside the gate. Without going inside he explained his mission and drew the note from his breeches pocket.

"All dead you say, saving old Jacko. Dear God, 'tis as bad as they tell then. We've none here - no plague that is. T'aint sense and us by the river. Runs with the water, they set store by that. Yet we'm here and well and all they bin taken. I thank you in coming. D'you go backways past Jacko's? Could 'ee tek him word? We got nothing here now. My man being dead these three years. We'd like fine to share un with Jacko. Our John's down at the boats. Helps he do down there for a shilling or two most days. But a farm! He'd surely love that."

Ainsley explained that he was for London - up the river himself and could not take a message back to the farm. "Leave it a bit," he suggested. "Plague's an uncertain devil, Mistress. Send word when you can, but stay here, your brother is best to bide alone for a time. Until the infection clears away. Maybe after the winter would be prudent. He's well enough. I've given him all the good advice I know. I've been a surgeon these long years and I'm hoping he'll come through. If so I expect he'll bring the pony and trap for you come spring-time."

She seemed satisfied with this and after taking his leave, he turned about and made his way along the street towards the river. Soon the Thames lay wide before him. He had never seen it so empty of craft. Two boats both barges stood at the jetty. On one a bustle of activity, as she made ready for off down stream. Her load of timber stacked on the small quayside, five or six of her crew busied themselves with her ropes. The other boat was larger and was of more interest to Ainsley. Her shabby decks were deserted save for the Captain, his peaked cap was pulled well down and the full black beard hid most of the rest of his face. He smoked a pipe, leaning on the rail and sending the smoke in a rising blue cloud which dispersed the myriads of gnats which swarmed above the water. He too was watching the men at work on the other vessel.

"A word if you please" Ainsley called across the jetty.

"Good evening stranger," the Captain swung round to rest inquiring dark eyes upon Ainsley's somewhat travel-stained person. He looked questioning but pleasant enough in spite of his somewhat intimidating bearded burliness.

Ainsley did not beat about the bush, "Are you going up river? I'm bound for London," he asked.

"Aye but I'll not take any stranger passengers - 'tis too dangerous these times. No plague here but yon devil's every where else. Not safe to harbour unknowns - Got my crew and my living to see after you understand." His answer was slow spoken but had a firm finality to it.

"I've no plague about me - I'm only off the water three days myself. I've been ship's surgeon on the *Janetta* these last four years. Just taken my ticket and making way back to my own people in the Midshires. I'm to settle in my own parishes as district surgeon," Ainsley explained quickly.

"I mean no offence; but 'tis the danger. None know how the Black Evil passes and none can say if she be hid secret in his coat. Crept in while the wearer sleeps often as not." Yet he seemed to waver a little to another sea-faring man.

Ainsley produced his trump card, "I've a golden guinea to settle the score and my own victuals and wine in my pack. When do you shove off? I only ask deck space to London. Drop me off where you will. Do you berth near the city?"

"Wait on the quay then, board when the tide turns and stay aft, above deck. We'm not intent on awkward inhospitality you'm understand, everyone likes to take care when times are so bad."

Ainsley thanked him and finding an old rowing boat upturned settled down to wait. It was two hours before the tide turned during which time he saw with pleasure that the local people seemed to be about their ordinary business and quite a number of people near the river bank. It was long past dusk and the sky had grown quite dark before the rising water freed them and the old boat began to creak her way up river. A crew of six or seven men had come on board from various parts of the

17

village, mostly young lads, rough dressed and strong looking. None came near Ainsley or attempted to speak with him. Each went below to stow his bag and then went about his business on the deck preparing for full tide.

Just before the ship moved away a young girl came running bare foot onto the jetty, her long dark hair was tied back with a loose ribbon, her puffed pink gown was worn but clean and neat mended, she stood in the half light close to the water looking round sharply for the Captain. He was below. She leant forward pushing her small neat head out towards the ship's side.

"Davey - Davey! Are you there?" It came as a low whisper.

"Kate - oh, Katy, you'll get me shot yet, you kelpie!". A fair faced curly haired lad came from loosening a rope. He sprang easily over the side, nimbly swarming down a rope still held fast. He took her hand and they moved into the shadows to embrace. Ainsley felt his own body stir - almost a pain sprang from his loins moving through him up into his chest which became so tight as to make him breathless. Elizabeth! Where he wondered was Elizabeth just at this moment? He turned away from the lovers his eyelids pricking. In a moment the feeling passed. The young man jumped back on deck, meeting his eyes for the first time with a merry grin.

The girl remained on the jetty to watch until they were under way, by which time Ainsley had settled himself on the deck out of the way of the crew. The girl looked forlorn as she watched the boat until it was lost in the darkness. The young man went about his work and never gave her another glance. Ainsley slept on the deck that night. He slept deep, the hard planks worried him not at all. His pack was his pillow, the air was very warm and under the boat the Thames tide ebbed and flowed in constant movement. A familiar rocking which he had unconsciously missed during the last few nights upon dry land. He woke to sun-up and found a bustle going on about him. He heard shouting and the raised roar of the Captain's voice.

"You board us at your own peril I tell you. Sickness is here! - Bad sickness!"

"We've heard that bloody fob off before Captain. We're after three young uns or two and one older. We're not two bloody particular you see. We shall leave you enough to crew you up river. Kings' Navy grows short handed. Black Death and the Dutch Fleet wipes 'em out as fast as we catches 'em. Can't be too particular". A harsh young voice this, Ainsley stood up to see the speaker. They were mid-river and over the ships side a small naval vessel bobbed in the water. Two sailors in the King's uniform were in her and two more, one obviously her Master, were just coming over the side. The barge Captain met them squarely, obviously furious. Both men carried a musket. The foremost brandished his weapon threateningly in the Captain's face. Both weapons were of the new navy issue of wheel-lock type Ainsley noted. His eyes narrowed keenly as he watched the outcome of the encounter; these were the dreaded Press Gang men who plundered every village and vessel for young and older men to be trussed up and then thrown into the hold of any of the King's ships in the area. Once far out to sea the unlucky captives would be sworn into the Navy to serve their time in the reluctant service of their King. Recent skirmishes with the Dutch had left the Navy short of recruits. The barge Captain stood firm and silent "There's a likely man - who's he - he'll do us for a start." The young officer glared at Ainsley over the Captain's broad shoulder. Ainsley drew his belt tight about his breeches pretending no interest - his eyes measuring the distance to his pack in which the knife he always carried lay gleaming and sharp.

"A landlubber and past your age in interest, he's only a by-day passenger. You're foolish to dally my young friend. Step you along the deck - there's a sight to prove my words." He drew back to make way for the officer. They both pushed past and strode along the deck swaggering a little in their braided uniforms and holding their weapons at the ready. Ainsley followed after first getting his knife and slipping it into the top of his breeches.

The small party moved forward and there to David's amazement an unexpected sight met their eyes: on the deck lay three white sheeted oblong bundles. Still and grim they lay in the early morning light. The outline of arms, legs and body showed through each roughly made shroud. Each face was close covered but between the loose stitches Ainsley's observant eyes caught the gleam of fair curls. The boy of last evening? He raised startled eyes to the Captain's, but the dark eyes met his in subtle warning, only the faintest gleam of amusement therein.

"By God 'tis the Death then!" Alarm registered in the young officer's tone. He backed off so quickly that he almost overthrew his partner in crime. A moment later he was tilting a tight-breeched leg over the side and catching the rope to slide inelegantly back into his own boat. His fellow officer was close on his heels, their craft made off down river without more ado.

"Aren't you even stopping for a glass, young sir?" the Captain shouted after them, but he was hard put to it to keep a great burst of laughter within his beard. There was no reply. All four Navy men had been in too much haste to cast off and make away down river.

"All well, lads - rise and shine," the Captain called softly. To Ainsley's amusement all three shrouded corpses at once stood up and pushed out their heads from the white linen. Three broad grins, turned to bursts of laughter from all parts of the deck as the rest of the crew emerged to join in the general merriment. "A good ploy, eh surgeon?" The Captain chuckled into his beard. "Now lads, get your breakfasts and be about the days work, and bring you a brace of eggs and a dish of pork slice up deck for our passenger - lest he fall dead of starvation - or Plague perhaps!

Ainsley made a good breakfast and felt much at home upon the old barge. Later that day it was with some reluctance that he took leave of the crew and went ashore onto the grassy meadows - now dried up in the heat-wave - just a mile short of the city of London.

CHAPTER II

CHAPTER II

It was evening when Ainsley reached the gates of St. Bartholomew's Hospital. Here he had come to be trained as a Doctor nearly eleven years before. Here he hoped to trace a few old friends. His walk across London had shocked him beyond belief. He found it impossible to associate this city of hot sun, blue sky, abominable stench and deathly quiet with the friendly active town he remembered.

In those happy times the square mile of the city, held within its walls so much to excite and interest a young man, newly up from the country. At night-times he remembered the cheerful noisy-voiced Watchman carrying his dim horn lantern as he walked the streets calling each passing hour. Then at first light he and his room-mate would often lie in bed in the little mews lodging house listening to London's waking. The Criers would be about at sunrise on every street calling their wares. Offering goods, milk, cream, fresh eggs and fish and every kind of provisions for the day's first repast.

At six o'clock shutters would clatter down along every street as the apprentices started their days work. Their shouted appeals to everyone who passed by had been a special feature of the city's vibrant life. "What d'ye lack?" "What d'ye lack?" the cry that had rung out along London's streets for hundreds of years past. Soon every thoroughfare would be thronged with lively vendors of all kinds. Fat country farmers' wives in spotless bonnets and aprons set down their great baskets of fresh farm produce on every street corner. They sat all day upon three-legged milk stools to sell their wares, joking the while with every customer. Odd job seekers ready to chop kindling, heave coal, mend shoes or sweep out an alleyway yelled themselves hoarse in their willingness to please. As now there had been no carriages or wheel traffic. None was needed when every housewife could carry her own basket upon her arm and wander at will to pick her fish and fruit, taste the cheeses and sample the items of her choice. Bunches of herbs, sweet lavender to slip amongst her gowns and linen. Thyme and Sage to flavour her meats. And all very cheap. Ainsley recalled oranges at a half-penny, fruit crops in abundance. A great loaf of fresh baked Wheaton bread hot from the oven for a penny piece.

Where was this London now? The press of happy joyful, noisy, quarrelsome, drunken people. Ladies of quality in beautiful gowns. Cooks and servants, sailors and travellers, jostling and pushing, thieving, and hissing, punching and brawling, as they had in 1661. Was it but four years? Today the streets stood silent. Refuse everywhere, foul dirt and stench in every alley. Some so filled with rubbish and dirt that they had been closed off. Houses boarded, the doors marked with the scarlet cross of Plague and written beneath 'Lord have mercy on us'. Men outside standing guard, grim faced and often drunken as they leaned against the doors. People shut within, doors and windows shut and nailed up fast. Children's white faces pressed against the glass gazing longingly out, in their faces utter bewilderment and fear. Sometimes a cry from within had rent through the shutters as he had passed by. So many, locked houses, their doors so marked, had he passed as he made his way across town, as to be countless.

He had seen hardly a human soul in the streets. Any he did see turned away. All who could, passed on the other side. None spoke. Fear was in every face, hurrying, scuttling away from contact with another human being. It had been a nightmare walk - only once had he stopped. Seeing a notice nailed at a street corner he had paused to read it in the fading light. A Bill of Mortality, that had been the caption and the previous day's date. Below long lists of names. Perhaps two hundred or more. His mind had closed on the thought. How often did these Bills come to the public's notice? Surely things could not be as desperate as they seemed. He remembered the bearded Barge Master's last advice to him, "Get straight to the hospital, touch no one, eat nothing, buy nothing! Reach your friends at the hospital, they will know, they will advise you. Enter no place until you reach St. Bartholomew's, keep from the St. Giles area at whatever cost, there is the most deep rooted seat of the pestilence, like flies they die there - this is what I hear - but the hospital will know better than I. God travel with you my friend and keep you safe in his hand!"

They had parted from each other without having touched hands or stood within a yard of each other. He was glad to find himself outside the hospital doors. As he entered the reception area he was at once stopped by a burly uniformed figure.

"No one in here, Sir - not without permit - Do you hold a paper, Sir? I can't let you pass unless."

"I'm a Doctor, my name is David Ainsley, I'm just home today from a stint in the King's Service - four years I've been a surgeon in the Navy. I knew nothing of London's plight until today. I'm seeking a friend, a Doctor who I believe to be here. His name is Fallon - Dr. Vincent Fallon?"

The man's face warmed at once to a smile, "Oh yes, Sir, everyone knows Dr. Fallon - he's one of the rare few - not many left like him. But he's not here - not at the hospital. He has a surgery in St. Giles. Very bad it's been there. I expect you know?" he looked enquiringly at Ainsley.

"I had heard something. But can you give me directions? I can surely find the way? Ainsley was tired now - it had been a long hot day. He longed for food and rest. Perhaps a little impatience was in his voice.

"Well Sir, it's not safe for you to make your way there in the dark. It's almost dark now and when the night comes the searchers and bearers are on the streets - those who must lift out the corpses, Sir - the risk then is far greater than in the daytime. The carts come to carry the dead. The rule is all to be buried in the hours of darkness. Often mistakes are made. The Watchmen who hold the keys to the locked houses are often drunk, they become cruel and offensive. Be guided by me, Sir, don't go on foot to St. Giles tonight. Let me find you a lodging. Wait a few minutes while I speak with the surgeon on duty." He paused, concern and inquiry in his eyes.

"Very well." Ainsley felt weary and unable to argue. The man left him for a few minutes, he looked round the once familiar hall and found its memories like some faded dream of long ago. Almost as though his time here belonged to another life. He turned at the sound of a voice.

"I bid you good evening." A short well built man in neat cravat, spotless white shirt, breeches and highly polished well fitting shoes, stood smiling at him. Ainsley was suddenly conscious of the pack on his back - his soiled appearance and travel stained clothes. He explained his presence all over again.

"London is not a safe place for the prudent traveller. I advise you to leave as soon as daylight comes. Seek out your friend upon another occasion. Go home to the Midshires, to the pure country air. All those with wealth enough to do so are long gone. Save for a few brave men. The King and all his court are all gone into the country in the first week of June, and wagon loads have followed since. None remain who need not. London surely is not a yoke you need carry my friend? I can give you host here tonight. It is not great comfort but a bed and a meal - to which you are very welcome."

Ainsley had been listening carefully. "I am not in fear of the pestilence. I am a surgeon - it's my work, just as it is yours - you are still in London - you have not fled, nor I understand has Vincent Fallon. May I accept your kind hospitality and sleep tonight upon our conversation. I am exceeding weary and it grows late for decisions."

"Of course. Come this way; my rooms are in the medics' building just along the street".

"I don't want to put you at risk. Who can say that they are free of infection?"

The other smiled wryly, "I too am a Doctor, we are all at risk, are we not?" They walked down the street together. Shortly afterwards Ainsley knew the comfort of warm water, soap and towels. He also had the loan of a clean set of clothes. He felt much refreshed when he took his seat at a table with a white cloth. He dined with his host and they enjoyed hot soup, cold meats with new baked bread and butter and several glasses of good red sack.

David learned that his host's name was Michael Brandon and that he had been at St. Bartholomew's for seven years. They talked for an hour or more and Ainsley learnt a great deal about Plague ridden London. The Bills of Mortality, such as he had seen posted up, were published every week and figures of two hundred and more were becoming common-place in some of the worst hit areas. The actual enormity of the total number of deaths was beyond estimation but Michael Brandon was certain that if the heat-wave continued the epidemic had by no means reached its peak. It made depressing hearing.

It was late when Ainsley excused himself and went to his

bed. He woke next morning much refreshed in body and mind. The sun shone in through the window of the small room with its plain furnishings and narrow bed. He lay a few minutes before getting out of bed. A sudden remembrance of Elizabeth's loveliness came into his mind. He was conscious of his healthy body, of its need and of his deep close love for her. Vivid came pictures of his home. His Mother's garden and the smell of the lavender which flourished in the border by the house. The fields at hay-time, golden with buttercups and cowslips. Meadowsweet thick as whipped cream about his bare thighs when as a small boy he had played and romped in and out of the Cliven Brook in summertime. He sat up shaking his head and shoulders in a physical effort to throw off the undermining and persuasive quality of those honey-sweet thoughts. Deep within himself he already knew beyond doubt that he had decided to offer his help for an unspecified period to Vincent Fallon in St. Giles Parish. Half of him longed to leave the hot dusty pestilence ridden city behind him, and set out at the earliest possible moment for the Midshires and home. The other half lay deep in his medical training, trapped in the ability he knew he possessed to help the sick. Here also were a series of clear pictures. A little red-dressed girl alone in a Kent Churchyard. The wizened dried up crust of an old man, Jacko, struggling to bury his dead. The young lad gathering in his arms and carrying indoors the infection ridden body of the woman who had fallen in the village street. Someone must stay. Why not he?

In the night he had twice heard the rattling wheels of the noisy dead cart in the street below. The hollow thump of wooden staves upon the doors. The harsh uncaring voices with the merciless shout, "Bring out your dead! Bring 'em out!". In the summer sun of this bright morning it seemed a far distance to nightfall. Yet every hour another night crept closer. Every night to those people shut in their over-heated, airless, stinking houses. Trapped amongst the sick, the dying, and the dead. Themselves waiting for death. Every night followed by another just as dreadful, and another beyond that again. Forty nights shut in by law! By rule of the King! By rule of his ministers! By rule of his Aldermen! A King fled to the country. A government set up in Hampton Court or Oxford or wherever plague did not live and breed and multiply. No one to help the poor! A handful of the brave to fight for those still alive. To strive for the dying. To make way for the dead into the grave.

Ainsley had never felt himself to be a brave man. In truth he had never thought of it at all. It was no more in his mind than that someone must stay. Michael Brandon had stayed - Vincent Fallon had stayed. He himself must stay. He was free to stay. His baggage, the bulk of it, he had sent home several months back - before his last voyage. Hence his present shortage of clothing. His parents knew his intention was to leave the sea. They knew nothing as to dates when they might expect him home. They would know no anxiety on his behalf so long as they didn't know he was in London.

In a month, perhaps less, the plague would reach and pass it's peak. Then he would no longer be needed here. If he left now he would count it a mark against himself all his life. As a free agent - unmarried! Elizabeth! God forgive me! This was a job for the unmarried men, if ever there was such employment. Settled then. Now to dress and find his host. He washed, shaved himself and dressed in the borrowed garments and went down to break his fast with Michael Brandon.

Seated at table he told of his decision. Michael Brandon showed no surprise when he learned that David intended to stay in London. "In my own case also, it was decided more or less of its own - I think the conscience dictates very strong in some of our profession. That's if it lives in a man at all!" He gave a short somewhat bitter laugh.

In daylight Ainsley found his host a striking man, short in stature, his head was crowned by a shock of unruly red hair. Beneath it very bushy eyebrows hovered over reddish brown eyes. These eyes were deceptive, they appeared to make sleepy mocking of every event. In fact they hid a keen alert mind and a quickness of judgment which had been the undoing of many a lazy member of staff working under him at St. Bartholomew's Hospital. Ainsley found himself taking a great liking to this little man, even upon so short an acquaintance.

"A month or two and the plague may be dead and finished, then we can all be about our own affairs once more," David suggested in a cheerful tone.

"Easy to see you're not long in London. Keeping good cheer is the very hardest task. It fails sadly after a round of calls amongst the locked houses. The bell never seems to stop tolling as person after person is snatched up and smothered under plagues black cloak. To say nothing of hearing the cart night after night, and seeing next day the pits filled to overflowing with the corpses of men, women and children: who only a day or two before had been patients one had striven to save; and in many cases thought one had saved."

A serious rather glum note was now in Brandon's voice. Watching him Ainsley thought how tired he looked.

"I think I shall find more reward in battling with the plague - however beset with failure, than to have remained in the service of the Navy to watch my patients torn and dismembered in conflict with the Dutch. I count myself lucky that my ship, *Janetta*, was so rotten bottomed as to demand a refit which sent her north to be heaved out of the water to lie on her back for many a month. It gave me my chance of my discharge, and I was glad to take it. In recent months we were twice in skirmish with Dutch vessels and the cost was five dead and two with limbs blown off. A messy business war, from the surgeon's standpoint." He paused in thought for a moment. "I fancy it gave *Janetta's* Captain a welcome escape route from the plague. I suspect that he and some of the crew knew well enough of the extent of the epidemic. I believe they kept the rest of us in ignorance lest we judge them 'coward' in their shyness of London."

"There's many like that. All the Court gone save old Lord Abbermarle and another one or two of like mind. Mr. Pepys stands firm here like a limpet, but whether from bravery or hopes of fortune it's hard to decide!" Again there was bitterness in Brandon's voice.

"Well I must make my way to St. Giles and find Vincent Fallon. It may be that he will decline any offer I make him. In the old days he was shaping a better surgeon than I; he may well remember the fact!"

"With upwards of ten thousand people at his door - he'll welcome you with open arms," Brandon's eyelids wrinkled in a smile.

"I thank you for your kind hospitality - it won't be forgotten

- and the loan of these clothes - I'll try to send them safe and clean back to you."

"No don't do that. Don't send anything from St. Giles here - pestilence is too easy carried by such means even in clean linen, besides they are a good fit and will see you better clad for your time in London. It's deuced difficult to find a seamstress, let alone a tailor in these times. Buy clothes - buy trouble - a good maxim in these times my friend."

Ainsley thanked him again and after taking his leave made his way out into the street. Once again it was fine. Quiet and dirt and glorious sunshine were together all over London in that desperate summer. His walk to St. Giles was uneventful. He saw only five living souls on the route. Three walking like himself took care to pass on the other side. The other two were ill-dressed workmen, occupied with spades throwing earth into a wide pit on a green area only a hundred paces from St. Bartholomew's Hospital. He knew well enough what they buried. They did not look up from their labours.

He soon found himself on the highway for Holborn. St. Giles Church stood sheltered and remote near the meadowland close to Bloomsbury, where the Earl of Southampton's great house stood. He had passed twenty or thirty boarded up houses with the scarlet cross upon the nailed up doors before he reached the city boundary. In two he saw white faces at the windows. Pressed as if seeking escape from the foul air within. He felt fury in his breast. It was against all his instincts for good medicine. This herding and close confinement. Pure air, clean water, fresh food. What chance for sick people so confined?

He reached St. Giles just before nine o'clock and immediately located the large room which served Vincent Fallon as a surgery. It had the wide double doors of a coach-house. Outside an oak tree shaded a patch of grass - dried now and brown, but having the vastly important advantage that it was in the open air. Forty or fifty persons stood waiting silently on the grass. All looked poor and many looked sick and undernourished. Few wore shoes and most were clothed in rags.

The double doors stood wide open as did the window alongside. The silent gathering shuffled to one side to let Ainsley pass. He mounted the steps and went into the large room beyond. Inside it was clean and cool. The stone floor swept spotless. Shelves ran the length of one wall, bottles, pillboxes, jars and flasks in neat array. There were two tables covered with white cloths. Behind one stood a plain wood chair. The chair stood empty. It's occupant was standing upon a short length of rush matting examining a young child held in the arms of a tall thin-faced woman. Her face was anxious under its rough grey shawl.

The man with his back to Ainsley was tall, thin, and wiry. His hair was fine textured and mousy in colour, cut short and neat above his white cravat. He wore knee-breeches and a close fitting white linen coat. Beyond him upon a low bench lay his long coat folded tidily. Beside it the gold headed cane which was the tally of his calling.

"Wait a moment please. I'm already engaged with a patient." He did not turn round or desist from his careful looking into the child's open mouth. His hands, holding the little girls head, were long tapered, and extremely gentle. Unhurried, he finished his task. "There little one." He patted the child's head and turned his attention to the Mother. "I can find no swelling to do with plague here - it is just the tooth grown too close against the small milk tooth. The tiny tooth will soon fall out. I'll give you ointment to soothe the swelling. Your home is free from plague?"

"Yes, surely we been lucky so far, it being all along the street."

"Then get home now - keep off the streets - away from others. Keep food clean and covered as I've bid you - mind your prayers but do not go to church or gatherings. Brush out your floors and pavement daily. Clean. Be clean - your lives depend upon it!"

He turned his head at last to meet Ainsley's eyes. He recognised him at once. "Ainsley! David Ainsley as I live! - I never expected to see you again. The Navy wasn't it? For a life of adventure as I remember! Just a moment let me get my patient's ointment." He went to the shelf and taking a jar, carefully spooned out some of the white substance therein into a small pillbox which he sealed with a lid. At the table he wrote carefully on the top of the box and handed it to the woman.

"Thank 'ee. I don't know what us 'un do without thee

Doctor." She bobbed a curtsey as she turned to go.

"Twice each day mind. That is two times each day - morn and night," he called after her. "Don't know why I write on those boxes, not one in fifty can read hereabouts," he explained turning to Ainsley, and breaking into a smile of greeting. But he did not extend his hand. "Not wise to touch - you understand. These times I'm very careful. See I have this dish to wash between each patient. I wish to God we knew how it is carried. I don't hold any one belief above another - save that it's not blown on the wind."

"I'm glad to find you alive in this doleful situation - but I feel I interrupt you in your work", Ainsley spoke briefly, his light blue eyes narrow and keen, as he studied his old friend's face. He found him much aged and weary, in spite of his brisk manner.

"Well - I've to see the rest out there - should be done by twelve noon perhaps. Then I take breakfast in my rooms upstairs - can you join me then? I'll tell you what, you go up and make yourself at home. The stairs are through that door," he pointed, "Up there there's wine - help yourself, I'll join you as soon as I'm able - Mary Ransome, my housekeeper, will see after your needs - you'll find her in the kitchen."

"Very well, we'll talk later." Ainsley left him to his next patient.

At the top of the stairs were four rooms. The first one Ainsley stepped into was a comfortable sitting room. Two windows faced St. Giles Churchyard, both were thrown open. Several well worn leather armchairs stood about the empty fireplace. A bookcase held a volume of Shakespeare plays and numerous medical books. A small rack held Fallon's pipes. Between the two windows was a table with a tray with glasses and two bottles of wine. A tin of wafers stood by the wine tray. This room exuded an air of peace and retreat. A book lay open face down on the arm of a chair, as though the reader would return at any moment to sit at his leisure and enjoy a glass of wine with the next chapter. The fireplace held cut logs and above the mantelshelf was an oil painting of an old man holding a basket of oranges out to two children. Faded red velvet curtains hung at the windows. A large rug of the same colour was before the wide fireplace. The rest of the floor was of polished oak boards. The room was uncluttered and tidy. A man's room.

Under one window a table was laid for one.

Ainsley put his pack down in a corner. He walked down the passage glancing in at the other rooms. Two were furnished very simply as bedrooms. Each held a wash-stand and had a cloth rug beside the bed. One room was obviously unoccupied, the single bed had a white coverlet thrown over it. The table and chair held no personal items. The other room held a double bed and a linen press. On the table lay several personal items including a well worn Bible. Both rooms were well polished and neat, brass candlesticks held each a fresh candle. Everything was in perfect order as was the rest of this small establishment. The kitchen at the end of the passage had the same air of clean well managed domesticity. A long scrubbed table stood lengthways and at it a woman in a white apron stood making pastry. Apples lay ready prepared in a dish. Ainsley greeted her and explained his presence. She was very small - under five feet tall. Her black hair coiled neatly about her head. Her round face and apple cheeks gave her a dutch doll look which was enhanced when she smiled at him, showing very small even teeth. He put her age at about thirty. She wore no rings.

"Do you come for a glass of sack, sir," the deep voice seemed odd coming from so small and dainty a person. There was a trace of a Welsh lilt in it somewhere.

"No - no. I'd prefer to wait for Dr.Fallon - if I might sit in the sitting room perhaps?"

"Of course sir, but are you to stay would you care to settle your bag in the small bedroom?"

"That has still to be discussed. I'll just use the sitting room until the Doctor is finished with his surgery."

"Very well sir - I'll just lay another place no doubt you'll take something when the Doctor breaks his fast."

"Thank you that will be excellent." He withdrew and went back to the sitting room. From the window on the landing, he could see that the number of patients waiting beneath the tree was gradually dwindling. He settled himself in an armchair and picked up a copy of the *London News*. It made depressing reading being filled with facts and figures relating to the Plague. The lists of casualties staggered him. St. Giles it appeared was the worst area of all and had been since the first week in June, when out of forty three plague deaths in London, thirty one had been in St. Giles. The third week of June had seen a hundred deaths within the parish.

In May the Lord Mayor of London had tried to contain the epidemic by ordering each and every householder in London to wash and sweep each and every portion of street daily if it abutted onto that householder's dwelling. The paper complained of almost total lack of success in this enterprise. Two weeks later a second proclamation had been issued stating that the streets now lay even deeper steeped in filth and charging the Alderman to severely punish all who did not comply. Obviously people had not done so. In the face of so many having fled to the country, great numbers of houses were shut up and empty. As the heat-wave continued and other houses were locked up with plague victims confined inside, so less and less people were able to comply with the cleaning order. Judging by Ainsley's own observations of the last two days, the filth piled higher daily. Rat infested heaps of refuse filled every dark alley and overflowed onto street corners. Many foul passageways had been closed off and others were shunned by the few reluctant pedestrians forced out by need of food or medicine. Or the foolish who would still insist upon joining in the funeral walks to lay their dead, mostly coffinless, into the pits. Thus people came close to one another and the plague continued leaping up, and St. Giles the worst of all.

St. Giles actually lay outside the city walls, but was so close-shouldered with the town that it was impossible to contain the infection. The *London News* seemed unable to suggest any remedy. Ainsley laid aside the sheet, his head confused by so many contradictory figures. Head back against the chair he relaxed in it's comfort and dozed. Aware that it was a long time since he had enjoyed the comfort for such relaxation.

He awoke just after noon when his host entered. The table was now set for two. Mary Ransome must have accomplished the task without waking him. When they were seated at table she came in to serve them, she bustled about in her blue and white striped kitchen gown which was covered by a spotless white apron. Ainsley ate little having broken his fast hours before. But Fallon ate well and took two glasses of sack. Ainsley was to learn that Vincent considered sack and well cooked meat, always roasted, were in no small way responsible for his continued good health.

"The sack to be best at middle age, fine and neat, bright and rosy in colour, and the tang of walnut in the flavour," he described his favourite.

"It seems to suit you - you look tired but very fit to me," David smiled into the deep grey eyes across the table.

"I fare well enough 'Twas worse at first especially when St. Giles ran fastest and worst in the plague race. This last week we are out stripped by Cripplegate. They now hold the highest death rate black spot on London's map. Mind it's still rampant and rising over all. Rain has been so little, I remain firm in my belief that this sweltering heat feeds the pestilence, and we shall see no great improvement until cold and frost are come. See, I'll show you my map." He reached a roll of parchment from the shelf and they studied it together - heads bent over the table. Ainsley looked younger by ten years, yet only twelve months separated their birth dates.

"See, wherever the streets lie close crammed with the eaves near overlapping; the dark streets with the foul air and filth shut in beneath, there the plague runs like fire. House after house with the cross and the locked door, and note that wherever open ditches run deep with blocked drains and stagnant water, there the plague lies blackest."

"Why must the people be shut in so? Surely it is inhuman, that when one or two are ill, the well are entrapped with the sick?"

"It's the law of the land and medics must abide by it, years ago it was shut up the house for forty days, then awhile back it was professionally agreed that plague ran its course in twenty-eight days. So Parliament by law lessened the period. Always there is plague in London in summertime, but often only minor outbreaks. Directly epidemic comes, as now, Authority at once panics and they at once enforce the forty day ban. There is no sense or compassion in it but they always do it nonetheless. Of course, it is always made far worse by tight shut windows 'To keep out Plague!' As if it flew by air. Shut in as they are and often filled with fumes of disinfectant, it is hard to understand how any survive. Enough now of my difficulties - let us talk of you. Are you quit of the Navy? Are you set for home and marriage? Perhaps you are already wed? I envy you if the countryside of the Midlands be your destination."

Ainsley explained his situation and his betrothal to Elizabeth Loundes. Vincent Fallon had stayed at Seckington Hall several times in their St. Bartholomew's days. He had met Elizabeth as a child on those occasions. He was deeply interested in the attachment between her and David.

"And does the Lady develop as much beauty as her childhood promised?" he asked, visualising the bright dark child with long lashed huge brown eyes, and tiny hands and feet, in little Maid's slippers.

"She is very lovely - I'm a most fortunate man. I've been away too long at sea - but that's not to say that another month will make much difference," his voice trailed off and then he resumed strongly, "If you've a bed, I've a mind to stay a few weeks and give you a hand, to see the peak of this scourge past?

"Good God man - I wouldn't ask you! You've no responsibility here - I'd count it bloody foolishness in any man who has no tie with London. Nearly all who can afford it are fled."

"Nevertheless I'd like to stay - I would leave the helm to you as Captain of course - but I'm not unversed. I've seen pretty bad times below decks before this."

"It's not that Ainsley, it's the risk - you have a lovely woman to go home to. Don't do it. It's madness. Our Parson, Robert Boreman - he has stayed, brave at his church throughout, but he's had to commission five great pits dug here, and that is just for this parish. They grow full daily, like sticks piled one upon another they lie there."

"There then - some must stay, allow me a week or two; then I may go with a clear conscience."

"You always were a stubborn fellow - very well, but I shall be the despot especially as regards our routine - by which I have kept alive these three months past."

"Of course - I'm in your hands." They smiled at one another, though Vincent Fallon shook his head. "Then let us begin at once." They stood up from the table and there began the partnership which lasted until the plague reached and passed its terrible peak.

CHAPTER III

CHAPTER III

Their daily routine was simple and demanding, but regular. They rose very early each day and at once took a dose of anti-pestilential electuary. They dressed each morning in fresh garments, clean cravat, shirt and breeches, before beginning their day's work.

They shared surgery in the open-air room downstairs. There would be fifty or more people waiting. After examining, prescribing and treating all these people, and having seen the last one discharged, the two men would break their fast in the sitting room upstairs, where Mary Ransome invariably had a good meal waiting.

The time until dinner was then spent visiting patients in their own homes. The watchmen in charge of the closed houses would bring the keys to open up the doors for them to enter. In each house disinfectant, usually Nitre tar and resin, would be burning in the hot ash of the hearth. The smell given off was over-powering, at all examinations the Doctors' kept a lozenge in their mouths as a protection against infection. Especially at first while he was unused to it, Ainsley found entering these houses the worst part of the business. The stench and suffering within was terrible. Plague poisoned the whole of a patient's system, the symptoms were many and varied, but all were horrible.

Most people felt at first just a little indisposed, but chill creeping over them and violent shivering would quickly follow. The shivering was frightening and always produced an unnatural feeling of terror and shock so terrifying to the patient that he or she became so low as to be terribly susceptible to the pestilence. This state would last perhaps half an hour, but sometimes much longer, after which began severe vomiting, so severe that those who had been ill for some hours were often claimed by death from sheer exhaustion.

The sickness and violent vomiting proved Plague beyond doubt, some then became comatose and slept as though drugged, unless woken they would certainly die. The next stage was high fever, any who had survived this far never escaped the fever. During fever, wildly beating hearts, violence in delirium, screaming and throwing themselves about, were frequent symptoms. People often had to be tied down to prevent them running willy-nilly here and there, carrying infection and injury to others. In this state they were mindless, recognising no one, often in this violent state a patient would suddenly fall dead, worn out by the intensity of the fever.

After the fever, those still alive often suffered 'blanes' or swelling in the groin or armpit. These tumours formed into an abscess, unless they were burst the surgeon must lance them to ease the acute pain caused by the trapped pus within. Poison-filled carbuncles also sometimes appeared. Great skill was needed to remove all the poison cleanly or gangrene would quickly destroy the patient.

The greatest fear came when the 'Tokens' appeared as happened in many cases. At the very beginning of Plague's infection a rash of tiny pus spots each with a red ring round often showed on the sufferer's skin. This was in no way to be confused with the 'Tokens', here a rash, bluish or reddish ran under the skin, sometimes only small areas were covered, sometimes the whole body, the neck, breast and back and thighs were the areas commonly showing Tokens.

Ainsley and Fallon dreaded the 'Tokens' coming on a patient's skin, they were the one sign that invariably meant death. They had to deal with all these dreadful symptoms every day inside the putrid little houses. Ainsley from the disciplined example of his companion learned to control the repulsion and quell his stomach from heaving. It was so much worse than he could have imagined. Often a Mother would be struggling with the whole of her family dreadfully sick, and then she in turn, would be struck down. The very scale of the epidemic was unimaginable, the doctors must touch, dose, lance, clean away poisonous matter, and most difficult of all give comfort where there was none, engender hope where almost certainly all would die.

When the daytime visits were done the two men walked home through the unbelievably sunlit streets, this walk in Ainsley's first days in London, was a respite from the dreadful sorrow within the houses. It was a short-lived reprieve. As the number of deaths increased, as it rapidly did during July's baking hot days, it became impossible for the mass burials to be confined to the hours of darkness. The carts, the searchers, the bearers and their dreadful cargo became familiar sights even in the afternoons. Ainsley saw scenes in the streets as well as in the houses, which he was to remember all of his life.

At home it was easier to relax and in some measure forget their work. Mary Ransome looked after them well, after each day's round of the houses, jugs of hot water would be ready for them. They changed their clothes and washed thoroughly. Mary kept the basement copper constantly on the boil. Into this all soiled garments were immediately flung.

Refreshed they would meet again in the sitting room, here they would sit over glasses of red sack, taking two or three each to disperse any beginnings of fever in themselves. Thus they would rest until dinner time when Mary Ransome would serve them a meal of well cooked roasted meat, vegetables and a sharp relish. At dinner each took more wine. Later it was back to more patients in the consulting room. After seeing all who came they would be back in the town until nine or ten o'clock at night, to visit any very sick who needed their aid a second time. Then home and an hour or two's rest before bedtime. As they walked home and dusk came the houses took on a new aspect. Where there was life in the houses, there was a candle lit and placed on the window sill at sunset, these were the emblems of London's courage. The courage of the very poor, a refusal to give in no matter how great the odds. It was something seemingly indefatigable. Ainsley and Fallon found in those candle flames the *raison d'être* of all their work and the daily risks they faced in every house.

Both men slept very well and only once during the time he was in London did Ainsley feel illness upon him. At once Vincent saw it and dosed him with increased draughts of sack. He then packed his friend off to bed where he slept dreamless and woke entirely restored.

Except for a short spell of rain the heat continued unabated. It was a hard, stretching, disciplined routine which David Ainsley and Vincent Fallon lived through those desperate weeks. Some of the sights and sounds they witnessed were never forgotten by either. Young women dying with their babies in their arms. Old people with their eyes wide in fear. The so called 'nurses' in the

43

houses, drunken, uncaring and dishonest, stealing from the living, waiting to steal from the dying. Vultures out for the best pickings when all in the house were dead. In the streets the bearers using their vile hooks to draw the dead from their houses, showing no pity for the living relatives who must stand and watch. Yet who could blame them when a single touch often meant death.

By the middle of August the church bells tolled incessantly. Each time reporting a death, as one clapper came to rest another would start in another bell tower across the town. The red and white wands which bearers and searchers carried and waved in front of them to keep the public at a distance, became a common-place sight even in broad daylight.

London had become haunted and empty. The river like the streets was also empty, the Pool of London deserted. A bounty was offered to any ship which would deliver grain into London. It was a farthing upon every quarter of grain unloaded. There were few who sought to 'take the King's farthing'. Between the fourth and the eighth of the month Ainsley and Fallon learned that over four thousand people had died within the City. All did not die of plague perhaps, it was however a terrible toll for a period of seven days by whatever means the count was done.

Both men went through periods of depression, they formed a deep and lasting friendship. When one was down and low spirited, the other was there to give cheer and friendship, they talked late over their wine in the sitting room, it was their salvation. Any subject under the sun was welcome to them save their work, which was never mentioned in the blessed quiet of the sitting room. They talked much about times gone by at St. Bartholomew's Hospital when as young men they had shared many happy times when London had been a crowded happy place.

Another favourite topic was holidays they had spent at David's home, riding and country pleasures seemed far away but they had many pleasant shared memories of those times.

On August the eighteenth news was brought to them one evening; it came from St. Bartholomew's, Michael Brandon was dead, he had died of Plague in one of the hospital's own beds. It saddened both men, especially since at last the numbers on the

St. Giles death lists had begun to decline. To have stayed at his post and then be taken so near the end was hard indeed. This news seemed to make Fallon anxious and edgy. A few days later, one evening as they sat late over their wine his thoughts burst forth.

"It's time David, your time's up! Get you gone, I'm well enough now. I'll never live with myself if aught happens to you now. Did you send letters to your people?"

"No - I wanted to but I dare not. It's the risk. The risk of infection."

"Well then go to them - they must grow anxious. No good news has gone out from London for weeks now. They may hear any evil rumour and fear for your safety. It's time man! Past time! It's my parish here - yours is in Seckington - you owe it to your family. Don't push Lady Luck too far, she is as fickle as any woman. I am well enough here, the worst of this is past. I have Mary - you know what I mean." He paused embarrassed. Ainsley looked keenly at his host - yes he knew - he had long since realised that Vincent Fallon with no wife of his own found much strength during the day and comfort in his bed at night from Mary Ransome. Her loyalty and love for him demanded nothing in return. She risked plague daily and nightly without a qualm bearing in mind his intimate contacts day after day with desperate illness. Suddenly Ainsley knew that he himself longed to go home. He looked up - the load slipping from his shoulders.

"Yes - Yes, I think it is so - you're right. I'll go next Monday."

"No! No! Go tomorrow early - for me - for our friendship and for Elizabeth Loundes. Promise! Promise me!" Anxiety was writ large on Vincent Fallons face.

"I promise - and thank you," Ainsley replied.

BOOK TWO
CHAPTER I

BOOK TWO
CHAPTER I

David Ainsley left London on the twenty-fourth of August 1665. Mary Ransome packed him food enough for several days and wine in flasks to drink with each meal.

"Drink nothing else. Take food from no one - keep to yourself for their sake as well as your own. Keep away from main highways - in any case every town has its watchmen on main routes, to keep out those without permits." Vincent was full of last minute instructions for his safe journey. At the last they made their farewells very brief, for both men felt deep emotion. They had been together on a tightrope over the pit of death through so many weeks that they were closer than brothers. Vincent looked at David for a moment intently and then flung his arm briefly across his shoulders. "God go with you, my friend."

"And with you - take care." David replied. They shook hands and Ainsley turned and strode away up the lane towards High Holburn and the open fields. He did not look back, if he had, he would have seen Vincent square his shoulders and go up the steps into his surgery and so out of sight.

David made for the open country beyond Lincoln's Inn and Holborn. It was his intention to travel on foot all the way in case he should carry infection with him. Every garment he wore and carried was fresh laundered and clean. He hoped that in the cool of the early morning he would be able to keep up a good pace and quickly get clear of the town. Clear of Plague too! His spirits lifted as every stride shook London's grief from his feet.

In his pocket a rough map defined his route, skirting all towns and setting course over the Chilterns. He intended to take his time, the past weeks had sapped his strength, He wanted to get home rested and as well in health as possible. He intended to keep careful count of the next twenty-eight days which would being him clear of risk of infection. This would mean a period of isolation when he reached Seckington Hall, before he could mix freely with family and friends. He wondered if Crab Tree Cottage in his Father's woodland still stood empty. He and his Father had talked of the idea of refurbishing it for his occupation. His Mother had felt that it was not large enough for Elizabeth, after living all her life at Upper Telso Park. So in the end nothing had been settled. For his own part he loved Crab Tree more than anywhere else on the Estate. Its position was hard to rival in beauty and privacy. The house which was larger than a cottage yet not so spacious as a farmhouse, stood about half a mile distant from Seckington Hall. A belt of woodland separated the two houses. Crab Tree was sited on a small rocky outcrop, scarcely a hill, facing down over acres of farmland towards Lower Telso hamlet, where the church and Parsonage House could be seen. Crab Tree had an orchard and paddock and a small set of stables at the rear. Its boundaries were formed by the woodland at the rear and a fast running stream with a waterfall and pool in the foreground. The stream began a hundred yards further up the hillside where springs leapt up out of the rocky escarpment. It was known to be the purest water on Lord Ainsley's estate.

The cottage stood amongst a natural garden of Silver Birch and heather, rocks and stream and winding paths amongst the close cropped grass, grazed by the Estate sheep. The house stood long and low under its rustic thatch. It's only vehicular access was along a mossy oak lined lane from the Seckington-Upper Telso road.

As David tramped through the open country he pictured Crab Tree in his mind in the utter quiet of the early autumn sunshine. Birds and wild creatures lived there undisturbed. He tried to imagine Elizabeth there waiting for him. He found much pleasure in day-dreaming after so long without a moment to call his own. With so much in his mind time passed easily by and the sun rose high in the heavens. London was far behind him. He was in beech woodland and it was cool beneath the trees. He rested and ate and drank from his pack. There wasn't a soul about. The wine drowsed him and he slept.

An hour or so later he woke and set off once more. New energy filled him. The fresh air in his lungs, the pure oxygen after London's rank air seemed to cleanse and refresh his mind and body. He walked until sundown and made his bed in the heather of a wild area of moorland. He had spoken to no one but was perfectly happy in his own company. Morning found him by a clear stream where he washed and broke his fast. The next few days passed in much the same way. Twice he passed the time of day with farm workers in the fields. Mostly he avoided human contacts, he would take no risks although he began to have a firm conviction that all would be well and that he was free from Plague. Elizabeth Loundes was in his mind a great deal especially when he reached the Cotswold Hills.

During the years in the Navy he had been with a woman only rarely. Once or twice desire had driven him hard enough to make him seek release. This had not been in London. There had been a woman at one of the small ports in Southern France. He had sought her out two or three times and found her body and company pleasurable. He wished her with him now - her yielding softness in his arms would have taken the edge off his need and left him steadier and better equipped to face his first meeting with Elizabeth.

Elizabeth looked always for strength and mastery in a man. He felt he would never be able to convey to her, nor indeed to his parents, the feelings which had prompted him to stay in London and take the immense risks he had done in throwing in his lot with Vincent Fallon. Yet he knew that at the time he had known no choice in the matter. Would he ever make Elizabeth understand that? He dismissed it all from his mind knowing that even given the chance of a woman, he could have no truck with her while he carried the risk still about him.

The hills and woodlands of the Midlands wrapped themselves healingly about him and his pace increased, as he saw the Cliven Valley open out before him. Soon the tower of Lower Telso Church came into view with the fields rising in gentle slopes up towards the thick belt of woodland beyond. Familiar land marks came thick and fast - a glimpse of the Cross Keys Inn showed through the trees above the Springs and Big-fields. Away to his left he could see the trees of The Park but the house was hidden from his view. He followed the brook round the hollow of Quarry Bottom. The gypsy settlement looked deserted save for ponies grazing near the caravans and a few bits of washing hung upon some bushes. Reaching Rock Bottom Lane he could see smoke rising from the chimney-pots of Wood Cottage. He climbed the stile into Low Wood and walked along the quiet mossy path which led upstream towards the ford.

At the bottom of Wood Cottage garden stood an old privy,

it's door hung on one hinge and it's roof was covered by a thick tangle of ivy. A dilapidated little place, yet facing due South it had a good spying view along Rock Bottom Lane towards the bridge. In the cottage lived the Dale family. Arthur Dale was Lord Ainsley's head cowman, a plain spoken family man. His wife Eliza was expecting her fourth child. They had already an elder daughter Ilsa who was sixteen, and twin boys, Sailor and Simon who were fifteen, Ilsa was in service at The Park. The two lads were amongst those fortunate young local boys working on the Estate learning a skilled trade. Simon, a quiet lad like his Father, was in a fair way to becoming a very good carpenter. Sailor was a lively lad forever after a lark and into every prank. The Estate stonemason was trying to teach him a trade, but getting the lad to apply himself was another matter. The boy took after Old Albert his Grandfather, a little wizened gnome of a man, who still, at eighty years of age, liked to see a joke in everything. He took a demonic delight in creating upset and disturbance about him, but most especially he liked to be the first with every titbit of news.

On the sunlit afternoon when David Ainsley crossed the lane and glanced at their smoking chimney, the lads and their Father were at work. Eliza was in the kitchen ironing her men-folks linen at the kitchen table. Her flat irons were set to heat on the kitchen fire. Kept burning summer and winter alike these fires were the hub and life blood of every cottage. Used for cooking, drying and warmth for the whole family.

Old Albert was in the privy. He often sat there for an hour on sunny afternoons. The broad scrubbed seat with its two holes - one set lower and smaller for the children was now little used. Albert, breeches down and buttocks settled firm and comfortable had been dozing. He woke and was chewing on the stem of his old clay pipe, unlit, he still enjoyed the habit and feel of it locked between almost toothless gums. His sharp old eyes saw a movement in the lane, leaning forward to the displaced board in the rickety door, he had a clear view.

"Yes - 'tis someone - I knew it! By God, can it be? Yes - well bugger me there's trouble if ever I clap eyes on 'en! Dang these bleddy breeches!" He stood up and struggled with tangled buttons and belt. "Gone up the woods he has - going home then -

and a right bleddy shock he's in for when he gets there. Mother! Mother!" His voice chirped out as he stumbled bow-legged along the uneven narrow path across the garden.

"Get out, Trip - you'll have me down, you dang dog - get out." His arms and stick flailed at the old sheep dog which romped to meet him. Hearing the commotion Eliza looked up through the open door.

"What's up, Old Dad then? You found gold or summit?" she grinned at him across the threshold.

"Hold yer tongue, Darter - you waits till you'rm heard the news! That'll set yer tongue still if anything will." His wrinkled old face was working with excitement.

"Get on with it old 'un! Spit it out! What you seen in the Privy then?"

"Not in the Privy, lass - in the lane. I saw 'im in the lane. Young Ainsley it were. Mr. David - sure as I stand here - come home he do be - carrying 'is bag - large as life. Gone up path to the Big House. This'll set the cat in the pigeon loft I'll bet yer! Ha! Ha! Ha! He! He! He!" He shrieked with delight jumping up and down in his mirth. Tears running out of his old blue eyes followed the runnels of his wrinkled cheeks and came to rest in the stubbles of his chin. His mouth kept opening wider and wider displaying two old tooth stumps amongst numerous gaps.

"Well I never! And us all took 'un to be dead. Lost at sea they said." Eliza's eyes started in her head and her mouth in turn widened, iron in hand, raised above the garment, she stood bewildered trying to collect her scattered wits and visualise the outcome of this alarming information.

"He be live and well then in spite of all the delay and the death eating up London."

"Course 'ee be. Didnee I just tell 'ee. Wish I be a fly on 'is Lordship's wall this next hour I does. Bloodshed! I shouldn't wonder! Nor blame 'ee - too hasty that's wot! Too bloody hasty some folks - an high falutin' over humble village peoples as well." He plonked down in the old basket chair by the hearth and reached deliberately for a taper.

"No good'll come of it. No good! You marks my words, woman!" He stuck the taper deep amongst the hot peats and lit his pipe, drawing in his breath in a deep noisy sucking movement. Grim satisfaction in his every movement.

David Ainsley unaware of the interest his return was already creating, made his way up through his Father's woodland until he reached the ford over Cliven Brook. Here he turned right onto the intersecting path which ran from Lower Telso across the fields and through the woods to Seckington Hall garden. Home at last. His heart leapt with pleasure. His pack was light now, the food and wine used up. It felt as nothing on his back as he began to run towards the garden wall. Suddenly he saw his Mother on the terrace above the lawn. He cupped his hands. "Mother! Mother! I'm home!" he shouted. He heard a faint cry as he pushed open the door in the wall. Once through it he saw her white dress billowing along the terrace as she ran. He was across the lawn to the bottom of the steps, his foot on the first stone step just as she reached the low stone parapet at the top. For a moment both stopped and stood frozen.

"David, my dear David" she whispered her face was as white as her gown, every beautiful feature perfectly still. Her curling grey hair piled close to her head, shaped the cameo of her small-made neat person against the dark background of the grey stone house behind her. The scent of the lavender bushes he had dreamed of so often was released by the brush of her skirts against the last of the late flowers at the side of the steps. "Oh Mother, I'm home at last!"

"We feared you dead these last three months - even I had given up. We had such terrible news of the Navy's engagements with Holland and then the Plague in London - and no word for so long." Her voice faded and tears began to rain down her cheeks. He began to mount the steps to put his arms about her. Suddenly he checked. This was madness - he must explain.

"Dear one - don't weep - I'm safe and well - but I must not embrace you - I mustn't come in the house or mix with anyone until a few days are gone past. I have been in London and Plague is rife there. I came on foot and have kept from human contact these six days past. All my linen and everything I carried was spotless - to take every precaution we might. It is yet not enough. I must isolate myself twenty-two days more to be certain. Look not so anxious - I keep well - I am well, I feel well - but we must yet be cautious. I wondered if I might spend the time at Crab

Tree. It's near and I can come into the garden to see you all. There's naught wrong with me that a sight of you and my Father and Johnny and the girls and of course Elizabeth - won't cure." His words tumbled out in his excitement and pleasure in being home.

Isobel Ainsley steadied herself - she was usually a calm woman -but it had been a shock - such a shock to see him - always her special favourite - coming across the fields like that - so unexpected. She put out her hand behind her, fingers spread, seeking and finding the low stone wall, and sat down upon it. The scent of lavender was all about her - strangely her mind paused to think about the flowers - they must be cut this week for the clothes' presses - its beauty was beginning to fade - it had been left and forgotten in the anxiety over David and Elizabeth and all the other business. Elizabeth? Oh heavens, what next? Her thoughts were in turmoil.

"Mother are you all right? I'm sorry I startled you - I saw you on the terrace and just ran." His voice seemed to come from a long way off.

"Oh yes! Oh David, I'm so glad. So glad you're safe. If we may not touch - how ridiculous it seems - let me fetch your Father. Sit here on the steps and take that heavy pack off your back, I'll only be a minute - he's only in the library."

"All right - I'll wait here - but where are the others?"

"The girls are about somewhere, but I'll fetch your Father first." She rose to her feet and hurried towards the house. David sat on the steps and stretched his legs, resting his back against the stone griffin which surmounted the rounded end of the curving stone wall above the steps. Home. Peace surged over him - he'd like to settle here for the rest of his life. He waited for his parents to come, but it was some minutes before he heard his Father's well-remembered step and saw the tall figure advance across the terrace. Lord Ainsley was alone. David frowned - he had expected his Mother and most likely his eldest brother and the girls as well. Most probably Esme squeaking with excitement at his home-coming. His eyes narrowed a little at his Father's serious face.

"My dear boy - I'm so glad to see you - I'm hard put to find words. We'd despaired, given you up. I wrote to the Admiralty twice but couldn't get any news of you, we knew of course that London is in turmoil with Plague and the King gone into the country with his court. Only today there is news of a great naval encounter with the Dutch, but much news gets abroad which is without foundation, it grows difficult to sort the wheat from the chaff. Your Mother says you must isolate yourself for days yet. Is it so? She mentions Crab Tree?" He paused, his steady grey eyes warm and welcoming in his calm aristocratic face.

David saw more - was there compassion, even pity in the strong face? Always an example in kindness and integrity, his Father was, in this small community, almost a king in his own right. David felt his manhood slip away and the echoes of boyhood return. Sensations much enhanced by his Father's great height towering above him on the steps. He felt as though caught in some misdemeanour of childhood. Something was amiss.

"Is something wrong Father, I'd rather you tell me straight out?" "I wish you had written" now definitely there was pain in Lord Ainsley's face. "I dare not. I've been six weeks in London with Vincent Fallon in the Parish of St. Giles, thousands die there - it is the blackest pit in all London. We have worked amongst the poor and lived cheek by jowl with the pestilence. I feared to send letters in case I sent death."

"Yet you are come now." His Father sounded anxious and perplexed.

"The peak is now passed by. Vincent is my friend, he was alone in dire straits, for old times' sake I could not do less than insist that he accept my help. It is my calling, Father, can you not understand that?"

"I understand it all well enough, except that you could take such risk when you were betrothed to Elizabeth - and to send no word?"

"Elizabeth. Is she well? Does she still..... ?" The question hung in the air between them. His Father's eyes met his squarely, they were dark with compassion, but steady in spite of it.

"Elizabeth has not waited for you." For a moment Lord Ainsley saw his son's pain, then David's blue eyes narrowed to slits, the dark lashes curtaining them in his attempt to veil his turbulent feelings. The sunlit picture of the house, the bright trees, the blue lavender and sky, the grey stone of the steps, seemed to swing and jumble together in a maze of kaleidoscopic colour. The whirling muddle refused to settle in his dull numb brain. He heard his own voice from a long way off.

"Not waited?"

"She thought you were dead, she was nineteen in May - many young women are married and bearing children long before that. She had heard nothing for so long, she is not entirely to blame."

"Is she gone from here, away from the village?"

"She was married ten days ago! They are to live at The Park. Lady Loundes has moved into Park Lodge."

"Married! Elizabeth married - but we are betrothed these two years - we were to marry on my return. We were . . . we are deep in love. Once again Lord Ainsley did not flinch or falter in his gaze, he answered in a low gentle voice, "It was Johnny - try to take it calmly, it cannot be remedied now. Try to see their side in this David. Don't let this split the family - it would kill your Mother - she's weeping in the house at this moment."

"Johnny! My own brother! - God forgive him, I doubt I ever will. Father how can I be calm - how can I accept it? If you knew how the last months have been, how I have hung my whole sanity upon her faithfulness. How I have dreamed - and longed, and planned. How could she? She does not love him, even from childhood he was cruel, greedy and demanding. Always he would take the best in all things, but she knew that too. It was something we shared from ten years old, always she and I together trying to be strong, trying to stand up to him. From babies almost we battled his arrogance." David began to shake, the shock, the long walk, all his hopes dashed in a single sentence - 'Elizabeth has not waited for you,' - turmoil raged in his mind. His hands sweating and clenched tight in his longing to hurl himself at his brother's throat, to hit him and hit him, again and again.

Lord Ainsley felt suddenly an old man, he stood watching his son's suffering and wondered if there was anything he or Isobel could have done to avert this tragic circumstance. It seemed to him the culmination of years and years of build up. His eldest son, always exactly as David had just described, if one stripped off the veneer which Jonathon so carefully cultivated, greedy, selfish, arrogant, taking all and giving nothing, unloved, even though they had striven for it to be otherwise, by Isobel or himself. Never even the favourite of either of his two sisters, yet somehow Jonathon had crept into David's shoes with Elizabeth. Playing upon her loneliness and longing for marriage. By gradual flattery and pushing persuasion he had won the favour of Lady Loundes, Elizabeth's Mother. A widow like that left alone, so vulnerable to a clever persuasive young man, and by reason of the entailment of the late Lord Loundes's estate, Jonathon would one day take the lands and wealth which came to Elizabeth as well. God help the tenants on that side of the valley when that day came.

Lord Ainsley stood silent his face bleak. "What a home coming for you - no wonder your Mother weeps, she cannot even put her arms about you to show her grief."

Something in his Father's voice reached out to a small sane strength in David's mind. This was a blow to his parents as well. He must pull himself together. Must have time to think. Must be alone. Make a show of acceptance, of calm. He lifted his head and raised his eyes. "I'm sorry Father - I mustn't cause you fresh grief. Let us not dwell upon it - what's done cannot be altered." He made a great effort to speak normally. "What about Crab Tree Cottage? Does it still stand empty? I wondered if I might live there until I'm the full twenty-eight days clear of Plague. It would give me time for thinking and for making some sort of plan for my future!"

"It stands waiting for you my son. Martin Bones has not spared his craft, he has made an excellent job of the alterations. There's a kitchen added and a pump to bring water from the spring, the roof is new thatched. Gibbs has done a fine job. The garden is fenced and the drive fresh gravelled. The barn has had the doorway made wider to allow passage for a carriage. The stables are tiled and set to rights. The only thing .... there's no furniture there - no comfort .... I never thought of you living there at once .... alone."

"I shall do well enough there, Father. I think perhaps at once would be wise. Give me time to reflect and catch my breath."

"Well, I'll go to your Mother now. Just a word to reassure her, and Esme too has been upset and anxious, she of us all would not believe you dead these last weeks. She is bitter against Elizabeth and Johnny. Refused to attend the ceremony - upset your Mother even more of course." David's heart warmed to his youngest sister - always the bond between them had been close.

"I'll get Jeffreys to get Jim Painter to bring a wagon, they can go before you with some bits and pieces together with provisions, they can be away by the time you get there. Meantime I'll have Cook make up a tray and wine to refresh you. Out here in the garden's best, we can talk while you eat, sit now and rest while I give directions and see after your Mother."

When he was alone David closed his mind to everything except his immediate future. Crab Tree Cottage - a place of his own - to find his feet again. A place he loved and only a step away from Seckington Hall. His Father returned to find him more composed. He brought a tray with sliced ham, home-made pickles and light crusty bread, a wedge of cheese and home-made butter completed the repast. At the side a carafe of wine. A little note lay beside the plate. David recognised his Mother's hand.

Bless you, my Dear David, be of good heart - I'll hope to see you in a few days - send word of all your needs. I go to give guidance to the men and cook for your comfort. My love always, Mother.

The words cheered him, as he sat down on the steps to eat his meal. His Father stayed with him an hour while he ate. They exchanged much news but kept away from all subjects concerning Jonathon and Elizabeth. The affairs of Seckington Estate seemed to have stood still while David's world had spun full circle. The harvest was good and the men on the Estate had enjoyed sunlit days to gather it in. In the stackyards Thatcher Gibbs the estate thatcher worked long hours to thatch and secure each rick as soon as it was made. Ten ricks of corn at the home farm alone gave indication of the bounty the soil had yielded. None need fear being unable to find their tithe this year.

His Father also brought him up to date with the Dale family's news. Eliza Dale was with child - after so long! The youngest, the twins were coming sixteen. Eliza was very shy about it, keeping inside the cottage. Her husband had his chest thrust out and talked of four or five more! Old Albert was still alive and well. Over eighty now of course. At the other end of Lower Telso the old witch Mother Ross, had been ailing by the fireside for some weeks and had not been seen about so much of late.

Lord Ainsley also told David that his eldest sister Charlotte had now got a beau. Irwin Saint from Dunsmore! Lord Ainsley laughed wryly as he told about it.

"He seems such a pompous fellow to me, but she is delighted with him and her Mother is not against the match, so what can a mere man do? My old mare, Melody had a foal in May - a little filly, the image of her Mother." And so came to David's ears all the trifling news of the Parishes. Gradually his Father's voice built up the picture of the small changes in this changeless place.

"Parson's wife is still unwell, I fear that she is consumptive - we've no surgeon and she needs help. The villages need you, David. There's no surgeon within thirty miles. If it is in your heart to stay. Your Mother fears you will go away again, it will break your Mother's heart if you do. But I must not press you, I only beg you to take your time before you decide, give yourself time, David".

"Yes - yes - time is what I need just now. Time by myself. I'll make way to Crab Tree. This tray? I'll put the dishes in my pack - it mustn't go into your hand again. It gets dusk - I'll go now, I'll come to the garden in a day or two. Tell my Mother - Tell her all is well." He stood up and carefully disposed of the contents of the tray into his pack. Stretching up again he smiled into his Father's eyes. Lord Ainsley felt deeply distressed he was not deceived.

"There's a time for weeping, son - but it passes."

"I know, Father - I know - Good night."

"Good night, my son."

David turned away, pack and tray beneath his arm. He walked through the door in the wall and was soon lost to view amongst the trees. Dusk lengthened the shadows and darkened the woodland. Lord Ainsley strained his eyes to keep his son in view until darkness swallowed him.

"Thank God he lives. We have that at least," he murmured as he made his way back to the house.

At Wood Cottage the coming of dusk saw the Dale family

sitting round the kitchen table finishing their evening meal. Arthur Dale at the head of the table was still a handsome man. At thirty-eight he was as upright and square-shouldered as he had been at twenty. In the warm kitchen his face was flushed into the roots of his red hair. His blue eyes beneath bushy brows, crinkled at the corners in his amusement at the chatter of the others. Eliza was busy slicing huge wedges of apple tart. The twins sat together at one side of the scrubbed deal table. A single candle held in a low pewter stick stood in the centre of the table, its flickering light found the laughter lines on the faces round the table. No one would have taken the two lads for twins. Sailor was a blue-eyed redhead like his Father, full of noise, laughter and bluster. Simon was different, quiet, dark and small made like his Mother, dark narrow brows over intent dark eyes, but he too could burst into laughter all of a sudden at some prank of his brother's or his Grandfather's. The only girl in the family, Elsa, resembled her Father in looks but had her Mother's quiet shy ways. She was not present tonight, being in service at the Park, she lived in. She had only been there a year and had been taken on by Lady Loundes. Now that Lady Loundes had moved to the Lodge, Elsa was employed by Jonathon Ainsley and his bride Elizabeth.

The Dales were a happy laughing family. Even Eliza with her rapidly thickening body, and a child, which she had neither expected nor wanted, coming to burden her in her thirty-sixth year, could enjoy a good laugh. They had been enjoying Old Albert's mimicry of David Ainsley's imagined conversation with the brother who had stolen his bride.

"Dash it all, Sir - Dash it all - it's not done, Sir - not in the best families, yer knows."

"Well, she was getting past it, yer see - needing a man - Well you knows - being a Doctor."

Old Albert rocked back and forth in his chair. Everyone laughed but Eliza felt enough was enough. Her mouth buttoned.

"Now then, Old Dad, don't get dirty now - enough of that sort of talk at our table. I knows you'm funning, but that Mr. Jonathon fair gives me the creeps - its 'is eyes. Greedy 'ee is. Allus on the take. I don't like to think of our Ilsa working for 'im. Miss Elizabeth's all right. Bit hoity-toity at times, but then she's

61

full young yet. Lady Loundes now - there's a Lady - I allus did like she. But that's all gone now - new times coming and maybe not too funny either, Old Dad."

She rose deliberately, gathered up and stacked the plates and carried them to the old yellow stone sink by the window. The men left the table and went to the fire. The old Dad to his wicker and a pipe. Arthur to pour another drink of tea from the pot, which for economy's sake remained stewing on the hob for several days at a time. Mostly they drank home made mead or cider from their own apples. Since tea had come to England a few years earlier, it had become very popular in the great houses. It was still very costly and far beyond the cottagers' purse. Ilsa had developed a taste for it along with the other staff under Lady Jane Loundes's roof. She had formed the habit of collecting all the used leaves from the silver teapots at the Park. These she would bring to Eliza, after drying them in the oven. Eliza Dale prized them greatly, stored them in an old tin box and used them sparingly.

The brew she made was strong and bitter but the whole family had taken to it, and Arthur preferred it to any other drink. The tin with the tea was left on the mantel-shelf, none of the family ever touched it except Eliza. They drank tea without milk, the boys sweetened it with a little home produced honey from Old Dad's bee skips, not that they were short of milk. Lord Ainsley was a good master. Arthur Dale as head cowman was allowed half a pint of milk each day for each member of his family. It was a great standby, milk and bread puddings with honey were delicious and filling. Milk came fresh every night in a closed can when Arthur came in from work.

Eliza saved the top cream to make a little butter for special days, usually they ate dripping on their bread.

None of the family went out much after dark, the two lads settled at the table, Simon was trying to learn his letters which Lord Ainsley preferred all his apprentices to do. Simon sat with a slate and lead, cheek upon hand, head bent. At the other end of the bench Sailor with a knife and nimble fingers carved a little fox from a fragment of oak.

"If lad'ud put half the skill 'ee puts in that thar foxy into them slabs o'stone, 'eed be a proper mason 'ee would." Old

Dad's easy grin showed his stumps of teeth.

"Now give over, you - let the young'uns get a bit of peace, Old Dad" Eliza wiped her hands on the hem of her apron and took her place in the single wooden rocker by the fire. She folded her hands over her distended stomach and held her feet out to the blaze. Arthur's eyes fell upon his family with pride. This was his favourite time of day, all the family together in the firelight. On the table the flickering light of the half candle, which was their nightly allocation throughout the winter months, this was the welcome respite before the hard grind of another working day.

The pattern of life in Wood Cottage was repeated all over the Estate to a lesser or greater degree according to the various abilities and temperaments of the tenants. All the Estate workers lived in poor circumstances and all worked long hours for low wages, their standard of comfort depended to a great extent upon the thriftiness of their women. Most were good cooks and good managers, nimble with the needle, the loom and the spinning wheel. Most of the men grew a full vegetable plot, skips of bees, apple trees in the orchard and a pig in the sty. Some had a goat if a patch of rough grass was handy. The women were adept in butter and cheese making and all baked several kinds of bread. Everyone had gleaning rights, this year the gleanings had been good - dry and heavy in the heads. After harvest everyone of the Estate workers could by right go gleaning on all Lord Ainsley's fields. All fallen corn was garnered, men, women and children all helped. Most of Seckington Estate had been enclosed into fields for almost a hundred years.

Lord Ainsley cared for the cottages and homes of his workers and tenant farmers. He also looked to their health and wellbeing, especially in times of illness and bereavement. After the gleaning all the corn thus harvested went into earthenware jars in the cottage pantries, lids secured against rats, come the winter, the women would measure out the corn to be carried each month to Upper Telso Mill to be ground, they brought it home as wheaten flour - full of nutrition and goodness, ready for a month's loaves both plain and rich. The plain bread was made with salt and water, the rich with perhaps a few grains of sugar or a spoonful of honey and a little pig fat rubbed in. 'Rich' loaves would be baked for Christmas or a wedding or any special feast days.

Pigs were regarded as community animals, the cottagers killed them only one at a time throughout the winter. The meat and by-products such as trotters, dripping, chitterlings, and poorer meat used for pork pies, was often shared between half a dozen or more householders in the village. Each home sharing when their turn came. Thrifty wives salted down most of the pork and bacon in the earthenware sinks which were built into every pantry. Care in planning could ensure meat for all the winter.

Game-keepers had the additional benefit of rabbits and pigeons off the Estate. These they could barter for apples or honey or a length of homespun cloth. Cowmen had milk as part-wage. All food whether home grown or given as bonus wages from the Estate was used in the village's unique and sensible system of barter. Lord Ainsley's shepherds - he kept five hundred sheep on his hill land, had the right to a couple of fleece each at shearing time. Everyone's clothes were rough. Hessian and a course rough flax linen were mostly used. The much prized wool was spun for baby-wear and best garments. Quilts were made of clean feathers, all feathers were carefully preserved for a dozen household uses. It was a happy community in which almost everything was made within the village.

John Price the blacksmith had his home with his unmarried sister Betsy in Wychwood Cottage. It was situated in Rock Bottom Lane almost opposite Wood Cottage. He was a giant of a man with huge hands and arms. He had taken over the Smithy in Upper Telso when his Father died years before. He could shoe a horse, mend a ploughshare, or fashion metal to any shape required. He had a fine deep voice and was always singing. Every morning at five o'clock, he would leave his cottage and stride up across the fields to Upper Telso. A bag of his grub for the day would be slung across his shoulder. His great voice would come ringing across the fields to waken the rest of the village to the beginning of another day. At the Parsonage House Andrew Mallard regularly wound his clock to the Blacksmith's alarm call. His sister Betsy Price was a tiny dumpling of a woman, rarely seen without her mop cap. She kept her house spotless and put a good hot meal in front of her brother every night on the dot of six. Yet she had no timepiece, and being a trifle deaf, most surely couldn't hear the church clock.

A little further along the lane stood the Church, an ancient building partly built in Saxon times. In the churchyard stood an old Saxon cross. Many villagers regarded it as a Holy Stone with the power of healing. About the churchyard the walled graveyard was completely encircled by a continuation of Rock Bottom Lane. The Parsonage House stood nearby, here lived the Reverend Andrew Mallard, his wife Harriet, their twelve year old son Luke and Maisy their ten year old daughter. Also in the Parsonage lived Lucy Fulton, who was cook-housekeeper, friend, nurse, and general oddsbody to the entire household. Andrew Mallard was a slimly built delicate looking man, but his looks belied a wiry strength and the tremendous Christian fervour and conviction which he used to the benefit of every member of his flock.

Harriet Mallard was a rosy-faced well built woman, but in her case looks also belied, in fact she suffered with her chest and was often laid up when the weather turned damp and misty. When well she acted as governess to both her own children and any others in the village whose parents wanted them to learn their figures and letters and stories from the scriptures, a back room at the Parsonage served as a schoolroom. They had very few books, but Lord Ainsley had provided them with slates, bibles and a great globe of the world, and several books from his library. Close by the churchyard were three thatched cottages, Glebe Cottage housed Swift, Carter and Acres. These three bachelors were frequently absent of a night drinking ale in the Cross Keys Inn. In the daytime they were Lord Ainsley's shepherds. Thatcher's Cottage housed Thatcher Gibbs handed down through four generations of his family, the men of whom had done all the thatching on the Estate for as long as anyone could remember. Thatcher was a young man of a serious turn of mind, his Father had married a Quaker and there was much of his Mother in Thatcher Gibbs. He was well versed in his letters, a loyal member of the church and a good friend and neighbour. He was a big made handsome young man and had recently become betrothed to Anne Barnes, of Hill Farm, Upper Telso. He counted himself lucky, she being the daughter of one of the most respected tenant farmers on the Estate. Her Father, Tarant Barnes, farmed with his son Arthur. Hill Farm was a holding of a hundred acres plus nearly fifty acres of hill land for grazing the sheep and goats and cattle. Arthur Barnes would no doubt step into his Father's shoes at Hill Farm when the time came, but Mistress Anne was a very good catch in any man's net and she was very comely with it. Golden curling hair, merry blue eyes and sturdy of bosom and thigh. No wonder young Gibbs went about his business whistling cheerfully all day long.

In Parson's Cott - a tiny dwelling built into the churchyard wall - lived Mabel Dunn, retired housekeeper from Seckington Hall, referred to behind her back as Old Nanny Dunn, she was actually only about fifty-eight. At the back of the Churchyard was a small thatched single room dwelling which housed Tom Hart (the Giant), tall thin and balding, he was not truly 'of the village' having appeared one day about fifteen years before. He had been homeless, ragged and barefoot and destitute. That had been in Parson Brady's time. Parson Brady had taken pity on the vagrant and installed him in Churchyard Cott as sexton, grave- digger and general odd jobber at the Parsonage. He had been there ever since. He cherished ambitions to move into Parsons Cott with Mabel Dunn, but he had never made clear to her in what capacity. She being sure that his intentions were not what she called, "Standing up in Church along of I," had steadfastly rejected his wooing and kept the door of Parsons Cott fast locked of a night as an added precaution.

Lower Telso also boasted a line of six cottages in a single row. These were situated along the lane further beyond the church, they were very poorly built, each consisted of a single earth floored room below and a loft with a ladder under the thatch above. Very low lying only just above the level of Bog End Marsh and the Mere, they were inclined to flood in times of heavy rainfall. The walls housed rats and vermin. Lord Ainsley had long intended to have them pulled down and new houses built above the flood level. No one had ever got round to the work and recent policy had been to house workers down there only until a better cottage came free somewhere else on the Estate.

In the early autumn of 1665 two of the middle cottages stood empty. At number one nearest the Church lived John Symes, his wife and three young children. John Symes was Lord Ainsley's ploughman. It was hoped to rehouse them before the winter. For the present the parents slept in an old wall bed downstairs, at the back of the kitchen cum-living-room. The bed was only five feet wide, and cramped for two adults. The children shared the loft above, the two little girls in a single low home-made wooden bed and the boy in a hammock slung onto the roof beams. Cathy Symes looked forward to a better home but she never grumbled, kept the place as clean as she could, she also helped Lucy Fulton at the Parsonage whenever an extra pair of hands was needed.

In number two next door, lived Martin Bones the Estate carpenter and builder. His wife was expecting her first child that autumn, they were due to move to a cottage in Upper Telso before Christmas. Number three and Number four stood empty and damp.

Number five housed Ben Hastly an elderly widower and his two unmarried daughters. Flossie and Pheobe were both in their late twenties, neither sought nor wanted the responsibilities of a husband, that is not to say that they did not like the company of men, indeed no sooner did Old Ben slam the back door of the cottage and make tracks to the Cross Keys Inn of an evening; and he had a well worn path from door to door in that direction; than the front door would be flung open. This was by way of an invitation to any single men who felt the need of a little free and easy female company. The single men were not the only ones, especially come the dark winter nights. Pheobe and Floss were lively, blowsy good hearted women who made no secret of their uninhibited enjoyment of rustic love-making. An hour's toss in the hay or under the trees of the wood was always for them a welcome interruption from working in the fields. Either would readily down tools at a wink or a sly invitation from a shepherd or ploughboy seeking a bit of quick pleasure.

In the last cottage at the very end of the row lived two women of a different stamp. Old Mother Ross and Jeannie lived their lives very separate from the rest of the village. Mother Ross had lived in the cottage longer than anyone could remember. She was very old and had been much confined to her cottage of late. No one ever went into the dark dirty interior. Few would go past it at dusk, and certainly never after darkness fell. Both were considered to be witches, their grubby looking house, be-cobwebbed windows, black clothes and secret ways, did nothing to dispel this idea. Mother Ross was going on ninety and rarely seen about for the last five years or so - rumour had it that she was ailing - or even dead. None dared either to ask Jeannie on her rare jaunts to the village, nor yet risk a peep through the window during her absence. There was always the fear that the old woman, or her ghost might fly out to greet the unwanted intruder with a witch's curse.

The only other household which could properly be said to be within the close knit small community of Lower Telso was Lower Farm House, standing opposite the glebe land near the Parsonage House, it was one of the best built dwellings in the village. It was a square house built of stout old timbers infilled with red bricks, it boasted four good sized rooms downstairs, a wide hallway with an oak stairway leading to a landing above. Upstairs there were four rooms directly above those below. The wall divisions were lath and plaster, all the doors, floors and woodwork, solid oak.

Outside a good barn, cow byres and walled yards for hay and corn stacks completed the picture of a prosperous farm homestead. There had been members of Francis Trewis's family at the Lower House Farm since 1475, a hundred and fifty years before the present house had been built. The earliest Trewis stone in the churchyard was close up against the Saxon Cross. Villagers swore that its close proximity to the 'Good Cross' was the reason for the family's continued prosperity in the community. The inscription on the stone was simple: **Francis Feltham Trewis born May 10 1404 - died May 10 1496** *A good master and a just man*. Obviously a tidy minded man to be born and to die so neat and trim upon the same date of the year, having reached a ripe old age. The present farmhouse and buildings had been built upon the site of a much older dwelling. It was built by the first Lord Ainsley when he had inherited the Estate upon the death of a cousin. The Estate had benefited from coming into the Ainsley family and many improvements had been made over the years.

The present Francis Trewis occupied the house with Amanda, his wife, four sons and two daughters. Ben, William, John and Armstrong were the four young men. Ben was now twenty-five, Arms the youngest was a year older than Velvet the elder daughter. Then there had been a long gap until three years ago when Hannah the baby of the household had been born when her Mother was forty-two.

Francis Trewis was a hard man, driving his sons, himself and his wife. Velvet was his weak spot - understandably - she was a beautiful qirl. Dark chestnut hair, sparkling brown eyes and a tomboy's temperament. She was a natural horse-woman with no sense of danger. She had been raised behind four strapping brothers and had learned early on that survival meant toughness of mind and body. She was spirited and determined, there was no job on the farm she would not tackle. Often she could do a better job than her brothers, she had a kind of aloof pride, mixing with no one. Most of the village men held her a bit in awe, partly because of her own attitude, partly because of her Father's jealous guardianship of his daughter. He felt none in Telso to be a match for his daughter, and made it all too clear to any would be suiter who showed so much as a sniff of interest.

Away to the South East lay the old stone Quarry. From here had been carted all the stone used in the building of Seckington Hall, the Home Farm and many of the old barns and agricultural buildings in the villages. Long disused it now formed a sheltered secluded hide-away where grass came early in spring and silver birches lined the banks of the Cliven Brook which formed one of the boundaries. Here lived the Romany community. As long as time looked back the Dyer's had held sway in Quarry Bottom Hollow. This was a truly gypsy settlement. Four or five painted Romany caravans stood beneath the oak trees, hidden from the eyes of the village. Caravans came and went in the nomadic fashion of gypsies, but Black Dyer, head of his clan, and his wife Jewel remained static, holding on like limpets to their tenure in Quarry Bottom. Ageing now Black Dyer had taken in his old age his cousin Jewel as his third wife, she was much of an age with Dyer's sons; Jason, Falcon and Saul. She was the mother of Mary the blackhaired, black eyed, one year old handful whose energetic shouts and cries were often heard as far away as the Parsonage House.

Also at Quarry Bottom lived Dyer's daughter by his second wife. Raven Dyer was sixteen, she had been raised by her

Grandmother now long dead. She had of late blossomed into a beauty. Black hair hung below her hips, black eyes could flash with temper as well as humour and passion. From a skinny unkempt little thing had grown a supple body, long thighs curved into wide hips, a narrow waist, above which her young breasts swelled and filled with a promise not to be hidden by the ragged torn dresses which were all she ever had to wear.

Jewel had begun to grow jealous of Raven from the first day of her marriage to Black Dyer. She had increasingly since then been forced to watch her husband's and his sons' eyes follow Raven about her tasks round the camp.

"Trouble that one - nothing but trouble," Jewel would mutter to herself, her mouth hardening into a tight line. During the months her belly had been filled with her young child she had wished that some man might be tempted to lift Raven's skirts and fill her, to swell in equal unsightliness. Since giving birth, Jewel had taken every step she knew to make herself desirable and always available to her husband, but not to become pregnant again. She went in constant fear lest his attentions stray to the younger girl. She knew her man. Even in age Dyer had a great liking for virgins. None could help but think Raven a lush ripe plum for the picking. It was an explosive situation with the two women for ever at one anothers' throats. The four men were amused at their antics but with not enough women to go around, each and every one of them was watching his chance.

They lived by peg making, snaring, poaching and fishing, they knew every inch of wild country about them and their exploits covered twenty miles distance in every direction. Their skill and cunning was such that they passed like shadows in and out of the Estates round about, almost unnoticed by the gamekeepers whose task it was to catch them. Lord Ainsley refused to have them driven off, he considered Black Dyer to be a king in his own right and by long custom, the Quarry to be his kingdom.

The Trewis family at Lower House and Dyers in the Quarry Bottom had held their land since time immemorial, long before an Ainsley had inherited Seckington Hall Estate. Such rights were not lightly to be overthrown.

And so at the time of David Ainsley's home coming, dwelt

the compact close knit community of Lower Telso; around and beyond it stretched Ainsley lands. On the hillside the sister village of Upper Telso was much more sprawling and scattered, although less close knit, most of the people on the hill felt themselves a part of the church and village in the valley. Between them lay the fields which were the basis of the villages' livelihood. Up on the hillside along the lane side were a scattering of cottages and the Cross Keys Inn, beyond stood the Smithy, where John Price plied his blacksmith's trade. By the side of the Cliven Brook, which ran and tumbled down amongst rocks beyond the hill, the Estate mill stood. It was powered by the tumbling water.

Alongside the smithy the harness maker Evan Sykes worked with his leather in a low thatched hovel. Along the lane to the west stood The Park. A small Elizabethan Manor House standing in its own acres of pasture and trees which had given the house its name. At its gates stood The Lodge, an old house which was used as a dower house for The Park.

Jonathon Ainsley had recently taken over this menage with his bride. Her Mother, Lady Jane Loundes had moved into The Lodge, taking three of her personal servants with her. Left behind at the big house in the service of the new Master were many members of staff who had served the Loundes family for many years. Ilsa Dale from Wood Cottage had only been with the household for two years, she was one of those who remained at The Park.

At the Easterly end of Upper Telso, Hill Farm stood in its green, windswept, well-husbanded acres. Here lived Tarant Barnes and his family. Tarant and his son and four workers farmed the land as Lord Ainsley's tenants. Marion his wife was mistress of the house helped by their daughter Anne and a couple of girls from the village. Anne was betrothed to Thatcher Gibbs. A strong bonny girl she looked after all the dairy work, milking, making butter and cheese for market. Marion hoped the young ones would settle in the farm cottage which belonged to the farm. It stood just along the lane near the farm gates. Anne secretly perferred Thatcher's own cottage near the Church, but at present she had not told her Mother this, fearing to hurt her feelings.

The hillside looked down across the fields and to the East towards a great belt of woodland. Amongst the woodland stood Seckington Hall with its stables, a group of workers cottages and the Home Farm beyond. It was a beautiful old house and buildings, built mainly of stone from the Quarry. Here was the hub of the Estate's functioning. Timber Mill, kennels, stables and cottages along with the great house forming a tight working force within the larger community of the village. All lay sheltered within the great trees of the old woodland, reached from the villages by crossing the fast racing Cliven.

In the shelter of Telso Woods, Crab Tree Cottage nestled peaceful, out of sight of all other habitation, it was so placed as to be suspended between Upper and Lower Telso and the Hall itself. It was to this out of the way community with all its loves and hates and happiness that David Ainsley had returned. It was to these woods and fields that he awakened under the thatch of Crab Tree on the morning after his arrival. He awoke to a sense of wonder, darkened suddenly in his thoughts of Elizabeth. He lay back stretching his arms above his head, and gazed across a sunlit patch of oak floorboards towards the open window. He could see the great trees, turning to autumn yellow at the edge of the woodland, then the ground sloped away across Big Fields towards Lower Telso Church and the old Parsonage House. It was a beautiful tranquil view. All bitterness seemed futile but the hurt was none the less strong for that.

"Face it, man," he muttered. "Face it." Face what? The fact that less than a mile away his own brother lay with Elizabeth in his arms in the intimacy of the marriage bed. That it was over for him. Everything he had imagined and fed on for so long was never to be. He must steel himself to face them both without giving way to his feelings. Pride would accomplish that. More difficult perhaps to convince his Mother and Father that his life was not in ruins. But in reality was it? Not if he applied himself to hard work - kept so busy as not to dwell on wounds which nothing could now alter, after all he had Crab Tree - these villages needed him just as he needed them. Work had been enough these last eight or ten years. He must see that it was enough again now.

He shrugged off his depression and spoke his thoughts

aloud. "Time to get up and explore." He ran down the stairs in his nightshirt and opened the back door. Looking out he saw a misty dew-decked world. The sounds of pigeons came to him from amongst the silver birches. Lower down by the brook he heard water tumbling into the deep pool below the rocks.

Glancing round the kitchen David saw something of a turmoil, several pieces of furniture on end and piled about. Boxes of clothes and household items in the hasty jumble of his Mother's necessarily hurried packing. The men had unloaded in haste in almost darkness, they had placed a low wooden couch with blankets upstairs as his make-shift bed, and they had set the kitchen table upright. On it several boxes stood waiting to be unpacked.

The stream had first call! He took his old towel from his pack and ran out of the door, the grass washed his bare feet as he ran, saturating the hem of his nightshirt. At the edge of the brook the noise was deafening as the water tumbled into the pool below. He threw off his nightshirt and dived into the centre of the pool as he had done so many times during the hot summers of his boyhood. Often with Charlotte and Esme. He had forgotten the icy quality of the spring water, it took his breath. He gasped and spluttered taking several minutes to get his limbs working properly, then he began to enjoy himself. For ten minutes he swam too and fro, diving below the clear surface and revelling in the contact of the water on his skin, and the clean sensation it produced in him. London was far away, he paused in his enjoyment to wing good wishes to Vincent Fallon, still prisoned in that Plague ridden city.

Raven Dyer walking silent and unnoticed through the woodland, barefoot and clad in her faded brown dress; she was as well hidden as a young fawn in the bracken. She had been sent to collect the unlucky beasts trapped in her half-brother's snares overnight. In this she was only half-hearted, any rabbits being quite dead she would carry home, any alive, she would free. It had long been her custom. No one at home knew about it, if they had she would surely have got a beating. Black Dyer found new pleasure of late in stripping her for beating, since the maturing of her body in recent months.

Raven came to the waterfall as one drawn by a magnet, she

loved the sound of falling water above all other country sounds. Just as she came clear of the trees she saw the man. He had done bathing and climbed onto the grass bank. He stood naked, his body was brown and sunburned, his wet hair curled and shining moist black. He reached for the towel but scarcely bothered to use it. The sun streamed down to dry him. He shook himself and drops of shining water flew off him in all directions. As he turned she fell flat to lie in the long grass, hidden from his eyes she yet watched him secretly.

Raven's contacts with men had been confined to the often unwashed sweaty bodies of her Father and step brothers' she held them all in revulsion, she longed to escape from them and most of all from the jealousy of her step-mother. She dreaded being sold to another of the Romany tribe to put a few gold pieces in Black Dyer's pocket. Seeing the clean beauty of David Ainsley's body suggested a new idea into her mind for the first time. To go to such a man might not be so bad - might even prove sweet. Did not the vixen crouch again and again for the dog fox to take his pleasure? But how to capture the attention of such a man? She knew he was the son of Lord Ainsley, she had heard Black Dyer speak of his return. Yet he had come to Crab Tree not to the great house. She puzzled in her mind as she watched him.

Within the wood another watcher craned his neck towards the sunlight as he tried to glimpse what had so caught the girl's attention. A poacher himself, Old Amos lived hermit-like in an old hut beside the Cliven Brook. Now in his seventy-fifth year he rarely bothered with much poaching. Pilfering instead amongst the Romany's snares and traps, he took only enough to barter for baccy and the few other simple things that he needed. A gnarled grubby, long-haired gnome of a man, a rabbit for the stew-pot was all he needed. He suddenly caught sight of the naked man in the sunshine.

"Welle! Welle! B'aint she a naughty wench, then. Bet she'd like to run a bit nearer to get a better peep! Not much Old Amos do miss. Never mind 'ee, missy, ole Amos won't spoil yer fun - knows how to hold his tongue does Amos. Aye, knows that well enough!" He picked up the brace of rabbits Raven had dropped by the tree in her first sight of David Ainsley. Slipping them deep in the pocket of his ragged coat he slipped away between the trees, as silently as he had come.

"I bet her'll get a shock when she do miss they bunnies," he chuckled wheezily in his chest. He was wrong, Raven's mind was filled with other things. The beating Black Dyer took pleasure in giving her that morning was for returning empty-handed. She hardly took notice of his belt across her back, her head was filled with other ideas.

In the stable yard at the back of Seckington Hall, Lord Ainsley spent half an hour that morning with Martin Bones and James Painter his head groom. Lord Ainsley, tall, grey-haired and clad in working breeches and cord jacket, spent some time selecting a horse for David's use at Crab Tree. In this he was guided by Painter as to the right animal to choose. What he wanted was an animal which would give David pleasure to ride, but at the same time prove reliable in the shafts should the need arise. He returned to the house well satisfied with the animal they had chosen. Beauty was a sure-footed kind-eyed mare, heavy enough built to carry a tall man over rough ground with ease. If they suited one another he would make him a present of her for visiting patients later on. Lord Ainsley hurried in to Isobel to tell her of his choice.

"Oh Richard - I'm so glad - what a good idea. How generous of you my Dear. Just the thing, a good horse - he will look so well upon her, very important just now."

"I agree - that was just what I had in mind, impress the tenants and give him some standing in the eyes of all the local people."

"His natural pride will carry him through anyway, but his own house and a first class mount will help. Did you send a nice saddle?"

"I've ordered one from Sykes - he makes a fine saddle when he's a mind."

"When will Painter take the mare down for him?"

"This morning, and the box of linen and food you ordered. Painter understands he goes no further than the gates, he can shout to David from there."

"He looked so handsome yesterday in the garden, I think

Elizabeth will wish these last weeks undone the moment she lays eyes on him."

"Too late now, she belongs to Jonathon."

"I hope she realises that."

"Jonathon regards her as his property now, he'll flay her alive if she so much as lifts a finger towards David. Elizabeth is a very spirited young woman - yet she likes dominance in a man - she might enjoy a whipping from Jonathon once in a while."

"You can't mean that."

"I do mean it. Young women are strange creatures, she won't respect Jonathon unless he keeps her in order."

"Maybe - yet I feel there's much in Jonathon that a woman or anyone weaker than himself might find cause to fear." Lady Isobel's face was troubled. They were interrupted by a light tap on the door, a little maid servant entered.

"Yes Ellen?"

"Will you take chocolate in here, My Lady?"

"No Ellen - We'll have it on the terrace. These sunny days cannot last much longer, let us enjoy the sunshine while we may." A beautiful smile transformed Isobel's face. Ellen curtsied and withdrew and they went out into the sunshine.

After his swim, unaware that he had been observed, David went back into the cottage. A great patch of late foxgloves grew on the slope below the dwelling, they were thronged with humming bees, working industriously up and down each purple 'glove' collecting nectar.

In the kitchen David spent an hour sorting out the furniture and boxes from the Hall. Crab Tree was built to a simple design but with its new thatch and fresh plaster it held the promise of a comfortable home. Downstairs it comprised three simple rooms. The kitchen with basement below contrived because of the fall away of land below the foundations of the house. Next to the kitchen was a large living room with a wide open fireplace. There were two windows, newly glazed by Martin Bones, replacing the old wooden shutters. The other room was an old parlour which had a door to the yard. David planned to use this room as a surgery for the use of his patients. He meant to model it upon Vincent Fallon's London equivalent. One wall to be shelves and cupboards for his medicines and books, a table and couch for examinations. Everything to be very clean. Windows open to the air whenever weather permitted. He found pleasure in the planning. He had known he would stay right from the start, right from his Father's words: "Elizabeth has not waited for you". At least it had been final, at once - no hope deferred - better that way, like a clean severed limb - one cut - finish!. The best, easier for the body to recover. How close ran the mind to the body. It took a medical mind to appreciate that. As he thought, he worked, finding relief in the tasks of his hands.

Soon the kitchen and sitting room were to rights. In the sitting room two old armchairs of his mother's stood either side of the fireplace. A rag rug thrown down upon the slab stone floor between. Two pictures, small oils of country scenes, taken from his old bedroom at the Hall hung on the walls, an old Venetian mirror hung above the chimney-breast. At the centre of the room a table of polished oak, round which stood four country-made chairs, the two other chairs which made up the set of six, he carried into the surgery, along with his old desk, its top ink-stained from long forgotten days of study, they began to give the room life. There was as yet no other furniture for the surgery. He shrugged - twenty or so days would soon pass, then his mother would gladly let him ransack the attics at the Hall to find a few more items. He needed nothing valuable - only a homely comfortable place. How different if Elizabeth were cominq here as his wife! The thought slipped in unasked. Well he was now free to make his own choices. This thought shocked him even more. Was there a sense of relief in him? Certainly it would have been difficult if not impossible to have brought Crab Tree to anywhere near the standard Elizabeth Loundes had been used to at the Park. Well all that was Jonathon's business now - no longer his own concern. Leave it. What about the kitchen? What about breakfast? He went into the kitchen.

Half an hour later he had fuelled and lit the fire from the stack of peat in the old stable. As it crackled cheerfully in the chimney-breast David sat down at the plain deal top table to his first meal. He found himself very hungry. In cook's hamper he found game pie, new bread, and fresh butter, milk and eggs from the home farm, cutlery and crockery and bottles of wine, all wrapped in clean laundered table linen for his use in the house. Wine glasses were folded carefully in a linen cloth.

Beside the newly fitted yellow stone sink in the kitchen was a dresser fitted to the wall at the side of the new iron pump. He worked the pump handle experimentally and out gushed water, clear and pure from the spring. He washed his soiled dishes together with those from his pack, left from the tray he had taken from his Father last evening. He set the crockery tidy upon the dresser and looked about him well pleased with his kitchen. The flames from the fire shone upon the clean dishes and the deal table. An old rocking chair was there from some long gone previous tenant - truly the place began to be home. He heard a shout and jumped up in surprise. In the yard he saw no one but again came the shout.

"Whoa, Whoa there!" He saw a horse and trap by the gate and James Painter, his Father's groom at her head, his hand upon the gate.

"Good day, James - how are you? It's been a long time."

"Aye, Sir, and Good day to ye - you'm very welcome home, Sir. We're all that glad to see ye back. Master says to keep the mare for riding and let her graze the stream bank. Her be Beauty - likely you ain't seen her afore - but she be a good mare. She'll see 'ee right. Her Ladyship had a few things put in the trap as her thinks you'm might need like. Is it right I dares'nt unload for 'ee? Seems strange like, it do."

"No, No. It's quite right - I don't think I'm ill but we have to wait the right number of days to be sure. Will you give them my thanks, especially my Father for the lovely Mare? Beauty you say? Indeed she is well named. I shall be able to ride on the moors and enjoy much freedom now."

"Aye, Sir - she's well named. I'll get back then, Sir, to me work - real glad we'm are - all at the Hall that is - that you're back among us again." He tied the reins to the gate rail and backed away a little embarrassed by the circumstances

"Thank you, James, I hope to see you again soon."

"Aye, Sir, that's right. By the way, Sir," he turned halfway up the lane, "Miss Esme do say as she'll come to the edge of the woodland at sunset to see you! All right?"

"Oh good, thank you, James, I'll look for her." David waited until the groom was out of sight, before he opened the gate and led the horse and trap into the yard. She was a fine animal, Chestnut, with a white blaze down her nose. Looking too fine to be in the shafts, yet she stood perfectly at ease while he unloaded and backed her up to rest the vehicle under the cart shed. Out of the shafts and harness she stood quiet and proud, the beautiful arch of her neck and mane, gleaming in the sunshine.

David went to her head, patting and stroking her shining coat."Lovely girl - Beauty girl - there's a good lass - what a beauty." She looked at him, ears pricked, brown eyes benign. It was the beginning of a life-long partnership for her. He turned her loose in the paddock by the stream where she began to crop the grass placidly.

In the unloaded boxes in the kitchen were two containers of clothes from pre-navy days. Some would not fit - he had filled out these last four years. There were also some pots and pans including a large cast iron kettle for his kitchen. He distributed all the items about the house. Everything he placed made it seem more homely - there were four candlesticks, a box of home-made candles and a bundle of thin tapers for lighting. He set them about, ready for nightfall.

Exploring the stables an hour later he found a pile of wood and some tools left by Martin Bones for his use. Seeing an interesting occupation for an hour or two he carried them into the proposed surgery and set to work putting up shelves. He soon became absorbed and the time passed quickly.

In the Cross Keys Inn that night, George Arms and his wife Esther were playing host to a dozen or more men from the villages. Old Ben Hastly sat in his usual place at the fire. George Swift, Tom Carter and Jack Acres stood ranged along the counter. Full tankards of ale had been placed in front of them. Zeb Mysen, the miller, had just come in, his fat girth was second only to the Landlord's. George Arms was also a big fellow but Zeb was always gloomy in outlook, while George had a perpetual grin about his florid features.

In the far corner Falcon Dyer and his brother Jason sat alone, backs turned to the rest of the company. Their black heads close in whispered conversation. Even here, they were markedly separate from the village, their independent almost tribal Romany arrogance isolated them. Coupled with the gypsy swarthiness of skin and eyes and a certain furtive slyness, they were as a race apart from all those present.

Andrew Tysen was also present, he was head gardener at the Park, he had held the post for over twenty years joining the staff as a stable boy in the late Lord Loundes time.

George Arms drew a pint of ripe cider from a barrel at the back of the bar and gave the tankard into Tysen's hand across the counter.

"Your usual then, Andy? And how are you liking your new Master, then? Be there gonn'a be changes, think 'ee?"

"Us outside see's nothin, and those inside say nothin. Us all waits and sees." Tysen folded his lips and felt in his waistcoat pocket for the money to pay for his drink, he put the coin deliberately on the counter, lifting his tankard he took a long swig and then wiped the back of his hand across his full mouth.

"Oh come on - that there's allus been a right bugger - movin' his bed a couple of miles 'ent likely altered that over much." Jack Acres entered the conversation.

"Now, Jack - kip out, 'ent nout t'do with us lot." Tom Carter, always peace-maker laid a restraining hand upon his friend's shoulder.

"Cum off it - I speaks as I finds. When yon bastard comes in for this Estate - I'll be the first off, couldn't work for 'im, I couldn't."

"By then, you'll likely have some lass to your bed and six or seven babbies to feed, then you'll be stuck here whatever." George Swift pushed his balled fist into Jack's shoulder in a mock punch.

"Never - I'd as soon stop single as get me trapped under 'is foot."

"Tis a cryin' pity as t'aint Mr. David as comes Boss here after 'is Lordship, now that'ud be summit like." A new voice broke in when Ben Hastly stood up and came to the counter.

"Another pint, thank 'ee, George - Don't likely reckon we'll live to see it, anyways up, eh, George? - You young 'uns'll have to sort it. We'll likely be under the daises by then."

"Now then, Ben!" Esther Arms bridled and shot him a quick

glance. "You'll give us another twenty summers more of your company, shan't you?"

"Wot I says is," Tom Carter drew them back to the main theme of discussion, "that we'm all damn lucky Mr. David is come 'ome - and to stay, if all I do 'ear is right, and that in spite of all the vagaries of women-kind and mind-changing which be their privilege, specially in the upper classes if I makes my meanin' clear. Wot we wants is a good Medic, someone as knows wot's wot, and cares for us and the old folks and childer here abouts. That's wot I says." He glared round at the company.

"I'll say Amen to that. Good sense that is. Let folks alone as do bide at the Hall to my way of thinking." Zeb Mysen's deep voice brooked no argument.

"We'm all of one mind on that Zeb - that's certain." George Arms closed the discussion by laying a cloth over his barrels.

"Now Gentlemen, if you'd oblige and drink up. 'Tis five minutes till this house be shutting - I must get my good lady off to bed of a night - that I must." He administered a promising slap across his wife's buttocks. A general laugh was lost in the scrape of boots on the stone floor.

At dusk David went out across the grass to the stream bank. Following the water course down amongst the rock pools until he reached a large slab of stone which protruded out across a deep pool. It was a favourite childhood haunt of all the young Ainsleys. From here there was a clear view of the path from the Hall which ran on across Big Fields towards Lower Telso. A small footbridge spanned the stream a few yards beyond the rock, the banks grew thick with meadow sweet, rushes and ragged robin. The scent of sun-warmed pollen and honeysuckle filled the air.

David settled on the rock to wait, it was here that Esme, his sister, would come at dusk as the groom had promised. He watched the sun sinking lower and lower over Windy Wood and the open moorland beyond. The last rays touched the barn roof at Lower House and the tower of Telso Church simultaneously, he could hear the distant quacking of ducks in the Lower House yards and guessed someone was penning them up for the night. In the woods behind him the birds called spasmodically as they settled in the darkening branches for the night. A sudden more shrill alarm call of a blackbird told him that someone was coming along the path from the Hall.

The sound came of twigs snapping and a small green-clad figure came flurrying out from beneath the dark trees, she leant on the bridge and peered over jumping about in her excitement. David was treated to a glimpse of bobbing brown curls and a pair of saucy blue eyes in a round rosy face. All were framed in the bright green velvet folds of her cloak.

"Oh, David! How do you do? How thrilling it is that we may not touch but must meet in the open. Puts me in mind of an adventure from a book. Truly it does. Father says I may come every day - but no nearer. Of course Charlotte will no doubt push me out when she gets to hear of it. Today she is with Mother, they are gone into Wesperton for cloth to stitch her gowns for winter, she grows very dull I may tell you since Mr. Irwin Saint from Dunsmore began to call, and he's so drab, David, and no wise handsome! Even a little fat to my mind!" She at last paused from lack of breath, gazing at him round eyed.

"Answering your first question - which no doubt you've forgotton in all this outburst. I'm well, thank you, and glad to be home. As to your last remarks, when you are as old as I am you will discover that girls are strange and like to becoming more so as they grow to women. The young man in question is no doubt a fairy prince in your sister's eyes, and she a fairy in his. It is always so in the best fairy tales. But what of you? You've become a day or two older perhaps?"

"Oh David - don't be such a tease! You are not near as old as you make out, and I am almost a young lady grown - see how my gown fills - and you call yourself a Doctor!'.

"I can see little of you above the wood slats of the bridge. It does not seem that you grow in modesty, sister!"

"Oh, David - I'm not vain - I spend only seconds upon my dress. 'Tis Charlotte peeps and preens. She do fuss so much, we are forever late when we go out, I must often stand in the hall and tap my foot until I'm near driven silly."

"Did you say driven? As I recall you were ever quite a 'silly dizzy' as a little one."

"Well, I'm not now. Father says he begins to see me develop

good sense and better manners each passing day."

"Well, keep in mind that you were ever the best cherry in the cake as far as Father was concerned."

"Oh David, don't be so tiresome. Here am I to cheer your loneliness and brighten your day and all you do ...."

"Yes," he interrupted, "all I do is admonish and reprove. Never mind, Dearest Esme - I'm only cross and nasty because I may not hug you and give you my accustomed kiss!"

"Oh, David, I do love you, and to have you home, when they all feared you dead! I knew you would come, I just knew it here." Extravagantly she pressed both hands against her heart. Her words ran on like the brook. "How Elizabeth could be so silly ....."

"No, Esme - I'll hear none of that. Elizabeth, or any lady in fact is free to choose. Elizabeth is now Jonathon's wife and our sister-in-law, there is no more to be said upon the matter."

"Well, whatever you say and no matter how you scold me - she was hasty and she is already in regret - I saw it in her eyes when she called and Father gave her the news."

"That will do, Esme" He sounded so angry that even Esme's tongue was stilled.

"I'm sorry David. I promise I'll not mention it again."

"Very well - now upon another matter - do you wish to be of help to me, little sister?"

"Oh, yes please."

"When you come tomorrow, bring writing materials and you can list for me the medical supplies I need for the Surgery, I'm furnishing at Crab Tree. Mother will send someone into the Apocathery at Wesperton to collect them. Father will stake me - I can repay him later. I have washed carefully all my coins but will take no risk. Do you think you can manage this task?

"Oh yes, of course I can. Also I've a basket here from the kitchen, I'm to leave with you. Only, I must run back soon, Mother said to be inside the garden gate by sundown, before it begins to grow dark."

"Yes, you run along. Put the basket on the grass by the path. I'll fetch it when you've gone. Be sure you thank Mother and Cook for me. Now run off quick and bless you for coming."

"And you - my dearest brother. Here's a kiss." She blew it with her hand as she ran away across the bridge. "Goodnight - I'll come tomorrow - a bit earlier - we'll need time to write your list - Goodnight." And she was gone. A flurry of pink skirts beneath the green cloak as she vanished into the shadows of the oaks.

At Hill Farm which looked out on the hill above Crab Tree the Barnes family settled down for the night. Tarant Barnes lay in bed beside his wife Marion, and settled his tired body into the comfort of the deep nest of feathers which formed their mattress. The rising moon crept as a finger of light through the uncurtained window and rested upon his wife's dark hair as she lay beside him. It held no hint of grey. He put out his hand and touched the dark tresses - he still found her desirable and their grown children would have been astonished at the love-making which they often enjoyed in the privacy of this quiet comfortable room. Marion turned towards him at once and placed her hands on his chest.

"What did our Arthur say then, Tarant?"

"What about?"

"You know what about! In the Cross Keys tonight."

"Oh, naught much - they'm all on about Jonathon Ainsley - you know how he's regarded. Seems most folks wish David were the heir."

"Well, I certainly do. I'm thinking we'll all wish it when the old Lord goes. A right bad one that Jonathon. Did our Arthur speak out in the Inn? It's as well he keeps a still tongue."

"No - he was with Thatcher Gibbs and young Gibbs holds a good head on his shoulders. Allus knows when to keep silent, that one."

"Yes - he's a nice lad - what about our Anne - d'you think she be right for him - they'm in a bit too much hurry for me!"

"Well, I was in a hurry at that age - so were you if I remember it right. Come on lass cease all this chatter - let's have a feel at you and a kiss or two. It'll be time to get up by you shuts up else!" They gave themselves up to the matter in hand.

Across the landing, Arthur Barnes stretched his long limbs in sleep. Flat on his back with the blanket thrown back he slept the deep untroubled sleep of those who work hard all day in the open air.

In her room at the end of the passage, Anne lay in her small narrow bed. Candle blown out, she lay watching the moon, her mind centred on Thatcher Gibbs. What a name, Thatcher! Surely she must choose another. She remembered his kiss earlier in the day, and the sense of excitement it had sent through her body lived in her again. She felt shamed at the feelings he roused in her, and that it was worse when he was in his work clothes than when he was dressed in his Sunday suit and came calling. When he caught her as he had today, dressed in his old work breeches and boots, the smell of the damp straw of his trade about him and with the sweat of a warm day in his armpits, tobacco upon his breath and dust all over him, then one touch and she turned to water in his hands. She had never known loving would be like this. This longing and wanting filling her mind with thoughts and questions about him, she shook her feather pillow and buried herself into it's softness, pretending herself in his arms. A few minutes later and she too was fast asleep.

In her vast beautifully furnished bedroom at the Park, Elizabeth Ainsley prepared for bed. She sat before her mirror and brushed out her long hair. It fell in silken folds upon the shoulders of her white nightgown. In the glass her eyes looked back at her, impassive, showing no emotion. Even to herself she was resolved that she would never again give way to her true feelings, least of all to her close family and her husband. Husband! For the thousandth time in the last few weeks she sought within herself the answer to how it had happened. Even before David came home. David! She forced the name to cross the passage of her mind quietly, as she must also learn to let it pass her lips in open company. Leaving no trace of anguish or emotion in her expression, she banished the train of thought and laid down her brush.

A moment later she stepped into bed leaving only one candle alight on the dressing table. She lay amongst the pillows - fine linen sheets about her, comfort and luxury on every side. She was a beautiful woman by any standards, she had the fine bone structure which had been the gift of all the women in her

Mother's family. It was not a meek face and it's strength lay in the clean cut perfect symmetry of every feature, even the eye-brows were perfectly matched. Dark smooth wings above the almond shaped eyes. Since her marriage there had come into her expression a kind of desperate calm. Almost a nun-like look of discipline which had not been there before. Only her mother had noticed this from the very first. Knowing her so well, it would have taken more than Elizabeth could manage in the way of deception to hide her feelings from her mother. Lady Loundes had herself weathered the stormy seas of thirty years prisoned within the walls of a loveless marriage. Now she feared for her daughter and knew herself powerless to help.

Elizabeth had never known that her Mother had not loved her Father, and now as she lay waiting for her husband she felt utterly alone, convinced that she was the only woman ever to give herself to a man, submit to his desires and wishes for the rest of life itself. Could anything be worse? How did it, how could it have happened?

Her thoughts were interrupted by the sound of his step and the door opening. He came in and smiled at her, suave, charming and courteous as always.

"There you are, my dear - I was longer that I intended - I had a few words with Cook - about the pheasant tonight - I was not at all satisfied. I fear that in times past, Mother, your dear Mother, failed to discipline the servants. Cook lays the blame upon Ilsa - Ilsa Dale - you know? Her Father is my Father's cowman I believe. Be that as it may - it appears that the girl selected the birds from the game larder. Careless, very careless. No taste in them whatever. Not hung long enough, I imagine. After all, I am Master here now. The servants must learn that I like things just so. After all, we might have guests - discriminating guests. I have told Cook that she may speak to the girl this time, but if I find any further fault or carelessness - then of course a good beating is the answer. For that, I shall assume responsibility. I like to keep discipline within my own hands - none but the master should discipline female staff. It so often gets out of hand if a man on the staff; a butler or someone is allowed a free hand, it can cause trouble".

"Jonathon," at last she interrupted him. "You don't mean

that you plan to beat Ilsa - for not choosing a pheasant to your liking? Why, it's nothing - I tasted nothing wrong at all."

"My dear - don't upset yourself, you are too gentle to be harsh with anyone. Leave this to me - it will show the staff the standard that I expect. I assure you it can do nothing but good." His thin lips closed in a harsh line.

"Please, Jonathon, don't make any more of this - Ilsa is very young - she's not been here long. Mother always found her a good girl, it may make bad feelings against you in the village. Arthur Dale's been with your Father's Estate over twenty years. I beg you leave it rest."

"Ah, very well, my dear - to please, you of course - but I mean to be Master in my own house. Even you must understand that. Our honeymoon cannot continue forever - much as I would like it so. And now we've talked enough my dear - let us close the subject."

He threw off his robe, he was clad for bed in his long nightshirt. He turned his back on her and went to the windows to open the long curtains. Looking at him she found it hard to realise that he, who resembled his Father in looks so closely, could differ from that kindly man in so total a way as regards every detail of character. Slim, tall and fair, a fine shaped head and well knit body, yet in his face there was much she was learning to dread. The thin lipped selfish mouth, at this moment the lower lip pushed out in artificial fullness, showing a sensual expectation in its contour, almost as if in a few moments under cover of darkness, he might allow saliva to dribble from the open lip. The thin white, ever moving hands, always cold in their touch. He moved across the room, blew out the candle and turned back the bed covers. A moment later his clammy hands were upon her.

CHAPTER II

CHAPTER II

The weather continued fine into early October. The villagers carried their gifts to church for harvest. The old hymns were led by John Price the farrier. Prayers of thanksgiving were said by the Rev. Andrew Mallard. He and his wife were much liked and respected in the villages. Andrew Mallard enjoyed getting his hands dirty, he was as able with a pitchfork in his hands as with a bible. He could make a rick of hay or of sheaves of corn, drive a horse before a plough or in the shafts of a cart. He would talk to a man, while helping him herd his cows or drive his pigs to market. If a man died and must be buried, he could conduct himself with compassion and kindness, as well as dignity at the grave-side. If a young couple had run ahead a little and wished to be married in haste, he could achieve the impossible. On the one hand he would not allow a rushed wedding in his church, on the other he could soothe all the parties concerned, read the banns three times according to custom; but also persuade the parents, the bride, the groom and the relatives not only to attend the wedding, but also to live peacefully, often in close proximity afterwards. This gift of being able to make people live together in harmony was rare. The villagers knew it, they loved Andrew Mallard for himself.

A few days after the Harvest Service at the church, the Harvest Supper was by custom held in the great barn at Lower House Farm. It was a great annual event for the villages. In the morning Lord Ainsley or his head man would attend at the old barn in Over Barns Field known as 'No Man's Barn'. It was across the fields from Lower Telso Village. A high building with a great hammer beam roof, it dominated the surrounding fields. Here by custom for close on two hundred years the tenants and tenant farmers had come to pay and be paid their dues from the Estate.

The barn would be swept clean and decorated with evergreens the day before. In the morning Lord Ainsley would sit at a long table at the end of the barn with his clerk in a chair beside him. In front of him the large ledger in which every transaction was carefully written. All the men, farmers, workers, and cottagers, no preference given between one man and another, would come from their homes and farms. They formed a line down the long floor space and went to the table each in turn. The farmers would pay over their rents for the last year. The workers would be paid over their dues contained in a leather bag of cowhide with a draw string at the neck. The clerk would write an entry in his book for each transaction. The coins, gold and silver would be piled in neat heaps before him. Lord Ainsley would shake each man's hand and speak with him for a few minutes before passing on to the next. It was a social occasion. Farmers and employees all in Sunday best would exchange news as they stood in line waiting their turn. The low buzz of conversation bringing the old building to life.

When it was over the men all went home to midday dinner, a meal especially cooked by the women to celebrate the harvest and a year's wages received. All would eat and drink well on this feast day.

In the afternoon villagers would go and prepare the barn for the Harvest Ball which was held at night. Others would go and set out the Harvest Supper which was held across the field in the smaller barn at Lower Farm House. Only essential work was done on harvest day. The women and girls would work hard setting out the food on the great lengths of boards set up in Lower House Barn. By nightfall the tables would be heavy with the weight of the food. Sides of roast beef and pork, chickens, geese and ducks. Fresh loaves of bread and great shaped pats of golden butter. Pork pies, pickles, apple tarts, great dishes of cream, jellies and sweetmeats crowded the tables. As much weight as the trestles could carry.

The men would set up barrels of cider and mead and sweet home-made wines for the women. At dusk the villagers would crowd into the barn. Candles and torches would light up the scene as over a hundred and fifty people sat down to feast and make merry. The founder of the feast would not be there. Instead Lord Ainsley's head man would sit at the top of the table. Frances Trewis sat at the foot. Children would run free about the rush strewn floor. Parents feeding them tit-bits from the table.

For an hour or more there would be nothing but chatter and eating and drinking. When the feast was done the women would carry loaded trays to anyone in the village too old or infirm to attend. John Price would stand upon his feet with a song, all would join in until the rafters rang, as the singing progressed it became more bawdy. The more the men drank the more bawdy it became. The women and girls would creep away taking the children home to bed before going across the fields to No Mans Barn to prepare for the dancing. Here they would tidy themselves and begin to light the torches and candles to give light to the dancers. A man was chosen each year as 'Watcher', his task was to keep sober and watch for the lights beginning to flicker in No Man's Barn. When he saw that they were lit he must stop the men in their drinking and send them across the fields for the dancing. This year it fell to Tom Hart's turn, he was more successful than most. The 'giant' could manhandle most men in the village. Any he found reluctant to leave the table, soon changed their minds after a good cuff about the ears and a quick shove into the cold night air. The walk in the open across the grass cooled the men down and restored every one to some degree of sobriety.

At No Man's Barn the fiddlers would be tuning up and the women waiting looking inviting and pretty in the torchlight. By midnight all would be engaged in the dance. Everyone, young and old, joined in the boisterous country steps. Onlookers sitting round on benches stamping and clapping their hands in time to the music. On that night in 1665, Anne Barnes waited near the door of the barn, she tried to look unconcerned as she talked with Lucy Fulton from the Parsonage. Lucy was engaged in pouring cider and lemonade into tankards from a couple of large pitchers by the table near the door. She set them in readiness for the thirsty dancers later on. Out of the corner of her eye Anne watched for Thatcher Gibbs to come and claim her, she had only danced with him once before. Village life did not find many opportunities. She was very conscious of her gown, it was of pale blue material and although not new, was so to her. Marion Barnes had cut it down from an old one of her own because the material was so good. It exposed Anne's arms and breasts more than any garment she had ever worn before. She felt herself blushing hotly at the direct glances of the men as they began to come noisily through the doors. Suddenly she found breathing difficult. Thatcher Gibbs was coming in with his friends, his eyes searching round for her, then he saw her and pushed through the crowd to her side.

"Well then, Lass. Are you dancing?" He took her hands and looked down at her and saw anxiety in her eyes. "Did you think I'd not come to you?"

"I ... I ... a girl never knows. Not to be certain."

"Aw, Lass - you can be sure of me."

"Yes - yes - I suppose so."

"Cum on." He drew her across the floor down towards the far end of the barn where the sets were forming up for the first dance. In his arms she at once regained her composure. With all the movement and exchanging partners and the to and fro of the quick moving country dances, there was no time to hold her close. Every time he touched her, however, and they came together, he held her hands close between his own, his eyes following her as they moved away again. Presently the music stopped and he drew her to the side of the barn to sit on a bench. There was much movement and din as dancers changed partners and prepared for the next dance.

"I don't like to call you Thatcher, it's no name for a girl to use."

"Well, call me Bill, then - me Mother allus called me Bill."

"Yes - I like that, it's nice, Bill," she said shyly.

"You'm a shy Lass tonight, you weren't so shy the other day - you've no call to be so with me - we're to be wed remember."

"I know - it's just all the noise and so many people - I never noticed before how rough and noisy the Barn Dance is. Always before it seemed like a party."

"Then you were a child, just a little 'un - now you'm nearly a woman."

She lowered her eyes and colour rushed to her cheeks. "That's only this dress - I wish Mother had cut it .... a bit more ... "a bit higher."

"No, No it isn't, Anne, it's you as is changin' - I am too - it's natural. We should be wed. The house is there - your Father's cot or mine, whichever we decide. I'll speak to him again - he'll understand - he's a man - here let's go outside for a bit - away from all these folks."

They stood up just as the music began again, and slipped

outside into the quiet night. Moving away from the great door he slipped an arm round her.

"I do love you so Anne. I wants you to be a woman - my woman, you know."

"Yes - yes, I know, but Mother wants us to wait a while."

"I don't mind biding till Spring - but no longer."

"I think they would agree to that."

"Well then - you know I want no one else."

"Yes I know - it's just I love you so dearly and I want to be . with you."

"Like now you mean?" His arms tightened round her and he bent his head to see her face. His mouth found hers and they clung together. The nearness of him was too much for Anne and he sensed and felt her sudden yielding weakness. He felt his own passion rise in him but was determined to curb his feelings. Tenderly he lifted his mouth from hers and bent instead to kiss the tip of her nose.

"Steady now, my lass - some things we'm going to save." He felt her soften and smile in the darkness.

"Let us go back to the dancing," she suggested.

No one from either the Park or the Hall attended the Harvest Supper or the barn dance. Lord Ainsley firmly believed it inhibited his workers when he attended such functions. All the staff from both houses had the evening off to attend. Ilsa Dale found herself dancing a great deal with Rust Bistock - a rather dull young man from Seckington. If she could have chosen she would have preferred one of the Romany men. The Dyers never came to the Harvest Supper but Jason, Falcon and Saul had, since being small boys, come to the barn dance. Though rough dressed they still managed to outshine almost every other man there. They were dark and handsome in their looks and all showed natural grace upon the dance floor.

Whilst Eliza Dale was forced by pregnancy to sit on a bench at the side talking with Lucy Fulton the Parson's housekeeper, she kept a sharp eye on Ilsa. In the event Ilsa dared not dance with one of the gypsies. Others were not so inhibited. Flossie and Pheobe Hastly both danced several times with the Romanies, and spent time talking and laughing with them on the side benches.

Ilsa danced on quietly with Rust glad of his lack of conversation, it gave her plenty of time to watch Jason Dyer. His hard dark eyes met hers more than once, he had seen her many times in the garden at Wood Cottage, when he had been unobserved in Witches Wood across the lane where he had a number of snares set. His interest was a natural Dyer male's interest in a virgin. It was no greater than that which he felt for his stepsister Raven. Just after midnight Jason took the hand of Flossie Hastly and pulled her towards the door in ungentle fashion.

"Come." His eyes told her his purpose and she was far from unwilling. He did not speak again but propelled her outside. Behind the barn it was dark, silently he drew her beyond the stone wall, his hands already beneath her skirts. She giggled a little in pretence of protest and even struggled once. It was not serious and was ignored by Jason.

"Let's have you agin the wall - that's the best." Her struggles ceased a moment later, turning to small moans and exclamations. A sound behind him in no way caused him to desist.

"Come on, Jason - get on with it - my turn now." It was his brother Falcon's voice and there was laughter in it. In no wise disconcerted, Jason turned his head.

"There, she's yours - I've done with she." Flossie struggled to drop her skirts as Jason's arms let her go and his brother's caught her up.

"None of that, come on in the grass - I'll show you who's the better man." Falcon bundled her over the low wall and they were lost from Jason's sight in a flurry of petticoats. He set his clothes to rights and went back into the dancing. He joined the set with Pheobe and found himself opposite to Ilsa. It was the first time he had ever been near her, let alone touched her. His hands caught hers in a firm grip as they executed the lively steps together. Jason's eyes laughingly sought hers and he saw that she had seen him go outside with Flossie and had guessed why. He felt her stiffen and recoil under his direct gaze.

"What? D'you wish it had been you, Missy? I'd like much to remedy that!" Scarlet-faced, she wrenched her hands away and they separated as the next formation began, they did not come close again. Rust Bistock claimed her for the next dance and she found relief in his cool glance and lack of interest.

By now it was long after midnight but the floor of the barn was still crammed with dancers. Rev. Mallard and his wife Harriet had gone home to their beds and the Publican and his wife had also left. The dancing continued until two o'clock in the morning when the villagers began to drift away. Most had to rise at five o'clock in the morning to begin another day's work. Tom Hart was last to leave, he took responsibility for all the candles and torches. As he extinguished each light the barn returned gradually to quiet and darkness. Along the lane and across the field paths to the cottages the sounds of laughter and good nights came back to him floating on the soft night air. The night was starlit and still, every sound carried. Tom closed the big old doors, and dropped the bar into the slots which held them fast. Then he turned his face towards Churchyard Cottage.

CHAPTER III

CHAPTER III

David's time of isolation passed quickly. By the time it was over he was much recovered in spirits from Elizabeth's rejection. His house and Surgery served to fill his mind and energy, both were now in good order.

The first day of his freedom to move about the villages at will, he saddled Beauty and rode to dine with Andrew Mallard and his family at the Parsonage. Andrew had been several times to the yard gate at Crab Tree since David had come home. They had talked and exchanged news with each other. The two men took an instant liking for each other and Andrew urged David to come to the Parsonage for dinner as soon as he was free to do so.

It seemed strange to be able to ride freely across the fields and along the lane knowing that now he could make contact with his neighbours. Old Albert Dale hearing the horses hooves, stood in Wood Cottage garden and raised his hand as Lord Ainsley's son passed by.

"Glad to see 'ee about, Sir. Welcome home you are for sure."

"Glad to see you too, Albert, and to be home for good."

"I think Arthur do want to speak with 'ee, here he be now."

Arthur Dale came out of the back door in his shirt sleeves, David reined in the mare and came close to the garden fence.

"Good day Sir - we're right glad you'm amongst us again, I was wonderin' like. It's my Eliza, you see?"

"Ah, Eliza expects a child, does she not? Is it my help as a Doctor you're seeking?"

Relief sprang to Arthur's face, his mouth widened in a broad smile. "We'd like it very much if you'd see after her, Sir - She b'aint as young as last time."

"Of course, Arthur. Tell her I'll call in a day or two - I shall be glad to look after her." He rode, on much pleased, his first patient - only pence of course, being cottage people but to be given the local folk's trust - a very promising omen for the future.

At the Parsonage he rode into a grassy yard. Tom Hart came out of the shed to take his horse,

"Good morrow, Sir. Lovely mare 'ent she?"

"Yes Tom - she's a Beauty all right and a grand ride. Lives up to her name".

"I'll tek care she'm right comfortable while you'm inside - they be expectin' you, Sir." He took the reins and led her away into the stable. David went through the wall gate and up to the front door. His tall figure was handsome in close fitted breeches, dark riding jacket and a frilled stock at his neck. Lucy Fulton answered his light knock. A round faced woman of about thirty, dressed in a white starched cap and apron, she bobbed him a cheerful curtsey. He remembered her from long back and much less stout. She ushered him into the plain dark-panelled hall and took his hat and riding whip.

"Well, Lucy, do you keep well?"

"Indeed yes Sir - thank you. You're most welcome back in Telso, Sir, if I may be so bold".

"Of course, Lucy, and thank you."

His hostess came to greet him. "How are you, Dr. Ainsley? Glad to be able to get out and about I expect."

"Indeed yes, Mistress Mallard, do I find you well?"

"Yes, yes - come along into the dining room, Andrew and the children are there. We can have dinner at once".

Soon they were seated at the table. Andrew Mallard said a simple grace, and began to carve a fine piece of lean beef in expert fashion. Maisy his daughter, a thin little Miss with her hair in plaits, carried the plates to her Mother for vegetables. She spooned peas and carrots before Maisy set the plates before each person, she came to David first, dropping a dainty curtesy after she had set his plate before him.

"Do you take gravy, Sir?"

"Thank you - yes a little, Miss - you must prove a good help to your Mother."

"I hope so, Sir." The plaits bobbed and swung.

"Are you settling in your new home, David?" Andrew laid down the carvers and began to enjoy his food.

"Very well - but I shall be glad to get to work - I hope to establish a small surgery at Crab Tree and find my patients in the district round about."

"You're needed here, Dr. Ainsley - if ever a surgeon was, there's no one these twenty miles distant. All are saying the same hereabouts." Harriet Mallard sounded enthusiastic. "Indeed, we in this house shall be glad if you will look after us, David."

Andrew smiled and his long thin face lit up.

"What about servants? If you are to be out and about you'll need at least one full time, will you not?"

"Yes - just one to begin - I have some savings but there are still things to be done to the house. I'm anxious to live independent of my Father, he has given me the house and my mare Beauty. He says the Estate will benefit from having a surgeon within the boundaries. The house is to be his gift towards that end. The mare was a personal home-coming gift to me. Both are invaluable, but I do not wish to burden him more." Ainsley flushed a little before continuing, "My entering the Navy was somewhat against my parents wishes but I was young and I desired the adventure and experience. Young men are restless. I have not returned with a fortune, but then neither am I penniless. Whatever the rights of it may be, I have gained much experience with a diversity of ailments these last four years, and a good deal of very unpleasant experience of the Plague in London more recently." David stopped speaking and applied himself to clearing his plate.

"Well I pray God you do not have occasion to use your London experience in England ever again," Andrew replied seriously.

"There's always been plague in England - none know the cause - until we do, we shall be hard put to it to stamp it out," Ainsley replied. The first course having now been eaten, little Maisy rose and began to collect the plates. These she removed to a side table. Harriet Mallard rang the bell and conversation lapsed until Lucy had bustled in and cleared all the used dishes away. She then set two large pies before her Mistress and a pitcher of custard sauce alongside. As the door closed behind her Harriet turned to David.

"Now, Dr. Ainsley, do you take a slice of cold apple tart, custard sauce or cream whip?"

"I have eaten so well with the beef - a little apple tart would be very nice thank you."

Harriet Mallard served them all and turning to David resumed conversation. "As regards a good servant, might I suggest Mabel Dunn? She is a clean cheerful body - very willing and honest. I think her age to be about fifty-five but no one

103

knows for certain"

"Do you think she'd be willing to leave Parsons' Cott?" David asked doubtfully.

"I think she'd be glad on one count at least." Andrew Mallard smiled impishly, making his face suddenly youthful.

"How's that?" David's dark brows were raised in quizzical amusement at his host's expression.

"Oh - just his nonsense - village talk has it that Tom Hart wants to court Mistress Dunn." But even Harriet was laughing. Both children had lost their 'seen-and-not-heard' expressions and were listening round eyed.

"I don't think Mabel is by any means certain that his intentions are honourable, she I'm sure would be satisfied with nothing less than what she calls 'a stand up in church do'. Tom is less worried about what he terms 'the fuss', that I fancy is the nub of the matter. As a result Mabel is at pains to let all and sundry know that she locks her door and slides the bolt each night," Andrew explained.

"Anyway she could be asked about a position as your housekeeper if you cared for the idea." Harriet wished to close any more talk about Tom Hart's intentions.

"Would you have a word on my behalf, Mistress Mallard? She could come daily as a trial - if she so wished. It would be mainly to keep the place tidy and set a good meal on the table at about three of an afternoon, which is the time I should expect to return from my round. She could then make the journey in daylight across the footpath."

"I should be pleased to speak to her and Andrew will come and let you know the outcome. Now, Dr. Ainsley, may I tempt you to a little cheese or a sweetbread?"

"Thank you - no more for me - I've dined well and enjoyed my meal."

"Another glass of wine with me, David?" Andrew rose and lifted the bottle,

"Just a half-glass please, you cannot imagine the pleasure it is to dine in company after so long confined."

"A pleasure for us too. Now, you children, bid your farewells and run away with you, I shall come as well if the Doctor will excuse me? I've household duties to see to and you two men can enjoy your wine and men's talk in peace." She bustled the children out and followed them with a rustle of skirts. David rose and gave her a little bow in answer to her kindly smile.

"Sit down, man - do you like a pipe?"

"No - I don't smoke." David settled again in his chair.

"Not even after the London experience?"

"No. The surgeon I worked with, Vincent Fallon, believed very firm in a pipe or tobacco chewed as a repellent to the pestilence. For my own part I believe in oxygen, to let in the fresh air and have windows and doors wide. Also keep clean the house and most especially food and drink. Mind, I carried lozenges at all times, and kept one in my mouth when examining patients. I came away unscathed. I count myself lucky in that as well as careful."

"It is well that you did for this valley's sake, I fancy we are deep in luck to get you David, very few country places boast their own Surgeon."

"It's good of you to say so - I shall do my best."

"Please know that we at the Parsonage stand behind you in friendship - any help we can give will be our pleasure." Andrew Mallard's kindliness shone from his eyes.

"There is something I wished to say while we are alone," he continued. "Harriet and I were much saddened at the news of your broken betrothal. I say no more but that we feel for you in your disappointment."

Ainsley's colour faded and his hand tightened upon the stem of his glass.

"The lady in question made her own choice. That choice is now made and over. Maybe the responsibility of building my career is enough for now, perhaps it is for the best."

"That is bravely spoken, my friend, and may hold more truth than you know. None can see round future's corner, it would be dull if we could would it not?" Ainsley's smile returned to his blue eyes.

"I'm sure you're right." Shortly after that he took his leave and rode homewards feeling that he had good friends at the Parsonage.

During the next few days David enjoyed to the full the pleasure of walking, riding and general freedom of movement about the village and too and fro between Crab Tree and his family home. He would saddle Beauty and set off for nowhere in particular with a lighter heart than for many years. Sometimes he called at the Hall to spend an hour or have a meal with his parents, they shared his happiness. Isobel Ainsley felt a great burden slip from her shoulders as she saw her favourite son so well recovered from Elizabeth's desertion, and his brother's devious courtship of her during his absence. In her heart she had never felt that Elizabeth was the right woman for David. At the same time she shared with her husband a growing fear concerning Elizabeth's present situation. They had not discussed it nor had they accepted any of Jonathon's invitations to dine at the Park. Isobel knew this couldn't continue. Lord Ainsley preferred to avoid the subject for as long as possible. Meanwhile their happiness lay with David.

There were only a few days of September left, the weather continued brilliant and sunny. Charlotte's suitor had spoken for her hand and Lord Ainsley had agreed to an engagement. There would be an official family gathering later, but Isobel decided to arrange a small party for David and Irwin Saint to meet each other. David dressed carefully choosing dark velvet breeches with a close fitting matching jacket. At his throat a cream lacy stock with matching ruffle in the cuffs of his shirt. As usual he wore no wig. Indeed his own dark hair low cut and curling about his ears became him better than any wig could have done. The last few weeks in the countryside all day long, fresh air and sunshine about him, had banished the pale skin and tired lines about his lips and eyes. All trace of strain was gone from him. His skin was more tanned and his eyes more clear and alert than on the day of his homecoming. His Mother's eyes shone as she looked at him seated at her table. It was a happy family gathering. Lord Ainsley was in fine form at the table top. Esme sat between David and her Father, she wore a charming young girl's gown of muslin, her curls gathered in a pretty ribbon, she chattered freely, first to one and then the other of the two men.

Opposite sat Charlotte and her husband-to-be. When introductions had been performed before the meal, David had been surprised to find himself drawn to the rather stolid looking Irwin Saint. Although his dress was somewhat foppish and flowery, inclined to a multiplicity of velvet ruffs and covered buttons, and a shirt befrilled from neck to waist, there was yet much to like about him. His speech was low and not very frequent. He wore a wig, but it was curled and trimmed to good shape. Immaculately neat, well kept hands held his knife and fork. His eyebrows were sandy and nondescript, but a blonde moustache adorned his upper lip giving it strength. The eyes beneath the sandy brows were brown, and held an expression of kindly concern. David noted with satisfaction that when they rested upon Charlotte which they frequently did, there was lit in them an expression of deep tenderness and love. Here, felt David, was the very man for Charlotte. That young lady herself, sat basking in her new found happiness, she wore her first woman's grown-up gown of dark blue silk. Plain cut into a deep point below the waist, billowing to a full skirt, its colour showed off her clear white skin, her dark hair which was straight in its growth was bound about her head in a shining coil. Her blue eyes, so like David''s seemed to have lost their former somewhat indolent expression. They sparkled bright as the only ornament she wore, her engagement ring, a large single diamond held in a cluster of pearls in a silver setting of filigree leaves.

David looking at her decided that she had grown up completely during his time away from home. Gone was the stolid, plump young girl he remembered. The main courses over everyone was enjoying trifles with whipped cream from the home farm. A whole cheese stood on the dark mahogany cheese stand. Cook had sent it to the table with a basket of new baked hot bread rolls. Lord Ainsley laid down his spoon and taking a knife began to cut into the cheese, paring off a large wedge onto a plate set at his elbow for the purpose.

"This looks prime ripe stuff, Isobel - is it one of our own?"

"Indeed yes - Cook says it's just at its best."

"Well, Irwin, may I pass you a slice?"

"No, Sir. I'm sure it's very good but I've eaten too well already."

"David, then? Come on, we can't disappoint Cook."

"Just a sliver to taste then, please, Father."

"Charlotte? Esme?"

"No - No thank you, Father, I shall not get into my wedding gown - no more for me thank you."

Isobel also refused and only the two men took cheese. When they had done eating, Isobel was about to rise to her feet as a signal for the women to leave the men to their wine, when sounds came to them of a commotion in the hall. Suddenly the door was flung open and a dishevelled figure burst into the room. It was immediately obvious that Jonathon Ainsley was the worse for drink. He made no apology for his sudden intrusion. He walked unsteadily to the fireplace and leaned his shoulder against the mantle. His hair was untidy, his clothes disarranged. No one had spoken. All had been shocked into silence by his sudden unexpected entrance. Isobel looked pale and apprehensive. The girls stared at their eldest brother open mouthed. The three men sat silent, momentarily, at the mercy of surprise. Evidently the unexpected visitor had pushed his way past Groves the butler. In doing so he had left the dining room door wide open. Groves, his face devoid of expression came into view for a few minutes and carefully closed the door. This gave the family privacy in which to deal with their guest.

Jonathon's eyes wavered unsteadily and then locked upon David. His face already blotched became dark red and flushed.

"Ha then - my dear brother - returned to the b'bosom of his d'devoted family. Is it the fatted calf then? Sh'd of - I should of brought my dear Lady wife. D'you remember Elizabeth? The beau-ti-ful Elizabeth? Oh yes! A bit of a sweetheart of yours one time of ..... one time of day, wasn't she? Well she's mine now! My bitch of a wife - my cold blooded little bitch of a wife." He rocked on his feet as he spoke.

All the three seated men leapt into action at once. David and Irwin Saint moved quickly to the fireplace, positioning themselves either side of Jonathon they began to man-handle him towards the door. He protested loudly. Lord Ainsley moved to open the door. Charlotte burst into tears and covered her eyes with her hands - her head bowed. Lady Ainsley moved to comfort her turning her back upon the struggling tangled group near the door. Jonathon, plunging about wildly to free himself, grabbed at a chair, it overturned falling against the table bringing a clatter of cutlery and plates down with it.

"Take your hands off me! You'll not silence me - not my fault. Not M...Master in my own house. Cold - that's what she is - welcome to her you'd be - cold bitch - even the servants laughing. All behind my back - leave me go - I know when I'm not welcome! No dignity. No r..respect. Every bloody sodding person against me ..."

At last they got him beyond the door. Lord Ainsley slammed it shut cutting off the sound of the tirade from the three women. Esme sat, tight lipped and angry, her hands over her ears. Isobel drew the shaking Charlotte to her feet, her arms about her.

"There, there, come along, Dear, don't let him spoil our evening. He has been drinking - he doesn't know what he's doing or saying. Faith, my dear, Irwin has more sense than to take any notice. Now come along, dry your eyes. We'll go the drawing room and have some tea sent in."

Charlotte was not to be consoled. "Oh - he's spoiled it all. What will Irwin think? Oh, Mother I'm so ashamed. Jonathon is wicked - wicked to speak so of Elizabeth, and to use such words in front of us, Mother! How can you be so calm?" Tears rained afresh down her cheeks.

"Because it's useless to be otherwise, you must be the same. A lady does not lose her good manners and self-control because someone behaves badly. Irwin will think naught of this if he finds us calm and behaving as ladies should in the sitting room in a few minutes time."

"I don't feel like crying - I feel I could kill Jonathon and I hope David gives him a good thrashing. How could he shame us so." Esme's anger burst out of her. She sat rigid and beat her two clenched fists upon the table top, unable to be still in her fury.

"Esme, pull yourself together at once - it's no help for you to start shrieking at the top of your voice." Isobel's voice was low-pitched but determined and commanding .

"Get down and pick up those knives and dishes - only one is broken. Give it to me - I'll dispose of it. Use a napkin to wipe up the spilled wine."

Esme set her mouth in a hard stubborn line but she did as she was told.

"Now, I'll ring for the maid to clear and we can order tea.

No doubt the men will have achieved quiet in the hall by now. Come along we'll go into the sitting room. Tidy your face, Charlotte, and put away your handkerchief."

"Yes Mother," Charlotte replied meekly, sniffing and mopping her cheeks. A few minutes later they were seated in comfortable chairs in the large room across the hall. There had been no sign of disturbance in the passage as they passed through. In fact once the men had closed the dining room door behind them David had taken charge.

"I'll see to this, Father - under the pump is the place for this idiot. Give me a hand to the side door, Irwin - we'll go through the garden - out of earshot of the servants."

Minutes later Irwin rejoined Lord Ainsley in the library for a few minutes quiet with a glass of port which Groves tactfully produced on a tray.

David and Jonathon were out of sight round the wall of the house. David, strong and used to lifting patients in all stages of weakness, swung Jonathon easily and none too gently across the yard to the horse trough. Heaving him with unceremonious roughness across the trough David then applied both hands vigorously to the pump. Water gushed out splashing in a cold stream full into Jonathon's face and shirt-front. The impact was startling. The stupid half drunk expression vanished replaced by one of fury and hatred as soberness returned. David kept pumping. Trying to escape the flood of icy water Jonathon twisted to one side, slipped on the wet bricks and fell heavily against the stone trough. He slithered down past the slimy wall onto the path. He was soaked, dirty and furious.

"Bastard!" The single word carried a weight of hatred through gritted teeth. "You think you're such a bloody virtuous prodigal son, don't you - wronged by the elder brother. Coming back and settling in that hovel of a cottage. Creeping in here, getting sympathy and no doubt money and valuables as well in due course". The sneer in his voice was offensive and became more so as it continued. "Well you just watch your step and keep out of my way. Elizabeth is mine now - lawful and wedded - and bedded regular - think on that. You'll never know the pleasure I get from taking her. She's my wife and she'll learn to toe the line. And servants - they'll learn to dance to my tune. A very different tune from my dear Mother-in-law's one, I may tell you. The Park's mine and all those in it so you keep your nose out. You meddle between me and Elizabeth and she will suffer for it, I promise you. I'll see you pay for this too - one of these dark nights you'll pay and pay dear, smarmy bastard that you are creeping for Father's favours."

Something snapped inside David's brain, he bent and heaved his brother up. Grasping the soaking body he pinioned the arms tight and flung him bodily across the trough. Jonathon struggled to free himself but David was stronger and fitter.

"Let me go, you mad bugger."

"By God, I'll kill you - never mind, let me go."

David heard his own voice mutter the words as he changed his grip. His hands gripped his brothers shoulders and pressed him lower over the water. A second later Jonathon's head was under, held there by hands like iron bands. David's knee came up and settled like a rock between Jonathon's shoulder blades forcing his head lower and lower in the water. All David's strength was thrust into his pent up anger.

"That's for Elizabeth, she's well rid of you." He heard the rasping hoarse voice whisper out and could not believe it to be his own. Suddenly two big hands caught him by the shoulders, shook him and lugged him backwards,

"Now, Sir - don't over do it. He's likely sober by now." Groves's quiet respectful voice was the same as usual. He overbalanced David, who lay back exhausted against the garden wall. He watched unbelievingly as Groves pulled Jonathon's head out of the trough. It flopped lifeless upon the sagging shoulders. Groves levered the inert body clear of the trough and bent to slap the half-drowned face sharply two or three times and then began to thump the shoulders and back. Water and slime spewed from nose and mouth and disgusting sounds of choking and vomiting came from his brother's lips.

"Give me a hand into the stable with him, Sir. Won't do for the maids to see him thus."

David staggered to his feet and between them they half carried half dragged the soaking man into the stable. There they dropped him down into the dry straw. David began to shake and shiver. Groves made no reference to the events of the last few moments.

"Now, Sir - you come inside with me - a glass of brandy, that's what's needed and a change of shirt and stock." His arm came round David's shoulders as though he had been a boy again. He found himself gently guided into the butler's pantry, where a glowing peat fire burned. David was pushed into a chair before the blaze and a glass of brandy thrust into his hands.

"There now, give yourself a few minutes and a drink, Sir - I'll away and find some dry clothes." David sipped the brandy and felt its comforting burning in his throat steadying him back to reality. By the time Groves came back he was almost himself. Groves helped him to change, brushing his coat and tying the clean cravat in place.

"There, Sir, good as new, only a little soiling on the coat - nothing to notice."

"Thank you, Groves. Thank you. God knows what might have happened if you hadn't stopped me." David's voice was not quite steady.

"Not at all, Sir. These things happen - terrible provocation, if I may be so bold as to say so, Sir. All just between ourselves, Sir, of course."

"Of course, Groves - but I'll not forget it."

"You get back to the ladies now, Sir. My Lady will wish it. In the long sitting room they are. The other gentleman and his Lordship have taken a glass of port in the Library. They have joined the ladies a few minutes back. I'll see after Mr. Jonathon, Sir. I'll send for James Painter, he can take Mr. Jonathon home in the carriage and his horse alongside. I shall say there was a mishap, I'll see to it, Sir."

"Bless you, Groves, and thank you."

David left him and went away to the sitting room. The rest of the evening passed uneventfully. Irwin showed himself a true gentleman,applying himself to make friendly conversation with his host and hostess and at the same time reassure his beloved Charlotte as to his continuing affection. This last he did with many kind glances and smiles and the most loving pressure of his hand upon her arm when he took his leave two hours later.

David was glad to get away and return to the quiet of Crab Tree Cottage. Esme's eyes had scarcely left his face during the latter part of the evening. When he bent to kiss her good night her arms had clung to him and she had whispered in his ear, "I hope you have killed him! He deserved it."

"I certainly did no such thing." Even in the denial he was well aware of the fact that but for the faithful Groves the position would certainly have been entirely different. But what of Elizabeth? What must she be suffering? It was something he knew he must not think about. Something to put away from himself for all time.

David began his work as physician very quietly. His first visit was to Eliza Dale at Wood Cottage. In spite of her age and the years gone by since her last child had been born, he found her very well. Her child was due within a few weeks. Examining her he advised her to rest as much as she could. Drink plenty of milk and walk daily in the fresh air.

"Will you take a glass of home-made, Sir?" Eliza asked him when the examination was over.

"Not just now, Eliza, I've several calls."

His next visit was to Glebe Cottage where he put a few stitches in George Swift's arm. The shepherd had cut it deep falling upon an iron stave in the sheep pen.

"Well, George - I've cleaned, stitched and dressed it, but it's nasty and deep. I'm going to put it in a sling and you can't use it for at least two weeks."

"Thank 'ee, Sir. Much easier now - we're not busy with the ewes at the moment. His Lordship being a good Master, it'll not matter if I'm away a while. Dare say I'll be head-cook-and-bottle-cleaner here at Glebe. Tom and Jack'll manage a week or two with the flock."

"All right - fine - I'm satisfied so long as you rest that arm. No lifting and keep it in a sling, come to me at Crab Tree in two weeks time to have the stitches out. Come sooner if it pains again."

David's next call was on John Price at Wychwood.

"Well, John, what ails you? I've never seen you ill all the years I've known you, let alone off work. How did the village wake this morning with no singer across the fields?" David's eyes twinkled as he looked at the big man in the chair.

"Well, I got a good lad mastering the trade now, young Matthew Painter'll carry on a day or so and do right enough on his lonesome." The big man put his hand up into the thick hair about his neck and winced at his own touch.

David went to him and with his fingertips carefully parted the thick black thatch of hair, again the blacksmith winced.

"Sorry John. Tender is it - ah! I see now - it's a nasty boil coming up near to bursting."

"By God, Doctor! It's dang tender, all down my neck and back I feels it, can you cut it or summat? I can't stick it much longer."

"Not cut John, but I can lance it for you. That'll release the pus and poison. It only needs a bit of sepsis to cause a lot of pain. All over the body it can run. Now we'll have to have clean rags and hot water for this job. At the kitchen table is best - come on, let's go in the kitchen."

In the kitchen Betsy Price bobbed him a curtsey and put the kettle on the fire.

"Clean rags, Betsy, and clear this end of the table where I can see what I'm at."

"Surely, Doctor, just a moment. 'Ee's been in such pain yet it don't look much."

"It's the poison, Betsy. It'll be a bit messy, are you squeamish? Can you help me?"

"Aye Sir - I don't mind."

"Well now, John, sit here by the table. That's it, now put the basin here and fill it - plenty of hot water." David opened his bag and took out clean swabs and a bottle of iodine. "A few drops will clean the water - must have everything very clean." David's deft fingers placed a towel across John Price's shoulder. Taking clippers he cut the hair from about the swelling. Next he bathed the boil with hot water, this increased the pain forcing a low groan from Price's lips, but it brought the swelling to a head. Washing the lancing needle carefully David positioned clean linen about the boil.

"Now Betsy, hold those steady to catch the pus - I don't want it in his hair. Bit of pain far a minute, John, forgive me." A single deep prick of the needle and all the matter broke away releasing blood, pus and stench.

"Lordy, that's relieved me, Sir! In a minute like that, it do feel wonderful that do, after three days gettin worse an worse."

"Good, good. Now I'll clear it out for you and put a dressing on. As to cause, I think you should wash your head every week. In your trade bits of metal fly up at you and in this case one has likely got into a cut or insect bite, and set up poison. Should come better quickly now. Keep it clean, Betsy, that's the main thing."

David took his leave and rode back to Crab Tree. It was just on three in the afternoon when, having stabled the mare he came into the kitchen. A bright fire of stacked peat burned in the grate? from the oven radiated a rich smell of cooking pastry and meat. Mabel Dunn had come into his service two days before and already he was feeling the benefit of her ample presence. A round dumpling of a woman with short thick legs and strapping arms, she seemed gifted of boundless energy. She bustled in from the sitting room.

"Ah, there you be, Sir. Dinner be ready. I'll just dish 'un up for 'ee."

"Has any message come this morning, Mabel?"

"Aye, that Mr.Bistock from Chalfont come down. His wife be took with fever and he do want you to call in there."

"I'll go this afternoon - but dinner first, Mabel. It's a good smell you've got in the oven"

"I 'ope so - nice bit of beef I got, I put it in a pie for 'ee."

"I'll just wash my hands, bring it when you're ready Mabel". A few minutes later he was seated at the round table in the sitting room. The windows were wide and the sound of bees buzzing in the honeysuckle outside came to him while he ate. The room looked polished and tidy. On the side a jar of lavender. His Mother had sent a few late blooms when she cut the heads ready to sweeten her linen presses. David relaxed over his meal savouring the pleasure of good food and good service.

Four o'clock found him in the saddle once more riding up across the fields towards Chalfont Farm. It was situated beyond the Hall on the brow of the hill part way to Seckington Village. After crossing the brook near the footbridge at Chalfont Well the track became rougher passing between whin bushes and rocky outcrops, Beauty picked her way, sure footed amongst the uneven flaking stones. He let her make her own pace, turning his head many times to look back at the much loved familiar view down across the fields behind him. Like a patchwork quilt knit together by green stitched hedges, lay the outline boundaries of Big Fields, Over Barns, Moles Run, Leg Field and Poacher's Plot.Beyond,Windy Wood was just beginning to glow with colours of autumn. The woodland rising to open moorland and High Bank above the trees. The view hazy and blueing in the distance. Away to the right Black Rock reared sharp and defiant above the steep slope of Windy Bank. The windmill now disused, spun and turned, uneven now with only three sails left intact. Below it the pastures round the Park lay in green tranquility up to the house. David paused as he caught sight of a figure moving between the great trees, scattering the grazing sheep. It was a woman on horseback, she was riding down Black Rocks towards the house. The slim black clad figure on the grey horse was unmistakable. The hair that flew in the breeze like a black mane would have identified her to him if nothing else. It was Elizabeth. He caught his breath, halted the mare and sat watching her. After so long and all the happenings in between, still she had the power to fill him with pain. Deep within his body it began, and spread through his loins to his stomach, rising suffocatingly to his chest and throat. He tried to clear his throat but only succeeded in producing a low sort of anguished half cough. He turned impatiently in the saddle bringing his knees sharp against Beauty's sides to urge her on again.

Five minutes later he rode into the yard at Chalfont Farm. The bad moment was behind him. Here was prosperity, the largest farm on the Estate and the tenant came out himself to greet David. Bernard Bistock was a well built man with sparse red hair and blue eyes. Clad in working breeches and waistcoat, collarless shirt and high boots, he looked what he was, a hard working man who had known struggle and hard times, and risen by his own tenacity above them.

"Good day! Doctor. I'm glad you've come - we've been anxious about my wife- never ill you see. Always busy and well, that's been Jane - all over our married life at least." He looked almost aggressive as though he might seek to lay the blame for his wife's ill health upon this new Doctor's doorstep.

"Well - let me take a look at her. It may be naught - we shall see."

"Rust! You there, Rust." Bistock raised his voice to a bellow, a young man came out of the stable door, a younger version of his Father this one. A bit more hair but otherwise the dead spit. The lad smiled a slow engaging grin disclosing large white teeth.

"Take the Doctor's mare, lad - get a move on - don't take all day. Time's money, yer knows - time's money." David dismounted and gave the reins into the boys hand.

"This way - my daughter will take you up - we'll go the back way she's likely in the kitchen. Taken charge there you might say - her Mother being so unwell. There's always a lot of work with a farm."

They went up three deep cut stone steps into a large kitchen. It was spotless, blue and white crocks adorned a huge dresser, shelves displayed shining copper pots and pans, jams and honey, chutney and preserves. Hams hung from the ceiling on giant iron hooks. A large yellow sink with a pump was built in the wall below a window. A scrubbed table with six chairs and a bench stood in the middle of the room. A great banked fire burned in the eight foot inglenook above which on the spit four fowls hung skewered and roasting. Brown fat dripped into a tray beneath. Standing with her back to them turning the spit slowly was a young woman. Well made and shapely, all they could see of her was the full curve of her hips in the long blue work dress which fell in deep folds to her feet, and the coil of her honey coloured hair from which escaped a few stray tendril curls onto the nape of her neck.

"Daughter, leave that awhiles - here is come the Doctor to see your Mother. Take him up to the best chamber. Make haste girl! Time's money hereabouts."

She turned without haste and swung the spit easily to the side away from the fierce heat, her eyes rested a moment on her Father and then came to David, looking enquiringly into his face. David saw that she was older than the roundness of her shoulders and hips had made him suppose. The thick honey coloured hair curled and escaped from the strong firm plait which wound about her head. Her skin, warm as a peach after leaning over the fire, was rosy and fair. The eyebrows and lashes a shade darker than the hair. The mouth was wide and serious formed. The chin determined and strong. But it was the eyes which caught and held him - not hazel nor yet honey coloured but somewhere between, they reminded him instantly of bumblebees and sunshine. Very direct - like a man's eyes he thought. Looked at you and into you at the same time. The rest of the face was modest - almost shy but not the eyes - those would be hard to deceive or hide from. Bistock made no attempt to introduce them. She came forward and introduced herself.

"I'm Rachel Bistock." She paused. "Will you please come this way." He followed her into the hallway and up the wide old stairway.

"Take care ?- mind your head, the beams are low."

"Thank you - I expect you know that I'm David Ainsley."

"Indeed yes - the village people have talked of no one else these last weeks."

"I didn't think I had such claim to fame." His voice mocked her a little.

"Well, it's only partly your being the new Doctor - your .. your local connections are responsible for the rest I dare say." She spoke calmly without embarrassment. David did not pursue the subject. They came to the end of a long passage which spanned the house. There was a deep-silled wide landing window facing the afternoon sun. Beside it a door stood closed. She paused with her hand upon the handle and spoke low voiced.

"Mother has been in fever these two days, it comes and goes, between she sleeps, but eats very little. Father says it is a sudden thing - but I think she has been ailing and out of sorts for several weeks. She works, we all work hard - there is much to do on a farm, Doctor Ainsley."

"Let us go in." His voice cut her short. The chamber was large and comfortable, the furnishings heavy but well made. David who always noticed such things, saw absolute cleanliness. The wash-stand hung with clean towels. The old four-poster dressed with fresh linen, the covers neat tucked, the pillows clean and fresh plumped behind the woman who lay there.

She was pale-faced and lay back in sleep - arm flung across the coverlet as if in exhaustion. David bent over her near to her mouth and smelt her breath. Gently he lifted an eyelid and then letting it fall took the thin wrist between his fingers. A few minutes later he folded back the bedding and lifted the patients nightgown. Her body was thin - over thin - but there was no rash or mark of any kind. He lowered the gown.

"Could you unbutton the top of the gown? I wish to examine her chest - has she had any rash or spot of any kind?"

"No Doctor - only sweating - when the fever comes she is wet through and cries out and throws herself this way and that. Unless I restrain her she would fall, then when the fever passes she seems to be very cold, for once it dies down it leaves her exhausted. Not even bothering to cover herself again."

"Have you been changing her gown after these bouts of fever?"

"Indeed yes - and the sheets. Three times yesterday - twice today - but she takes no food, Doctor - that is what gives me cause for most anxiety."

David tucked back the gown and bedding gently and moved away from the bed before he spoke. "She will not want food until the fever subsides. This weakness and inertia is caused by lack of fluids in the system. So much sweating loses body moisture which we must replace. Quite right to change the clothes - she must not be in wet things - very dangerous - after being so hot. If she lies in wet things pneumonia will likely develop." He paused frowning. "I think this to be a fever in the joints and muscles - there being no rash or marks upon her body."

"What can I do for her, Doctor?" The girl's face puckered in concern.

"Continue as you have been, keep her warm - hot bricks in the bottom of the bed are good. There she will not kick them out. Put three in the hearth - two sets is a good method. Three in the bed - three in the hearth. Change them every two hours - wrap each in a strip of blanket. Change her gown and bed linen after each bout of fever. Make a jug of lemonade - a little honey makes it slip down easy - try to get her to drink all you can, six or seven pints a day is not too much. I would like to have more air in the room. Do not fear to open the window - it is not cold, the oxygen in her lungs will help circulation which in turn will clear the body system. Does she have much pain?"

"Indeed yes - her arms and legs and back have been bad at times."

"Well, I think this to be a fever to do with rheumatism of the joints and muscles, with care it will pass, the danger is not to others. This will not be passed to contacts. Here the danger is the high temperature run by the patient in fever followed by clammy cold experienced afterwards, causing pneumonia. I will send you a draught which will help her resume normal sleep instead of this exhausted semi- consciousness. Do you have anyone to help you with the nursing?"

"Not living in the house. There's a girl from Seckington, Mary Gibbs - she comes on wash days to help."

"Would she come at night for a few nights, to sit with Mistress Bistock? You must get your rest and someone should keep watch in case she throws off the bed clothes in the night." David stuck to his point firmly.

"I'll ask Father, but I shall do well enough." The long mouth tightened and the firm chin was much in evidence. David picked up his bag and they went down to the kitchen: It was empty.

"May I wash my hands?" David asked pleasantly.

"Yes - let me pour you some water." She raised the kettle from the hob and half filled the dish in the sink. Working the pump easily with her strong capable hands she cooled the water down and handed him a small towel from the hob-rack. David felt her eyes on his back as he swilled his hands. Sure enough she met his eyes steadily when he turned round.

"Thank you for coming - my Father will be much relieved at your verdict," she said.

"Yes - I'll see him before I go, I'm anxious that you shall have help."

She flushed a little at his words. "I assure you I can manage perfectly well."

"That's hardly the point - I don't wish for two patients - it is too much for one. How many are you in family?" He asked abruptly, a coldness in his voice.

"Only the three menfolk, my Father, Charles my eldest brother and Rust - you saw him as you came in."

"Do you do any outside work?"

"Only the poultry. I care for the hens and geese. Normally

my Mother and I share the housework."

"What about your Mother, when she is well that is?"

"She helps milk and tends the calves - we both milk at times. Harvest and haytime, threshing - when the men are busy."

"Well, your Mother will not work so hard again - even when she's better and able to be about once more. I'll speak with your Father - is he in the yard?" David did not intend to sound so peremptory. He saw the independent toss of her head at his words.

"Yes - he'll be waiting to see you, I dare say." She turned her back and went to adjust the spit over the fire. He spoke again cheerfully, ignoring her obvious annoyance.

"I'll call tomorrow to see your Mother again, meantime I'll send a boy with the bottle of physic. I'll bid you good day, Miss Bistock." He gave a small formal bow and turning on his heel went out and down the steps.

She watched from the window and saw her Father in conversation with Dr. Ainsley across the yard. After a few minutes they clasped hands and Ainsley swung into the saddle of his horse which Rust had brought out for him. The Doctor rode away without a backward glance. His mind no doubt already on his next patient. When her Father came in a few minutes later Rachel was surprised at the mildness of his tone when he spoke.

"Well now, daughter - your Mother is to have every care just as Dr. Ainsley has instructed. It appears the matter is more serious than you or I dreamed. Give her your full attention and follow every instruction. I've sent our Rust to fetch the girl Mary Gibbs, she can come until your Mother mends. I do like a man who knows his trade and that fellow Ainsley is such a one. Toughened him up - altered altogether since a boy. The King's Service - time at sea, that's what's done it. Capital! We're in good hands there, Daughter." He was striding about the kitchen slapping his thighs as he spoke his orders.

"I'm sure I could have managed, Father - he did say that I had done right with my nursing."

"Nonetheless we shall do as he says. No use paying for advice of the first order and then refusing to take it."

Rachel recognising her Father's mood changed the subject.

"I've just been up, Mother's comfortable - I'm just going to the poultry," she said

"Um - yes - I must get back outside."

Rachel took a basket from the pantry and ran out down the steps. In the barn she fetched a bucket of corn carrying it on her arm with the lazy strength of a country woman. She made her way to the orchard enjoying the feel of the soft air and sunshine on her face. She scattered the corn for the hens, driving off the geese by little flag-waves of her skirts and much shooing and pushing her basket at their hissing bills. At last she penned them in the small area set aside for the purpose. She poured the last of the corn into their trough and took the bucket to the water barrel filling from it the long stone sink in the goose pen? leaning over the wall to reach. The birds guzzled up the corn then ran to the water trough tumbling over one another in their eagerness to fill their bills and sluice down the corn. Back and forth they went, it was a comical sight as their webbed feet slipped on the wet stones. Rachel watched them a moment smiling and carefree, then took her basket to collect the eggs. She knew every nest, climbing amongst the hay, up and down ladders into mangers and all about the farmyards. If David Ainsley had seen her he would have laughed aloud. Her pleasure in the work was a youthful letting off steam after the time of confinement indoors. She lifted her skirts and tucked them into the waist of her dress, this made easy the slithering up and down the hay stacks which she did with a child's abandon. All too soon the basket was half full and the nests all visited. Pulling her clothes to rights she returned to the house.

The next day when the Doctor arrived to see his patient, it was to find Mistress Bistock much improved. Rachel greeted him at the door.

"Good day to you Doctor! I think the fever to be less - will you come up?"

"Yes indeed - did you begin with the potion I sent?"

"Certainly. Father said you were to be obeyed in every detail." Her eyes were demurely cast down as she spoke. The voice low and soft. He looked at her keenly. Did he detect a hint of malice in her tone? He raised his brows quizzically.

"I'm glad to have happened upon so obedient a nurse!"

She looked up sharply to find his eyes steady and unsmiling

upon her. It amused him to see the quick irritated swing of her skirts as she turned about and preceeded him into the hall. She mounted the stairs quickly and did not speak again until they were in the bedchamber. Jane Bistock lay back on the pillows; but Ainsley's experienced eyes took in at once the more relaxed limbs and the slight colour in the cheeks.

"Well, Mistress, I can see that I find you in better spirits." His voice was kind and concerned. His patient opened her eyes and regarded him questioningly.

"It's Dr. Ainsley, Mother - he is to take care of you now - our new surgeon - you recall? He is come to live at Crab Tree."

"Oh, I remember. Lord Ainsley's second son is it not? I remember him as a boy, Is he to stay even though Elizabeth Loundes has broke the troth and married that ne'er-do-well?"

"Hush, Mother. Hush! Dr. Ainsley is not concerned with wagging tongues - his medicine has done you good."

"Have you been taking plenty of liquids, Marm? I want you to drink all you can, no wines, mind - lemon water or home-made cordial." Ainsley took her pulse and laid his hand upon her forehead. Rachel noticed his strong hands with the long tapering fingers. "I think you've almost done with the fever - but stay in bed, two, perhaps three more days - then a chair at the window if this good progress continues. I'll call again tomorrow and see how you do. Good day, Marm. I'm glad to find you so much improved." He bowed and went out carefully lowering his head beneath the low lintel. Rachel followed him downstairs.

"She mends, it will be slow - the high temperature weakens all except the very young." He looked searchingly round the kitchen, "Did the girl come?" he asked sharply.

"What girl, Sir?" Deliberately misunderstanding him.

"You know which girl! Don't fence with me, Mistress Rachel. The girl, Mary Gibbs, who was to come for a few days to reside here while your Mother mends."

"Oh, that girl?"

"Yes, that girl, where is she?"

"She's in the orchard Sir, hanging the linen on the line. Do you wish me to call her - that you may make sure of her presence?" Rachel spoke softly but her eyes sparkled defiance at him.

"That will not be necessary. Do you always behave so? To antagonise every visitor that calls here?" His light blue eyes held the merest twinkle in their depths. She reddened and pursed her lips.

"I find you somewhat over-bearing Sir, and do not wish to be treated as a child or low-brained servant." She roused his anger, as had been her intention.

"I can assure you that no servant in my employ - however humble - has ever complained of my treatment."

"Well, if you were wont to lay your instructions on so heavy with Elizabeth Loundes as you have done here - I can understand why she preferred your brother!" The moment she had said the words she could have wished to bite her tongue. She turned away, her head lowered to hide her shame. "I beg your pardon, Sir, - it was not my place to speak so - especially when we are in your debt so deep for your attendance and care for my Mother".

But the previous words could not be unsaid. His face had whitened and the muscles were tight about his jaw and lips. He picked up his bag and riding crop and turned to the door,

"You are entitled to your opinion. Good day, Mistress." She turned to say more but he was gone down the steps. He waited to speak to no one, fetching his horse from the stable and throwing himself into the saddle. He rode at a gallop down the rough road, "Impudent young woman! Well, likely he would not be needed at Chalfont after tomorrow. Women were the Devil. Ordinary friendliness could be twisted. Sound advice ignored by female perversity and yet they could turn one's words making themselves the injured party in every argument." He guided Beauty off the rough road and turned her head sharp West across the pastures towards Upper Telso. He put her to full gallop over the soft grass and cleared each fence as he reached its rails The hard ride gave release to his anger. By the time he reached the road his natural good humour had returned. His next call was at the Smithy.

John Price's young apprentice had some days before, dropped the weight of his hammer upon his thumb, it had been sore and had blackened. Ainsley had been calling at the Smithy to dress it most days. Today he found John Price at work shoeing a great shire horse from Hill Farm. Tarant Barnes held the great beast while John expertly cleaned and pared its feet. At the back of the Smithy, young Matthew Painter worked with bellows fanning the fire to a great blazing heat. John came in and began to beat and shape the first shoe, thrusting it in and out of the fire, fashioning the molton metal with his hammer.

"Well, Surgeon - how do you settle amongst us?" Barnes's rough but kindly voice asked.

"Very well. It's a great pleasure to be amongst my own again."

"Surely - and the best place for a man to be - his feet planted in his own earth." John Price looked up a smile on his red hot flushed face.

"Can you spare the lad a moment that I may change his dressing?"

"Aye - fire'll not hurt for a few minutes." Matthew laid aside the bellows and came to the doorway. Ainsley opened his bag and took out fresh dressing and scissors. These he laid out clean on a small roll of oil-cloth which he always carried. He unwrapped the thumb and examined it.

"Comes cleaner now, Son, does it not? Has it done paining?"

"Yes, Sir."

"The nail will fall off later but it heals well, this will be the last dressing but use this leather thumbstall to jacket the thumb when you are at work. Tie a bootlace round the top to secure it in place, just until the nail falls and the new one grows hard below. I shall not need to see it again."

"Thank you, Sir - what debt do I owe 'ee?"

"I'll settle with Doctor," John Price interrupted. "Tell 'un to mind where he do drop the hammer next time - on the metal nail be best!" John Price grinned as he set the first shoe in place on the shire's hoof. The acrid stench of burning hoof filled the air, but the horse never moved, only dead hoof being in contact with the hot metal. Price eased the great foot between his legs, resting it on the leather apron he wore. He began to hammer it in place with the square headed nails from his apron pocket. The skill, speed and precision of the country craftmanship pleased Ainsley. He watched for some minutes before riding off for home.

125

CHAPTER IV

CHAPTER IV

Ilsa Dale was no longer happy in her work at the Park, in fact she was a frightened young woman. She had no outlet for her unhappiness and fears. She was allowed one day off per month on which to visit her family. Of late these days had not been easy ones for her. Her Mother was so near her child-bed as to make it impossible to confide in her in case she became upset and harm the coming child. Ilsa had no sisters and could not bring herself to speak to her Father or her younger brothers.

Her worries had begun on the day when Lady Loundes had left to take up residence in the Lodge and the new Master had returned from his wedding trip with Mistress Elizabeth. Ilsa had hoped she herself might have been chosen to go with Lady Loundes to the Dower House, it was not to be. Lady Loundes took only her old maid Martha and a younger man servant with her. The elderly cook from Seckington Hall had also joined the Lodge staff, leaving a younger woman in charge of the more demanding work at the Hall. When Ilsa tried to pinpoint, in her rather muddled childish way, as to when her troubles had begun, she found it hard to pick on an exact moment, yet she felt that she had first become frightened when with the other house servants, she had lined up in the hallway at the Park to welcome the new Master. She had of course, ever since childhood known Jonathon and David Ainsley by sight, from the garden at Wood Cottage, she had seen them ride by on their ponies. Sometimes their little sisters would be riding behind. She had even found the two boys handsome, especially the elder, tall and fair, boyish as he had been in those days. Dressed in well cut riding breeches and brandishing his riding whip. David had sometimes called a cheery greeting to those in Wood Cottage garden. Jonathon never had. He had earned a nickname in the village of 'That young prideful buck' or even less respectfully as 'Snobby boots!' For Ilsa he had been a part of the 'they' at the Hall, and as such totally separate from the 'Us'n' of the village. As such she had taken little account of Jonathon Ainsley.

In the large hallway at the Park he had immediately singled her out, an attention she had not been quick to forget. He had entered the hall just behind his newly wed wife, posturing and swinging his cane. Elizabeth coming home to her own after a singularly difficult honeymoon; had warmed to the sight of the servants. Most of them had known her since babyhood. She had moved along the line introducing them each in turn by simple format, "This is Burns our cook who provides most delicious meals - Burns this is the Master." Each in turn they had bobbed a curtsey or given a bow according to their sex. Elizabeth had for each a friendly word and smile. The Master had a smile for no one, merely passing a searching critical glance over each new face. When it came to Ilsa's turn, he had paused, his face hardening.

"Dale, did you say, my Dear? Is that Arthur Dale's daughter?"

"The very same. Ilsa is not long with us, but such a good willing girl, my Mother tells me."

"And did not your Mother insist that she appear clean and tidy before her Master and Mistress?" Like ice the cold words fell from his lips. His eyes had settled firmly upon the girls full breasts and then slid down to her rounded hips. She had glanced up at him, a little fearful, not understanding the criticism. Her work dress had been clean on less than an hour since. She was shocked by the look she surprised in those cold bleak eyes. It was the same look she had seen in the Romany eyes of Jason Dyer at the harvest dance. She had not liked it then, but in a gypsy it had only repelled her. But in the Master - a 'gentleman' it frightened her deeply. Then the look had been instantly gone and she had wondered if she had imagined it.

"She has a soiled dress on and her cuffs need freshening." Jonathon Ainsley's voice had sounded completely indifferent.

"To me she looks most neat and trim," Elizabeth replied quietly.

"Do let's continue - this grows a deadly bore. Do I need to acquaint myself with every slut and scum that works for us? I yearn for a change of clothes and a meal."

Elizabeth did not reply being taken up with hiding her shame and hurt at his words; from the servants who had served her Mother so loyally in the past.

It had been a bad beginning. As the days went by and turned into weeks - every person in the house and grounds became aware of a deep and growing dislike of the new Master and his methods. On every possible occasion he found fault with all and sundry. At first only the household staff knew of his mean cruelties. Gradually word escaped, as it always will in villages, until behind closed doors in every cottage he became hated and feared. At first he confined himself to the young male staff. Seeking out faults and insisting upon administering the subsequent inevitable whipping. Always in front of the outside staff, it was done in one of the stables. The lad concerned would be stripped, even of his breeches. His hands fastened by thongs to a door post and ten or fifteen lashes administered with the long whip which Master kept in the library for the purpose. Afterwards the Master would stride away unconcerned as to the state of his victim. Other members of staff would release the breechless lad. Usually Mason, the butler, would be on hand to help the boy dress; having bathed the lash marks on his body. Mason would then take the lad to the butler's pantry to sit at the fire with a tot of brandy to get over the shock, and it was a shock. They had known nothing like it before. The Park had always been a happy place to work sons following Fathers down the generations in serene secure service.

One morning it was discovered that two of the young stable hands had run away. One had taken a severe beating the day before. Both were local, but neither went home. They had fled the district. Jonathon Ainsley when he heard was furious. Elizabeth was frightened, thinking of times ahead when no one in the district would come into their employ.

One morning about a week later, Ilsa was dusting in the hall when the Master came out of the dining room. He stood watching her at work. After a few minutes she became so nervous that she knocked over a small vase which had been standing on a side table. It fell to the tiled floor smashing into a kaleidoscope of tiny fragments. The Master loomed over her like a dark shadow, blocking off the light. He gripped her wrist in a cold tight grip. A scream came up from her throat and not to be stifled, rang through the hallway. Elizabeth in the morning room started up and laid down her pen. She rose quickly and ran across the room, as she came into the hall, Mason the butler appeared from beyond the baize door which led to the kitchens.

"Has there been a mishap, Sir?"

Jonathon Ainsley had moved six feet away from Ilsa, who cowered white faced against the wall.

"This careless girl has broken a vase, now she seeks to make further disturbance by indulging in hysterics."

"Are you unwell, Ilsa? You are so pale." Elizabeth went to the girl and took her arm in concern.

"No, Mam, no, I'm all right - just the shock - I'm sorry, Mam, I've never broke nothing afore."

"Of course not - it was of no special value in any case. Take her to the kitchen, Mason, and have cook make her a hot drink. Ask one of the maids to clear up the mess. Please see to it, Mason."

"Yes, Mam - come along, Dale, you come away out to Cook."

Ilsa escaped gladly thinking the incident closed. She kept out of the Master's way for days after but he was too clever for her. At every turn he found fault with her work until it seemed that every day cook would be reproving her, or Mason would be questioning her about this, that, or the other small wrong-doing. The effect on her nerves was distressing. She began to sleep badly and to make mistakes in her work. She would be awake in her narrow bed in the attic room she shared with two other girls. Tears would begin to fall and she would stuff the corner of the blanket into her mouth lest her sobs wake the others. She longed for dismissal but was not clever enough to engineer it. She yearned for the simplicity of life at Wood Cottage and the homely company of her Mother and the family.

One morning when her Mistress had gone walking to the Lodge house to visit Lady Loundes, Ilsa was at work in the library. Her Master had gone out early dressed in riding apparel. As always when he was not at home the household relaxed. The room was full of sunshine and for once she felt light-hearted. She did not hear him come in. She knelt at the hearth, brushing up the fallen ashes. Suddenly she heard a distinct click of a key turned in a lock. Turning she saw him. She tried to rise but could only stare at him, trapped by her own fear.

"So, at last." He bent over her and pulled her roughly to her feet. There was no struggle - she felt faint with fear and would have fallen but for the vicelike grip of his arm across her back.

"Did you think you were going to get away with your misdemeanours?"

"What - what have I done wrong?"

"All the unpunished careless slipshod work. It is my custom to beat those in my service who refuse to obey me and mind my orders. We strip them and the other servants are present so that they also learn a lesson. A good beating would no doubt be good for you, but first I've something else in mind." The cruelty in his voice was unmistakable. His hand moved to the buttons of her dress, fondling her breasts, she began to struggle, but his arm tightened, the other hand busy at her dress. The cold fingers slipped beneath her clothes, squeezing and roughly pummelling.

"No use to cry out - these walls are thick - besides the maids are always counted the Master's pleasure, and you are ripe for it if ever I saw a wench so." He tired of her breasts and lifted her skirts and petticoats. She felt his body now - forcing her backwards, his hand thrust between her thighs, parting them.

"After I've done with you - a good beating - and you unclothed. What a morning's pleasure and none to know of it." His voice was low and rasping in his excitement. His breath hot and close to her face. His mouth slobbered as he licked and sucked at her. A moment later his breeches were open and he was pushing and fumbling amongst her garments. Her struggles increased but he was a big man and she a small girl. A moment later he had opened her and gasped in his pleasure as a scream came from her. Her struggles ceased and he pushed in deeper in his rapacious enjoyment. When at last he withdrew he muttered and moaned to himself

"Ah, you began to pleasure with me at the end there - by God you're as sweet naked as any I've had, but that don't spare you a whipping." He pulled himself off her and fastened his breeches looking at her nakedness without conscience.

"The big whip is for the men. The riding whip will serve me best for this. Now miss - every cry you utter will mean an extra lash."

The next few minutes were never clear in her mind - so shocked was she that nothing other than submission occurred to her. He threw her across a chair and began by handling and fondling her again - opening her clothes to expose more flesh.

Reaching then for the riding whip he raised it and brought it down again and again upon her back and buttocks. She felt the pain and knew that she cried out. Roughly he flung her over and she felt the sharp cut of the whip across her breasts time and time again. In the end she slipped away from the chair and fainted at his feet. He threw aside the crop and the repulsive glassy eyes he turned upon her were not those of a normal man.

"That's your punishment, Elizabeth - cold bitch that you are - should be you I'm beating - one day, by God, it will be you - meantime this must do." He picked up a vase of flowers and threw the blossoms into the hearth. Turning he dashed the water into Ilsa's face. She moaned and moved. He kicked her with his foot turning her onto her back, bending to pick up his riding crop. He left her then striding across the room and unlocking the door. Once outside he set the key in the lock and turned it. Pocketing the key he walked away down the hall and out of the front door. Brisk now in his walk he headed for the stables.

Sometime later Ilsa dragged herself to her knees and lay weeping against the chair. Her clothing was in shreds and across her back and breasts and stomach red marks swelled and bled and blackened.

In the kitchen cook was busy preparing dinner, "Where's Ilsa? She's a long time in the library. Us'll never get dinner on at this rate. Just go and hurry her on, Mr. Mason, if you please."

The butler went to the library and tried the door. It was fast locked "Ilsa, are you there? Cook's asking for you. Bin so long you have - open this door, girl."

There was no reply. He bent to the keyhole and saw daylight - no key in then? He heard a sound - sobbing! Not loud but gasping and somehow terrible to hear. His good sense told him that something was deeply amiss. He returned to the kitchen and drew cook to one side

"Mrs. Burns, come with me. The library is locked and the key's gone - but someone's in there - weeping they be, weeping terrible."

"Whatever d'you mean, Mr. Mason? I haven't time to leave dinner now for some silly servant's prank!"

"This is no servant's prank, Cook. This is something bad. I don't like it. Something perhaps best kept between you and me.

Come now - best if there be two of us. I'll get the bunch of Master keys from my pantry."

A few moments later they entered the library. Neither could believe what they found. For several seconds they were stunned. Then cook pulling herself together ran to kneel beside Ilsa, her bulk spreading her skirts and apron in a balloon all about her. "Oh, my Deary one! God save us all!" Ilsa did not feel the loving arms about her, she had slipped again into merciful unconsciousness.

"Christ almighty! Has someone broke in? We never heard no sound in the kitchen."

"Never mind that - fetch a blanket and send young Robin for the Surgeon."

Cook cradled Ilsa in her arms, tears streaming down her face in the shock of the last few minutes. Mason fetched blankets and they wrapped the girl about, placing a folded blanket beneath her head. "Did you send Robin?"

"Aye, he's taken the pony. Us must move her out of here!" Mason's face was a grim mask.

"Tis'nt wise, leastways until Mistress comes - 'tis near dinner time. Where's Master?"

For a moment Mason didn't speak; his hard expression deepened. "He went riding early - question is, did 'ee come back?"

"You don't think ... ? You're not meaning ... ?"

Mason went to the window and tried the door to the garden. It was held fast by two stout bolts on the inside. They both looked at the bolts and then at each other. Mason exploded. "Bastard - should be hung that one. Likes of him ent fit to be Master over decent folk. He's had it in for this lass ever since he came here - an' all this whipping - the lads is bad enough. This here's bloody cruelty just to satisfy his own evil body urgings." Mason paused for breath, his face scarlet with anger.

"Don't keep carrying on so." Cook heaved her bulk onto her feet, panting in the effort. "All I knows is, it'll kill Miss Elizabeth - us must hide it from she, whatever."

"How can we with the Surgeon coming and Ilsa so bad?"

"Get her to her own room or the kitchen - open the bolts on the door to the garden? Then it 'd look as if some one could've come in - some robber or passing tinker after thieving."

"A thief might have beat the lass but not .. . not ...."

"No need for any save the Surgeon and you and me to know the full of all 'as happened in 'ere, be there?"

"No, you're right. Here let us'n lift her gentle like. We can tek her to my pantry - lay 'er down on the couch. There's a good glow in the fire in there. Doctor, he'll know what's best. Let him see after matters when he do get here."

It was not difficult to lift Ilsa - she was a small slight girl. She moaned again and again on the laborious journey to the couch in the Butler's room. Having settled her there and rekindled the fire, Mason by now recovering his scattered wits took charge of the situation.

"You see after dinner, Mrs.,Burns, I'll set the library to rights and slide those two bolts open. If the mistress comes in I'll give her word as Ilsa has had an accident and us have sent for the Surgeon to come."

"That'll upset she for a start being as she was once to be wed to Dr. Ainsley - I don't think she's laid eyes on he since he came home."

"It may keep her mind from Ilsa and what's befallen the lass, which would be naught but for the best."

"Does this mean Masters to get off scot free then?" Cook bridled at the thought, her mouth working furiously.

"No it don't! Fer I intends letting Master know as you and I knows well enough who it was done this devilry! Gives us a fair hold over 'ee that do. Maybe that'll curb him in future".

"That's if 'ee don't hang for Ilsa Dale's murder," Cook replied tartly "I wish that Doctor'd mek haste, she's real bad - breathin' low and shallow she is."

"Now be calm, Mrs. Burns. See after the dinner and keep the rest of the staff away! You mind after your kitchen and I'll see after the front door and the Doctor."

As it happened, David was riding quietly home across the fields towards his own dinner when he saw the boy from the Park galloping across the pastures after him. He reined in and turned Beauty in her tracks.

"Whoa there! Steady Boy. What's amiss?" He smiled as the young lad drew level gasping for breath as he pulled on the reins and babbled out his message.

"Tis Mr. Mason at the Park as sent me, Sir. There's been an accident. One of the maids, Sir. Ilsa Dale from Wood Cot. She'm hurt real bad. Can you come quick, Sir?

"Yes, yes of course - do you know what manner of accident, Boy?"

"No. Mr. Mason just said to come quick, Sir."

"Turn you back, lad, and tell them I'm coming. I'm so near my home - I'll get a few things in my bag - I may need more than I carry here. I shall surely overtake you, the mare will be more fleet than the pony."

"Yes, Sir. I'll go then," He swung the pony round and trotted away across the field.

Ainsley ran quick hands along his neat stocked shelves in the surgery. He collected extra bandages, suturing thread and a phial of laudanum and other items. He thrust his head round the kitchen door.

"I've an urgent call, Mabel - don't wait if I'm not back."

"Very good, Zur. I'll put en in the bottom oven against you comin' in late." Only minutes later Ainsley caught up and overtook the boy at the Park gates, and urged Beauty into a gallop up the drive. It was some years since he had entered Park House. It was a low stone built house of rambling proportions and part covered with a vine creeper. The leaves were turning rosy scarlet all over the front wall which faced due South. In the early afternoon sun it gave the appearance of sheets of flame upon the building spreading like fingers between the stones. Ainsley dismounted and gave the mare into the hands of a boy who had run out from the stable yard to meet him.

"Mr. Mason says you'm to go straight in, Zur."

"Thank you." Ainsley took his bag and ran hurriedly up the wide stone steps to the heavy metal studded oak door. It was wide open, inside he was met by Mason the butler.

"You sent for me, Mason?"

"Aye, Sir, will you come this way - the girl's in the back. Cook's with her, she'll explain." Mason's voice faltered, he looked very anxious and ill at ease.

"Has she fallen or something?"

"No, not rightly, Sir - you'm best see her afore us speaks."

137

Ainsley walked briskly after the Butler, he did not ask after his brother or the Mistress of the house. In the Butler's pantry Cook stood waiting beside the low couch twisting her hands in the folds of her apron. Ainsley smiled at her, briefly extending his hand to move her away out of his light. He bent to examine his patient. Her face and hands above the blanket were colourless but unmarked, He was therefore unprepared for the sight which met his eyes when he lifted the covers. It had been quite impossible for cook to either dress or further undress Ilsa, the beating lashes being so raw and bleeding. David Ainsley's expression did not change but the movements of his hands did. Gentle fingers skilfully lifted each garment away with the utmost care, examining but not touching. It was typical of him that he asked only one question. "Are there other whip marks on her back as well?"

"Aye, Zur - all about her they be, poorly lamb." Cook's voice shook and she removed her eyes from Ilsa's injuries.

"Will you bring me some very clean linen, bowls of warm water and a large pair of your Mistress's sewing scissors?" He spoke so quietly. "Oh and a clean nightgown and a candle - I shall need a good light."

"Aye, Zur - there's candles here.," She took a taper from the rack and held it to the fire. Her hands shook so much that the candle did not ignite. Ainsley took it from her and lit the candle himself.

"I'll bring the other things to 'ee now, Zur."

Ainsley re-covered Ilsa with a blanket while he waited. He could not have said how it was but he was immediately certain that it was his brother Jonathon who was responsible for Ilsa's terrible injuries. His Surgeon's training kept his mind calm and capable, holding himself apart from the situation. Thinking back over Jonathon's behaviour in the past, as though he were considering a stranger, not even an acquaintance let alone his own flesh and blood. Suddenly he was aware that even as a child this had been there, lying dormant, waiting to spring. A violence and cruelty of that sadistic quality which looks always for a victim weaker than himself. Jonathon's cruelty had always been there. David knew that it had been whispered in the cottages and feared amongst the villagers. Was this the culmination of a bestial nature or was the culmination yet to come, centred round Elizabeth and a marriage gone wrong. A secret hidden knife-point turned a little within David's breast - imagine her beauty subjected to this! Just as bad for this poor girl. His mind jolted back to his patient.

When Cook returned he had moved a small table alongside the couch. "Thank you," he said as Mrs. Burns set down the tray, "Are ... Are your Master and Mistress at home? When do they dine?"

"No, Sir - Mistress is with my Lady Loundes - Master is away ..... away riding I think, Zur. Dinner be ready to dish, they be due back now, both they."

"You see to your duties in the kitchen - I shall do well enough here - it'll be slow work in any case. Say nothing - I shall wish to speak to your Mistress later - and to you and Mason. I'll let you know when I've done here." The stern voice dismissed her and he turned his back on the softly closing door. David Ainsley bent to his task. He was glad the girl was deep unconscious - it made his task easier without causing too much pain. It allowed him to escape from observing the shamed, damaged look in her eyes which consciousness must surely bring. As he worked it passed through his mind that every wound the girl had suffered must be paid for by someone. During the Plague in London he had many times seen terrible sights which had moved him to deep compassion; but then the enemy had been the pestilence, that black creeping unknown horror. This was so different. That had been 'something', this was someone. No not someone. Jonathon! His own flesh and blood - brother, born of the same seed, fruit of the same womb. God, what this would do to his Mother! Perhaps they need never know, but this deed must not go unpunished, and what of Elizabeth? No, I am a Doctor - set these thoughts away - the job, the task, only the task. Empty the mind of all else. He set to work, using scissors to cut away each garment. Tender as a woman he washed the blood from the long torn strips of skin. Patting dry with his finger tips encased in the clean towel. Bandaging and using healing ointment where bandage could be used. Loose linen where, as on her breasts no bandage could be held in place. One heavy lash had cut her nipple and into the breast above and below, this he sutured as carefully as a seamstress stitching fine linen. He turned her gently onto her face moistening the inside of her lips with laudanum and listening carefully to the uneven breathing. He turned her face sideways resting her head on a towel to leave free the air passages to mouth and nose. Two places on her back had to be sutured. Nine long raised weals on her back, all in places with the skin broken and ripped. All ran from shoulder to thigh. It was slow painstaking work. When it was done he eased her gently upon her back again, even now he was not finished.

Evidence of the brutal sensual attack was obvious, the vaginal entrance was torn and bleeding. Again he repaired the damage. Anger rose again in him. The passage of a child in difficult birth could scarce have done more mischief. The tear took eight stitches in its mending.

Then began the cleaning up. Again warm water purified with a few drops of iodine served him best. Soft cloths wrapped the stitched area. Satisfied at last with his work, he eased the nightgown over her head, lifting each limb separately to give her more freedom of movement and comfort when she became conscious later on. Three times he moistened her lips with laudanum and now her breathing seemed to grow more regular and to deepen within the chest cavity. On the butler's tray a hair brush lay amongst the orderly array of collar studs. Ainsley brushed Ilsa's hair and sponged her hands and face. He replaced the blankets and felt his task completed. Methodically he packed his bag. The garments he had cut from her he folded and wrapped in the outer apron she had been wearing - placing the bundle beside his bag.

Closing the door quietly behind him he went into the kitchen. Dinner had evidently been served. Two maids were replacing plates on the dresser while another carefully settled silver-ware in a basket. Copper pans stood draining on the sink board. Cook stood by overseeing the work. She flashed a warning glance in Ainsley's direction.

"Oh, Doctor, will you step this way? Mr. Mason's in the old housekeeper's room. There 'ent a housekeeper now but we still keeps it tidy." She marched through the door and along the passage. Seemingly she had recovered herself in the mundane task of serving dinner. In the tiny housekeeper's room Mason rose at once from a chair near the window. David Ainsley went into the attack at once.

"I have done all I can for my patient. It is my opinion that she will mend - at least in body. That in no ways alters the seriousness of the situation. She has been given the most brutal beating it has ever been my misfortune to examine, either in peace or in war. Also her virginity has been taken in the most beastly and cruel fashion - as if at the hands of a madman. There is enough medical evidence in her condition to condemn whoever her attacker was to a long term of imprisonment, if not to the forfeit of his life. Speak therefore with care for what you say, Mason .... I suggest you tell me ...."

"She was in the library - cleaning, Sir, - she'd been in there so long, Mrs. Burns she did ask me to call Ilsa to help see after getting the dinner dished. The Mistress being expected back any time, down at the Lodge she were. Master had gone riding - he 'ent back even yet." Mason paused to draw breath.

"Is your Mistress back yet?"

"Yes Sir, my Lady's had dinner on her own - she did ask to see you, Sir, when you done seeing to Ilsa."

"Does the Master often absent himself from meals?" He carefully avoided saying 'my brother'.

"Oh yes - he be ...... he be a bit of a law unto himself, Sir, if you sees what I mean." The more flustered Mason became the more he reverted to country speech.

"Now, let us get back to my patient - she was in the library, you say?"

"I couldn't get no answer Sir, locked the doors were - and no key - I saw light through the lock - then I heard this weeping - terrible - like a sob, low like and on and on."

"And then?"

"Then I ran for Mrs. Burns and we fetched the big bunch of keys as hangs in my pantry. Ready against loss they be. Then us opens the door and finds her lying there, and the room all of a mess. Flowers tipped up and blood all over the chair and carpet."

"Was there a whip anywhere, a riding whip perhaps?" Cold emphasis lay on every word.

"No Sir, only the big whip on the wall, as Master do use to ...." Mason's face drained of colour.

141

"To WHAT?" the words cracked out.

"Master do sometimes beat the stable lads and garden boys if they be slack in their work."

"I see. Now I wish to see the library."

"Yes, Sir. Come this way." Mason moved towards the door.

"You carry on with your duties, Mrs.Burns - I'll see you again before I go if I need you."

"Thank you, Zur - I'll be in the kitchen."

In the library Mason stood uneasily just inside the door while Ainsley walked across to the fireplace. "Where did she lie?" The words came sharp and clipped.

"Alongside this chair, Zur. The cover was down - dragged off like. I tidied up - against Miss Elizabeth - the Mistress - she might have come in!"

David Ainsley walked to the window his blue eyes hard and narrowed. "Think before you answer, man! Were these bolts drawn, or did

you draw them?"

Mason's gaze dropped and his face grew red, his reply came very low and stumbling. "I undid they, Sir. I was feared for the Mistress." He spoke lamely, shifting his feet.

"I understand! But do WE understand each other, Man? That's the question?"

"Aye, Zur." Mason looked the Surgeon full in the face at last. "May I speak out, Zur?"

"Certainly - we shall make little progress else."

"Mrs. Burns and me - we both think it was the Master, Sir - did this dreadful thing, I mean. It's been a bad time for us ever since 'un took over the Park. You and him is chalk from cheese in a manner of speaking. He b'aint a normal man in his ways. Too many beatings and us all knows Miss Elizabeth be a changed person since her marriage. Cook and me - we wanted to spare Miss Elizabeth. We bin here since she were just a toddler. I had it in mind to let Master know as Cook and I knows his evil doings. Tell 'im as I opened the garden door to air the room or summat like that, threaten him a bit. It 'ud likely curb his hand, if you sees what I mean. Then Miss Elizabeth need know nothing." Mason finished speaking and waited respectfully for the Surgeon's answer.

"Very well, Mason, but I'm uncertain as to your Mistress's safety in this house. You agree with me, do you not, that what Ilsa Dale suffered was not the work of a normal man?"

"Could you speak to her, Sir, tactful like - warn her?"

"I can only speak to her as a Doctor, Mason - and also you must realise that the girl's family will have to know."

"Yes, Zur - could they be informed that the door was unbolted?"

"Implying that it might have been an intruder?"

"Aye, Zur."

"We can do it but it won't wash, Mason. Already the village has it as common gossip that your Master beats his workers with a glass in his hand. I myself have crossed swords with him recently because he was drunk with too much brandy. However we advance nowhere in our talk. Go and ask your Mistress if she will see me now?"

"Aye, Zur."

A few minutes later David Ainsley tapped lightly on a door leading off the hall.

"Come in." The low gentle voice he had yearned to hear over so many months had little effect on him now. His mouth was hard and his eyes those of a stranger as he advanced to meet her across the rich carpet. He saw before him the same beautiful woman he remembered. She wore a green gown trimmed with seed pearls. It was vastly becoming as was her black shining hair dressed to fall in ringlets about her ears. She held out her hand to him but he made no move to take it. "How are you David? I'm deeply upset at the nature of your visit."

"Elizabeth! Let me speak first. I must tell you that I am here only as a Surgeon. Your man, Mason, sent for me in your absence. I came because I understood that your servant Ilsa Dale had met with an accident, I find it to be a far more serious matter. Sit down please, Elizabeth, for what I have to say is not pleasant."

"Oh David!" She moved to a chair near the window. "Will you not sit down and let me treat you as a guest. Jonathon would not like ... "

"Jonathon would not like me to be here," his answer came very sharp on her ears, "and I prefer to stand. In fact it is of

Jonathon that I must speak."

"Jonathon? What has he to do with this?" Her eyes grew very dark as she spoke.

"Everything," he snapped back. "Ilsa has been subjected to the treatment of a madman!" He paused to give weight to his words. "She has been robbed of her virginity in the most bestial way - that alone occasioned eight sutures in its mending, then her assailant stripped off her clothes and subjected her to a brutal and prolonged beating, after that he left her half-naked and alone, unconscious and in a most grievous state in your library with the door locked. I have absolutely no doubt that this was the work of Jonathon. It lies heavy upon me that he is my brother, but heavier still that he is your husband."

"Will Ilsa live?" The question was scarcely above a whisper.

"It is my hope and belief that she will, but as my patient I wish her removed from this house"

"Where? Where will you send her?"

"To her family - they must be told, with them she will be safe. My advice again as a Doctor would be for you also to leave this house. Go to your Mother and seek her protection."

Elizabeth said nothing - her face was colourless and it struck David that she was far thinner and more frail than he remembered her. He spoke into the silence.

"Well, that of course must be your own decision - it is nothing to do with me. Mrs. Burns and Mason know of my opinion about Ilsa Dale's injuries, they entirely agree with me. They also tell me that your husband has been beating severely any of the staff here who displease him. He may consider that to be his right - also perhaps before long to treat his wife likewise. That cannot become my responsibility even if I wished it so. My care must be for my patient. Sadly we cannot undo our mistakes in this life Elizabeth. Even you must realise that." His voice remained cold and devoid of feeling. Still she remained silent - eyes downcast in misery, again he resumed speaking. "Will you do me the favour of summoning a carriage from your stable to transport the girl home in some degree of comfort and privacy?"

Elizabeth felt the hopeless tears rise in her breast - could this be the lover she used to dream of? Had this stern man grown out of the little boy who had taken her part so many times against

Jonathon's bullying arrogance when they were children at play together? For the first time she had an inkling of how she had hurt and wronged David Ainsley. She forced back her tears and stretching out her hand rang the bell.

While they waited in silence David was aware of the widening of the gulf between them, separating them finally in the chasm of her ill-fated hasty marriage. Mason knocked and entered. David went to the window, his back turned, and stood gazing out at the garden.

"Mason, will you have my carriage sent to the front door and give Doctor Ainsley every assistance to take Ilsa Dale home to her family?" David heard Elizabeth's every word although she spoke almost in a whisper.

"Yes, Mum, I'll see to it at once." Mason bowed and withdrew.

David Ainsley turned. "It's best that we say no more, Elizabeth - I shall not name Jonathon to Arthur and Eliza Dale - nor to anyone else - but think well upon all I have said to you. There are some things which cannot be hid even from ourselves."

Elizabeth made no reply. David walked past her and left the room closing the door behind him. It was only a few minutes later that the carriage with its frail, pathetic burden lying upon the seat was driven away from the front steps. Ainsley, mounted now, drew Beauty in alongside matching his pace to the slow progress of the carriage. He did not look back. Elizabeth let the curtain at the parlour window fall back into place as the carriage reached the lodge gates and vanished from her sight, then she sank into a chair, crushed and dejected, there was no one to hear her heart-broken sobs or heed the tears which fell onto her clenched hands.

David Ainsley did not in fact take Ilsa home to Wood Cottage. Having in mind the nearness to childbed of Eliza Dale, and the cramped conditions in which the family lived, he decided his patient would fare better at Seckington Hall. It was a decision which was to have far reaching results. David diverted the carriage beyond Seckington Village. There was no direct route for wheel traffic between Upper and Lower Telso. Those on foot or on horseback used the track across the fields which opened between two massive oaks opposite the Cross Keys Inn and ended in a grassy lane near the Church in Lower Telso. Wheel traffic, having crossed the Cliven brook beyond Hill Farm, Upper Telso, had to wind its way over poor winding lanes round the perimeter of Lord Ainsley's Estate. The way passed through several small hamlets eventually bringing the traveller into Rock Bottom Lane, re-crossing the Cliven brook into Lower Telso. Fortunately Ainsley was not faced with transporting his patient nearly so far. When the carriage had passed Hill Farm, Ainsley shouted to the driver to turn the horses first right after the bridge and head for Seckington Hall. The entrance gates were about one and a half miles beyond Chalfont Farm. Progress was slow the road being rough. Ainsley was the subject of many curious glances from the cottagers. At Chalfont he looked across the yards, raising his hat and bowing stiffly as he saw Rachel Bistock. She was carrying a basket of laundry from the orchard. She allowed herself a brisk nod in his direction before hurrying on into the house. Her long shirts were tucked up to allow freedom of movement, and he was treated to a glimpse of a pair of trim ankles encased in dusty brown buttoned boots. Her Mother was now up and about, but he was due to visit at her Father's request to collect his fee for his services during her illness.

When the carriage reached Seckington Hall Ainsley bid the driver wait while he told his Mother the facts of this unusual situation. Isobel Ainsley was well used to dealing with many and various family upheavals. Fifteen minutes later Ilsa Dale was installed in the disused Nursery wing of the Hall. Hot bricks at her feet and a fire lit in the grate ensured comfort. Her care had been entrusted to Jenny Bains, the kindly woman who had served as Lady Isobel's personal maid for over twenty years. David in some relief dispatched the carriage back to the Park. He then left nursing instructions with Jenny and turned Beauty at last for home. He told no one any more than that Ilsa had met with an accident. Before riding away he spent a few minutes with Arthur Dale in the cowshed, advising him to refrain from seeing his daughter until the morning and to keep the news of her illness at a low key within Wood Cottage, bearing in mind Eliza's nearness to her time. Arthur Dale was no fool. '"as that bast ... beg pardon, Zur, but 'ee be terrible disliked in these parts?"

146

"That's all right, Dale - there's no love lost between my brother and me - never has been really."

"Has he ... touched her, Zur? He do beat the young lads real bad at times."

"Leave it rest today, Dale - she's going to be all right and she's in good hands. She won't go back there, I promise. When she's well I'll find her a better position in a happy house - I give you my word. When there's no proof, it's best to keep a still tongue at times, you know."

"Aye, Sir, mayhap you'm right - especially with her Mam as she is just now."

"I shall see her again later tonight and take all the care of her I can, Dale."

"I know that, Zur, and I thank 'ee for it."

In the quiet of his sitting room Ainsley discarded his coat, cravat and riding Boots. He enjoyed his solitary meal in stockinged feet; although covered by a dish, it was somewhat dried up but, being late and hungry, he enjoyed every mouthful. He washed it down with two glasses of red wine and cut a slice of cheese from the wedge on the pantry shelf. This with a red apple from the basket served him as a second course. Afterwards he lay back and closed his eyes. The day had been warm and dry like so many of late, but now in the cool of early evening it was pleasant to relax. He was conscious of his dusty dirt stained body and the damp sweat marks on his shirt. A blood stain on his cuff reminded him of Ilsa Dale's broken body. He pushed the memory away and decided to take a plunge in the pool below the waterfall. Lazily he sorted out a clean shirt and breeches from the press. Taking these and a length of towel he went out of the door pulling it half shut behind him.

The orchard and path to the pool were bathed in sunshine, peaceful silence filled the air. Beauty grazed amongst the foxgloves and whin bushes near the trees, enjoying being free and unsaddled without his weight upon her back no doubt. Reaching the bank by the pool he threw off his clothes and lay on the warm sun-drenched grass spreading his arms and legs in freedom from the confines of close fitting breeches and coat in the heat of that trying day. He must have slept, for the sun's rays had moved on when he next opened his eyes. What had disturbed him? He lay dreamy listening. Laughter! A child's laughter! He rolled onto his face and raised himself onto his elbows. Now he could see right into the pool.

At the deepest place and almost below the cascade of falling water a head and shoulders bobbed about. The child's hair was pushed into a scarlet cap, its body clad in an old voluminous shirt or dress of some kind. The material flowed hither and thither like the fins of a fish, pale in the dark waters of the pool. Ainsley watched the antics of the swimmer for some minutes before making his presence known. Lithe as a seal the young swimmer moved in the water, out of sight in the depths and then reappearing unexpectedly beneath the fall of water from the rocky shelf above or further out where the surface was calm and placid. Ainsley was reminded of an otter at play in the river bed. He raised his head and shoulders above the bank and shouted to be heard above the crash of falling water. "You trespass in my pool, Water sprite!

The red cap bobbed up. "Aye Sir, but I was used to bathe here before ever you was come."

"Well maybe I shall let you remain as you have so prior a claim."

"I do no harm, Sir."

"Are you a male Water Sprite?"

"Aye, Sir - 'tis so."

"Then I shall join you." David got up brushing prickles and grass from his body and legs. The red cap ignored him and dived deep beneath the water. He raised his arms and dived in dropping easily the fifteen feet into the deep water. He came up spluttering and gasping; as always the icy chill of the stream was sharp on his body, leaving him breathless. He looked round but couldn't see the child. He shrugged and swam about strongly to warm up in the cold water, making towards the far end of the pool. After four or five bouts he turned at the farthest point and saw the red cap bob up almost beneath the falls. Red cap was eight or ten feet beyond where the curtain of water torrented into the pool's deep worn rock basin. Behind the fall itself the water lay deep and dark. Ainsley dived under and came up behind the falls. It was suddenly quiet, the dim light greenish; there was a dry ledge just above him, otherwise the rocks came down slippery and black into the depths beneath. He trod water - there was no footing here. Hundreds of years of falling water had smoothed a great deep dish in the rock. As his eyes grew used to the gloom he looked about him for Red Hat. He couldn't see a sign of anyone. He was about to dive under to emerge again outside when from almost beneath his feet the flash of scarlet bobbed up beside him. The child's laughter rang out.

"How in Hades do you stay under so long you, young Devil?"

"Oh, I'm used, that's all - I've come since I was six and me Dad threw me in to learn me to swim."

"Well he made a damn good job of it anyway." Ainsley smiled into the impish face before him. He was totally unprepared for what happened next. Slender young arms flung themselves about his neck and a young mouth fastened itself upon his. Then he felt a slender very feminime body pressed against his own. Small firm pointed breasts pushed against his chest through the thin garment that she wore. Slender legs wound about his thighs. Her whole endeavour seemed to be to drag them both to the bottom-most depths of the dark pool. As they went down one of her hands reached up and caught at his hair, using her pull upon it to draw him even deeper beneath the surface. He strove to release himself and fight up to the daylight and air. His lungs felt they must surely burst and noise raged like a lion's roar in his ears. He jerked his head to free himself and began to kick out hard with his feet. As suddenly as they had gone down they came up again coughing and spluttering to the surface. The arms still clung to him and he'd no strength left to throw her off. She was scarcely even out of breath. Seeing him gasping she pulled him towards the rocks.

"Here, move in against the rock - there's ledges where you can plant your feet - close agin the overhang. Like steps they is to climb up on them flat rocks. She pushed him from behind and he found footholds and scrambled up to lean against the slippery surface above. He closed his eyes and lay panting, his heart thumping against his rib-cage.

"You'm not much good under water, is you?" The tone was almost insolently casual.

"You . .. deceived me ... you ... little ... beggar . . you've no business." He rasped out the words.

"'Twas the only way I could think on."

"To do what, for God's sake?"

"I watches you bathe ever so often - I wants a man - and I choosed you - that's what I done - very simple it be."

"Very simple it may be to you but you damn near drowned me, to say nothing of the fact that I'm a respectable Doctor with a reputation to keep up."

"None need know - I don' want much - I got no man of me own. Don't 'ee understand?"

"I understand well enough - but you're just a child. What would your Mother say if she could see us now?"

"She's long dead - I got a Step-Mother now and she'd be glad of any man takin' me. She hopes one of me brothers'll do it soon - in case me Dad gets first chance. He will, too, soon - he watches I every day - like an apple goin' red in our orchard. Ready he is to grab it off and get first bite."

"That's appalling! Why don't you run away?"

"Where to? Romany girls get no coins and me Dad 'ud soon catch me and bring me back, or send Jason - that's me brother."

"Well I'm growing cold and since you've seen me naked these many times it won't count for much if I climb out and get rubbed down. Come on, I'm off. It'll soon be dusk and I've a sick girl to visit yet before night." He pushed her away and swam under the waterfall and across to the bank. Red Cap was there before him. He scrambled out and wrapped his towel round him and then took his first look at her.

"Haven't you anything to dry yourself with?"

"I never bothers - I runs back through the woods to the Quarry."

"You said something of the Romanies. Are you one of the Dyers? Black Dyer's daughter?"

"Aye, I'm Raven."

"Here, take my shirt." He picked his soiled shirt up from the grass. "Go behind those bushes and change out of that wet garment".

She took it from him and examined the frilled cuffs. "It's right pretty," she said.

150

"It's sweaty and not even clean, but it has the merit of being dry. Go and put it on."

"Here's as good as anywheres." She peeled off the wet shift and flung it on the grass. The red cap was dropped on top of it. Black hair straight and long fell to her waist. It did little to cover her naked, unashamed body. No man could have helped but admire her body. Slender almost to the point of thinness, she was yet beautifully made. Small boned hands and feet gave her a fairy-like daintiness. Her neck and shoulders sloped into the curves of her small well-formed pointed breasts, the nipples of which were firm and mature. Her skin was clear and pale and fine grained. Her belly was as flat as a boy's, the female hair a triangle of down between the long smooth thighs. She held herself with completely unconscious grace and was without vanity. The lovely smile and white teeth were childlike and pleasing.

David Ainsley allowed his eyes to pass over her only briefly but she missed nothing of his glance. Her black Romany eyes held mischief.

"I does please 'ee - I does." She struggled into the unaccustomed shirt sleeves as she spoke, the garment hung almost six inches below her knees. He refrained from smiling at the picture she presented and continued rubbing himself down briskly. He tried to ignore her provocative behaviour as he shrugged into his clean shirt and pulled up his breeches.

"Thee run off home, young woman and forget these foolish fancies," he said firmly. She looked so disconsolate, he was forced to laugh. Before the sound had died from his lips he heard another sound just above them on the grass bank. It was as if someone made a sharp intake of breath. He glanced up just in time to see the flounce of a lavender blue skirt and the glimpse of a pair of startled eyes under a lace- trimmed bonnet, before they whisked away out of sight amongst the long grass and bushes in the direction of the orchard.

"Oh Damnation!" he exclaimed. The honey-coloured curls spilling beneath the bonnet had left him in no doubt as to the identity of the girl who must have stood - for Heaven knew how long - looking down at them.

"I've got a patient waiting - you get off home at once." His voice was sharp and cross. He scrambled up the bank and began to run in the direction of the house.

Rachel Bistock had a good start on him, also she was furious, which lent wings to her feet. He caught her up as she fumbled with the garden gate.

"Did you require something, Mistress Bistock?" He was unable to keep the amusement out of his voice at the sight of her scarlet angry face and flashing eyes. At first she refused to answer and continued plucking and hitting at the clasp on the gate.

"Allow me." He took her arm to propel her gently to one side in order to get at the gate. Her fury burst forth as she flung him off.

"Don't you dare lay hand on me! Why, you're disgusting! Bathing with that ... that gypsy trollop and not a stitch of clothing on either of you! How dare you pretend to be our Doctor and come amongst respectable folk? Dressed up smart and riding about giving advice to all and sundry, and you being his Lordship's son and all as should know better." At this point she rounded on him and glared up into his face.

"Doctors," said he, emphasising the word as he opened the gate and swung it wide, "are much as other men, Missy; they have an eye for a pretty face." Pausing he allowed his eyes the benefit of a sweeping glance at her from top to toe, then went on, "And they like a sweet word and a kiss as much as the next man. You must guard against jumping to hasty conclusions, and that quick temper of yours will surely get you into trouble one of these days. As a Doctor," and again he stressed the word, "I advise you to find a nice young man and do a bit of courting yourself. A few kisses and a toss in the hay would soon bring you down off that high horse and stop you making wild judgments on other people, especially when you know none of the circumstances." He stopped speaking and smiled at her in a superior and almost fatherly way. She stood for a moment dumbfounded. She had expected him, at least, to attempt to defend his actions and try to explain away the incident by the pool. Instead, he stood there calm and sure of himself and quite unperturbed by her furious anger; she boiled over again.

"Oh! Oh! I can't just stand here listening to you, I'm going home again." She swung away from him, tossed her head in the air and ran along the path which led round the house.

His eyes twinkled as he watched her, and just as she was about to vanish round the end of the building he called after her, "Did you come for something? Will not your Mother think it strange you return empty handed?"

"Oh, bother." She paused and stamped her foot as she turned round. "My Father has strained his knee - he sent me for a linament to rub in, if you can spare the time?" This last spoken very icy from a pursed up cross little mouth.

He caught up with her. "Let us go to my surgery and I'll make you up something - I have the very thing - that is if you feel you may dare trust to my judgment in the matter?" His face was impassive.

"Oh, you are impossible! I never said you were not a good Doctor."

He led the way into the Surgery and went to the shelves. "Please sit down." He indicated a chair.

"Thank you, I prefer to stand."

"Oh, yes." He poured from two bottles into a small measure and began to mix a potion. "No doubt you feel safer standing up so that you can run for your life if this rake of a Doctor should decide to make an improper advance?" Still he showed no glimmer of amusement. She blushed furiously and glared at him.

"I am not in the least afraid of that - I know how to behave, even if you do not." She raised her eyebrows contemptuously. At first he made no reply, concentrating on pouring the mix into a bottle and writing a neat label. When the label was in place on the bottle he went across the room and placed it on the small table by the window where she stood.

His next action surprised himself as much as it did Rachel. He laid his hand on her shoulder and catching her by surprise? swung her round into his arms. He drew her close and held her with such firmness that it precluded any struggle. Her bonnet tipped back and he kissed her firmly on the mouth, taking his time about it and leaving her breathless and limp. His kiss was warm and gentle; when he drew a little away from her he looked down into the lovely honey brown eyes and saw an unexpected spark there.

153

"And that, Mistress Rachel, is the first kiss that I have given any maid these last two long years. No doubt you will not believe that, but it is the truth nonetheless." He still held her in the prison of his arms and the sudden weakness she had felt at his kiss prevented her from trying to free herself. He spoke again. "Are we always to squabble when we meet?" He spoke softly, wooing her with his voice. "Seems a pity, does it not, and you so pretty - far prettier than that .... er, gypsy trollop? Was that your description?"

She came to herself in a gasp of anger, flinging him off with all her strength. "Oh, you are a beast! A hateful beast! Give me that medicine. Father can come and pay you himself - I'm going." She snatched up the bottle and half running half walking flurried out of the door. He followed her into the yard, watching until she was lost from sight beyond the trails of wild rose and honeysuckle which enveloped the hedgerows above the grassy lane. "Good evening, Mistress Rachel - keep well!" he called after her.

In the cool of the evening David walked through the woods to the Hall. The sun's last rays touched the early autumn colours in the oak and beech leaves all about him. A cock pheasant rose up from the bracken at the side of the path winging away amongst the trees. The sound disturbed others in the high branches and there was much rustling and crackling above his head. A squirrel leapt from branch to branch, hurling beech nut shells onto the mossy woodland floor below. Once or twice the little animal sat on a twig, keen eyes trained on the human below. The slim almost hand-like claws cupped round a nut as he held it up to his strong jaws. Balancing on the branch with his hind-quarters, the beautiful plumey brushed tail curved in a copper arc over his back, he was a delightful sight. Delicately he scattered the nut shells and used his sharp teeth to bite deep into the sweet kernel. David watched his antics on his way down to the ford across Cliven brook. The water ran slower since the dry summer. Ainsley crossed by springing from stone to stone, not bothering with the wooden bridge which his Father had had constructed some years before. David strode up through Dumble Wood with renewed energy. The encounter with Rachel had somehow given him much pleasure. He liked her spirit and quick temper. Little Red Cap's part in the adventure he couldn't help but find amusing even though he must set to mind some means of freeing her from that old devil of a Father of hers before either he or her brothers brought trouble on the whole family. Obviously her desire for 'a man of her own' was her way of seeking escape. While his mind mulled it over he reached the garden and climbed the steps. No flowers now purpled the lavender, the bushes were clipped back to form a neat curving grey hedge bordering the stone slab path. In the house he went straight to his patient in the nursery wing.

In the old night nursery Jenny Bains sat in an old basket chair by the bed. Two old brass pricket candlesticks were standing on the table,their light was insufficient to reach the darkest corners of the room, yet they cast two areas of light which recalled David to his childhood as soon as he stepped over the threshold. Years ago he had occupied this room and from this very bed had lain watching the comforting friendliness of the candles as he waited for sleep. The table was standing in the middle of the same threadbare red rug. The old green table cover beneath the candlesticks still fell skirt-like in folds to the floor. On the shelf between the windows the four worn tattered children's books which nurse had read to them time and again, rested against the old clock which had ticked away the hours of his childhood. At the windows still hung the faded blue curtains he remembered. One was torn at the hemline. In the hearth a peat fire glowed red.

Entering quietly David put his bag down on the table. "How is she, Jenny? Is there any change?"

"I did think she slept more peaceful this last hour, Mr. David. Her eyes opened once but I didn't think her knowed me - not to be sure I mean."

"I'll just take a look at her, Jenny - you get a bite to eat. I'm hoping to give her laudanum - the more she sleeps the less the pain when she wakes. I don't want you to have to sit up. Have you a bed near?"

"Yes - made up it is, just through the door in t'other room."

"She should sleep till morning if I can get the dose down alright."

"Have you a glass, Sir?"

"No - a feeding cup - here in my bag - I can manage and I'll be here a good half-hour. You come back then, give yourself time to eat your meal."

"Thank you, Mr. David. I'll tek the bucket and bring a few peats back. Keep the room cosy - goes chill do the nights now."

"Very good, Jenny, take your time."

When she had gone he turned to the bed. Ilsa lay flat on her back. Her round country girl's face, usually so rosy, was devoid of colour. The brown wavy hair spread over the pillow. Ainsley lifted the covers, listening to her chest. He determined to change no dressings until morning. Rest and sleep he felt to be much more important. Jenny had left a dish on a side table and a kettle hung on a small brass trivet over the fire. He lifted it and poured a little hot water into the bowl and a few drops into the feed cup. Strips of clean linen lay to hand. Drawing the chair nearer to the bed he prepared the measured dose of laudanum. Ilsa moved in her sleep when he sponged her face and hands with warm water. A moment later he took her hand in his and spoke to her gently.

"Ilsa - I want you to drink this - just a warm draught to make you sleep. Here, let me lift your head a little." She moaned and shifted a little in the bed. Holding her head, he gently slipped the spout of the drinking cup into her mouth. By slow tipping he emptied the contents. Some was spilled on the cloth he put under her chin but some was swallowed. Against her throat the drug must have burned a little bringing her back to consciousness. Her eyes opened slowly but they did not focus and her gaze wandered vacant and dream fashion settling on nothing long enough to see it properly. He removed the cup and wiped the spillage from her mouth and chin.

"That's a good girl - rest again now - you are quite safe here. Jenny's going to sit with you." He soothed her like a child. There was no way of knowing how much she was aware of his presence. When Jenny came back they turned Ilsa over onto her side and resettled her limbs.

"Best if she does not lie too long in one position. I think she will rest now until morning. She is in no danger but she is none the less quite ill, Jenny. Keep the room warm and bricks to her feet. I'll come first thing in the morning. If there's any change during the night, wake a boy and send him for me. It is only ten minutes if he comes by the woods with a lantern."

"Aye - I'll see after the lass - I ask no questions, Mr. David but 'tis a bad business all ways. I've two bricks in the hearth and peats for the fire. We shall manage very well I dare say."

"I'm sure you will, Jenny - I've never left a patient in better hands. God rest you, Jenny. Good night."

"Good night, Sir."

After spending a few minutes with his parents Ainsley set off back across the garden. A brilliant moon lit his way. In the dingle bottom the water glistened under the wooden bridge. A great white barn owl flew out of the buildings at the back of Crab Tree. The soft whirring of it's white wings passing just above his head. He went to bed and soon fell asleep. Outside the owl resumed his hunting.

David Ainsley woke early and made his way to the Hall at first light. Both patient and nurse had passed a quiet night. The bedroom curtains were open to the first fingers of sunlight. The fireplace was brushed up and neat. A cheerful blaze crackled up the chimney.

David first dismissed Jenny to her breakfast and then turned his attention to his patient. Having prepared the table with his requirements he began methodically to dress her wounds. He saw to his satisfaction that the healing process had begun, although considerable bruising was now visible along the sides of the whip lashes, yet scabs had begun to form on all save the very deep cuts. The cut in her breast which he had had to stitch had closed very even and the nipple which the whip had missed by only a fraction was undamaged. He put on a fresh dressing, securing the linen bandage behind her back. Some weals he left uncovered to heal themselves. The stitches at the broken vaginal entrance looked clean - the skin lying firm together each side of the wound. His task was almost done when a light tap came on the door. Not waiting for a signal his Mother entered. Ilsa lay on her side and her back was exposed. Isobel Ainsley's eyes gazed steadily at the injuries and then turned her head to meet her son's eyes.

"She has been most wickedly beaten. Does she mend?"

"Aye - indeed she does." David smiled gently.

"Are there... are there other injuries?"

"Why should you think that?"

"Your Father has spoken with a groom. It is about the village that she has also been ravished."

"And do they name the attacker?"

"No! No! But if 'tis true, then in my heart I need no one to name the man." Her voice was very low. He moved round the bed and took her into his arms.

"Face it, brave Mother - he likely is not normal in his mind - to do such a thing." She struggled free of his arms and began to pace the room.

"That makes the matter grievous worse not better. If he has lost his reason then all are in danger from him. What of Elizabeth? Does she know?"

"I have told Elizabeth, but I am by no means sure that she fully understands the dangers."

"Do you intend to inform the Magistrates? Must it be so?"

"I have little or no proof, Mother, Mason and Mrs. Burns know as much if not more than I. It is perhaps best to let them put what curb they can upon Jonathon and wait a few days. It is not murder, for this girl most surely mends."

"What of her family, are they to be told?"

"I've spoken with Arthur Dale, and we are agreed it shall be kept as an 'accident' so far as Ilsa's Mother and the rest of the family are concerned. Arthur Dale is coming to see Ilsa this morning."

"The poor girl seems deep unconscious - should it be so?" Isobel went to the bedside and bent anxiously over Ilsa's still form. David replaced the bed covers, his task complete.

"She is under drug but I shall give her no more. She will waken to some pain and bruising but mercifully she may well recall very little of what happened."

"You take it all so calmly, David - considering that Elizabeth is so closely involved it must be very hard."

"That is all over and done with, Mother. I found myself able to confront her with only the Surgeon's face. When we are young and parted, we tend to hang upon imagined images and dreams. As we grow older we learn to accept the imperfections of reality.

Romance and undying love can become very faded words." There was a trace of bitterness in his voice.

"At the risk of your anger, David, my dear, it was never certain in my mind that you and Elizabeth would have found much happiness."

"I always knew that you did not entirely approve but could not understand the reason for it."

"Elizabeth had been raised in luxury and spoiling from her parents. You, and indeed any Doctor, need something more. You were raised to comfort and plenty - yet you opposed your Father and chose the hard life of the Navy, to ply your trade and gain experience. I was proud of that in you - I would like you to find a woman who loves you enough to throw in her lot with your dedication to being a good Surgeon. Someone not too wrapped about with luxury." Isobel smiled very sweetly at him as she spoke.

"It is not in my mind to marry - I am very well as I am," he replied.

The conversation was broken by Jenny's return to the sick room. Leaving instructions that he was to be sent for at once when Ilsa awoke, David went with his Mother to the dining room where they joined his Father at the breakfast table.

David Ainsley went later that day to collect his settlement for his services from Bernard Bistock at Chalfont. The last time he had called, Jane Bistock, much recovered had received him herself, she had been sitting in a chair at her bed-chamber window as he had instructed. The girl Mary Gibbs, had been peeling potatoes at the kitchen sink, giving him a sly smile as he passed through on his way upstairs. Mistress Rachel, she had informed him, was away in the pony and trap to market with her Father.

Today it was a sultry still afternoon in the valley with hardly a breath of wind, the leaves on the trees hung dusty and wilted. Continued drought had taken the life out of the grass and flowers. Even the wild birds hid in the low branches of the drooping hawthorns, their song stilled. David let Beauty make her own stride and as they jogged along his mind went over his time with Rachel Bistock at Crab Tree the previous day. He

159

looked forward to seeing her again and wondered how she would greet him. Bernard Bistock was in the yard and came at once to meet him.

"By God, Medic, this heat never finishes - our well runs low and even Cliven grows shallow. All day gets spent carting water to thirsty beasts. 'Tis time wastin' work, no mistake." Indeed the farmer looked overheated himself, his brow was florid and sweaty, and the thin red hair stuck to his head. His shirt sleeves were rolled high and his collar was open at the throat. Ainsley also wore no coat and his cuffs turned back.

"Yes. It stifles, this humid air - please forgive my shirt sleeves but riding is a sweaty business today."

"Nonsense, man - we stand on no ceremony here, you'll be thirsty, Doctor, come in and take a glass of sack - then I'll get out of debt for my wife's illness."

It was cool in the kitchen where Rachel was lifting eggs from a basket into a stone crock. She kept her eyes lowered as she gave him a small bow.

"Good day, Mistress Rachel. I trust you keep well. How are you enjoying the hot day?"

"Well enough, thank you, Sir, with the fire down low it is cool in this kitchen."

"Daughter, haste you and fetch up a bottle of red sack from the cellar and serve us a glass in the parlour. Where is your Mother?" Her Father spoke in his usual assertive way.

"She's gone across the paddock for a breath of air Father."

"Oh well, no matter. Come through, Doctor, 'tis cool and pleasant in the parlour."

The parlour at Chalfont proved to be a large roomy apartment with its two windows wide open to views across the Lower Telso valley. Like the bedroom David had seen upstairs the furniture was somewhat heavy, but the feeling was of homely comfort. Rachel followed them in with a tray and poured the wine handing them a glass each. David watched her out of the corner of his eye, noting her comely shape and neat movements. She poured no wine for herself, and left the room immediately, closing the door behind her. Never once did she look at David directly. Bistock went to the drawer of a large desk which stood in the window.

"Sit down, man, and enjoy your wine." He spoke over his shoulder. David took a chair by the table. His host brought a small leather bag to the table and spilled its contents of golden coins upon the cloth in a small shining heap. "I'll not ask your bill, Doctor. I'm thinking this will meet the case." He pushed a number of coins across to David, gathering the rest in his big rough hand and tipping them back within the bag. The coins he had left on the cloth were in value twice the sum David had had in mind to charge him.

"That's too much, Sir. I expect far less."

"You must often be paid very frugal at the cots where money is tight - I dare say it often happens you receive nothing. I am not a wealthy man but we do very well here, and it's been a good harvest. You'd please me if you pocket the money. My wife comes better every day, for which I thank God and your very good service. Pick it up, man, put it in your pocket." His natural impatience reasserted itself.

"Very well - thank you, Sir," David replied.

They talked a few minutes longer over their wine about the farm and its welfare, the pheasants in the coverts, and other local matters. It was his last call of the day and dinner waited at home.

In the kitchen Rachel surprised him by speaking to him directly. "How does Ilsa Dale? The village hangs fire with rumour, but none can say truthful if she really mends."

David looked at her keenly letting his eyes linger on her mouth just to gain the pleasure of seeing her blush. He was not unrewarded, but his blue eyes were a little cold as he answered her question "What is your interest Mistress Rachel? Or do you seek to ferret news for your neighbours?". His voice sounded harsh. Colour flooded her already over rosy cheeks and neck but her temper did not fly as he had expected.

"Oh no, Sir. Please don't think it so; Ilsa and I were always friends - as little ones - our birthdays fall on the same day. I was wondering if I might visit her? If she is well enough that is?"

"In that case, in a few days she'd be glad to see you I'm sure. She is in my Mother's care at the Hall. Jenny Bains is nursing her in the old nursery wing. Tell Jenny I said you might call. Just a short visit - she is weak yet - and no questions, she is not fit for it yet."

"Thank you, Sir." She gave him a small curtsey. David noticed her new found gentleness and could not but admire the picture she made in her buttercup yellow gown with its close fitting bodice. Even in her work dress the girl was certainly very comely - all that corn-coloured hair - the very full breasts and honey coloured skin with its bloom and country maid's freshness. His eyes suddenly met hers and again his mind turned to honey bees. The hazel flecks sparkled at him and mocked him a little, as if she read his thoughts. Unbidden his Mother's words came into his mind: "I would like you to find a woman who would love you enough to throw in her lot with your dedication to being a good Surgeon, someone not wrapped about with luxury." He turned away, dismissing the thought.

"Well I must be off. Good day to you." He went out down the steps and untied Beauty from her tether by the gate post. As he rode away he glanced up at the kitchen window. Rachel stood there watching him, she did not raise her hand nor yet turn away.

Two nights later David lay in bed, it was bright moonlight, he was unsure of the time but he guessed it to be well beyond midnight. A sound had woken him, he waited for it to be repeated. Almost immediately he heard it again, a muffled but insistent knocking on the back door. He rolled out of bed and reached for his breeches

"All right. All right - I hear you," he called as he lit a taper and made his way down to the kitchen. He slid the bolts and opened the door to look out, a ragged small boy was on the doorstep.

"Are you in trouble, lad, that you call so late?" he asked the lad quietly. The child stood firm and fearless on short stocky legs. He wore a ragged shirt and breeches pulled on over his nightshirt.

"'Tis Mistress Bones, Sir - she be come to 'er time - me Dad said to fetch 'ee."

"And who might you be, son?"

"Me Dad's John Symes, me Lord's ploughman, Zur. We be in cottage row down along the Glebe Yard. Mistress Bones be next door - her man be Martin Bones, Zur."

Now I have you placed, son - come in and wait while I get my bag and put some clothes on. Did you run all the way?"

"Aye, Zur - b'aint far," he added stoutly.

"You can travel back in front of me on my horse, boy," said David smiling, as he pulled on a shirt and jacket.

"Be that the big mare - I seen you about on?"

"Surely, the very one." David slipped his feet into his shoes.

"Have you ridden such a horse before?"

"Nay, only the cart horses when me Dad is in the fields. Often I gets a ride upon the collar at harvest and the like."

"Well, we shall see how you merit a riding horse then, shall we not? Now, my bag - is this Mistress Bones's first child?"

"Aye, Zur, and me Dad do say she's a long time about it."

Ainsley collected all the things he could recall needing for a birth. As he stowed them in his bag he was anxiously aware that it was a long time since he had delivered a child. None of course during his time in the Navy. He had helped Vincent Fallon once in London, but the mother had already been a victim of the plague, with little chance of survival in the closed up house in which the confinement had taken place. In fact both mother and child had been dead within six hours. It seemed an ill omen to be remembering. As was his way he closed his mind firmly and went with the boy out to the stable to saddle up the mare. Outside it was brilliant moonlight, giving the child his bag to hold, David fumbled his way round the tack room where the saddle and bridle hung. With them over his arm he went to the orchard gate and whistled softly to the mare. A soft whinny answered him and she came trotting to him out of the shadows. It was the work of just a few minutes to put her bridle on and slide the saddle over her back. Five minutes later they were heading down the footpath which ran beside the tumbling brook to the footbridge. David gave the mare her head, letting her pick her own way. At the footbridge the footpath was intersected by the wider bridle way which led either left to the Northeast and the Hall, or right to the South across Big Fields to Gleaners Acre and so to Lower Telso. The mare hastened her pace as soon as she felt her feet upon the wider smoother path. Ainsley tightened his arm about the boy's waist to prevent him slipping off the saddle. The child laughed aloud in his pleasure at their increased pace. He clung onto Ainsley's bag with his small rather grubby hands, they passed through the gap to Gleaners Acre and reached the lane a few minutes later. David leaned down and lifted the gate's latch letting it clang shut behind them. They followed the lane which curved round the Churchyard wall past the Parsonage House, standing in silence and darkness close by. A dog barked at the sound of the horse's thudding hooves. From somewhere within the yards at Lower House Farm another barked in answer. The lane dipped down sharply and a moment later they reached Cottage Row. The low thatched buildings looked poor enough even by moonlight. Having dismounted Ainsley sought a post and tethered Beauty securely. He turned and took his bag from the small boy standing waiting. "Is this the house son?"

"No, Zur - this be our 'un. Bones be next door. There .... " He pointed. David turned to a door by a small dimly lit window. As he moved forward two rats ran across the step almost under his feet. The boy took no notice of the vermin but ran forward to tap on the door.

"I'll manage now, son - you get home to your Mother, and I thank you for fetching me so quick."

"Nothin' to it, Zur, and I did like fine to sit on your mare." He smiled showing white uneven teeth in the darkness, then he vanished into a darkened doorway.

David pushed open the door of No.2 even as a dishevelled young man in shirt sleeves pulled it back to greet him.

"Come in - come in, Zur. I be might glad you've come - she be ... so bad." He nodded his head towards a wooden bed in the wall where a young woman lay, obviously in advanced labour. She looked little more than a girl, white and frightened. Beside the bed another young woman stood holding the girl's hand, she was plain dressed in a dark working day gown covered by a white apron. Her black hair was worn in a close plait about her head. On her feet were rough clogs which Ainsley associated with farm women. She looked he felt far too young for this sort of work. He voiced his thoughts. "This surely is no place for you. You look very young."

"Indeed, Doctor, I've helped with a good many. Started with our cows and worked up, you might say. I'm Velvet, Sir - Velvet Trewis from the Lower House."

164

"Ah, I see now - you must be Francis's daughter, you have the Trewis look and colouring."

"Please let Velvet bide, Zur. She been right good to Martin and me, she have." The small weary voice came from the bed.

"Very well - now let's have a look at you. Can we shift this table a bit, Bones? Then I'll have room to open my bag and a space to work in."

The cottage was primitive with signs of poverty - none the less it held a homely air. A half candle in a dish and a low burning peat fire were the only light source. A pile of peats was stacked alongside the open chimney. The earth floor was rough swept but dry. Along one wall the couple's few pots and pans hung on nails. A wooden box stood on its side in one corner. On the top of it a large crock basin. Nearby a bucket of water stood uncovered, a measure for baling hung from the metal handle. The bed was clean but the rough linen sheets were well worn. The mattress was covered with worn ticking. It was of straw. Two rough home woven blankets were the only covers. A chest stood against one wall, on the top rested a small pile of baby clothes and a few strips of clean torn woollen blanket material. One drawer of the chest stood pulled out, it had been lined with hay and a sheet folded neatly inside. Velvet saw Ainsley's quick eyes take in all these details. They came to rest on the drawer and he smiled.

"There's a good many babies get put into worse cribs than that," he said gently answering the anxiety in her eyes.

"Now, Mistress Bones." He bent over her and drew back the covers. He examined her carefully and without haste, questioning her as he did so. "How long have you been in labour?"

"I started this morning - I didn't think 'twas the baby but after Martin come for 'is dinner and I couldna' fancy none - then pains got bad and Martin run to fetch Velvet. She bin with me since - aw, aw Doctor!" She braced herself gripping his arm as a shaft of pain racked her body. Sweat broke on her forehead, the muscles in her thin shoulders tensed under the ragged nightgown.

Ainsley lifted her in the bed, easing her position. The pain passed as quickly as it had come. After that the labour spasms came quick one upon another. Between whiles Velvet sat by and

165

comforted Emmy, holding her hand. Ainsley sent Martin Bones out into the night to wait under the moon, promising to call him as soon as his child should be born. David then took the largest pan down from its nail and filled it with water from the bucket. He set it at the side of the fire and at the same time topped up the kettle which already hung from an iron hook above the fire's heat.

"Is there a clean towel?" he asked Velvet.

"Surely, Sir, I carried it from the farm, and scrubbing soap and a clean sheet for the bed after," she replied.

"Good girl," Ainsley approved her as he reached over and opened the drawer. He spread a towel on the table and took the few things he would need from his bag. He laid them out methodically as was his way. He then wiped out the crock basin and set it down on the other end of the towel.

"There now, you can clean the baby up when he makes his entrance, Velvet."

Before Velvet could reply a gasping cry from the bed told him they would not have long to wait. The grip of Emmy's hands tightened on Velvet's.

" I can't - I can't do no more, tired so tired."

"Yes you can, Mistress Bones - just one more effort now and we shall have the child safe." A moment later with a sharp cry from his Mother a small scarlet scrap of humanity slipped into David's hands. He surprised himself in the excitement that burst over him at this, his first childbirth in the village. Emmy sank back, stretching her legs and belly in the joy of relief from the tight pushing force within her.

"Is it a boy?" Her eyes fixed on David's face.

"It is indeed - and a fine strong little fellow he is." David reached for the scissors and cut the cord. Then he lifted the child, the baby cried out at once.

"Oh, God be praised! Isn't he lovely!" Velvet reached for the slippery messy bloodstained child enthusiastically, holding him as a precious burden. She began to clean the remnants of womb from the child's body, nose and mouth. She handled the baby firmly and in so experienced a fashion that Ainsley revised his earlier opinion that she was too young for such work. Emmy gave a last small groan as the afterbirth slid from her. The last pang from her first born child. A scene of quiet activity followed. Velvet lifted the baby into the basin of warm water and thence into a warm towel on her lap by the fire. She sat on a three-legged stool to dry him and dress him in the few poor garments at her disposal. Ainsley sponged his patient and rolled away the soiled linen.

"I'll tek all them soiled things - us can put 'em in the copper at the farm, Sir." Velvet smiled broadly as she wrapped the child in a blanket. "Here, Mother - here's him that give 'ee so much trouble." Gently she laid the little bundle in Emmy's arms. Emmy made no answer, the pain was all forgotten in the joy of this tiny infant.

David Ainsley and Velvet smiled at each other in the enjoyment of a job well done. "I'll lift her, Velvet - you slide the clean sheet below her will you?"

"Surely, Sir, you'm a good Doctor - 'tisn't many as lifts a hand to help clean up after - that I do know."

"I like to see birth more than anything, being away at sea, this is my first delivery in a long time - but the pleasure in it doesn't pall, Velvet, made more so if anything."

"Aye, Sur - 'tis the same for me. Very satisfying it be. Calves, foals, chicks or babes - lovely they all be to me."

"You've been a good help here and I thank you for it. Will you look in at times and see them right here. I shall send a basket with a few things tomorrow - bits to eat and perhaps an extra blanket."

"I've a pie done for tomorrow for they, down the farm pantry it be. Martin can step across and fetch it here. His Lordship did say Martin was to have the day off after the baby came. He knows they be on their own."

"Yes, I shall speak with him - I don't like the state of these houses. The whole row lies damp and rat ridden - not fit for a young baby."

"His Lordship plans to knock them down and move folks up near the Cross Keys. There's one cot ready there now, p'raps he intends it for Martin and Emmy." Velvet looked at David questioningly.

"That I don't know. As I say, I'll talk to my Father about it and we'll see. Now I'd better call in the proud Father."

Martin Bones came in a few minutes later for the first sight of his son. The child was at his Mother's breast, sucking and content. Martin stood looking down at them joy in his eyes.

"Our job's done Velvet," Ainsley said. He gathered his things together and turning his back went out to his horse. Beauty had stood tethered two hours or more, but she greeted him with her usual whinny of welcome. "Good Lass - Bonny Lass. Up there then - Up there."

Martin Bones came out to watch him mount. A tall rangy ill-knit young fellow, awkward in his appreciation. "We'm real grateful, Zur - coming like that - night time and all."

"Think no more of it, Bones. Both well and strong, that's all I ask. Reward in itself that is."

"Good night, Zur - dawn be breakin'. I see the light in they trees back o' Dumble."

Ainsley turned his eyes east. "Another day then, Martin." He lifted his hand and flicked the reins, Beauty snorted with pleasure to be on the move. Martin Bones turned and went back into the cottage to his wife and son.

CHAPTER V

CHAPTER V

At the Park Elizabeth had found her life easier since Ilsa Dale had gone from the Estate. After the dreadful assault on Ilsa Jonathon had not come home until far into the night. He had not then come to Elizabeth's bed but had slept instead in the dressing room along the passage. For the first night since their marriage he did not claim from her the satisfaction of his body's needs. She knew such a release could not last but nonetheless it was a respite. In her mind it pointed to two conclusions. Firstly, that her husband **was** guilty of Ilsa's injuries and **was** ashamed to face her. Secondly, that if the abnormality which David had warned her of, did exist, then the whippings and cruelties, when he indulged in them, served to appease the hidden frustrations of his twisted nature. Perhaps if her theory was correct, she might now expect a respite from the many subtle unkindnesses and sexual degradations which she had suffered at Jonathon's hand of late. The next few days would show her if she was right. The next few days did prove her right. They passed uneventfully by, there were no beatings in the stables. Jonathon resumed his occupation of the marriage bed but did not keep up the pretence of a lover on honeymoon. Instead he came to her bed and took his pleasure, masculine, selfish and quick, withdrawing immediately and leaving her without any show of affection. It was for her, easier to face but she gave him no hint of her feelings of relief.

During the day he treated her with exaggerated courtesy, bowing his greetings, opening doors for her and complimenting her upon her dress in front of the servants. Yet she was still aware of a deep sense of fear. Never once since Ilsa's going had he given her one smile or glance or kiss showing love. She was suddenly deeply afraid of him. She felt as though she stood on the edge of a precipice, awaiting she knew not what. The worst part was that she felt so alone. She remained aloof from her Mother determined not to cause her worry. From the Ainsley family, life long friends until now - she was cut off by reason of David's return and their previous betrothal. Her pride prevented any communication with the servants. She had no way of knowing how closely Mason guarded her and kept watch upon his Master's activities and movements both day and night.

At the Hall Ilsa Dale continued to mend in body, but rarely spoke a word. Even Jenny, in her company so much, could not be sure how much her patient's mind had been hurt. Isobel Ainsley was even uncertain whether Ilsa really remembered the attack. Each day now Arthur Dale spent an hour with his daughter. She was up and dressed and ate her meals at a little table in the nursery window. She spent time in the garden with Lady Isobel, weeding and tidying for winter.

Lord and Lady Ainsley were of one mind as to her future, both wished to protect her and wanted her to remain at the Hall in a capacity to be decided later. Largely it would depend on her mental and physical condition, and that, David insisted, was dependent upon the passage of time and absolute quiet and peace for mind and body. Lord Ainsley had great faith in his son's ability. "Give her time," he said. "Time will tell."

Another young girl in the village was passing through the happiest time in her life. Anne Barnes lived for the quiet hour of dusk at the end of each warm day. Thatcher Gibbs would come every evening at sundown across Big Fields and through the woodlands to a copse of trees near Chalfont Well. Anne would slip away from the farm and run along the lane and across her Father's paddock to meet him. He would stand beneath the trees and watch for her coming. She would lift her skirts and run through the grass into his arms. There by the stream they would lie in the high grass, his arms about her in the sweetness of first love.

Many a man in the flush of his passion would have spoiled it all for her. Thatcher was made of better stuff and his love was deep. He was an only son, his parents long dead but he remembered their happy home where he had been a small boy. The love between his mother and father lived with him still. For him Anne was the cornerstone of that love being rebuilt in a home of his own. The realisation of all his dreams, she was his future, his hopes and his joy, the looked-for Mother of his children. He had little money and few possessions. His gift to Anne was his gentleness, his rustic chivalry, his steadiness and his love. Long years after, when Anne was an old woman she was to remember those precious kisses by the stream, her courtship memories like jewels, to be taken out and held as treasure trove. In many ways she was luckier than most.

As the evenings began to draw in, the men of the villages began to gather of an evening in the bar of the Cross Keys Inn. The talk at the bar often turned to Jonathon Ainsley. At home behind the cottage doors there was much speculation on the facts which lay behind Ilsa Dale's so called accident and Dr. Ainsley's removal of her to Seckington Hall. Almost everyone laid the blame on Jonathon. It was to be expected. He was a much hated master. Then there were the whippings. The two lads who had run away from Jonathon's service had caused indignation throughout the villages and many tongues had wagged. Other lads had gone home with the marks of the lash beneath their shirts. Although Jenny had kept a still tongue, it was whispered that similar lash marks were upon Ilsa's body. It all sharpened the men's hatred and resentment towards Jonathon Ainsley.

In the bar lowered voices would grow rough with anger at the mention of his name. '''ee wants a taste of 'is own medic.

"I'd like to strip 'ee naked and run 'un across the moors and me with a damn great carriage whip in me 'and."

"Naw! 'ee needs public floggin' in front of all they as has had beatings from him, the miserable bastard."

"And that 'ud be too good, I says."

"Never knowed two brothers so different."

"Nor I. Chalk and cheese they be, no mistake."

"Summat 'll happen, 'ee'll get 'is deservings, that's for sure."

"Well, I just 'opes I 'as a share in the giving."

In his chair by the fire old Ben Hastley emptied his tankard in a single gulp, wiped his hand across his mouth, smacked his lips and had the last word as usual. "Mad! That's my opinion! Bloody mad 'ee be, that Devil. Clean out of 'is mind, that's wot." He turned his head and spat neatly into the hot ash on the hearth.

Lord Ainsley sat at his desk in the library at the Hall. He had inherited from his Father a deep interest in the affairs of the nation. He maintained regular correspondence with several men of letters in London. Since the plague these letters had been much interrupted, in truth he had been very reluctant to handle and open such mail, lest it should put the family at risk. Little news had come from London since David's homecoming, so it had been with mixed feelings that he had heard from one of the servants that a rider had come from London with letters.

Remembering David's advice, he had held each missive over a dish of warm vinegar, turning each for several minutes before reading it. The reading provided much news. There had during September been a great victory by the Navy against the Dutch, many ships and much plunder had been taken. There had been much stir in Court Circles, but as yet this excitement had left the City of London untouched. The Plague, though past its peak, had not yet abated enough for the King and his court to return or Parliament to meet again at Westminster. The total figures of those lost in the pestilence were not yet available but fears rose that it would be close on a hundred thousand lives.

Lord Ainsley found it impossible to think in terms of such tragedy, it brought home to him the high risks which David had faced, with such courage, by staying so long in the city. Lord Ainsley burned the letters. Once read it was better so. He determined to keep the bulk of their content secret from his wife.

At the time that his Father was reading his mail David was on his way to the Parsonage House. He carried a little bottle of physic for Harriet Mallard, who had been laid up very chesty for several days. Beauty was in fine fettle and it was a pleasant ride from Crab Tree. In the lane near the churchyard few people were about. He passed a pedlar with his pack and tray. Strangers were rare in Telso and inclined to be mistrusted. David gave the man a close searching glance and decided he was harmless enough.

"Good Day to thee, Sir." The man doffed his battered hat.

"Good Day, have you come far?"

"Come far - go far; allus travelling, 'tis my living, so one place be much the same as next, you might say."

"Did you come through the towns unrestricted?" David was thinking of his own journey from London. He remembered Vincent Fallon's warning of Watchmen posted on the outskirts of towns keeping people away.

"I come by the wild ways - the hamlets be my trade. I has little truck with the townships. I can travel by green rides here to Kent and back. I goes in a big circle, comin' to each place once in a twelve-month."

"Interesting way of life, you must meet many on your travels."

"Born to it I was - never done no other."

"Well, I wish you safe journey."

"Thank you, Sir."

David went on his way. At the Parsonage he spent some time with Andrew Mallard who pressed him to a glass of red wine. He found Harriet very thick upon the chest and advised her to remain in bed. In the study the two men sat opposite each other.

Andrew spoke of his work. "There are bad Christians and good Christians here, like elsewhere, I expect. Do you continue with going to Seckington Church with your family since your return?"

"Oh, there you have me, Andrew! I'm ashamed to admit that I've not heard a sermon since I was on board ship. In London I placed myself entirely in Vincent Fallon's hands and he would not allow it safe for either of us to attend divine service. I think he feared more what we might carry amongst others in the congregation than that they might infect us."

"Well, a man's conscience is his own, David, but I'd be glad of your support in this church if you have a mind. We have a simple service here, suited to the ordinary folk hereabouts. Of course, when times are bad more folks come than when, like this year, the harvest is good and the villages are not near so much in need of comfort. I went to see Martin Bones and Emmy and the new babe yesterday." Andrew changed the subject not wishing to press his friend.

"And how did you find them?"

"Well, and of course in great happiness over their son. I understand that they wish to call him David. For you, I fancy!" Andrew's thin face broke into a smile.

"It was a pleasure to me to deliver him - my first childbirth in the district." The blue eyes lit in David's face as he spoke.

"They come to bring him for Christening on Sunday."

"I'd like to be there - my first attendance at Church. Very suitable wouldn't you agree?"

"I should be much pleased."

"I wish they were in a better cottage."

"Does Lord Ainsley intend to pull the row down? It was in his mind last year when he spoke to me about the Symes family."

"Ah! The young lad who fetched me in the night to Emmy Bones - he was a Symes."

"That would be Peter, he's the only lad. There's two little lasses, Kate and Mary. They need a bigger house. In all those cots there's only one room downstairs and a string ladder to a loft in the roof. She's a clean enough woman, Mrs. Symes - but it's a poor place - enough to dishearten anyone. With three youngsters it's impossible."

"I thought the whole row a disgrace - rats ran free across my feet the other night."

"The thatch is very poor and the floors only dry because of this long dry spell. Winter time the damp creeps up from the Mere and even the bedclothes are damp, strive as they may with fires."

"Who lives in the rest now? There are six dwellings there, as I remember it."

"Two stand empty - the two middle ones. Your Father moved the families up to Upper Telso about two years ago. Of course the two empty cots worsen the position. There the rats run in the walls and no one drives them out or cleans the place up."

"Sounds as though all the people there should be moved to better places. Who's in the two at the far end?"

"That is, I'm sure, what your Father intends. One difficulty is those very people. Number five houses old Ben Hastley and his daughters. The other gives home to Mother Ross and Jeannie."

"Good Heavens! Does that old witch still live? She must be a hundred." David's dark eyebrows rose in an expression of comic amusement.

"That's a good question? No one has seen her these last weeks and Jeannie says nothing. She's not about much either. Old Ben's all right, he likes his glass of ale over much, but he's harmless. His daughters are harlots of course - but clean harlots, if you understand me!" Andrew leaned back in his chair and

176

laughed as he spoke.

"I'm not sure how to take that - coming from the cloth, so to speak." David smiled.

"Well, it has been my habit to close my eyes to their activities. You see, to my mind, Phoebe and Floss supply the needs of most of the local men who might otherwise go to the town and pick up disease, or even to another local man's wife. All very irregular - but the lesser of two evils perhaps?" He raised gently enquiring eyes to David's face. David's heart warmed to this man's honesty and wide ranging outlook.

"I can understand a Doctor like myself taking that view but it surprises me in you, Andrew."

"Well .... " Andrew paused choosing his words. "I take the view that my duty here is to bring people into Christ's Church and teaching - but at the same time I must care for the people and be a good shepherd having an eye for their wellbeing. Wellbeing of the body as well as the mind and the spirit. Of course, I'm against these men taking their pleasures as they do, but Flossie and Phoebe know what they are about and I suspect that they rarely take much money for their services. But of course, I'm in favour of all those cottages being knocked down if Lord Ainsley is willing. Even if some of the tenants prove difficult to rehouse.

"I shall speak to him about it - I think they should all come down and no replacements should go on that site. It lies too low for good health."

Their talk turned to other things and shortly afterwards David took his leave and rode home to Crab Tree and his dinner.

Two days later Ainsley was summoned to Glebe Cottage. It was the home of Lord Ainsley's three young shepherds, George Swift, Tom Carter and Jack Acres. David wondered if Tom Carter's arm had not healed as well as it should. It was not all that long since he had dressed it after an accident in the sheep pen. He was a little surprised therefore when his knock was answered by Tom Carter himself.

"Well, Tom, who's unwell? I thought it might be that arm troubling you again."

"No, Doctor - it's come good that has. B'aint me this time,

'tis George is sick and us don' rightly know what ails 'ee. Come you in, Doctor - he's at the fire - he can't seem to feel warm and his belly keeps hold of nothing." Tom showed David into the large chamber which was the only room downstairs at Glebe Cot. It was a far better built dwelling than those in the Row. Thatcher had laid new thatch to the roof along with his own a few yards along the road, less than a year ago. The floor was stone slabs, an improvement on earth. The square window was of good size with a wide stone sill. The ladder which led to the large roof bedroom was solid wood and fixed to the wall. In the roof a dormer window gave air and light to the bedroom, there were three simple home built cots each with a straw mattress. In addition each man had a square rough fashioned wooden box in which to keep his few possessions. On each bed was a thick homespun wool blanket. This last was a luxury, rare in workmen's homes. It was a product of the mens' calling. The wool was from Lord Ainsley's flock, each shepherd was entitled to a good blanket.

The living room was also very simple in its furnishings. A scrubbed deal table, three country chairs and a couple of shelves for pots and pans. A stone sink in one corner held an earthenware bowl in which the washing of their bodies, clothes and pots was all done. A few pewter tankards and plates and a small barrel of cider lodged on its side completed the picture.

It was warm within these walls but the man by the fire shivered in his chair. He was crouched low ever the fire, ashen faced, a bucket between his legs. There was the smell of vomit in the room. Some strange immediate instinct came to David Ainsley.

"Open the window, Tom - and leave the door wide." He spoke over his shoulder to Carter, who stood in the doorway.

"But he's chilled, Sir - he's never stopped shiverin' these last three hours."

"The air's warm, Tom, that won't make him worse. I want fresh air in here while I examine him. Now then, George - let's look at you. When did this sickness begin?" George Swift looked up slowly, his eyes were sunk in his head and a look of dazed incomprehension was on his face. Even as he tried to focus on Ainsley a fresh bout of sickness took him. He bent heaving and shaking over the pail. David held his head and waited until it passed. George sank back exhausted.

"'Tis the sickness, Zur - I'm so afeared of this sickness - never been like it afore - always been a well man, you might say." Again he began to shake and shiver.

"We all get sick sometimes, George. Now I want you to get to your bed where you can rest. Tom and I will help you up the stairs."

"I don't reckon I can stand, Zur. Oh, beg pardon .... " He began again to vomit.

"Tom, go up and turn the bed back and find a clean nightshirt, if you have one." David's voice was calm and kind.

"Aye, Sur." Tom went up the wooden steps, ten minutes later George Swift was in his bed. The two men had to half carry him up. David helped him out of his clothes and into the rough cloth nightshirt. David folded the blanket about him and leaving him lying back exhausted went downstairs to where Tom waited anxiously.

"He's real bad, Sur, 'ent 'un?"

"Yes, yes, I'm afraid he is, Tom. Now there are things we must do. First where is Jack Aires? Up at the Home Farm?"

"He's further off than that - up on the moor - his Lordship got a hundred sheep up over Seckington Way. Jack's gone with the lad to see after they, two days they bin gone."

A small sigh of relief escaped Ainsley's dry lips. "When does he return?"

"Sometime tomorrow - when they be done shepherding - they got the dogs along of they."

"Well now, Tom, first we need a second pail. Have you any disinfectant? Something you use for sheep perhaps?"

"Aye there's some out the back." Carter went unquestioningly to find it. He was back in a few moments.

"Burn a little in the hearth, Tom - there are several things I want you to do. Keep the windows wide and the door, save at night. Dig a place in the garden and bury the vomit and all that comes from our patient. Wash out the pail and, if need be, have two pails and use them turn and turn about. Drink the cider from the barrel - don't drink any water for the present. Wash your hands frequently especially before you eat. Cover your food with a cloth and don't keep anything stale by you. But most important of all - let no one come near."

"Can you tell me, Sur, what ails him? What is this sickness?" Anxiety was writ deep in Tom's face.

"I do not know how it may have come, but I fear it is the Plague, Tom. I've seen so much in London."

"God's mercy, Sur! How came it here?"

"None know its travelling, but do all that I've told you - I may yet be wrong. There's no mark - no spots upon George - so there's a chance I may be mistaken. Yet I fear this has the smell of it. One learns to recognise it, but it has many faces, Tom, so we can only wait."

"Is there no medicine, Sur?"

"Nothing at this stage - just fresh air, quiet and cleanliness. Has anything come new to the house, yesterday or today? Any stranger perhaps?" Even as he spoke David remembered and knew what Tom would reply.

"I never saw 'un, but George said a pedlar come - on foot, you understand."

"Yes - I saw him myself. And did George buy aught?"

"A . .. a parcel of cloth. A skirt length for George's lass - some bits of things - a jacket for his own use - just a bundle it were."

"Where are the things - not gone from here?" David tried to keep the anxiety out of his voice.

"No, they'm still here. They was damp so he hung them agin the fire to dry. Later 'ee was took bad and he bundled 'em in the rush basket, where we lays the dirty linen. It lies under the roof at back." "Show me, man. They went out and found the coat and cloth as Tom had described.

"Don't touch! Have you a shepherd's crook or iron bar?" Ainsley's face was grim.

"That's something we all three of us have, Sur. Here - by the wall they stand."

"Bring you a torch from the peats - anything - a bundle of rolled straw - as long as its well lit." David hooked the basket on the iron crook and swung it away from the house, across the vegetable patch, and down on the bare soil. He lit the basket with the flaming torch Tom brought to him. They stood and watched it burn away to a pile of black ash.

"A few pence he paid, said it would make him a winter jacket."

David did not reply. In his mind her heard Michael Brandon at St. Bartholomew's saying to him, "A jacket bought cheap can cost a first born son's life." How many precious lives might that jacket cost in the weeks to come? How many homes had the Pedlar visited in the village? He squared his shoulders and went back to his patient in the loft.

Presently George ceased to vomit and began to turn and twist upon the bed, hot and cold by turns. Grimly David recognised the beginnings of fever. They moved Tom's bed down to the ground floor. David went outside the front door and called to Thatcher Gibbs, home from work, in his cottage along the lane.

"Thatcher, would you do me a favour?"

"Aye, Sur - very willing."

"Will you take the mare and go to Crab Tree for me - turn her loose and bring me a few things I need. Keep away when you return - we have grave sickness here. Set down the things on the grass yonder. I'll take them up when you've moved away."

"I'll go straight - shall I ride the mare, Sir?"

"Surely - it'll be quicker. She's quiet enough you'll find."

"What is it you're needing?"

David listed the things, including lozenges, physic, red wine and clean linen.

Soon after that Thatcher came and untied the mare, mounted, and looking curiously at Ainsley standing in the doorway, urged her into a trot along the lane and away through Gleaner's Acre.

David stayed with his patient all night, he gave what comfort he could bathing George Swift's sweating face and hands. Trying to soothe him in his wild imaginings, when, in the grip of a raging fever he complained of being tormented by black beasts at his throat and phantoms lurking in the dark corners of the room.

"God, it makes such weakness - it turns grown men to children," David muttered to himself as he strove to prevent the half demented man from doing himself a mischief in his delirium.

As suddenly as it had begun, the fever ended. Just as dawn broke and the light became strong enough for David to douse the candle, he noticed a change. George suddenly threw himself backwards and lay glassy eyed and comatose on his mattress. David splashed water on his face and shook him in a desperate effort to waken him. So many had he seen die in London, in just this way, worn out by the violence of the poison in their bodies. It was no use - George Swift had no strength left and no spirit to fight for his life. His breathing became low and harsh and David knew that he could do no more.

He set the bed and room to rights and closed the lids on the open, vacant, still living eyes; as though at a signal the lower jaw dropped a little and the big hands on the blanket spread their fingers wide, pressing down as if their owner would rise up. The eyes did not open again and a moment later George Swift fell back dead. David stood looking down at him with sad bitterness in his heart. He felt he had fought in a great battle which in the end he had lost.

The news of the death passed through the villages like a fire through dry grass. The small population was numbed. The first glorious touch of autumn was in the woods and fields. The sun shone, the birds sang. The countryside remained unmoved in it's exquisite unblemished beauty. But George Swift - yesterday a virile young man with a ready smile and a taste for ale and a comely wench - was dead of the plague - a townsman's illness - he was five and twenty. At first none could believe it. Then Dr. Ainsley ordered that a red cross be painted on Glebe Cottage door. Those passing by saw it, even though Glebe Cottage windows and door stood wide and, on Ainsley's orders, Tom Carter remained there. He kept in the open air all he could and stayed in the garden away from his neighbours, yet there was a silence about Glebe which provoked fear. Tom spent his time digging over the vegetable plot. He did not shout his customary greetings to anyone who passed. It was a lonely fearful time for him. Ainsley came frequently to visit him, calm and encouraging, automatically taking all the precautions he had learned so well under Vincent Fallon's tuition in London.

In the churchyard 'The Giant' Tom Hart dug George Swift's grave. Lord Ainsley's carpenter at Home Farm fashioned a simple oak coffin of planks taken from trees which had grown in Telso woodland. The Hall also sent a simple linen shroud. At Ainsley's instructions these were left on the grass at the cottage garden gate. He and Tom Carter carried them within the house and upstairs to the bedroom where George's body lay beneath a blanket. Ainsley alone prepared the body for burial, and he let no one near until the coffin lid was nailed fast in place.

Within the hour big Tom Hart came along the grassy lane trundling the Parish Bier. He came to a halt at Glebe Cottage gate. He helped manhandle the coffin down the awkward narrow stairs, out onto the path and up onto the bier, before making his way back to the churchyard. In the church he began to toll the bell. Andrew Mallard dressed in his priest's robe and with his prayer book open stood waiting on the sunlit pathway. He led the small procession along the lane. David Ainsley and Tom Carter pushed the bier. During the short walk to the graveyard there was no sound save the squeak of the bier wheels and the tolling of the bell. All across the valley the people heard the bell tolling out the twenty-five years of George Swift's young life. They came out of their houses and cottages and stood in silence. At the Park, Elizabeth Ainsley and many of her staff came out onto the smooth circle of lawn in front of the house. Lord and Lady Ainsley did the same in the farmyard at Home Farm where George had worked since his tenth birthday. The Cook, the maids, the farm-hands, cowmen, carpenters, grooms and keepers stood in the sunlit yard with their Master and Mistress. With them were the two young ladies, Miss Charlotte and Miss Esme. No word was spoken. A little way off stood Jack Acres, the third shepherd, who by reason of his work on the moors had missed the touch of plague's black fingers on Glebe.

Up at Hill Farm, Anne Barnes stood with her family by the yard wall beyond which the land fell sharply away to Lower Telso. From here she could see the two new thatched roofs of Glebe and Thatcher's Cot. She drew in her breath as if in pain as she saw how close they were one to the other. Her hands gripped tight together in a silent prayer for Thatcher Gibbs's safety. Her Father's eyes searching to see the coffin pass by the churchyard wall saw what tormented his daughter. When the tears burnt against her lids and lashes he placed his arm about her shoulders in a rare gesture. "Don't fret, daughter - 'tis but one died. The good Doctor will see after the rest, never fear."

In Upper Telso the Inn stood empty. George Arms and his wife together with John Price, the blacksmith, and his apprentice stood heads bowed in the lane by the gate which looked down across the meadows to the church. All along the lane people had been drawn from their homes by the tolling bell. The women left their work to stand straining their eyes to glimpse George Swift's last journey. They could see the white flutter of Andrew Mallard's vestment against the hedge-line and for an instant the light wood of the coffin and the white stuff of David Ainsley and Tom Carter's shirt sleeves as they turned in at the Lych Gate. Then they became lost from sight beneath the dark yews of the churchyard.

There was no service in the church. Dr. Ainsley wanted the coffin buried as soon as decent respect allowed. They went directly to the grave. Andrew read the simple words of the 23rd Psalm, followed by the prayer of interment. The bell had ceased and Tom Hart came from the vestry door to help with the coffin. He brought two stout ropes with

him. It was fitting that Doctor, Priest, Sexton and Friend took each a rope end to lower the coffin into the tender dark earth which George had loved and served all his life. Presently there were only two sounds to be heard: the clatter of stones and earth from Tom Hart's shovel as he filled in the grave, and the gentle repetitive cooing of the pair of wood pigeons which inhabited the dark yews nearby.

The village settled back into an uneasy peace. The normal traffic between one cottage and another was little in evidence. The men went to work and did their stint as usual but few went to the Inn at nights. The cottage families kept themselves to themselves. None wished to show their wariness one of another, but all knew the restraint which George Swift's death had laid on them. The following Sunday Martin and Emmy Bones brought their baby son to be baptised. At David's instigation, Andrew Mallard did not perform the ceremony at morning service. Instead, it was done in the early morning - only the parents and godparents were present, and what should have been a small rejoicing in the village, passed by almost unnoticed.

At the usual Sunday Service many overcame their fear of coming near their neighbours, there were more in church than usual. It was the proof of Andrew's words about the Church being better filled in troubled times. Andrew stood at the door to bid them Godspeed after the service. He noticed that many laid a hand on the Saxon Cross - the Healing Cross - as they left the churchyard. Others cast fearful glances at the new turned earth of George Swift's grave. None stayed to chatter at the gate.

The respite was short lived. Three days later, Tom Carter fell sick, and later David found the dread rash of 'Tokens' on his body. Within two more days he suffered swellings within his groin and armpits, which festered. In spite of David's untiring care in lancing them and keeping the flesh as clean as possible, the poison outstripped all his efforts. Tom Carter died very suddenly on the sixth day while David was heating him some beef broth over the fire. Harriet Mallard had made the broth and sent it round hoping to tempt the invalid's appetite. He never tasted it. Exactly eight days to the hour, Saint John's tolled its grim message again to the villagers. That night no candle burned in the black square of Glebe Cottage window. David nailed boards across the door and fixed a chain about the gate.

The sight of the dark cottage awoke in Thatcher Gibbs an idea. He took a candle, lit it and set it in his own cottage window sill. Close against the glass, its light shone out. Anne, he hoped might see the little glow down across the fields and know it to be a sign of life, that all was well with him. In a few days the other cottagers began to do the same and David, visiting a patient at night, would often draw comfort from the small, steady burning flames. It reminded him of London. The idea was not new, it had long been the custom during the black months of the Death for a candle to stand lit in the closed houses of London. A proof that life and hope still existed within.

In early October the first sharp frost came to the valley. David woke to white crisp rime upon the trees and bushes around Crab Tree. His view to the Springs and Big Fields was of grass and rushes bespangled with frost. The trees were turned brown and red and gold over night. He saw it with relief - the onset of cold weather would halt the pestilence within their midst. For two nights the frost came sharp before first light. Ponds were covered with thin ice. The last of the flowers drooped and faded in Seckington Hall gardens. Villagers carting peat and carrying water in the early morning saw their breath cloud the sharp air in front of them. On the farms troughs had to be freed of ice before horses and cattle could drink.

On the fourth day the sun shone less hot and clouds began to blow in across the sky from the West, promising rain. Storms built up in high dark masses all day, with a strong breeze piling the clouds into black unearthly shapes by sunset. The sun dropped pale and unnoticed over the horizon.

Next morning the countryside woke to torrential rain. It ran off the dry fields and poured into drought-ridden brooks and streams. The noise from the waterfall below Crab Tree was deafening. Until the coming of rain David had swum every day. He had become used to the cold water and hoped it would rid his body of any traces of the pestilence which might linger. Only once did he set eyes on Red Cap and she had at once splashed out of the water and run away. Evidently her passion for him had been short lived. Perhaps she had found a lover amongst her own Romany people. At any rate his thoughts dwelt little upon her and even less upon Elizabeth during that autumn. His mind was taken up with his work and with his enemy - Plague. He tried to keep a watch upon everyone in the villages. He paid special attention to those in Lower Telso whose homes were near the empty closed up Glebe Cottage.

Lord Ainsley had found lodgings for Jack Acres in Seckington and he had not been back to Glebe. The village grapevine had it that Jack Acres was now courting Betty Groves, the young niece of Lord Ainsley's butler.

It rained almost non-stop for two weeks before the clouds finally lifted and, under clear skies, it became cold once more. David was much within his own house. He visited people's homes as little as his work allowed. He was very conscious of his recent close contacts with death. The folk of Telso did not shun him, it seemed that with his time in London and since as their Surgeon, they held him to have a charmed life. It was certainly so in the case of the Dale family at Wood Cottage. David was called there one frosty October morning.

The time had come for Eliza's child to be born. It was an easy quick birth. The waters broke as David entered the bedroom, five minutes later a strong well formed lusty boy pushed his way into the world. In doing so he split open the skin of the womb entrance that had given him shelter. In truly masculine fashion his uncaring rosy mouth latched immediately onto his Mother's milk filled breast. Ainsley was left to neat stitch the untidy passage he had come by. Eliza was delighted with him and quite unworried by his hurried manner of entry.

Arthur Dale missed his youngest son's arrival, being at work in his Lordship's cowsheds at the time. Old Albert sat at the fire in the kitchen smoking his clay pipe. He came stumbling noisily up the cramped stairs when the child cried out.

"It's a lad if 'is voice is that bleddy good!" shouted the old man. "Well done, Lass, and no messing about at it either!"

"You make his Mother a drink of that precious tea of hers and let's have less noise," Ainsley reproved him cheerfully.

The child's coming lightened the heart of the village and some kind of normality returned to Lower Telso. Ilsa Dale, now much recovered, came often to Wood Cottage. She loved the new baby and would nurse him by the fire in the kitchen, playing with him and talking to him in her soft gentle way.

"You pick him up so much - you'll have 'un proper spoiled," Eliza would chide her. In truth, Eliza did not mind, she was pleased to see Ilsa smile again and begin to grow well. The girl, now established as a maid at the Hall, never mentioned the Park or her time there. Dr. Ainsley still watched over Ilsa, as did his Mother, Lady Isobel. Her physical wounds were healed, her left breast carried a scar alongside the nipple. Ainsley did not think that it would ever be entirely gone but time would fade its harshness. Her monthly flux had come uneven at first after the vicious rape, but mercifully Jonathon's semen had found no seed in her and gradually her bleeds became normal and steady once more.

Old Albert also took pleasure in his new grandson. "Brave he be - real brave," he would boast to all and sundry. "Grows so quick and lively with it. That 'un teks after me, he do, no mistake about that!"

"The Good Lord forbid! One like you's more'n enough in one family," Eliza would remark sharply. She was forever at the old man.

"Get from under me feet. I got to get dinner on for they three men that works to keep old fools like 'ee sitting on back-sides smoking dirty old pipes all day long!"

It was good natured sword-crossing. Wood Cottage was a happy place that autumn.

The other baby in Lower Telso also gave his parents much joy. David Ainsley had not tried to move Martin Bones and his wife and baby or their neighbours, the Symes family next door. The plague had been too near. Infection could be hidden in any cottage in Lower Telso, waiting, crouching and secret, to leap up when least expected. David would not risk either family unwittingly carrying death to Upper Telso. Lord Ainsley had sent his workmen to prepare two cottages near the Cross Keys, but it was not planned to move them until after Christmas. By then bitter cold should have laid the Plague's dark ghost.

Emmy Bones was content where she was. Martin had made a crib of wood for the baby and had lodged it firm in a recess in the wall of their room. The baby would lie sleeping in the flickering firelight. As the dark evenings came Martin Bones came home early. He and Emmy were making their home more comfortable. The wall bed now boasted two good blankets woven since the baby's birth. Emmy had made them on her own loom. Martin had made the loom himself with the skill of his hands. Emmy had become adept at weaving. His Lordship allowed Martin to buy a fleece from the Home Farm sheep at cost price. Emmy would wash it and clean it and then spin it on her long dead Mother's old spinning wheel. It was a laborious task, from fleece to blanket, but rewarding in itself, especially so when they lay snug beneath the blankets in the wall bed.

When the baby was some weeks old they lay so one night in the glowing firelight. Martin spoke soft - not to waken the child.

"You'm so lovely, Emmy - now the child be come - your belly so flat - 'tis good to see you so - it do tempt me. What you think?"

He had not taken her since the child's birth, she being sore and bruised.

"I dare say it wouldn't hurt none."

"Suppose I swells your belly agin? Don't seem right so quick, but I do so long to be in you, Lass."

"I don't mind - I loves babies - you know that well enough."

"Oh, Emmy, you be a good wife to me - I don't deserve such."

His hands fumbled below her nightgown and pushing it up fastened on her breasts, full and heavy now since the child was so much sucking. He drew her to him and felt her warm arms go round his neck. "Oh Emmy - I've got to!" he muttered. A moment later her body opened to him and he gasped with pleasure. His arms pressed her closer prolonging the satisfaction of his hunger. At last he was done and lay at her side with his arms still about her. They did not speak again but drifted into sleep as the fire burned low in the cottage hearth.

After three weeks of frost at the end of October, when most of the leaves had fallen, it came very warm. A few days of Indian Summer sent Bernard Bistock and his sons Charles and Rust into the stubble field behind the house. Each had a team of two horses behind a plough. As they began to cut out the furrows, the black earth was turned up rich to the sun and wind. Seagulls from far away seas followed the ploughs. It was a pretty sight. Rachel stood and watched them one day in the afternoon sunshine. She wore and old faded blue gown and her lovely corn coloured hair was windblown, escaping the confines of a crumpled ribbon. On her arm a basket of stone bottles, empty now since the three men had stopped on the headland on their last bout to slake their thirsts with the home made cider she had carried to them.

Rachel lingered in the sunshine reluctant to return to the house. The Cliven ran tumbling along its course at the end of the field and her eyes were drawn to its sparkling surface. She heard a sound and caught sight of a rider coming over the bridge along the lane from Seckington. She saw at once who it was and felt a movement in her breast. "Fool girl," she admonished herself, "he's not for the likes of you - he's for some fine lady such as was Miss Elizabeth. If anything, he holds you in some dislike." Her heart still beat fast and a blush came to her cheeks. Her thoughts did not show in her face. She regarded him with steady eyes as he came close. He wore no hat and his thick hair shone black and curling against his narrow head. His eyebrows lifted at once in recognition. The light blue eyes sparkled between the thick short lashes as they flattered her country girl's charm. He reined in his horse and leaned down to speak to her.

"And how does Mistress Rachel on this fine day? Sweet in spirit and temper, I hope?" The blue eyes laughing at her took in every detail of her bonny country girl's demeanour and found her very pleasing. As always his slightly teasing way with her started off her quick roused nature.

"Meaning that I was bad humoured at our last meeting, I suppose?" Even as she spoke she blushed in the memory of his kiss at Crab Tree.

"Never! Surely such charm could not bespeak a sullen nature - such sweet lips must," his voice lowered, "indeed, do hold sweetness for any man fortunate enough to taste them."

"You tease me, Sir. You always make me wish very much to strike you in the face, Sir."

"I hope most sincerely that you will manage to restrain yourself in that. I was never a very brave man!"

"Do you never speak serious, Sir? Or is it always your custom to treat everyone as a child?"

"Not everyone, Mistress - only those very pretty young ladies that in part are children still, and especially on a sunlit pleasant day when the world looks good on every side." He added this last as an after thought.

"Oh yes." She forgot her ill humour. "The warm sun is so good - the world so lovely! I did not wish to go indoors. It is such a special day, is it not? Like a gift before winter. A day to run in the grass and listen to the larks on the moor up there! Her honey brown eyes sparkled as she turned and pointed upwards towards the wild moorland above Chalfont. There the fading heather showed purple fingers hazing into the skyline beyond.

"Shall I take you up on my horse and gallop you up amongst the rocks and heather? Then you could run through the grass, and we both might hear the larks and watch them rising." His eyes flirted with her as he spoke, his firm mouth bent to sudden sweetness. Her eyes dropped and he had the pleasure of seeing the colour flood her face and neck. The long lashes hung like curtains and her free hand came up to her mouth to hide her confusion.

"My Mother waits - I must be gone, Sir" She turned and almost ran from him along the fallow edge of the ploughing. He watched her out of sight along the hedge line.

"Well, well, a warm heart lies deep somewhere within the little wayward wilful Miss. Let that be a warning to men with bachelor leanings such as myself!" He rode home in high spirits.

The Indian Summer carried them into November and when that month was a week old it was still mild. Ainsley spent half a day cleaning out the harness room and stable behind the house at Crab Tree. He wanted to be able to get Beauty in at night, later on, if snow came to the villages. He was near done with his job when William Trewis of Lower Farm House rode into the yard.

"Good Day, Doctor"

"Good Day to you also, William,is it not? William Trewis?"

"Aye, Sir - that's right. We keeps well of late - no cause to send for 'ee, not since you come to us as medic. Being four of us brothers, folks do get muddly tryin' to sort which be which!"

"I know you and Johnny well enough; Albert and Arms - I'm none to certain. Your sister Velvet I regard as my assistant, she being so good a midwife!"

"She'd be pleased to hear you say it, Sir. 'Twas her as sent me, matter o' fact."

"Oh yes. Is someone ailing then?"

"Well, Sir, not amongst us, like. Not at Lower House. 'Tis Velvet do worry. It may be nought. 'Tis them cottage women, Mother Ross - she as they calls witch and Jeannie as lives along of she." He hesitated.

"Are they ill? Has Mistress Velvet seen something?"

"It''s more what she aint seen. We often goes weeks and sees neither. Sometimes Jeannie do come to our back after a can o' milk an' a few eggs. She 'ent no witch! Just how folks be, you knows - village clap - all talk. Never says much - not talks a lot - smiles pleasant enough - that was first of it."

Ainsley began to despair of getting to the bottom of the matter.

191

"Has she been today?"

"Who? .... Oh, Jeannie, you means. No she 'ent - she 'ent been these three weeks. Our Velvet do say she 'ent seen none of her since usual. And now our Velvet have been watching - watching they chimneys days past, and it do seem strange. It be warm now but it were cold some days back. They'm allus had a fire - all these years, and then there's the cat." The boys voice became emphatic on the last five words, as though they were conclusive.

"What about the cat?" asked David patiently.

"Their little ole cat do come in our milk house under our feet all hours she do. Cry she do for milk and our Arms does usual pour 'er a drop in the trough. Never used. Never come about our yards afore. Jeannie was used to fetch milk for 'er times past." William closed his mouth, mopped his face with a rag, and sat back on his horse, relief etched sharp on his round face. His communication was at an end. He stared enquiringly at David.

"So, it seems there may be something wrong in the end cottage. I expect Mistress Velvet wants me to go along and find out. Is that it?"

"She was hopin' p'raps Reverend might go along of you?"

"Did Mistress Velvet suggest that?"

"No - me Mam - she did say - she wouldn't go her sen - none of us do like to go that way. Jeannie be all right, 'tis t'other is a bad 'un."

"Ah, I see. Well I dare say I'd be safe enough going with Reverend Mallard," David said somewhat drily.

"That's what Mam says - tell them to take Reverend's cross - she says." William Trewis's reply was delivered with stolid seriousness.

"Tell Mistress Velvet and your Mother we'll look into it today, William, and thank you for your trouble in coming."

"That's nowt, Sir, hour away from mucking out cowsheds - that 'ent much hardship to I!"

David, much amused, watched the young man ride away.

David finished his work in the stables by stacking the straw battens which his Father had sent from the Hall. Behind the stable was a small lean-to; with the straw in there it would be easy to bed Beauty down snug on cold winter nights, especially if snow should come. He finished and went in the house and found it to be two o'clock. In the kitchen Mabel Dunn was ready with his dinner, she had become very much part of his life at Crab Tree. She carried his dinner in now with a cheerful smile.

"Here you be then, Doctor. Enjoy it while it's good and hot." She deposited roast beef with a dish of carrots in front of him. "Carrots be a gift from Mr. Bistock up at Chalfont. Young Rust brought 'em down yesternight."

"That was a kindness - I must call and thank him."

"There's a slice or two of cold goose, if you fancy it after."

"No. No. This will do nicely."

She left him and went to clean up in the kitchen. As a rule she went home about four o'clock. At the time of George Swift's and Tom Carter's sad passing David had been tempted to ask her to come and live in. There was room enough, but something had kept him from making the suggestion. Truth to tell, he enjoyed having the place to himself at night.

He did not dally over his meal; he felt uneasy in his mind about the two women in the end cottage. He himself had not seen the old woman since before he went into the Navy. She had seemed very old then and that was years back. He remembered her as a thin stick of a woman in the black flapping garment of poverty, and above it a narrow dark face and hooked shepherd's crook of a nose. No wonder the village dubbed her witch. He had no recollections of Jeannie and was in doubt if he had ever seen her. His meal finished, he drained his glass of red wine and went up to the bedroom. He threw off his breeches and shirt and took clean ones from the press.

Fifteen minutes later, mounted on Beauty, he came in sight of the Parsonage House. As always since Glebe Cottage had been closed up, he had ridden by with a great lowering of his spirits. Had he been right to put the Red Cross on the door? It was very necessary to keep people away, so he reminded himself. Andrew Mallard was at home. Ainsley explained the visit he had had from William Trewis.

"Surely I'll come with you. Wait while I get my coat. Where's your mare?"

"I took the liberty of putting her in the stable - there was no one about."

"No, I expect the boy's in the garden. Tom Hart's been lifting our turnips. Shall we make way on foot then? It would draw less attention to our mission." Andrew pulled on his cloth coat as he spoke.

It was a cool blustery afternoon, in the lane leaves and twigs whirled and eddied about their feet, rustling as they walked. Across Back Drop and Poacher's Plot fields the trees in Windy Wood were more than living up to their name. The West wind whipped across High Bank, through Black Rocks and down the bluff, laying flat the grass and whin bushes in its path. The scots pine and beech in Windy Wood bowed and creaked. The old lane was more sheltered but grew more grassy and rough as they advanced. They came in sight of the row of cottages; against the wild windy backdrop of woodland they looked poor hovels indeed. The two end cottages, where John Symes and Martin Bones lived with their families, did not look so bad. Effort had been made to keep the grassy area outside neat and tidy. The cottages further along the row were a different story. As David Ainsley and his companion passed by they could see in through the dilapidated open doors of the two middle dwellings. The thatch had begun to cave in, clods of earth sprouted to grass in the doorways. Recent rains had left mud and puddles beneath the holes in the roof. Litter and dirt from previous inhabitants lay piled in corners. Ainsley's mouth hardened at the sight. They came level with Ben Hastley's cottage. The door was tight shut and it looked uncared for but better than the two near ruins they had just passed. They moved on towards the last cottage, the difference here was that there were no doors or windows on the front of the house. Being the end house, the builder, for some reason best known to himself, had put the door and small square window in the end wall.

David and Andrew Mallard turned the corner of the building into the force of the West wind. Wild marshland faced them and overgrown nettles grew almost up to the house wall. There was something threatening in the dark woodland swaying in the wind above the marsh. There the great trees moved in wild disarray. Above the trees the open moor hung dark and menacing. Ainsley turned his attention to the door and window. The single cracked pane was black with grime. He rubbed a small circle to peer inside. To no avail, inside hung a dark strip of cloth. Andrew moved on and knocked at the door. It was unpainted and half off its hinges. There was no sound from within.

"Great Heavens, Man! No one's been here for days. See there's not a single footprint in the earth. Nothing!" Andrew rapped again on the door with his fist.

"Here, let me push it, it's near dropping off anyway."

David Ainsley pushed his shoulder to the rotting boards, there was a splintering of wood and half the door fell away under his weight. He pushed his head through the gap in the boards. The stench which met him almost caused him to vomit. He drew back and flung his arm across in front of Andrew to prevent him moving in closer.

"For God's sake, keep away, Andrew, leave this to me."

"But, man ... what is it - are they?"

"They're dead - both of them. In there on the floor - and the rats have been here before us."

"But, shouldn't we go in and cover them? Drive the rats out? It's degrading to human remains." Andrew had not seen - he could not comprehend.

"No we shouldn't! The old woman lies half naked - she has swellings on her which I know to have only one cause. It's Plague, Andrew! The pestilence has been here before us. If we go in without disinfectant or proper precautions we may carry it all over the village."

"Can it be so?"

"It can - of course, it can. Did I not wage war with it in London - week after week? Just when we think it gone it bursts forth again in some new quarter."

"What now, then? I am in your hands David."

They stood in the wind and faced each other. Ainsley took his friends arm and led him away. "Come on, there's nothing we can do here. I'll explain my course of action as we walk up the lane." They strode away putting distance between themselves and the horror of the cottage.

"My duty as the Surgeon in the district is clear and simple and cannot be avoided," Ainsley explained as they walked back to the Parsonage.

"And what is it you must do?"

"First, I must seal that cottage, unpleasant but necessary. The door must be hammered fast and the window boarded. All entrances tight closed. They must be marked with the red cross to keep others away. That I must do at once - can you lend me a few boards and a hammer and nails?"

"Yes, and I'll help you tackle the task. There's paint also in the Parsonage stable."

"No, Andrew - I don't want you, or anyone else near that building again. I'll see to it myself."

"And what of the dreadful corpses - who will see after what's left of the women?"

"That's my next task. I must ride into town and see the magistrates. The house, once all in it are dead, becomes their responsibility. My duty in this case is to the living - more particularly to the three who live next door - right within the clutch of the Death. Also the two families at the far end of the Row."

"Can you move them away?"

"That is no longer my choice - the magistrates have jurisdiction over close neighbours' houses - but at least they cannot shut up the folk within their homes - at least not until there is Plague actually in the other cottages."

Andrew's face had lost its colour and looked drained and sad.

"God save us all - it is indeed a dread situation. Do you think it will pass to the other houses? Is it inevitable?"

"No one can say. I can warn them and guide them in every way of prevention that I know, but no one knows how it spreads. It creeps where it can strike deepest. That is why it is so hard to fight against."

"What, in your opinion, will the magistrates do? How can those wretched women be given Christian burial without risk of spreading the pestilence?"

"They cannot," replied Ainsley bluntly. "It seems likely the magistrates will send men to inter the house and the women together in one heap - it would be my advice if they asked me." David tried to speak cheerfully.

"Yes, indeed yes, I see your point. The Surgeon must

safeguard the living - and you are right of course."

"I hope so." David's face was tight and tense. "But, in any event, it is the law of the land and we shall have no part in the choice."

"And will you ride to town today?"

"Yes, and I must make haste - for some part of the journey must already be in darkness."

"Let me get together the things that you need." They had reached the yard gates at the Parsonage. It took David half an hour to complete his gloomy task and fetch his horse from Andrew's stable. He went back to Crab Tree as soon as he was done at the old woman's cottage. There he changed his clothes - plunging all he took off into the old copper in the kitchen. He washed his body well and tossed off two glasses of red sack before setting off on his hard ride.

It grew dark as he rode out along the Seckington road. There were lights showing at Hill Farm and across the fields at Chalfont as he went by. He pictured Rachel in the farm kitchen, at the spit. A picture of the curls escaping under her mop cap came clear to his mind and drew a smile to the firm set of his lips. His way lay nine miles to the North.

At first his pace was slow - the road being rough in the gathering dusk. Presently the moon, at her half, rose behind the hills. Beauty put herself into an easy long striding canter.

The journey proved uneventful. The chief Magistrate took a gloomy view of David's news, but agreed that he and his subordinates must see after the issue. After a little more conversation Ainsley found him more helpful. He was treated with the respect due to a Surgeon, when the identity of his Father and his time in London was mentioned. They parted on good terms. Ainsley went away with the promise that help would be sent at first light.

The man proved as good as his word and shortly after dawn broke over Lower Telso a dozen men came with picks and shovels and axes. They were led by a giant of a man with two great horse drawn wagons filled with quicklime. David Ainsley was there to meet them. So much traffic was unheard of in the narrow lane and, although the men in the row were gone to work, the women came out, much disturbed by the noise and bustle at their doors. Cathy Symes and Emmy Bones stood watching, Cathy's children clung about her skirts. There were carts and men everywhere. The dogs at Lower Farm House yelped and barked behind the closed gates.

"What's afoot then, Doctor? Is the marsh to be drained at last?" (It had long been under discussion).

"No, Emmy, it's something else. Take the children inside, both of you, and close your doors. I'll call in directly and explain."

David Ainsley spoke with firmness and authority, addressing himself to both women. Emmy looked anxious and as if she would say more, but in the end she turned with Cathy and they both went back into their homes. Doors closed behind them. Flossie and Phoebe Hastley and old Ben were not yet out of their beds. Ainsley rapped upon their doors loudly. A moment later Flossie's tousled head was thrust out of the tiny dormer in the roof.

"What the Hell's all this bleddy racket?" she shouted, then seeing the Doctor she grinned sheepishly. "Beg Pardon, Medic - thought it was just they workmen. What's going on here then?"

"Serious business, Flossie. Get your Father and your sister up and dressed but keep them inside until I come to you. It's important, Flossie - so mind my words." Flossie nodded briefly, withdrawing her head from view. The window banged shut.

The workmen had begun, they made haste to be done with their gruesome task. The instructions had been direct and simple. They tore down the boardings at doors and window, smashing in the glass with the back of a shovel. One of the loads of quicklime was then hurled with all speed in upon the foul, loathsome corpses. Next, the rough low roof was pulled down with long grappling hooks. As the thatch fell in so the lime rose up in a thick cloud of white dust. It burned the eyes and throats of the men, making them cough and sneeze, but the stench of death was gone, lost in the purifying lime. When the roof was open to the sky, the mud walls were pushed in and levelled with the hooks. A second load of lime flung over all completed the task. The mud walls had fallen before the swinging hooks and picks of the men in a fog of dust and lime combined. Now the second wagon of lime covered all and left a white mound. The men flung two cart loads of peaty soil on top to hide the eyesore. Now there was only the earth mound, as of a vast grave amongst the trampled nettles. The wall of Hastley's cottage stood stark and exposed, the peak of thatch torn roughly away, the wall covered in dirty peeling lime-wash.

On David Ainsley's instructions, the rest of the lime was thrown in through the doors of the two empty middle cottages and their doors and windows tight boarded. The whole distasteful task had taken less than two hours. David saw the carts drawn away up the lane before he went and knocked on the Hastley's door. The first of his three calls to tell his grim news and to advise and instruct those left, in the best way to preserve their own lives.

News that plague had struck again in Lower Telso was quick to reach all parts of the village. None regretted Mother Ross's passing - she had been feared by many. The greatest impact of the two deaths and the macabre nature of their burial was felt by those families still left in the Row. The most troubled were naturally old Ben and his two daughters. The women were frightened. Death stood on their dorrstep. Perhaps dwelt in the very walls of their home. For days, each watched the other for some sign of illness - ready for a secret flitting at a moment's notice. Ben himself was more philosophical.

"I be had 'un good life - an' I reckons my pipe do keep I free of them pestilences what flies about. Doctor do say fresh air, well they floosy daughters do sleep now danged cold with attic shutter ope'd wide. I b'aint such foolish - tek a freezin chill and us'am dead any road up. Six feet under in yon Chruchyard you be; dead then, by plaguey or pnewmony - wot's difference? Answer that?" He would then light up the weed in his pipe and puff smoke about in vigorous fashion, as though that must of a certainty build up a wall of protection against all ills around him.

Had Phoebe or Flossie decided to run off it would have to have been a secret flitting, The Magistrates sent out the same printed notice as Ainsley had seen many times in London. Copies were nailed on all the doors in the row and on the Parish Notice Board outside the Church. On them it was clearly stated that Plague had been in the immediate vicinity and residents must stay where they were for 40 days passing. This being the law since the cottage walls all joined, being built in one block. No one in the row could either read or write but David saw to it that all understood the need to obey the warning.

David was thankful that the Magistrates had not resorted to panic measures. Measures such as locking all the families inside their houses for forty days. As it was, John Symes and Martin Bones continued going to work. Both worked in the open air, which in David's opinion was the best antidote to plague. Cathy Symes and Emmy Bones placed implicit faith in the Doctor's judgment; they went calmly about their daily lives - kept their houses as clean as they could, opening doors and windows to let in pure air. They covered their food with clean linen, they cooked the food very thoroughly, all water was carried from the Parson's well on the Glebe. Lord Ainsley sent men to cover the old well below Mother Ross's cottage, which by custom all the cottage dwellers had used until now, Ainsley felt it was suspect being so low lying, only just above the level of stagnant marsh. Also it was fearfully close to the women's burial ground.

All three Symes children were told that they must play in the Parson's orchard on the Glebe. They must not venture further down the Row than Mrs. Bones's door, on pain of a sound thrashing from their Father. There was little temptation. Glebe land had chestnut trees and a see-saw and until now had been closed to all children except those from Parsonage House. Cathy's two little girls and eight year old son, regarded it as a great treat to be allowed to play there every day.

One outcome of the second ugly appearance of plague in Lower Telso was the effect it had on Flossie and Phoebe and their amorous exploits. None of the men, who had previously come once or twice a week to avail themselves of the earthy pleasures which the two had so enjoyed giving, came any more. Most took themselves instead to the cottage of a young widow in Seckington who was also known to be obliging and ready with her favours.

If it had been summer no doubt Flossie and Phoebe could have obliged in the woods or a dry ditch and so arranged their assignations and kept their suitors, as it was they were shunned and bitterly resented it. Their bad humour rubbed off on old Ben who complained over his ale in the Cross Keys.

"They be like young heifers kep away from the old bull - forever moving and moping and chuntering. 'Tis enough to drive any peace lovin' man plain daft. This bleddy plague do have much 't answer for! That's the truth!"

For several weeks David Ainsley waited anxiously. Daily he expected some fresh case of sickness in the lower village. One thing ran in his favour: the weather changed. November went out in a burst of cold. The wind changed and veered to the East - bringing sun by day and hard frost by night. Dumble Wood crouched low under the bitter East wind. Round Crab Tree at night the wind sighed and moaned. The piles of leaves, which had lain damp and golden, turned black and stiff with the encrusting frost. At dawn rime sparkled on every twig. Squirrels and hedgehogs slept dreamless in their chosen warm habitats. On the moor the hares' coats turned near white as they shivered in their frosty forms. Foxes hunted by night in the woods growing brave in their hunger. At Chalfont and Hill Farm and Lower House the women let the traps down before dusk on the poultry lest Reynard get too saucy. Rachel Bistock had twofold problems. She must needs get her geese in their pen just after noon and then the water froze so quick in their trough that she had every day to carry four or five pails to them, across the slippery yard, before dark.

In the wood the foxes hunted and barked. In the houses the men stacked up the peats and clung about the fireside for warmth.

CHAPTER VI

CHAPTER VI

The foxes were not the only ones hunting. This was the season for shooting. Lord Ainsley would organise shoots for his friends. The gentlemen would come in fancy coats and breeches to enjoy the sport. Village lads with bright kerchiefs at their necks would beat the woodlands and coverts, bringing the birds into the open, within range of the guns. By night a different set of actors took the stage in the woodland. As soon as darkness fell, gamekeepers and poachers began their eternal battle for top dog. Once the frost struck really hard, the gamekeepers began to put down grain in the woodland, to attract and fatten the pheasants. They became tame as farmyard fowls.

It was the signal for Black Dyer to plot and plan his strategy for the coming winter. His sons and daughter did most of the work but his was the master mind behind every manoeuvre. Dyer knew every woodland, every path, every haunt and perch of the birds. Their feeding grounds and habits, the special shelter they found in roosting in a certain thick low bowed yew tree or amongst the high branches of the thick berried holly bush. His finger was on the very pulse of the forest. Windy Wood, Dumble Wood, Telso Wood, Witches Wood and Low Wood were all his hunting grounds. All served him well for winter poaching.

It was not enough to know how to slip a hand round the legs of a perching bird and yet keep it quiet. To be able to drop a sack over a plump cock pheasant in the total blackness of a moonless night, or even to set a snare or trap so that sharp eyed gamekeepers on the watch for just such ploys would pass by unseeing. There was another vital factor in the war that raged, silent, fierce and constant between the keepers and the Romanies from first frost until springtime.

It was the Patrols. As long as anyone could remember, the gamekeepers had carried out night patrols in all the woodlands on the Estate. The head keeper, knowing the cunning of his adversary, took care to devise a constantly changing pattern of patrols. Some nights here - some nights there. Sometimes before midnight, sometimes near to dawn. The patrols consisted of up to half a dozen men in each. All carried guns. All were good shots. Orders were to shoot only if the quarry ran away. Mostly the quarry did run away. Punishment for poaching in 1665 was whipping, imprisonment or death depending on the severity of the Magistrate who deals with the case. To outwit such well balanced arrangements for putting him and his sons out of what he considered to be their rightful business, Black Dyer needed second sight, or, a spy in the camp of the enemy. Although Dyer's wife, Jewel, made a steady bit of money during the long summer days tramping round the local towns telling fortunes, selling pegs and good luck charms, Dyer had little real faith in her ability at foretelling Head Keeper Anderson's plans for the patrols. He preferred a more accurate peephole into the carefully mapped out movements of Anderson and his men. For ten years past Black Dyer had found just such a spy in the unlikely guise of Old Amos. It worked in a very simple way. Old Amos - an expert poacher himself in times long back - now lived in semi-retirement (he robbed Dyer's snares if they were close to his hut in the dell by the Cliven). The hut had always been accepted, no one knew its origin. It seemed it had always been there and, for most local people, so had Old Amos. Lord Ainsley himself could not remember a time when Amos had not lived in the small stone bothy on the stream bank. Just as by custom a good plate of hot cooked dinner and a jar of ale was always carried to Amos on Christmas Day. A servant would be sent on this errand, usually one of the maids.

Amos was not without his friends amongst the servants at the Hall. Servants are often pretty maids. Even gamekeepers are susceptible to pretty maids. A kiss or two, a glimpse of a trim ankle was a very pleasurable price to pay for a word or two about times and paths and ways to be followed on the next night's patrol. What then more natural than a kindly little housemaid taking poor old Amos a few apples or a slice of fat, please cook - left from the meat, or a couple of eggs from the nest in the stack. And from Amos in return, of course, a little repayment, in his case always the same, a penny for her pocket and a sly pinch of her knee. This was invariably followed by a half mug of his sweet cowslip wine, which he kept in four stone kegs on the floor at the back of the hut. The wine was potent, it loosened her tongue and did wonders for her memories of what the young gamekeeper had told her in the barn.

Early in the morning every day during winter it was part of Raven Dyer's work to run through Low Wood across the stream to Amos's hut. She would learn from him the route and timing of the coming night's patrols. She would run home, checking her brother's snares along the route. The beauty of Black Dyer's scheme was that nobody knew too much about the others involved. Also, of course, nothing was written down. Indeed, none of the people involved could read or write. None thought of it as spying or being dishonest. In most country places men like Lord Ainsley had a curious kind of respect and liking for the Black Dyers and their kind. They treated them with humorous tolerance, provided the Keepers kept the poaching within bounds. All this works well and all goes along happily until someone gets caught. Once caught, the offenders become outlaws. Then they become villains and felons. Then they are dealt with by the Magistrates, who are often men like Lord Ainsley. In the courtroom, previous tolerance must be set aside in the pursuit of law and order and justice.

All schemes which are dependent upon a number of human beings are fallible. One night in the bitter winter of 1665 a last minute change of plans was made in keeper Anderson's night patrol. The word had come to Black Dyer that Telso Wood and Low Wood had been chosen for a patrol from ten o'clock until midnight. After that the keepers were to return to the Hall for hot soup and a warm round the harness room fire. Then most would get off home to their warm beds. Anderson himself and two others were to ride on horseback across by the Park to Black Rocks and down to the top end of Windy Wood. Here one man was to have charge of the horses and the other two patrol on foot through the woodland from North to South. This was a good ploy. Windy Wood was on a steep slope, a wide grass ride ran down the centre. It was far easier to flush out a man and chase him down hill. Especially as he must run onto open marsh at the bottom. The grass ride widened and a gate at the bottom gave way to open track winding away round the hedge line of Poacher's Plot and Middle Field, and thence via Back Drop into the lane near the Glebe land. The man in charge of the horses was to ride his own and lead the other two, skirting the woodland

and waiting for his companions at the bottom of Poacher's Plot. This plan had served them well many times before. Taking the horses saved the men, often overtired with night work, a lot of walking over rough lanes back to their warm beds.

Black Dyer had enjoyed a good week, his outlet for game birds was twenty miles away. It was a small meat shop far enough distant to be discreet and safe from local prying eyes. The birds were transported by Falcon and Jason Dyer in leather bags slung either side of the saddles of their horses. They travelled, always separate, usually before first light. They used untrodden paths, lonely byways. The price they got for the birds was fair, considering that the Butcher knew well enough that the game was poached. That week they had transported forty brace of birds. It was tiring work and sleep was in short supply for them all. Tired men make mistakes, so thought Black Dyer. He decided to leave Telso Wood and Low Wood alone for a night. It had the merit of less work and giving his sons all the hours until midnight to poach Windy Wood with no chance of interruption. They could be back at the caravans by midnight and be under their blankets before Anderson's Patrol even finished supping their soup at the Hall.

It was a week before Christmas. Very cold and frosty, there was no wind and the moon swung near full in the sky hidden once in a while by the sparse fluffy clouds. At ten o'clock, nine keepers including Anderson, moved into the top of Telso Wood, they split into three groups and began to walk the long rides which ran from just below Cliven Brook to and fro from Big Fields. It was a still night, when even a twig cracking underfoot could be heard fifty yards away. There was no talking; it was a rule of Anderson's. In any case, every man was concentrating on looking and listening for any intruders. Their progress was necessarily slow. There were forty acres of woodland to cover, the ground was uneven, in some places the undergrowth was dense. They walked with care in the darkness under the trees. Each man carried a loaded gun.

Across the valley, three dark clad figures moved unseen across from Dale Meadows into Bog End. Jason, Falcon and Saul Dyer had the similarity of face and form which instantly marked them as brothers. All were big made, long in the leg and quick of movement. All had the dark skin and eyes of the true Romany. Black thick hair and hatchet, hook-nosed faces. Jason was heavier in build than the two younger men, his features, especially the nose, slightly thickened and course. Falcon, who had a hard closed look to his face, was much inclined to pick fights. His temper could flare at nothing, but die away just as quick. Saul, the youngest, was slim and graceful - he could outrun any man in the villages. He had a lean handsome face and a ready smile which revealed good teeth. He liked women above all else and because of his good looks did not lack for their company.

Always for night poaching they were dark clad in warm close fitting breeches and jackets. Black kerchiefs about their necks, stout boots on their feet. Each carried a short thick club-like stick and several long hessian game bags. No one spoke until they had passed by the village which lay across the field to their right. They came then alongside the Mere below the dark outline of the cottages in the Row. A dim candle shone in the windows of numbers one and two. Cathy Symes and Emmy Bones still lit them nightly as a ritual against Plague. The men moved on past the last cottage and saw in the moonlight the ghostly mound which was all that remained of Mother Ross's cottage. They moved instinctively away from it's dark undulations and passed by below the well which had been boarded over since the Death. They kept silence until they had climbed the stile into Marsh Meadow. This was pasture - hard and white now under foot, They struck out across it straight for the wood.

"They candle flames give me the creeps," Saul said.

"Why? They be provin' life inside."

"Never bin afore. I likes to see them houses dark when we be about our work."

"'Ent no one about. You gettin' nervy?"

"Never - no call to say such. I just don' like they lights - someone might be watchin'. "

"In this bloody cold! Never. Symes and Bones be abed, lying up close their women and busy at it, I shouldn't wonder." Jason's course laughter was low in his throat.

"Which way you want us to work the woodland?" Falcon

Dyer spoke for the first time.

Jason was their natural leader; he replied at once. "We'll keep together and work up the field side, those firs along Leg fence be the best cover, full of birds they was, last picking."

"Are us to carry birds along of us or tek un across to the grass way and leave un hid agin us coming back down?"

"We've plenty o' time. Saul can ferry 'em across to the halfway path. When us comes back down the moor side, us can pick birds up then."

They moved into the darkness of the overhanging trees. Fanning out until they were each fifty yards apart, they worked through the woodland with the practised skill of men used to working as a unit. Each knew every path, every bush and every tree. All the likely roosting places for game were visited and the best pickings taken. They used light nets, lengths of twine and cleft sticks to haul in their quarry. The birds scarcely realised their fate before they were taken and silenced. Each birds neck was expertly and quickly broken. Plump corpses were then passed into the waiting hands of Saul. He bagged them in the game bags held to his shoulders with a buckled strap. While Jason and Falcon moved further up through the thickets, Saul crossed and re-crossed through the trees to the wide grassy ride which ran down the middle of the woodland. He hid the bags close along the path amongst the bracken. Such was their experience that small birds were left to roost in favour of plump prime victims. There was always another night.

They reached the top of the wood just as the church clock struck eleven. It sounded clear in the frosty air. They paused a minute or two to catch their breath. Saul crouched down on his heels, the others leant their backs against two massive oaks. An owl hooted somewhere away to the north, in the vicinity of Black Rocks, another answered it from close by.

"That old woody owl do know none's about." Jason stood and strained his eyes to stare along the rocky ridge. The path ran on that way protected by the curve of the rocky hillside. It wound deep under Black Rocks and then broadened as it entered the grounds of the Park, through stone pillars and an iron gate. That was the way the gamekeepers would ride when they came to these woods. All was quiet. Jason could hear nothing.

"Well we'm half done. 'Tis a fair bag we got."

"Reckon we shall be done and off afore they buggers gets 'ere."

"Aye, that'll be it. Come on, lads, best be at it." Jason turned and went back amongst the trees and hazel bushes. They had one empty game bag left.

"You mun pick up as we goes down, Saul. You'll have some weight on by you gets down bottom. Don'ee bother none with us. We'll work down steady and join up with 'ee down along."

Saul was gone before Jason finished speaking. He moved quickly and silently, plucking each bag or net as it might be, out of hiding. Unerring in his choice of the exact place where he had slipped them under the fern. His pace slowed as soon as he had a few brace of birds hanging about his person.

Jason and Falcon began to work down through the woodland, the thickets were very dense on this side of the wood. It was good roosting country for pheasants, but more difficult to locate their perchings.

Across the valley, the patrols had made good time. Keeper Anderson heard the church clock strike. He and two other men were on the path near the footbridge. He heard crackling in the undergrowth and knew someone was close by. Probably three of his men.

"Who's there? Speak, if you be keepers," his voice barked out. It was the standard arranged challenge.

"Aye, Sir, Hendrick here." The burly figure of the under keeper moved into the half-light.

"Ah, Hendrick, where are the others - have you seen they?"

"Above the ford, I think, Sir. By the Cliven, I reckon."

"Good - we've made good pace. You take your men and work on up to Crab Tree. Meet up with the others and get off home. We three'll get back to the stables now - get a quick sup of summat hot and saddle up for Windy. That way we should all be near done by midnight - it's bitter cold. We've seen neither man nor beast. 'Tis too cold even for they bastard poachers."

"Very good - aye, you're likely right." Hendrick turned away.

It was half past eleven when Keeper Anderson reached the

Park. Black Rock rose before them stark in the bright moonlight. The three horsemen skirted the rocky bluff a few minutes later and came to the wood's entrance. The middle-aged man, Ames, remained mounted. Anderson and young Davie Heston dismounted and gave their reins to Josh Ames. They watched him out of sight. He rode away at walking pace round the long curve of the headland to Leg Field. The two riderless horses walked quietly alongside.

Anderson turned to Davie Heston. "Now, lad, your gun - see it loaded and safe. Let me keep afore - only two of us remember"

"Aye, Sir."

They moved along the ride under the dark trees. Their eyes quickly became accustomed to the gloom. They moved silently, only the occasional snap of a twig broken underfoot told of their presence, it was enough. Away to the right and in front of them, Jason Dyer laid a hand on Falcon's arm.

"Psst! I hear sommat." They both froze and stood listening intently. Falcon heard nothing. "Someone's on the ride - coming' down hill - two at least, I reckon."

"What about our Saul?"

"Young bugger - he'll likely not hear 'em till they has his coat-tails."

"What's to do then?"

"You tek these - there's only ten birds - you'll carry 'em easy, get you out onto the moor. Run down into the marsh - 'tis dry with frost. Wait in the oaks at the bottom an' try to get ye home."

"And you?"

"I'll cut through 'ere, get young Saul off that bloody path afore 'ee gets 'is breeches shot off 'is backside. Get you gone - Quiet now! Quiet!"

They separated. Jason, his hands free now and empty, moved out of the thickets into the oaks, he made good speed to the lower part of the wood without actually running. He came out two hundred yards from the bottom where the grass ride opened into the meadow. The gate stood wide in the moonlight. He breathed his relief to see it so. He couldn't see Saul or anyone else.

"Where the bloody hell's that Lad?" Jason whispered to himself. He waited listening intently for a moment. He heard some small sound but was not sure if it was human or some small animal in the underbrush. He began to move slowly back up the hill towards where a curve in the wide grass path hid all that lay beyond. He had almost reached the bend when everything happened at once. A shout rang out from further up the woodland.

"Who's there! Speak if your business be lawful!"

At the same time, Jason heard the quick thuds of his brother's running feet.

"We've seen you, you thieving varmints! Stand or I fire!" Anderson was running as he shouted, knowing his quarry was not yet in range. He could not have raised his gun while running downhill. Could not have carried out his threat. Jason knew it and leapt into the path. Saul came pelting down the track, bags of birds slung round his thighs banging against him. Twice they nearly brought him to the ground.

"Christ! You've cut it bloody narrow. Quick, give us some." Jason heaved an armful of bags onto his shoulder and turning they both pounded on down the track.

"Quick - we've got a minute afore they comes round the bend - then they'll fire on us like ducks off the bloody pit!"

"Don't let's leave our birds lie unless us has to."

"Surely not for them buggers to pick up."

Hearts thumping and legs at full stretch, the two men covered a hundred yards. They were now fifty yards from the gate.

"Stand! Stand, or I fire!" Anderson pulled up at the curve in the ride and raised his gun. "Shoot at their legs if you can, Lad," he panted. "Master won't want 'em dead."

Jason was a yard behind Saul. "Quick - sharp right into the hedgerow - there's a gap into the marsh in the thorn bushes. T'aint many yards. Slip that road and get in they bulrushes." Saul heard his brother's instruction from his bursting lungs. A shot rang out through the woodland and a moment later another.

"Ahh! God's Buggery!" Jason clasped his shoulder as he reeled under the hawthorn hedge. He fell to his knees in a small dell amongst the grass.

"Cum on - ye can't give up!" Saul gritted out the words through his teeth, heaving his brother up. They grappled a moment swaying, the bags of birds swinging about them. Saul shifted his bags to leave an arm free to shove round beneath his brother's armpit. They lurched along and mercifully came at once to the gap they sought. It was not wide. They pushed through, letting the thorny twigs spring back behind them. They were at once deep in reeds and rushes.

"Get down - keep low - us needs to git a few paces into they tall rushes," Saul whispered, wriggling away from the hedge.

"Me bloody shoulder's broke - I reckon - I'm nigh beat." Jason was on his knees again,

"You'll be a dang sight worse if that ole bastard Anderson gets his hands on 'ee." Saul felt no sympathy. His own arms ached with the weight of the bags and his legs throbbed with fatigue. In his chest his heart seemed risen out of its socket to wedge itself in his throat. Every breath was agony. They lay thus for several minutes listening to Anderson and his companion in the gateway not twenty yards away. The keepers looked this way and that coming out into the moonlit marsh. The Dyers' luck was in. A great slow moving cloud rolled leisurely and dark into the moon's path. Deep shadow crossed the marsh like a wave coming in from the sea. Saul saw his chance and gathered all the game bags into his arms. Through the gloom he wriggled away almost on his belly. Twenty-five yards ahead was an old clay pit, mostly flooded and marshy, but a good low place to give cover and hide the birds. He found the place - near dry in the recent hard frosts. The bank dropped steep and under it several hollowed out holes curved into the frozen clay. Saul dropped down and thrust his load into the nearest.

"Talk about set a bloody thief to catch another." It was a low chuckling voice he recognised.

"That you, Falcon? We'm in proper trouble this 'un." There was yet amusement in Saul's tone.

"I heard 'un shots. Be Jason hit? Have they buggers got 'un?"

"Not yet. He got it in the shoulder. He lies just up yonder in the bulrush - about done, I reckon."

"Moon's covered - can us get 'un, think you?"

"Ah, but come quiet. Anderson's only along the track. They must 'ave the 'orses along Marsh Meadow. I heard one of them nags asnorting just since! If the moon hadn't clouded they'd had us for sure."

"Quick, then, while yon clouds hides us."

Jason lay where Saul had left him. In the field over the hedge they heard shouts and horses' hooves on the track.

"By God! There's hundreds of the buggers! Get shifting!" They heaved up Jason's heavy body. He responded with a low groan. Saul felt the sticky wetness of blood on his hands as he tugged at the dark jacket. They couldn't crouch down and sustain so much weight. Falcon swore under his breath throughout the hundred yards of their struggle. Jason moaned and gasped with pain. Saul merely gritted his teeth and saved his strength for lifting his brother's weight. Minutes later they half fell over the bank and dropped onto the hard soil below.

"Up 'ere with 'im, 'tis a deep 'ole and dry." They rolled their burden under the overhang.

"Find another for yer 'sen - I'll stop here by brother, but he do shout out." Saul tore off his kerchief and held it ready to stuff in Jason's mouth. Like foxes running before the pack they crept into their holes and lay waiting and listening.

A little way off, in Marsh Meadow, Anderson too stood silent and listening. The only sound was the shifting feet and snorting breath of the horses, still held by the assistant keeper. He had dismounted and the three stood together.

"Damnation take the moon - that cloud spoilt my chance of another shot - we nearly had them." Frustration raged in Anderson's voice.

"How many were there? I heard you fire twice."

"Two. Two, and I winged one - that's certain, but it was blasted dark and they running like Hell."

"What about the birds? What happened to them?"

"They had some bags - didn't drop anything that I saw. Go back up the ride and see if you can see anything lying, Lad." Anderson's arms flailed angrily as he waved the young Davie back towards the woodland. Then he swung his big body back towards Jack Ames. "For God's sake, don't just stand there, man - did you see anyone as you came out of Poacher's Plot?"

"I didn't come that way. I come through the rails along top

path - above the bank - below the trees, seemed easier on the horses."

"We're out of luck tonight, no mistake. There's forty acres of this bloody marsh, else they be long gone away across Back Drop and by the houses. Us could search till morning and never find 'em. Let's get mounted and away to our beds. 'Tis a thankless bloody job this, us goes weeks and sights no one, then we has two on 'em in our grasp and they slips us!" Disgruntled and tired he threw himself heavily into the saddle and rode on ahead. Davie Heston came back empty handed. The two keepers mounted with shrugs and turned down lips, they rode after Anderson.

Ten minutes later the two Dyer brothers who were still sound in wind and limb, rolled out from their cramped positions. Once on their feet they pulled Jason from beneath the turf overhang. Bits of ice and grass clung to their hair and faces. Jason's jacket was wet and sticky with blood. At that moment the moon appeared again in her full brightness. Jason's face was drawn and pulled. His good arm reached up, the fingers grabbling about his face brushing off the debris. "You two buggers tryin' to bury me? Better fit you gets I back 'ome."

"Can you get on yer feet?" A grin crossed Falcon's dark face.

"Better we fetch the mare - tek the birds across the Dale and then fetch un home across her back. Marsh be froze hard, mare'll carry un easy enough." Saul was tired and cold with lying under the bank.

"Right. As you say, only for God Almighty's sake get a move on afore I bleeds ter death or freezes agin this ice bank!" Jason rasped out the words and then lay back and closed his eyes resigning himself to waiting.

He did not have to wait long. The brothers reached the vans in Bottom Hollow in under ten minutes. Saul was glad to find no one about. He had half feared Anderson's men might have come to flush them out. Those in Authority had a habit of laying any unlawful happenings at the door of the gypsies. A brown mare grazed near their Father's van, she was tethered on a long rope. Saul went for a bridle to the van he shared with Jason and Falcon as sleeping quarters. Falcon went to his Father's van and entered after tapping lightly. Jewel, his stepmother, lay in the ornate painted bed. His eyes took in briefly her dishevelled appearance and bed gown with it's full open bosom. Lying back she watched him in lazy amusement. Black Dyer was fully dressed. Seated at the table his big hands played idly with a miniature set of nine pins on the scarlet cloth. His heavy shoulders lifted as he stared at his son. Plainly he had waited their return.

It was a very well kept caravan. Finished in true Romany fashion. Fresh bright coloured paint on the furnishings, sparkling copper and brass pots and pans and ornaments. A brass stick held two lighted candles which sent a circle of glowing light round the walls. Two pairs of dark eyes stared at Falcon. For a moment no one spoke.

"Anderson altered the times." Falcon never wasted words.

"Ah! And what befell?" Black Dyer's swarthy face hardened.

"Jason took a ball of shot - maybe two - in the shoulder."

"Where is un?"

"Saul's getting the mare, it unt far. Reckon us can get un over 'er back. He lies in the clay pit amongst the bulrush."

"Moses in the bulrushes, eh? What about the birds and your nets? Did you leave aught lying?"

"Nothing. Birds are hid in the quarry cave along of nets and bags. The usual way. I was feared Anderson might come snooping and sniffing."

"Right - get you gone. Lay him in your van. I'll come and look at un. Maybe Raven'll have to get waked up to tend 'ee." Falcon turned and went out.

They heaved him across the Mare's back and he managed to hang on. It was a slow painful ride for Jason. Falcon lifted him sack fashion off the mare when at last they reached the Quarry. Amid oaths and swearing they manhandled him up the caravan steps and in through the door. They lowered him none too gently into his bunk. Black Dyer sat waiting for them. A candle burned in a dish,Dyer had drawn the curtain across the window. The van struck cold to Jason as he shivered in his weakness. He had lost a lot of blood. It hung about him in dark stains spreading through his clothes. Dyer stood up and bending close examined his first born.

217

"You b'aint in much fettle - but first things first. You two great clouts, get yer things and git out. You beds down in Martin's van - it stands empty. I'll fetch young Raven t'this job, but I ent trusting you young stallions along o' her. I don't reckon Jason'll be much use under a skirt for a night or two." He gave a harsh bellow of laughter, disclosing yellow teeth.

"Right! Get you out! I shall likely lock you in Martin's later, so no tricks!"

Dyer moved his heavy form out of the van and down the steps. A little way away from the other vans stood a small gay painted one. Dyer thrust his hand deep in his breeches pocket and took out a bunch of keys on a rough string. He selected one and fitted it into the lock. He shoved the door with his foot and it swung open. The van was in darkness. He pushed in through the door. A gasp came from within. Dyer grinned to himself in the darkness.

"Get you up, daughter - I ent come to break you in - much as it 'ud pleasure me. I'm saving you for summat else, it so happens. Our Jason's been shot - seems your message from Ole Amos weren't right. Never could trust that beggar Anderson to stick to 'is word. You'll get a whippin' for bringing wrong word in the mornin', I dare say. Tonight you teks care of Jason. Bathe 'is wound - see how bad 'ee be. There's a drop of strong stuff in our van - I'll set it out on the steps. Don't come worryin'. You know Jewel's way, she don't like you in our van. I'll hear at daylight how you've done. 'Tek care on him." Black Dyer turned on his heel and left her.

Raven wriggled out of her blanket and felt for her rough work dress. She pulled it on over her under-dress and shift in which she slept. An old shawl lay on top of her blanket. She had piled everything she could lay hands on onto the top of her to keep warm. Since Jewel had turned so much spite on her, Raven and her little half-sister, Mary, had not been allowed a fire in the van, although there was a little hearth and a chimney. Raven tried to move quietly. Little Mary slept in the small corner bed and Raven loved her. Raven bent now to look at her in the cold shaft of moonlight, which shone on the mop of black curls above the blanket. The child was in deep sleep and felt warm.

Raven pulled on the red cap that David Ainsley would have

recognised, and flung the shawl about her shoulders. She slipped her bare cold feet into her clogs. They were worn thin and let wet in but were better than nothing in the bitter cold. When she reached Jason's bedside she was frightened by his appearance. She did not love her brothers. They looked at her as men look at women they desire, not as a sister. She lived in fear of her Father and Stepmother. There was very little in life for her to love. Baby Mary and the small animals of the woodland, the foxes, the rabbits and the squirrels - all were persecuted and trapped by men. Gamekeepers, Poachers, Gentlemen;killers and ravishers one and all, in Raven's mind. Her attachment for David Ainsley had been brief. She had liked to look on his clean naked body diving into the pool, she compared it with the dirt-stained sweat smelling bodies of the Dyer men. She was sexually asleep still, but she had watched the wild creatures, the dog fox and his vixen, and seen their mating antics. It was only a matter of time before one of her brothers or their Father used her in the same way, then she would swell even as the vixen, then she would be even more vulnerable to whipping and to Jewel's strong cruel hands upon her. To her David Ainsley would have been an escape - better a clean beautiful man, she had never seen him shout or swear, reach for his belt or a whip. When he had laughed at her and repulsed her she had accepted his refusal at once. He was a 'gentleman', one of the 'they'. Perhaps gentlemen did not seek such pleasures. She had shrugged her shoulders and left it at that. She took life as it came in her small world, and questioned nothing.

Now she stood in the candlelight and looked at the big ungainly body of her brother. He lay on his back, weak as a kitten. His eyes opened. "For God's sake help me." It was a low growl. Her fear began to leave her as she realised he couldn't touch her. She leant her body forwards and turned back his coat front, undoing the buttons. She tried to pull it from him, but he had it fast below his shoulders. He was too heavy.

"Cold - so cold," he muttered.

"Oh .... a drink! Father said, - wait a minute." She ran out and returned with the stone jar from Dyer's van steps. Lifting a tankard from the shelf she half-filled it. "Here, then." She raised his head and he drank deep while she held the vessel. He spluttered and choked over the strong spirits.

"Oh, that's better!" The hot burning in his throat revived him.

"Tek my knife - it's in the pocket, cut this bloody sleeve!"

She felt in the pocket and drew out the knife. Using the sharp blade she began to tear away the seams of the coat. The shirt beneath was soaked dark red, this also she cut away.

"Ahh! Better!" He expelled a deep sigh and rested back against the wooden bed-board. She pulled the blanket from under him and covered him as well as she could.

"Can 'ee get a bit of fire on?"

"Aye. Give us a minute till I cleans you up some." Fearless now, her small hands worked busily, pulling away the pieces of the blood stained garments. The shoulder lay bare and bloody. A blackened hole below his shoulder welled blood every time he shifted his body. His arm and chest were dirt stained and the mat of black course hair in his armpits stank of sweat. Raven overcame revulsion and fetched cloths and a wooden bucket from the shelf. Kindling lay heaped at the hearth and a black kettle hung from a chain above. She lit a taper from the candle and coaxed the small leavings of the last fire into flame, raking out the ashes to create enough draught underneath. Soon flames caught the dry sticks and she piled on more, lowering the kettle over the heat. While it warmed she searched and found another blanket from Saul's bunk. She laid it round Jason's shoulders and back, covering his upper parts except for the wound. Pouring water from the kettle into the bucket she doused a clean cloth in and out until it felt warm. Then she began to bathe Jason's upper parts. At first she was very tentative and cautious. She had never touched a man in so personal a way before. After a bit she found it much akin to cleaning up baby Mary when she had been at the mud pies. Raven grew bolder, rubbing off blood, dirt and sweat with energetic vigour.

Jason suffered it all in silence. When it was done and she felt the van begin to grow warmer, she looked again at his wound. It looked ugly and still the blackened hole oozed blood. An idea was forming in her mind. She took the water away and tidied up.

"You dun look better - but that be bad - that 'ole - I can't do nothin' to that 'ole. I gonna go for Doctor - that's what, he'll know well enough how to see after that hole."

Jason woke into wide-eyed horror and began shouting, "Don't you bloody dare - he'll fetch Anderson - and I'll be catched good and proper. Be you mad, Sister?

"No - No, he won't - he's .... he's a friend of mine - he'll tend 'ee and say nowt."

Jason's eyes narrowed, "Have you bin' ..... with him?"

"Wot?"

"Have you bin with him - lying in the grass - you knows well enough."

"No, I have not! But he be a gentleman - he wunt tell on us."

"Well, I hope to God you're right. Get un then, but be quiet about it. If the old man gets to know - he'll bloody murder you - that's for sure - and me an all, likely."

She ran across the Quarry and over the lane, swift and quiet as a deer, past Wood Cottage garden and alongside the stream. Her feet followed the sheep track - never stumbling. She reached the footbridge and crossed it, turning sharp left under the trees. On the path again, she hastened on. In Crab orchard Beauty lay beneath a tree, silvered with the frost on her coat.

"'ello then girl - don'ee fret, Lass." She patted the mare and ran on. At the house she hesitated. He'd be abed. Her eyes searched and saw the strong twining creeper up to the window. She kicked off her clogs and swarmed up the rough branches. She could see nothing through the thick glass. She lifted her hand - pausing, unsure of herself. The discomfort of her position forced her to bravery. She tapped boldly on the glass. Ainsley woke with a start.

"What the Hell? Who's that?" He rolled out of bed and crossed the room, a shadow against the pane blocked off the moonlight. "Good God! Has the witch risen?" He thrust open the catch and nearly dislodged her from the sill. "What on earth are you seeking? Who is it?"

"It be I - Raven Red Hat - you knows. Our Jason's been shot - he looks like to die. Can 'ee come right away?"

Twenty minutes later they were in the caravan. Ainsley examined Jason's wound, carefully, without speaking. Jason had given him no greeting and an expression of sullen brooding anger was on his face.

"Lift the candle nearer." David turned his head to Raven who stood fidgeting in the background. Her hands shook a little as she held the candle's dish above her brother's chest.

"Mind how you goes, Sister! I don't want to be boiled in fat," Jason barked at her.

"Well, at least you're far from dead," Ainsley observed drily,"but something will have to be done at that wound, otherwise it will fester - then you could easily be dead indeed."

"Can you see to unt?"

"Yes, but it won't be pleasant."

"Get it done, never mind so much talk about it."

"Very well." He turned to Raven. "I shall want a dish of clean boiling water and some clean linen."

"I'll get them ready, Sir." She busied herself seeing to the kettle. Ainsley set out the things he would need on the table. Presently all was ready.

"Do you have any spirits, Mistress Red Cap?"

"Aye, there's some in here." She lifted the stone bottle onto the table.

"Good - have it to hand."

He cleaned the wound and the skin round it with warm water. Then he dabbed it with a pad of linen soaked in whisky. He began to search deep for the ball of shot, working delicately with fine pointed forceps and probe. Jason drew breath sharply once or twice but did not cry out. At last Ainsley touched metal and eased out the cause of the pain. He dropped it into the candle's dish with a metallic plop.

"You've got it!" Raven exclaimed.

"Yes, now I must dress the wound, it may still bleed a little. It's of no account and it will clean away any particles I've missed." He folded a fresh pad of linen and strapped it firmly to the severed circle of skin and torn flesh. "Now it needs a sling - like this - keep the hand and wrist high, you can't use the arm for some time. I'll see it again in a day or two. Come to Crab Tree in three days."

"Not in daylight! You must know how I come by this!" Jason spoke as though the words were forced from him.

"That's where you are in error. I have no idea how you received this injury, and I have no wish to know. However, if you so desire - you may come to Crab Tree after dark one evening. I'll bid you good night - or perhaps good day would be nearer the mark. Good day, Mistress Red Cap." Ainsley picked up his bag and left the van without another glance at Jason.

Raven ran after him. "Thank you - thank you for coming' - I don' rightly know how I'd 'ave gone on without 'ee."

"I haven't seen you much of late, too cold now for the water?"

She flushed at his words and hung her head. "I was a silly girl then. A child - like you'm did say."

"I thought maybe you'd found some handsome prince."

"No. No. None like that. My Father .... "

"What about your Father?" He spoke sharply.

"He hasn't done told me - but I've a mind he means to sell me within the travellers. He'd have took me himself by now else."

"Sell you? What are these travellers?"

"One of our own - a Romany - one of our own tribe, a man came once a whiles back. A cousin of my Father's. He looked at me a lot. He'd .... there was much talk in the van with my Father and my Father's wife. She do hate me - wants me away."

"Was the man your Father's age?"

"Aye - he was old - but if there's gold pieces in it the Old un 'ent likely to hold back. Romanies likes to tek young girls when they grow old, then they gets strong sons." She spoke simply, without shame, stating the facts as she knew them. They walked together across the quarry floor as she spoke. First light was showing in the sky, beyond Dumble Wood the sun showed its beginnings in a half-ball of orange fire in the cold frosty air.

"Do you like to live this life, Red Cap?" David asked giving her a searching glance.

"I'm a Romany. Romany girls lives on the bottom, below every man and boy, below every older woman. 'Tis how it be!"

"Would you not like to live in a house - to have a room of your own, to work perhaps for a little money of your own?"

"T'wouldn't be so. The old un would tek the money off me."

"I might be able to find work for you - a servant perhaps - but you would be free of your brothers and escape your Father's beatings."

223

"Would my new Master beat me?"

"Not if you worked well and I found someone kindly."

Raven shook out her dark hair and looked unconvinced. "I mun go back now." She lifted her hand and ran from him before he could speak again. He watched her go back towards the ring of caravans under the high cliffs of the Quarry.

Christmas came and passed with the weather still cold and unrelenting. Ainsley, much to Andrew Mallard's pleasure, attended Lower Seckington Church for Christmas Day worship. There were a good many there. It was a joyful occasion and the old church rang with Christmas hymns and carols. Afterwards the congregation streamed out into the churchyard. They stepped into the first snow of winter. It lay thin in a white coverlet, unsullied and beautiful. It hid from view the two new unturfed graves of George Swift and Tom Carter. The Saxon Cross by the main door commanded the eye, a pointing grey finger to the open sky, to low clouds heavy with snow.

David walked to the Hall and dined with his family at three o'clock the same afternoon. Isobel had supervised a very good meal, a great side of roast beef, a huge goose and plum porridge, puddings and mince pies. It was a merry happy company. Irwin Saint was there, and Charlotte and Esme were full of laughter and chatter. Small gifts were exchanged. For David it was his first Christmas amongst his family for five years. He walked home through the snow at eleven o'clock at night. It was a strangely different silent world. His footprints were the first in the unblemished whiteness of the woodland. At Crab Tree, the mare Beauty greeted him with a small whinny of delight from over the door of her warm stable.

"Wait a bit, Lass, I'll get you a treat." He went into the kitchen, pausing to knock the snow from his boots against the door scraper. He fetched a double handful of carrots from the thrawl in the dairy and carried them to Beauty's manger. She nuzzled his hand as he fed her, munching contentedly on the unaccustomed delicacy. He left her and went inside to his bed. Looking out over the snowy landscape from his bedroom window he found it hard to believe he had only lived here for three months. So much had happened. Some good some bad.

A little later, lying in bed waiting for sleep, his mind ran over the unanswered questions which during the full busy days he pushed determinedly away from him. How did Elizabeth fare at the Park? None of his family had seen her or had any news from the Park in weeks. And what of his brother Jonathon? He had not been to see his parents since his drunken intrusion which had ended in the ducking in the water trough. David had heard unsavoury rumours that Jonathon had been much seen about with Lady Margaret Wartrusan - a lady of doubtful reputation, whose elderly husband was a local laughing stock. Also local gossip had it that the ale houses in Wesperton were now reluctant to serve Lord Ainsley's eldest son since he was so often drunk or half drunk that he caused them nothing but trouble.

And what of the Plague? Was he done with the battle against his unknown enemy. Had the recent bitter weather wiped out the pestilence or was it lying hidden deep in some secret concealed pocket of warmth ready to pounce again in the first flush of Spring's warmth? He turned and tossed in the bed, unusually restless. His brain was wide awake. His body yearned sleep - or the comfort of a woman. Since Elizabeth's desertion he had not allowed himself to think of women. Did he want the involvement that a woman would being into his life? Not enough to look for marriage for marriage's sake.

Of course, if he met someone. That was nonsense - he met no-one, none of his own kind. Well, that was of his own choosing. He preferred a working useful life. There was no wish in him for the round of the Country Houses and the idle pastimes, balls, hunts and trivia, which satisfied so many of his kind. Then why was he so on edge and unsettled tonight? He turned again in bed, tempted to get up and indulge in a glass of wine. No, he was warm in bed, he would turn his thoughts to something pleasant, after all it was soon to be a new year - there was much to hope for. His work was widening, he was becoming a success. More and more families were turning to him in cases of sickness. He was now making visits outside the villages. Beauty frequently carried him twenty or thirty miles in a day. The family at Chalfont farm had recommended him to a number of their neighbours beyond Seckington's boundaries. It had been after Bernard Bistock's wife's illness and her excellent recovery from the fever. It had considerably increased the number of his patients. Into his thoughts unbidden stepped Rachel Bistock. He remembered the day he had seen her on the plough land .... what was it she said? "A day to run in the grass and listen to the lark up on the moor." Sweet sentiment that - a pretty face she had, full of life and sunshine. It was the lovely eyes and the honey coloured hair that caught a man's attention. Also her spirit and independence. He had enjoyed rousing her anger. Of course, he didn't feel for a child like that as he had felt for Elizabeth. He began to drowse and his thoughts became confused. There was a lot to be said for freedom from ties - but it was long since he had been with a pretty woman.

CHAPTER VII

CHAPTER VII

Heavy falls of snow continued into January. It had the effect of separating Upper and Lower Telso. The long road route round the lanes was impassable for weeks. The track across the fields was variable. After each fall of snow the villagers shovelled and worked to keep the way open at least for pedestrian traffic. When the wind blew from the East the snow would be blown to build into deep rolling drifts across Big Fields and Over Barns. John Price the blacksmith used the path daily between work and home and somehow managed to get through. His great legs carried him over the drifts but he was often in up to his waist. For the women and men of small stature it was impossible.

There were few social gatherings in January. The country folk passed the short days in the confines of their cottages and outhouses, intent upon domestic chores and survival. Wood had to be chopped for fires. Peat in stacks which had been cut and carted in summer was more often than not frozen solid in the stack. Few people had the good luck to have it under cover. Most had to hack it out with picks and cart it into the wash house to thaw. People with livestock were faced with a daily battle in caring for their animals in the appalling weather. Water froze solid in troughs and pumps. Hay and fodder had to be cut with the heavy hay-knife after being dug from under two or three feet of snow.

The men who worked for Lord Ainsley had the daily battle of getting to work through the drifts and back again before darkness fell. David Ainsley walked miles each day. Beauty had often to be left in the stable. Drifting snow covered holes, ruts and pitfalls. Ainsley would not risk so fine an animal breaking a leg or coming to grief in a ditch. His own lane leading to Upper Telso was not too badly affected. The hedges were high and kept the snow out. Getting to Lower Telso was a different matter. In the middle of January there were three foot drifts along the lane near the Vicarage.

During the worst of the weather Amanda Trewis, Velvet's Mother, fell on the slippery ice, down the back steps at the farm. The result was a broken arm. Francis Trewis, concerned for his wife, sent his eldest son Albert to fetch the Doctor. It took Albert two hours to get to Crab Tree and nearly as long for the two men to get back to Lower House Farm. By that time it was past two o'clock in the afternoon. Mabel Dunn had been unable to get to Crab Tree for over a fortnight so no meal would be waiting David's return.

Carefully David set the bones in Mistress Trewis's arm. It was done in the farm kitchen where a great fire burned. Velvet was at the fire turning a roast of meat over a grease tray on the spit. She greeted Ainsley as an old friend.

"Do ''ee take a bite along of us Doctor? T'would be a pleasure to us," she asked smiling.

"Aye, you'm welcome, for surely you done us a good turn. My arm be easy now with the splint on, since you'm tended it." Amanda Trewis, a faded fair haired little woman, sat by the fire, her arm in a sling. She watched Velvet at work with the dinner. On the floor Hannah the youngest child - a chubby three-year old - played with her toy. It was a wooden horse on wheels which she pulled along, clattering round and round the kitchen.

"Thank you - if it's no trouble, I'll be glad to stay." David replied.

"Pick the Bab up, Lass. She'll get under your feet. Stick her in the little chair then you can get to lay the plates."

Velvet bustled about setting plates and cutlery on the well scrubbed table. At that moment the men came in. Francis Trewis and his four sons seemed to fill the kitchen. When they were all seated, Velvet put the roast of meat onto a dish in front of her Father. He carved it with the speed and skill of long practice. Velvet busied herself with heaping vegetables onto each platter. She was so quick that all were served with a very hot meal. Indeed the brothers, hungry and impatient, rashly filled their mouths only to burn their tongues and lips. The main course was followed by a huge boiled pudding, taken in a cloth from a steaming pot on the fire. Again hot enough to burn the mouth. The fruit in it was bursting from the pastry. The rich smell of apples and cloves filled the kitchen, there was no conversation while they ate.

Francis Trewis worked his sons hard. They came to the table ravenous and took their eating as a serious business. When the last scraps were cleaned from their plates, Velvet placed a mug of home brewed ale before each man. She then drew a red hot poker from the fire and plunged it into each mug in turn. The metal mugs exuded a hiss of steam as the hot poker and the liquid came in contact. David tasted his cautiously but found it to be very good. Francis Trewis lay back in his chair patting his swollen paunch appreciatively.

"Well you'm done well, our Velvet, with the cookin'," he said, a broad grin on his dark face.

"Tis goin' to be too much for Velvet, with the churning and dairy work an all. If I'm to be laid by a whiles." Amanda looked anxious.

"We'd be hard put to find any help this time o' year. Ent as though Emmy Bones could come, now she got the brat to tend."

"What about young Arms here? He'd look well enough in our Ma's apron," Albert suggested. Arms Trewis flushed scarlet, at just turned sixteen he was an awkward shy lad.

"If I may make a suggestion?" David Ainsley spoke for the first time.

Francis looked surprised but raised his eyebrows questioningly. "Aye, D'you know some one?"

"The Romany girl - Raven Dyer. I think she'd be glad to get away from her Father and Stepmother." All eyes turned on David during the silence that followed.

"We never had no truck with the gypsies." Amanda's eyes had flown wide open.

"Her Father'd never let her away - cause trouble that would," Albert Trewis the eldest son gave his opinion.

"Say nothin' of they brothers of her'n. We'm don't want a rough house with they lot!"

"Keeper Anderson be after they for poachin' in Windy Wood a few weeks back. Tis said that girl - that Raven be linked in with the poachin' and all."

"The girl is only just turned fifteen - if she got away from the family tribe she might do well enough," David suggested mildly.

"She'd be proper dirty - I saw her one day with a basket of pegs at Mistress Dunn's door. No shoes she had and hair matted and filthy."

"That's b'aint agin her - we've a good pump - I don't mind strippin her off and cleaning 'er up. If, you'm looking for someone for the job," Albert broke in again, a ribald grin on his face which at once provoked his Mother's wrath.

"If she should come this ways I'll thank you to keep your great hands to yourself, you great goof."

Francis Trewis silenced his family. "Black Dyer likely has his own plans for her - she being ready for marrying. If she be a pretty wench then he'll find a gold coin in it for himself somewhere - if I knows the score with them Romanies."

"If she could come - if I could arrange it - would you give her a trial?"

"Aye, so long as we don't get they gyppo's breathing down our necks."

"Would you give her a wage and a room to herself?"

Francis looked across at his wife. "Us could manage a shilling a week and a clean bed in the attic on her lonesome - if she do work hard. Us all works hard here. Aint no room for idle hands. Clean mind - she'd have to start clean. We arn't gentle folks, but we has a clean house place here." Francis rose to his feet.

"Come on you lads - tis time to see after they cattle, be dark else."

Chairs scraped and the men trooped out, nodding to Ainsley as they went. He turned to Mistress Trewis to take his leave.

"I'll see Raven Dyer and her Father tomorrow, if it prove that anything can come of it I'll bring the girl to you. Thank you, Mistress Velvet, for a good dinner."

"My arm does ache, Sir, but I must expect that I dare say."

"I fear so - I'll see it again in a few days."

A few minutes later Ainsley came out into the yard, he was met by a blustering wind and a snowy walk home. None the less his spirits were high in the hope that life might soon be easier for Raven Dyer, away from her villainous Father. During the walk home he put his mind to planning the means by which he hoped to make this possible.

The next day found him in the Quarry once more. The snow lay in deep drifts like fantastic giant organ pipes where it banked up against the cliffs. The Romany horses and men had made a hard track through to the circle of caravans. David Ainsley

232

followed it to Black Dyer's scarlet painted door. It was opened by Jewel who glared at him for several seconds without speaking.

"Who is it woman?" Dyer's voice came from within.

"'Tis the Medic - the Gentlemen's Medic!" Jewel's voice was a sneer as she said the word 'gentlemen'.

"Let un in and you can bugger off for a bit." Jewel swung her hips down the steps brushing past him. She tossed her head and walked away towards the other vans. There was no sign of any of the rest of the family, yet Ainsley thought that he saw a curtain move at the window of one of the small caravans. Likely Raven was watching with interest. Ainsley stepped into the dim lit interior and found it more pleasant than he would have expected.

A cheerful fire burned in the small hearth, Dyer sat smoking his pipe in a worn old chair, his thick legs, clad in dark breeches, stretched before him. Round him the brass and copper gleamed and the wall bed provided a splash of colour with its patchwork covering.

"And what might the Gentleman Doctor want with Black Dyer? T'aint often the Gentry comes calling on us. Sit you down, us aint proud." David sat down in a chair at the table. Every movement he made was slow. He sought to gain a moment or two to size up Dyer and assess his likely reactions to Ainsley's proposal. Dyer was not to be drawn. He said nothing more but sat and waited. His nearly black eyes were intent, cunning and watchful. He saw before him a man who was indeed a gentleman, yet he also was a man hardened and toughened by his chosen way of life. Dyer looked at the strong face with its firm jawline and clear blue eyes. He at once felt respect for the strong healthy muscular looking body, which carried no excess weight and which gave the impression of a countryman - born and bred. Ainsley, returning his look, saw a hard man. The face grim lined, the skin so dark and rough as to be leathery. Thick set and heavy muscled. A formidable opponent - a difficult man to bargain with.

Neither man gave away his assessment of the other. David Ainsley spoke first.

"I came about your daughter, Raven I believe she is called."

Black Dyer's thick eyebrows shot up, he had not expected

this.

"She's bespoke."

"Is she now - is it settled finally?"

"It is - she is to wed a member of our own clan. Tis a most happy match. The Romanies mostly marry with their own - we don't mix with did not miss the implication. He ignored it.

"Is he a young man?"

"That aint your business - but no harm to tell you. No, he's a widower - lost his woman in child-bed. He needs fine sons. Raven will provide them. She's strong and a good worker. Obedient too - I trained 'er mysen. Also she's comely - a pleasure to any man's bed - my cousin is well pleased with his bargain."

"Bargain? Was it a matter of purchase?"

"Between cousins there is of course friendship - but no man expects something choice for nothin' paid - times being bad."

"I understand. It is a pity. It seems I am too late." David Ainsley's face was impassive. He made a small movement as if to rise. Dyer did not miss the movement, he spoke quickly.

"Of course, under the bargain Raven will leave here - me cousin is from Kent. We should have liked her nearby. No man likes to see his own goin' aways." A crafty look was in Dyer's eyes. He looked, David thought, like a pirate. David said nothing. He took a leather bag from his pocket and set it down on the table beside him.

"Mind, I've never bin a man to break me given word." Dyer did not allow his eyes to stray to the bag. Still David said nothing. He took a second bag from his pocket and plumped it down beside the first. The coins within made a pleasant sound to Dyer's listening ears. He pursed his thick lips and thrust his face towards David's side of the table.

"D'you intend t' wed Raven?"

"No."

"Makes no matter. But you munt cast her off when you'm done with she. Leastways, goes she to you, then she doesna' come back here, you understand?"

"Perfectly - I do not want her for myself."

"You mean - you bargain for another?"

"In a way yes - but you do not give me your answer."

"How much do you offer? Ent shown the colour of the

234

money yet. Bags is bags, can hold pebbles, silver or gold, us knows."

"The bags hold gold. Do you wish to count it?"

Dyer leant across and his fingers like leathery brown claws closed on the bags. He lifted them and weighed them in his hands. After a moment he replaced them on the table. He lifted his hand, closed the fist and thumped it down with a crash on the table. The bags jumped and resettled. The caravan shook with the force of the blow. David Ainsley did not blink an eye.

"When would you tek the wench? Her stepmother holds her in dislike. You know how it runs with women kind?"

"There is another matter to be settled." Ainsley's voice was firm and low.

"What?"

"Raven will go to a local family as a worker. I would want to be sure that you would leave her in peace and cut her off from your family. Also that the family she goes to would not be prey to you or your sons. Your sons have some unsavoury habits .... poaching and so on."

Dyer's face flushed with anger. "None shall speak agin the Dyers - we'm as law-abiding as anyone in these parts. Anderson and them keepers have no crime they can hang round our necks." His mouth hardened lips thrust out as he glared at Ainsley.

"Have a care - I have enough evidence to hang a rope round your son Jason's neck, should I be forced to use it." David's voice was mild.

"Blackmail is a tool no Romany will stand under. Men have a habit of being found dead with such talk."

"Let us not dispute - there is no question of Jason's injury being ought but an accident. I told him as much when I removed the ball of shot from his shoulder just before Christmas. Surely we both have your daughter's welfare at heart."

"I have - certainly I have." Dyer visibly calmed down as he continued, "Ah well, that's as maybe. Still, 'tis money in hand, as they do say. Did ye say you'd tek her today?"

"I didn't - but I'm quite willing."

Dyer made up his mind suddenly. He leapt up nearly overturning the table. His size when on his feet was enormous.

He thrust out both hands, the left hand clawed up the money bags and thrust them deep in his breeches pocket, with the right hand he smote Ainsley's extended hand with a blow which well nigh over-balanced him.

"A bargain, Medic! You have Black Dyer's hand 'ont!"

There were no farewells. Raven accepted that she was to go with him without question. It took her but a few minutes to gather together her meagre few bits. She came out to him on the snowy path and a poor thing she looked. Her tiny bundle was wrapped in an old kerchief, it couldn't have weighed more than a couple of pounds. She wore the threadbare torn green gown that David remembered. About her shoulders the old grey shawl clung. On her feet the worn down at heel clogs. They were so low and down at heel that as she walked he could see the red sores of chilblains and chaps on her feet from contact with ice and snow. It became obvious to him as they walked in the enforced close proximity of the narrow cut path through the banked snow, that she had not bathed for a long time. The hands that held her bundle were engrained with dirt. Altogether an unsavoury prospect to present to Mistress Trewis. By the time they came out of the Quarry, Ainsley had reached a decision. Instead of going along Long Bottom Lane towards the village, he led her along the narrow path within the wood towards Crab Tree. She followed him at once, keeping her attention upon picking her way through the snow. Neither spoke until they reached the footbridge. Walking was easier in the woodland where the great trees had held off the snow. There was a bitter East wind which struck cold even to Ainsley, warm clad as he was in thick breeches, long coat and warm stock at his neck. Far worse for Raven, he guessed, in her poor thin garments.

"Do us go to Crab Tree?" she asked at last.

"We do - to get you cleaned up."

"Do you tek me to your woman then?"

"No, I don't! You are to go to Mistress Trewis at Lower House Farm, to help in the house and the dairy."

A warm flush of pleasure crept into her grubby cheeks.

"I don't go to no man then?"

"No, certainly not!"

"I be that glad." She said no more.

When they reached Crab Tree, Ainsley took her in by the back door to the kitchen. He felt deeply thankful that Mabel Dunn was still prevented from coming by the lingering snow. Raven stood tongue-tied looking round the kitchen. She gazed at the stacked peat fire which burned day and night. Then at the scrubbed table and white dresser with its load of shining pewter pots and pans and plates.

"Sit down, Mistress Raven, while I see to things."

She sat on the very edge of a wooden chair. She had the uneasy look of a house sparrow ready for flight before the claws of a hungry cat. He smiled at her cheerfully and began to make his preparations. He carried hot cinders from the fire and with them lit the fire under the copper in the back-place. This he filled with buckets of water from the pump at the sink. He heaved down the circular wooden trough, which served him as a bath, from its hook by the copper, trundling it on its side into the kitchen. He set it before the fire. Next he fetched towels from his clothes press. Raven watched, spellbound at the sight of what to her was so much luxury. He took a knife and sliced off thin slivers from the bar of yellow soap at the sink. When he had a good pile he scooped them up and threw them into the bath tub. The block of soap and a clean linen cloth he set down on the table. His preparations completed he turned to face her.

"Now - I'm going to Seckington Hall to find you some more suitable garments. I shall take the mare and go through the lane. The way by the garden is deep in snow, it will take me some time - perhaps two hours. While I'm gone you watch the water in the copper. When it is hot, fill the bath with the bucket. Then get into it - and get clean. Your hair too, mind! All of you! And first pile your old clothes in a heap in the back place - you are done with them. They stink and do not befit your new life. At Lower House you will be expected to wash your body every day and to smell about your person as sweet as the floors and furniture that you have charge over."

"Yes Sir - I does like to keep clean, but 'tis hard in cold times - when even the Cliven be froze over."

"Aye, well there's a pump at Lower House and soap too, I make no doubt."

"Be that soap?" She reached out a tentative finger to touch

the yellow block on the table.

"Surely, and it won't bite you. Use it well upon your body - especially in the corners and creases."

"Aye, Sur!"

"Right! Just one more thing." He strode out and returned a minute later with a woollen blanket.

"Wrap up in that when you're clean; do not don any of those filthy rags again. I shall bring you back ample clothing."

He left her and rode out of the yard a few minutes later.

Raven tried the copper's heat with a tentative hand, it steamed and grew hot. She baled six great buckets out in the wooden pail and carried them, slopping a little on the floor. The first one she poured into the tub rose up in a froth of soap suds. She had never seen such and sprang back in alarm. When it subsided she fetched more water until the bath was almost to the brim.

She stripped off her gown, petticoat and shift and threw them with her clogs and shawl in a heap on the scullery floor. Clinging with one hand firmly to a beam at the side of the hearth, she lifted her foot and gingerly tested the water. The pain from her cracked chilblained foot was sharp for a moment, but she left her foot underwater and a moment later the healing and balm of the hot soap suds warmed and sent pleasurable messages up through her leg. She stepped in with both feet and lowered herself into the bath tub. Never had she experienced anything so good. She reached for soap and cloth and began to clean herself. She slid up and down, in and out, of the hot suds, relishing the feeling of the warm water on her skin. She ducked her head under - but disliking the soap in her eyes, lifted it quickly out, feeling for the towel to mop her face. Instead, she rubbed soap into her scalp and cleaned it by dipping in and out, keeping her eyes clear. She felt like the young otter in the Cliven, such was her pleasure in the soap and water.

Isobel Ainsley was much amused at her son's request to find him some garments suitable for Raven Dyer to wear in the Trewis household.

"Do you turn to Sir Galahad, that you rescue all the young

women in distress? First it is Ilsa Dale, now it comes to a gypsy princess. As I recall, Raven was a pretty babe. Does she grow to a pretty maid?"

"'Tis hard to know - she is covered in dirt. I left her about to get into my tub full of hot soapy water."

"'Tis well Mabel Dunn is away - very unseemly it is to put young women into your bath! I had thought I reared you better!" She went away laughing to search the clothes closet.

David went to partake of a glass of wine with his Father. Lord Ainsley was in fine fettle.

"There's news from London - the Plague is dead. The King holds court, and balls and entertainments are much in fashion. The victories against the Dutch are the excuse. The tradesmen are all again at work. The capital seethes with merchants once more.

"'Tis pleasant to hear such news, David, is it not?"

"It is indeed, but I should like much to have it confirmed by my friend Vincent Fallon that Plague is truly dead amongst the poor also."

"I dare say he will send word directly - when this weather improves and all the roads are again open. Another glass, David? This is quite a good flavour, is it not?"

"Yes, it's very good - but no more thank you. Do you hear any word of Jonathon?"

"None .... and I'm glad of it for your Mother's sake. News comes to me that he takes too much wine and is oft from home with women of the wrong sort."

"Aye, that's been on the village tongues all winter." David frowned as he spoke.

"Very little we can do. I shield Isobel from it all I can. He's long past coming to manhood and must make his own way."

"I agree, but I am saddened for Elizabeth."

"She made her choice, my son - would you wed her now, were it possible?"

"No. 'Tis done with. A romantic dream. 'Tis not that I feel her .... sullied. Only that I have no feeling for her in my breast any more."

"I'm glad. Someone else will come along - and you will judge her wiser for your past experience".

"Very likely - but at the moment I do not seek it - I must be gone - I've much to do."

"Come again soon, David, we delight in your company."

Isobel Ainsley was in the morning room. On the table she had a varied assortment of garments. She looked up smiling as he entered.

"Jenny Bains has sorted out two of her old gowns which will serve for workday use. Charlotte is slim built and she has thrown out much since her betrothal. I think your girl to be in luck."

"Is she to have all this? It seems a great deal. Are you not being too generous?" David fingered the garments.

"There is some small wear, shifts and petticoats and three warm nightgowns. Then there is one gown - this dark green which is a better one. She can keep it for Sundays. We were uncertain about shoes. Our maids wear pattens all summer and boots for winter. There are two old pairs of pattens here and one pair of Charlotte's old buttoned boots. Also some much mended hose. You say her feet are sore. She must then have been poor shod. I don't see how she may do you credit if her feet hurt. She must try for size. These clogs were found by the boots boy in his cupboard. I know not where they came from. They may do perhaps for the farmyard."

"I'm sure she will be grateful, she has nothing - just rags which I shall throw upon the heap."

"There are two things I have added. Here an old hairbrush and mirror of mine with a bundle of ribbons. Also this old quilt. It is faded but warm and colourful. It will make her attic more homely to her, will it not? We can wrap everything within the quilt and put the bundle in this old leather holding bag which Charlotte flushed out of the attic."

"You're a wonder, Mother, and I thank you for it." David laid his arm about her.

"Get along with you, and ride careful through the snow - I wish it gone - I long for Spring."

He took his leave and set off for home.

When he came into the house at Crab Tree he found Raven at the fire drying her hair, All was tidy in the kitchen. She had cleared all away save the heavy bath tub and the pile of dirty clothes. She had washed out the scarlet cap he had first seen her in and hung it to dry on the end of the oven-spit. She was wrapped close in the blanket he had left for her. The parts of her he could see were agreeably cleaner.

"Here," he said, dumping the bag on the floor. "Get dressed decent, but the dark green, Lady Ainsley says, is to be kept for Sundays. Go into the sitting room and sort the bag through. Then we shall eat here in the kitchen. Make haste now, I'm desirous of getting you to Mistress Trewis in the daylight."

While Raven sorted delightedly through the bag David raided his larder. He set out cold roast meat, bread, cheese and a crock of butter. He heated some mutton broth over the fire, it was the good smell of this last which wafted to Raven and speeded her in her dressing. Presently she came shyly in and stood before him. He was thankful to note that she had had the sense to choose plain garments. The clean blue work dress was a good fit if a mite short. Beneath it she wore black hose and the boot boy's clogs. Obviously mindful of the afternoon's walk in the snow to Lower House. Her hair, clean now and shining blue-black, was tied back tidy with a blue ribbon.

"Well, that does show an improvement - you become quite a young lady, Mistress Raven." David smiled at her.

"Oh no, I be just the same - 'tis only that I be clean."

"I'm sure Mistress Trewis will be satisfied and pleased. She has a little one, Hannah, about two or three years old she is. I think it likely you will be expected to share in the care of her."

This provoked an unexpected response. Without warning Raven suddenly sank into a chair and burst into sobs.

"Good God girl - what ails you? Are you not pleased with the change we have made?"

"T'aint that, Sur - t'aint that. 'Tis little Mary, Sur - she be my little half-sister - Jewel's babe. I did look after she - allus from born I did."

"Never mind - dry your eyes and come to table. You cannot in life have everything, you know. In fact it has been my experience that everything good must be hard won and paid for every step of the way. Be thankful you no longer need fear your Father's whippings and perhaps worse!"

"You'm quite right, Sur, and I be real grateful for all you done, and to your Lady Mother for these fine things. I never

241

wore such pleasure on my back afore and my feet be like heaven after so sore."

"Good, then eat up your broth and let us be cheerful."

They did not talk over the meal and afterwards set forth across the fields to Lower Telso. It was freezing still and Ainsley was amused to see with what care she tucked up her dress to keep it clean before venturing out. She still had no outer garment, so he gave her a good brown wool blanket to cast about her shoulders.

"Mistress Trewis will perhaps furnish you with needle and thread, and Mistress Velvet help you fashion a cloak with a hood from it," he suggested.

It was half-after three when he delivered her at the Lower House. Mistress Trewis and her daughter Velvet were alone in the kitchen. Baby Hannah slept on a small settle by the window. Ainsley stayed only long enough to examine Amanda Trewis's arm and make the necessary introductions. Raven, he thought looked scared to see him go. Well she would soon settle down in her new surroundings. She was not moved into town. With all the farmyard and country noises about her she would surely be quick to find her feet.

To Anne Barnes it seemed a long hard winter. The dark evenings had put an end to her secret meetings with Thatcher Gibbs long since. It had still been possible for him to come courting to the farm each week. They would sit together on the oak bench in the kitchen for two hours or more every Sunday evening. Under her parents' eyes there was little chance to kiss and cuddle. At least she could see him, feel the pressure of his arm against hers through her gown, catch his eye now and again and exchange sweet secret smiles.

The snow had ended even this yearned for time together. Thatcher was much taken up, like the other Estate workers, with scrambling through the deep drifts to and from work. It left much of the care of his own cottage, his pig and his few hens, until Sundays. Once he had managed to come to Hill Farm through the drifts. The two following Sundays had seen heavy falls of snow in the valley. It had been impossible to make the journey up to Hill Farm. She had not seen him for three weeks.

At Hill Farm also there was much cold hard work to be done. Anne must take her share like the rest. What with chapped hands, ice to break in every trough, hay to carry to hungry beasts, frozen milk in the buckets, she longed for the end of each day. The uncertainty as to when she might hope to see her lover again put her in very low spirits. Her Father and brother teased her and called her 'the lovesick maid' and similar titles. Her Mother, Marion Barnes, knew better, she left the girl alone, remembering her own sensitive feelings at the same age.

Anne was hardly aware of any of them. For her it was one long cheerless day after another. The only respite, the dreams she could summon beneath the warm blankets in her bed at night.

The second week in February brought a slow thaw. The frozen edges of the Cliven gave up their packed ice to the rushing torrent of thawed snow which began to come off the moors. The paths, which the villagers had cleared to and from work, widened over night giving way to muddied flattened grass. A warm wind and the gradual increase in the sun's power melted great patches of snow. It began in the morning sun's path, with Windy Bank, Daw Lake and Up Tops'. Then it spread rapidly across The Springs, Big Fields and Over Barns. The much looked for grass areas widened and expanded. By the end of the week the snow lay only in shaded ditch bottoms or a few rapidly shrinking rolls of dirty white where the biggest drifts had been.

Beyond the marsh, near the Mere, the cries of snipe and curlew were heard once more. Raven Dyer, at her window in the attic at The Lower House, shook her duster and heard the birds singing in the orchard amongst the hazel catkins on the nut bushes. She listened with joy and longing, wishing for escape and to know again the freedom of the wild creatures in the woods and on the moor. To be free of the confines of rooms and walls. She quickly stifled the longing. As young ones can always do, she had settled into her new life. Her own room, with its view over fields and woods, good food and clothes, and rough but kindly company. Learning every day - how to churn butter, separate cream, bake bread, milk the cows and a dozen other tasks, all had her enthralled. She had put the old life behind her, she was a farm girl now. She was happy.

At the Park, Elizabeth Ainsley was at the other extreme. She was so unhappy that the days and nights flowed into one another and she seemed caught in a sort of limbo of terror and misery. This state knew neither night nor day. Jonathon's cruelty was so diverse. She was trapped in a net of his weaving. She could not have said when it was that he began to abuse her to the point of degradation. It did not go on all the time. He would be away, sometimes for two or three days together. Always on his return he would boast of his conquests, forcing her to listen in detail to how he had carried out this or that sexual perversion with whatever low creature he had picked up during his time away. This was not the worst. He would come to her bedroom and lock the door, and force her to lie naked upon the bed. Then he would compare her with the women in the brothels he frequented. He would talk of the diseases some of them carried and threaten her with the likelihood of her contracting the same. He would satisfy himself with her sexually, making her submit to him in full daylight or with the candles close pulled to the bed. Afterwards he would rebuke her for her inability to satisfy him, blame her for his need for other women, it always ended in the same way. He kept a whip hidden in the bedroom. He would become excited and slobbering in his abuse, then he would tie her to the bed and whip her. Sometimes she would slip into merciful unconsciousness very soon after he raised his whip. Sometimes he would only bring the thongs upon her once or twice before he became bored. He then became suddenly calm and cold.

"Oh God, to be saddled with a bitch like you - not even worth beating." Then he would rip the tapes that tied her undone and leave her alone, locking the door behind him. She would creep under the covers to weep and moan like an animal in pain. She now no longer knew how long and how often these tortures happened. She slept but knew not when nor for how many hours. She dressed, went to the dining room and to the parlour. She ate so little that the house staff believed her ill and perhaps failing in her mind. She was so much under Jonathon's dominance that she told no one. She had not been seen outside for seven or eight weeks. Even her Mother was barred. When she called, anxious about her daughter, Elizabeth kept to her room, saying she was unwell - that she had the sickness - that she had eaten bad food. It was all excuses and Elizabeth was so low that she was hardly aware of having made them. She longed for death and merciful oblivion. Escape. Yet she was to weak and dazed to resort to taking her own life.

She was not quite so alone as she believed. Mason the butler did not know how bad things were, but he knew them to be very bad. He knew the new Master's insatiable appetite for cruelty and that it had to find it's outlet. Mason had seen that in the beatings of the stable boys in the early days. Then there had been Ilsa Dale and the terrible assault upon her. Since then .... nothing. Now the Mistress .... suddenly behaving so strange - near mental at times. Yet she was not mental. At least, Mason did not believe so. One of the maids complained on two occasions of finding the bedroom door locked during daylight hours. Why should such be the case? Mason put two and two together. He watched the Master like a hawk. Saw him come in the worse for drink. He never heard Jonathon order Elizabeth upstairs during daylight, but finding her nowhere downstairs on one such afternoon, Mason crept upstairs half an hour later. He listened on the landing - nothing. He moved silently along to the bedroom and tried the door very carefully and quietly, It was locked. Mason breathed deep, eased the handle back to the closed position and bent to the keyhole. The key had been taken out, but he had no clear view of the room. He listened intently. Jonathon's voice came to him low and harsh. The words being said turned Mason's stomach. He heard the low terrible rasping sobs which were Elizabeth's only answer to Jonathon's assault. It was in Mason's mind to break open the door and rush to his Mistress's assistance. Only once before had he heard such sobbing. Ilsa Dale's flayed broken body came before his mind's eye. His mouth became hard. He stood upright, his portly body quite unheroic in its solidity. Well, there were more ways. Secret evil must be matched with its own weapon. The Master was a big strong young man, more than a match for a middle-aged servant. Mason retreated silently to the ground floor. There, in the seclusion of the Butler's Pantry, he pondered the situation and began to form his plans.

A week later the high winds which so often heralded the beginning of March swept across the valley. Branches and dead trees in the hedges and woodlands fell before the wild purging wind. Jonathon Ainsley had been away in Wesperton for three days. He returned a little before midnight much the worse for drink. He drove the small fashionable light chaise which had been purchased new as a wedding present for Elizabeth. It was drawn by a single horse. Normally a quiet easy handling animal, the gelding was frightened by so much use of the whip and the whistling of the high wind. Jonathon stood up behind the guard rail and urged the animal to increase its already hazardous pace in such narrow lanes. He cracked the whip and yelled abuse at the horse. His words caught in the screaming wind which lifted his cloak and billowed his clothes about him. They reached Seckington lane approaching Hill Farm corner. The animal knew the lane corner and was used to the groom slowing down to take the bend. Automatically, Blacky broke his gallop into a canter. His driver uttered fresh oaths and cracked his whip down on the horse's flank. Jonathon heaved hard on the horse's mouth. Again the whip came down. Blacky, really frightened now pelted again into a gallop. He raced hell bent along past the Smithy, the Inn and the cottages. The vehicle swayed from side to side as the wheels tried to find grip on the muddy uneven road. The wind ripped at the horse and the man. It took Jonathon's plumed hat and hurled it away over the hedge top. They reached the lodge and again from habit Blacky slowed.

"Get up - you lazy bastard! The gate stands open! Get up, there," Jonathon shouted. The gate was not open. Blacky tried to draw up sharp, the gravel shifting and spraying beneath his hooves, but a collision was unavoidable. The horse crashed into the gate, coming to a halt amidst splintering rails and shafts. Fortunately the gate burst open and they passed through into the Park. Blacky came to a halt winded and fighting for breath. Jonathon rose in fury, half-thrown from his position by the impact with the gate. He had lost his grip on the reins, and the long whip hung slack in his hand. He leaned down to regain his hold on the reins and whip. He never knew whence came the sudden heavy weight upon his back, pressing down his shoulders and head towards the board beneath his feet. He felt the sudden twist of the whip thong, snake-like about his throat, as it tightened he fought to free his hands from the entangled reins. Again the thong coiled and tightened about his neck. One hand came free and he clawed at the ever tightening choking leather strands. As Blacky began to trot on across the Park, Jonathon's glazed eyes saw the lights flickering in the house windows. Then the air in his windpipe was stopped as the thong twisted its last full circle about his throat, cutting deep into the flesh beneath the collar of his cloak. Blacky, undriven now, trotted on across the Park. The reins slithered down and dragged along loose on the gravel between the wheels. The driver lurched to and fro with the movement of the chaise. His head lolled like a man drunk. His shoulder leaned forward, strangely unnatural.

In her bed in the Lodge House, Lady Jane Loundes turned uneasily in her sleep. The dog in his kennel in the yard gave a low growl and then lowered his head to his paws once more. Two nightjars called harshly to one another in the beech trees.

In the harness room David Dale dozed over the dying fire trying to keep awake in case Master should return. Jonathon insisted upon such attentions from his staff. None knew what time he might come. The head groom had instructed David to wait until half-after midnight. Hearing a sound, he raised his head, the light clip clop of a horses hooves on the drive and the squeak of turning wheels.

"Must be dead drunk to cum in so slow - generally do come clack-clatting in, wakin' up whole bloody house," the boy muttered as he came out of the harness room into the cold of the yard. He pulled up his braces and heaved his slim shoulders into his jacket. Blacky came to a halt in front of his own loose-box door, and stood quiet. Young David swung the lantern, holding it aloft, he saw the slumped figure in the driving seat and the white sweat frothed on the steamy horse's harness.

"Whoa, Blacky, then. Good lad. Stand you fast." Blacky pricked his ears hearing a well-known voice. David went to the horse's head and found the reins loose. Had the Master been so deep drunk as to drop the reins? David pulled them free beneath the horse's belly and hitched them safe to the shafts. Turning, he then went to the side of his Master, not knowing quite what to say. "Shall I give you'm a hand down, Sur?" He lifted the lantern and drew closer to stare up into the face above him.

"Merciful God! He be choked with his own whip! Strangled by his own hand!" The boy stood frozen, his arm high, the lamp jiggling in his shaking fist. It was a fearful sight. The swollen purpled face, the gaping blue mouth, the tongue protruding, the lips drawn back above the teeth which were wide open. Like some great deep sea fish about to swallow its prey, and worst of all the eyes. Wide and staring like flints, frozen in an expression of horrified realisation of the manner of his death.

At last David pulled himself together and stiffly drew down the lantern. He stumbled away towards the groom's quarters, seeking help. Blacky stood quiet in the shafts, waiting to be unharnessed. Never again would Master raise his whip over Blacky's back. Never again would he raise his whip over anyone's back.

Dr. Ainsley was not called upon to make an examination of his brother's body. The Magistrates came from Wesperton and brought the local Surgeon from the town to do all that was necessary. It was perfectly clear to them that Jonathon Ainsley's death had been an accident, having taken too much of the bottle, he had strangled himself with the thongs of his own driving whip. There were marks upon the chaise wheels and upon the Park gates. Also damage to the shafts and a cut along Blacky's side. All these thing clearly indicated that for some reason, almost certainly intoxication, Lord Ainsley's eldest son had driven full pelt into the closed gate of the Park. The impact must have been such that the unfortunate man had lost his footing, and became entangled in the whip thongs. The horse had moved on forward, driverless, while the thongs wound tighter and tighter about his throat, thereby cutting into the windpipe and extinguishing life.

The Magistrates came in a fine carriage drawn by two black horses. They were townsmen, black breeches and long coats, highly polished black boots, high hats, white stocks and curled wigs, leant them due weight and authority. They drove up in fine style. Arrived at the Park, they viewed the body and consulted with the Surgeon who had accompanied them. They attempted to condole with the widow, but she was indisposed and could not see them. So they condoled instead with her Mother, Lady

Loundes. They then drove away completely satisfied with themselves, to enjoy at the town's expense a good dinner at the Stag Inn in Wesperton.

One person was not satisfied. The head groom at the Park, Tom Brown, was a careful man, he had himself made sure that the Park gates were wide open any night that his Master was from home. It was not a rule but it was a responsibility he had always taken upon himself. He remained unmovable on that one point. The gates had stood wide at sunset. There was no stock grazing in the Park in winter. There was no need for the gates to be closed. There was every need for them to be open. The Master was likely to return, they had been open at sunset. Who then had closed them? No one cared. The house staff were in turmoil preparing for the funeral. The Magistrates were satisfied and had gone home.

Jonathon Clarence Edward Ainsley's remains were interred in the family crypt beneath Seckington Church. As was the custom of the times, no women attended. The day was cold but dry. Lord Ainsley and his son David followed the coffin. A handful of local gentry and farmers came to show their respect for Lord Ainsley and his family. From Chalfont, Bernard Bistock and his eldest son Charles. From Hill Farm, Tarant Barnes and from Lower House, Francis Trewis and Albert Trewis. From the Park, Lady Loundes's brother from Hertfordshire represented the widow and her mother.

It was a brief service with no music save the tolling bell which rang out the twenty-nine doleful chimes which counted the years of the dead man's life. With the closing of the crypt door there ended a shameful chapter in an honourable family's history. For the staff and family at the Park the black clouds would begin to disperse. There were none who mourned Jonathon Ainsley. Though his mother grieved deeply and wept often for the little boy he had once been.

CHAPTER VIII

CHAPTER VIII

In the last days of February there came a mild spell of weather to the villages. The cold winds dropped and the warm sun shone across the woods and fields with gradually increasing power. The woodlands began to come alive. Squirrels woke and stretched their limbs and left the warmth and safety of their drays. They raced up and down the leafless tree trunks searching amongst the brown leaf mould in their efforts to find nuts buried and forgotten last autumn. The blackbirds and thrushes sang in the hazel bushes in their ardour and joy at the coming of Spring, they shook the yellow pollen from the newly opened catkins. By the Cliven, pussy willows danced to and fro above the sparkling water. Raven Dyer carrying corn to the ducks, discovered the first few pale primroses in the bank in the orchard.

Thatcher Gibbs whistled about his work, he was laying new thatch to No Man's Barn. The sun was warm on his back, he threw off his jacket and laid it in the hedgerow. Up at Hill Farm Anne Barnes caught sight of his white shirt sleeves against the barn roof. She dropped her buckets and ran down the fields to him. He saw the flying figure in the white apron and came down the ladder two rungs at a time to meet her. It was their first time alone together in weeks, she flew into his arms.

"Cum you out of sight a minute, Lass." He half carried her round behind the barn. They clung together in a long kiss.

"My dear, dear Lass - I have missed 'ee." He spoke low, holding her close.

"Oh! Oh! and I you. When .... when can we be wed?" Feeling herself immodest, she dropped her eyes and bit her lips.

"Sooner the better, I reckon - we best tell to yer Dad next Sunday, as ever is. Dost think he'll agree?"

"He must, I'm sixteen now - 'tis surely time I were free in my choosin'."

"Aye, Lass - I knows that - you knows that. It be him us've got to convince, ent it?"

"Come on Sunday and we'll see - now I must run, else they hens'll eat all the pig swill. I just see'd thee and run, dropped the buckets down all anyhows, I did!" Her lips parted in a rosy smile.

"Get you gone, then - tek a man's mind from 'is work, you does." He gave her bottom a sound slap as she turned from him. She squealed and ran back up the fields.

In Stackyard field behind the Lower House thirty ewes began to drop their lambs. Johnny Trewis had charge of them. So far there were twenty two lambs. David Ainsley thought them a pretty sight when he rode Beauty into the yard to take the splints off Amanda Trewis's arm.

In the kitchen Velvet was preparing bread for baking, she was hot and sweating with the work of throwing and thumping the dough into shape on the table top. At the sink Raven Dyer was peeling vegetables, Baby Hannah was playing with a Dutch doll at the hearth. Amanda came down the stairs with her arm still in a linen sling.

"'Tis fine to see the Springtime be come, Doctor, after all these bad winter times," she greeted him cheerfully.

"Yes indeed, and you've some fine lambs, I see."

"Oh well, our Johnny - he be very concerned for his flock - they gets best of everything this time o' year."

"I've come to unstrap your arm - if it's mended. Shall we have a look?" She still wore a sling and bandage strapped tight to splints of wood.

"Shall I sit here by the table?"

"Just so." David began to remove the sling and bandage.

"Oh - 'tis stiff - will I be able to straighten it?"

"It's bound to be stiff." He felt the elbow and forearm carefully.

"Seems quite a nice knit together to me. Now you must move and use the fingers and work the elbow as well - look, like this." He flexed his own arm up and down, massaging it with the fingers of his other hand. "We'll leave the splints and bandage off now. Just wear the sling when it gets tired. No lifting, mind, but use it all you can about the house. That's the secret." He smiled at her cheerfully.

"Now I must go - I've to see the Bones baby, and later I'm to dine at the Parsonage."

"Be the baby sick?" Velvet looked up from the tray of loaves she had finished shaping.

"No, he was very well last time I saw him, I just like to keep a close eye on the babies. Mistress Raven seems to settle amongst you? Is that right?" David smiled again, this time directing his blue gaze towards the girl at the sink. Raven looked up smiling.

"I be real happy - thank 'ee, Sur."

"She's learnin' all the things, 'tis a real help to us that is." Amanda's faded face lit up for a moment.

"Good day to you all." Ainsley nodded and went out.

Emmy Bones was stirring a pot over the fire, a pleasant aroma of rabbit stew reached his nostrils. The baby lay sleeping in his crib by the open window.

"Come you in, Doctor - don'ee stand out there." He bent his head under the low beam. "How are you? I see you've put him to get the air. That's right - best thing for him. Well, he grows a big boy doesn't he?" David bent over the cradle. "What do you call him?"

"Well, we calls him Bill - but he was named David - for you, Sur - us hoped ye'd not mind. Seeing you bringed him into this world."

"No, of course not - he was my first baby delivered in the village here - so perhaps it's fitting."

"Aye Doctor - there'll - well that is - there's another coming this back end - us hopes it 'ent too soon!" She flushed scarlet.

"Often happens that way, Mistress Bones, you are a strong young woman. I don't see you taking any hurt from childbearing yet awhile. Well, I must be on my way - I'm due at the Parsonage. I'll be in to see you again."

"Us never pays 'ee, Doctor - would you tek this jar of honey? Clover honey it be. Martin looks to the bees for his Lordship and we'm allowed one hive for oursen."

"Thank you - that is a kind thought. I'm fond of honey and it's long since I tasted any."

"Just so; Sir, and good day to 'ee." She bobbed a curtsey as he went out.

David spent a pleasant hour with Andrew and Harriet Mallard. The Parsonage was strangely quiet that day. The two children, Luke and Maisy, had gone to spend a month with their Aunt and Uncle at Banbury.

"We're glad to have them out of the way for a while, if the truth be told," Andrew explained.

"How's that?" Ainsley asked. They were seated at their fireside, David enjoying the unaccustomed leisure, stretched out his long legs to the blaze. Harriet had gone into the kitchen to help Lucy Fulton, the meal was finished.

"Well, we've reached a point where their futures must be decided. My wife has been teaching them with other children from the village." Andrew looked troubled and thoughtful as he spoke. David said nothing, waiting for his friend to express his anxiety.

"The trouble is, both Harriet and I have both reached the limit of our ability in teaching them, so it is either school or some other form of tuition, or training of some sort. Difficulty is that School is beyond the purse of a country Parson."

"Would you send your girl, Mary, to school?"

"Oh no, only the boy - but even that would be too much. For the moment their Aunt in Banbury is to teach Maisy to be a little better with her needle and introduce her in some small way to town society. If the two of them settle happy, they may remain there for a time. Luke might try for a Scholarship to the day school there - we would manage that I think - and it's a good school."

"What does he want to do later on?"

"He wants the Navy - but I doubt we could afford a commission - much as I would like it."

"I might be able to help a bit in that direction later on - of course, more schooling would give him better footing in the Navy, or any other venture he fancies - come to that."

"He's been set on the Navy since a baby almost. I don't see him changing. But it has to be a step at a time in our financial position. Enough about us - How does your experiment with the Romany girl prosper?"

"She settles well - I was at the Lower House this morning, seems it was worth the effort."

"Yes - I'm glad she's away from the Quarry settlement. Of course, the Travellers are a law unto themselves. None the less, they are part and parcel of my flock and I feared her proximity to her Father and brothers now she grows older. There's much incest among the gypsies - although it never can be proven."

"In this particular case, I think Black Dyer intended to sell her off and pocket the gold, to his cousin from Kent who is well over fifty."

"Well, I don't know how you did it, but it must have cost you, David." Andrew's eyes twinkled as he looked at his friend.

"Well it did - a bit - but worth it, I think. Well I must go, my horse has stood three hours today and she yearns for the open orchard, now the sweet grass begins to come."

"How pleasant to see the countryside in Spring dress once more." Andrew rose, a thin spare figure, to see his visitor away.

As he rode home David found himself in complete agreement. Just the pleasure of walking Beauty along unencumbered by snow was a joy. The heart lifted to see the grass and the trees beginning to answer to the warmth of the air. The dark days of winter had been long and lowering. In the hawthorn hedge of Gleaners Acre a charm of goldfinches darted amongst the buds, giving a flash of colour as they sped from bush to bush.

March came in mild and sunny, the pink buds on the sycamores opened and each leaflet unfolded in dainty greening sweetness. Primrose clumps perfumed the sheltered lane from Crab Tree cottage. A pair of robins carried moss and began to build in the old pump handle in David's back yard. The old men of the village looked glum and forecast a bad end to the month. Ben Hastley gloomed over his mug of ale in the Cross Keys

"'Er to come in like a lamb, then 'er shall go out like a lion. Allus is so, any road up! Terrible winds us'll get back end of month, you see if I 'ent right!" The rest of the village continued to enjoy the mild sunshine and began to dig over their patch ready for tatty planting.

Simon Dale, one of the twins from Wood Cottage, came to Crab Tree to ask Ainsley to call. His Mother, Eliza Dale, was ailing he said. She was still suckling the little one and was fretting lest her milk should upset him. David was visiting in Seckington so Mabel Dunn took the message. David went along after his dinner. He went on foot - it was a pity to saddle Beauty again for so short a distance. He had only the one call to make.

When he reached Wood Cottage he found Eliza Dale pale and distressed. She was lying on the old couch in their big room near the fire. The baby lay in his crib. The twins were both at work, as was their Father. Old Albert was up at the Hall. It was a regular Springtime task for him to help dig over the large vegetable garden at the Hall. In spite of his age, Albert could still tackle any task with a spade and make a neat job of it. Betsy Price, the blacksmith's sister, was in Eliza's kitchen doing some washing at the sink.

"Sorry to be botherin' you, Doctor - but I been so poorly - my head and that. I'm feared about the babe, being as I'm still suckling he - in case I upsets him. Betsy have come to see after the men's dinner - I couldna' have managed else." Eliza spoke anxiously, sweat on her face. David smiled at her and at Betsy, the little woman's round rosy face beamed back at him.

"Let's have a look at you, then - can you unbutton your dress?" David began his examination. "Have you any pains in the chest or stomach?"

"Well, I do feel sick and chilled - like as if I can't get warm - but no a real sharp pain." David took her pulse and found it a trifle fast, otherwise he could find nothing.

"I think perhaps you've eaten something that's disagreed with you," he suggested.

"I only had the same as the others, Sur."

"Just the same, I think to be on the safe side you should rest and keep to a light diet. A good broth - if you have any. Don't put the baby to breast, give him a little cow's milk - boil it and give it to him when it's cooled, but plenty of rest for you - I'll come again in the morning

The next morning David Ainsley rose early as was his custom. Mabel Dunn was before him, she had cold roast and fresh wheaten bread on the table ready for his breakfast. A bright fire burned in the grate. He was learning to love this room and to find peace and respite within the walls of Crab Tree. Even through the tragedy of Jonathon's death he had found solace here with his books, the lovely view across the valley and the quiet comfort of his own home.

He ate his meal and went into the Surgery for his bag. A frown creased his brow as he concentrated on his requirements for the day. He went methodically round the shelves collecting what he needed. A soothing draught to soothe Eliza Dale's upset stomach, lint, bandages, ointments, forceps, scissors and a dozen other items. Ten minutes later he set off for Wood Cottage. As always it was a pleasure to feel Beauty's easy movement beneath him.

"We're lucky, Lass - you and I." He bent forward to pat her neck. They splashed through the stream, sending up a sparkling shower of droplets as they went. At the gate of Wood Cottage garden he dismounted and tethered the mare to the rails. Along the narrow path to the door clumps of white snowdrops dangled their delicate pearls of blossom above the black earth. David walked round to the back and entered after giving a light tap on the door.

Betsy Price was alone in the kitchen with the baby. He was awake and lay kicking happily in the cradle.

"Well, he's fit enough, anyway. How's the patient?" David asked.

"I made 'er stay in bed, Sur - she do feel badly, I only got John's dinner to do - it's no trouble to do they dinners and the babe do need someone about."

"I'll go up and see her." He made his way carefully up the narrow stairway. It opened into what had once been one large room in the roof. Then it would have been lit by two dormer windows facing the lane. With the birth of the twins, fifteen years before, Arthur Dale had divided the room down the middle with a rough wooden partition. David Ainsley now came up the open stairway into the area where Sailor and Simon slept. There were two sturdy oak home-made beds along one wall, an old chest of drawers stood between the beds. There was no other furniture. At one end of the room was the small window, at the other end, a recess in the wall where a curtain hung across, contained a wall bed. Here old Albert slept and had done for over fifty years.

In the centre of the partition a rough door opened into the other half of the roof. Ainsley stepped through, noticing how clean and tidy everywhere was, even though so sparsely furnished. The room he now stepped into was the exact replica of the first save that here there was only one large country-made bed. Beside it a large chest in which all the families clothes and bed linen were stored. On the chest stood a pricket candle stick, it was the only ornament in the room.

In the bed, Eliza Dale lay with her head resting on the single bolster, a bowl stood on the floor close to the bed-head.

"Have you been vomiting Eliza?" David spoke gently, his eyes on the white frightened face in which the eyes pleaded for his help.

"Oh, Doctor, thank God you'm come. I .... I know 'tis foolish but I'm so afeared - am I going to die?"

"Have you been sick?" He repeated his question gently.

"No - no - only I felt so - I didn't want Betsy to be cleaning up after me. She's bin so good - with the baby an all." Slow tears began to run down her cheeks. David smiled reassuringly.

"Now, now, try not to be upset. I'm here to get you well. Have you managed to eat anything since I was here?"

Eliza's voice trembled so much she could hardly bring the words out, "No, I can't seem to get it down. Betsy did make some lovely broth - but I keep worrying - about the baby - and my Arthur and the boys."

"Of course, that's natural - now, let me examine you again." He helped her with the strings at the neck of the course nightgown. Beneath the gown, on her back and breast, Ainsley found a dozen or more hard central spots, about each was a red ring. He looked no further. It was a shock, his enemy was awake. With the warm weather, the Plague was back seeking vengeance. Here, where the house was so clean, the food mostly home grown. A dozen questions threw themselves round in his mind, a jumbled shocked turmoil. He thrust them from him, time enough for that later. For now - just the patient. Nothing was in his face, only kindness, he spoke again quietly as he helped her back into her nightgown.

"Now, I want you to stay in bed, but you must take nourishment, milk or broth, no solids, but as much liquid as you can, even if you vomit at times."

Eliza stared up at him, seeming not to take in what he said.

"What are they? What are they spots, Doctor?" Her hands shook as they clutched at the bedclothes. Then releasing them, she caught at his hands. Sweat broke out on her forehead, beseeching eyes were wide now in her unnamed fear.

"Please - Please - it 'ent me - I've had my life - 'tis the babe! Can you? Can you tek the babe somewhere's safe? I knows, yer see - I knew yesternight, I don' know how. T'was why I wouldna' let Arthur lie by me last night - I made excuse, said I was too sickly, but I knew, see! Don't try to keep it hid, Doctor. 'Tis the others yer see, the boys - I know what it be - 'tis Plague!" It was out. The dread word that she had lived alone with since yesterday. She sank back, tears and sweat intermingled upon her ashen face. David's voice came to her, quiet and commanding.

"Now, Eliza - I shall not permit you to give up - as you say, I fear it is the plague risen again - but we have some things on our side this time. In London, I lived with Plague for many weeks. There it is breeding ground for disease. Dirt, very hot weather, filthy food, bad water, closed houses, people herded. Here we have fresh air, good food, a clean home, room to separate people. We must use all these things to help us fight. We shall fight it together, you and I. I shall not leave you alone in this. Now, put the family from your mind and try to be brave - if you can keep up your courage, that will be half the battle. Can you be brave, Eliza?" He took her hand again. "Will you try for me, Eliza?"

"Why has it come to us? - Why us, Doctor?"

"If I knew that we should have already won, it strikes often where it is least expected."

"Will I be worse? Will it be very bad?"

"No one can say - it has so many ways, we must wait and see and take care of you. Now, rest quiet a few minutes while I see after Betsy and the babe downstairs."

"I didna let Betsy touch me - nor the baby - I never picked him up - not since early morning yesterday."

"Good - that was brave - now lie a few minutes."

She fell back with her eyes closed but the tears still spilled beneath her lashes. David went downstairs with a heavy heart. In the kitchen he did not beat about the bush.

"Betsy - I'm sorry in my heart to have to tell you, but I fear 'tis the plague with Eliza - she's not too bad at present - but it will be worse yet - whatever comes of it." His voice was quite calm, which in some way forced calmness upon his listener.

"She knew - didn't she? That's why she wouldna' let I near. Oh, Doctor! God have mercy on all of us."

"Yes, Betsy - we must pray and hope, but we must also be watchful. It's country air here - much different from London - we must look after ourselves and each other. There's a lot we can do if we are sensible"

"Country air didn't save young George Swift or Tom Carter, an' her spells and witchery didna' help Mother Ross. Is this from them, Doctor? Can plague be sleeping so?"

"I can't say, Betsy - no one knows, but listen to me now - because those four died does not mean Eliza will die too. Some recover. Some never catch it at all. But first we must plan what must be done."

"What about the babe? Surely we can get him away - such a dear wee mite - I can't bear thinking."

"Would you take him across the lane to your cottage? Your brother John already stands in risk since you were here yesterday - you should go anyway. Your home stands by itself - there's no close neighbours - only here."

"How should I go on? His feeding, I mean?" The round face puckered with anxiety.

"Baby Edward is almost four months, Betsy. Feed him cow's milk with a spoon, or I can let you have a feeding cup. Boil the milk and then cool it. Put a drop of honey in it. Keep him in the air - by an open window. It is my firm belief that fresh air and clean food can do wonders. Will you take him? Mind you - there is some risk, there has to be some risk for all of us." David paused, giving her time to speak. Betsy smiled, the round face sweet and certain in it's expression.

"Course I'll take him - must I go now?"

"In a few minutes - first, could you bring some bricks from the outhouse and set them at the fire. I shall open the windows - I want clean air through these rooms. That may make it cold for Eliza - I want hot bricks at her feet and more covers on the bed. She shivers now - later there will be fever - but warmth is important for her now.

"Surely, Sur - I'll fetch the bricks now. There's two spare blankets in the chest by Eliza's bed."

"I'll fetch those - don't go upstairs again. When the bricks are at the fire, take up the boy just as he is and take him across the lane. If there are any clean baby clothes down here, take them with you. Don't take the cradle - John's a good fellow - he'll knock you up something. And Betsy, if you or John or the baby feel ill - come to the gate. I shall watch for a sign. If all is well set a candle in the window at dusk. We shall see it. I shall not leave here while Eliza is so sick. Tell John to keep away from others as much as he can until all this is past. And bless you, Betsy - God go with you."

"Aye, Sur - and thank 'ee. 'Tis you will save us if anyone can - us knows that."

"I shall strive to do so, Betsy - now let us be about our tasks - and, Betsy,"

"Aye, Sur?"

"Don't use the well, either here or your own - get water from the Cliven. Running water is purer - safer. John will carry it - 'tis wiser in these times. And boil it - and keep your food covered with cloths, there's a good Lass."

"Yes, Sur - I'll tell John when 'ee comes in."

David Ainsley spent the next hour making his patient more comfortable. Hot bricks wrapped in cloth at her feet. A flow of soft pure air through the open casement. Two extra blankets over the bed. He sponged her face and hands several times. She still displayed the irrational fear he had seen so many times in London. He thought she seemed a good deal more reassured when he told her that Betsy Price had taken the baby across to her own cottage. David then had the satisfaction of seeing Eliza lie back under the covers in an attempt to relax.

At six o'clock the twins and their Father came home from work across Big Fields, Old Albert with them. David heard them come clumping up the path in their farm boots, and the murmur of their cheerful conversation. He felt a wave of sadness as he waited in the kitchen. The door stood wide. Arthur came in first, anxiety in his face the moment he laid eyes on the Doctor.

"How be she then, Sur? my Eliza, how she be?"

David broke his news quietly, but nothing could soften the blow he gave them. All were shocked into silence. No one spoke for a few minutes.

"If this be so - how is it none of us be took bad?" Arthur's voice was hoarse and confused.

"The testing time will be these next few days," David said

gently.

"Is Eliza very bad - can I go and be with she?"

"She's poorly - I expect her to have a fever before long - I cannot say how soon or how long it may last. There are many symptoms with the pestilence - some people only suffer a few - others suffer greatly. We can only wait and see how she goes along. She needs careful, cheerful nursing." He went on to explain his views, a light diet, milk, eggs, good broth, plenty of liquids, fresh air, open casements, warm blankets, hot bricks. It was necessary to convince people of the need for fresh air when all the cottagers lived behind closed doors and shutters to save the warmth from the hard come by peats and logs.

"What about little Edward, what of the babe?" Arthur's thoughts came back at last from his wife, to fix upon his young child.

"I've sent him across the lane with Betsy - it seemed the best - she will keep away and care for him until this is past."

"Surely. Betsy be a good friend - allus a good friend to us."

"I think you should all keep away from other folk as much as you can. Especially you, Arthur, if you feel able to nurse Eliza. The rest should keep outside the sick room and keep in the open air as much as they can. It would be my suggestion that Simon and Sailor continue at work. I will see my Father and arrange that they are found jobs outside all the time. But I think, Arthur, as you will be needed here as nurse full time, it would be best if you stay away from work until we see how things go here at home. You are too much indoors at work - being a cowman. I also advise that none shall sleep upstairs, for the present at any rate. Move the beds down into the living room. The wall bed of course cannot be shifted, but this couch would give rest for you, Albert" They all seemed stunned by his suggestions at first. It was Albert who recovered his wits.

"I cud sleep in the wood shed - clear it up a bit and knock up a cot - plenty of air in there, any road up." His crinkled old face attempted a smile. Arthur followed his Father's lead, shaking his head and shoulders in an effort to rouse himself.

"Surely us'll do our best to act wise - us'll need thee to guide us, mind. We be poor understanding such fearful illness. But you says we mun eat well. Seems best if I keeps away from the

264

cooking pots and leave meself free to mind after Eliza."

"I be dang sure I can mek as good a stew as Betsy. Sides, t'will give me summat to keep me busy." Old Albert found his tongue. Suiting words to action, he went to the fire and lifted the stewing pot lid. From the pot came a rich smell of gravy intermingled with onions and stewed mutton. Betsy had left them a good dinner. It cheered and steadied them all. The two young lads fetched platters and spoons to the table. Arthur made to go upstairs. David detained him.

"I'll go back upstairs - while you get a good dinner inside you. I can't make too much of how important it is that you all eat well and regularly. Also there's the water. I want you to cover the well and for the present carry water from the Cliven. It is wise to use running water - especially since it is so easily obtainable.

"That's an easy matter. Sailor and me, us can carry water of an evening - fill the copper for washing and that, keep the buckets for drinking."

"That would be very good, but keep the drinking water covered - a cloth of linen is sufficient."

A few minutes later David returned to his patient. She was very wretched, unable to be still, and while he was with her began to vomit for the first time. Watching her struggling body, Ainsley was conscious of both pain and anger. He could give so little help. When the wretched heave of vomiting was over he again wiped her face and mouth. It had grown towards dusk and he lit the candle at the bedside. This action roused her, she extended her hand, he bent to listen.

"I grow so warm - a drink, please?" It was scarcely above a whisper. He gave her a drink of the water he had boiled earlier, resolving to bring some red wine later. She gulped the liquid thirstily. It was an encouragement to him. She seemed easier afterwards.

"Through the window - I can see a light - is it Betsy? She has a candle on the sill, does she not?"

David went to look. Sure enough, in the dormer sill of Wych Cottage across the lane he saw a light. A small flickering beam shone out like a tiny beacon in the deepening darkness. He went to the bed and took Eliza's hand.

"Indeed it is, Eliza. Betsy promised that so long as all was well with her and the baby, she would set, a candle where we should see it at night time."

"It do give me good heart to watch it. Will you put our candle the same, so Betsy shall know us safe also?"

"Of course." He lifted the pricket and set it in the corner of the wide sill.

"It is a comfort that - a real comfort." She closed her eyes and lay back. Her limbs still twitched and she sweated, but she lay more content. Ainsley left then soon after. The mare, Beauty, had stood four hours - she gave a great whinny of joy at his coming. He turned her for home. To wash. To change his clothes. To drink red wine. To rest and breathe pure air. To practise again the strict disciplines that Vincent Fallon had instilled into him in London.

Charlotte Ainsley stood in the old still-room at Seckington Hall. She wore an old print gown and a kerchief tied about her dark hair. If anyone had told her a month before that she would ever be hard at work in the servants part of the house, she would have laughed in their face. Life had changed for them all in the last few weeks. The plague had altered the lives of almost every household in Lower and Upper Telso. The Hall was no exception. Indeed, it had become the hub of the parish. The unused rooms behind the great house had been made over into what amounted to a supply depot for the villages. Lord Ainsley had put the rooms at David's disposal when it became clear that Eliza Dale's was not an isolated case. Within days of Eliza being taken ill, plague had risen in three other houses in the villages. In the row of cottages where the two women had perished earlier the pestilence had again struck. Flossie Hastley had been taken ill one evening and her Father, old Ben, that much loved old gossip, had also taken to his bed an hour or two later.

More serious perhaps, because more people dwelt in the one house, was the sudden illness of Arthur Trewis at Lower House Farm. Up at the Hall itself a maid servant and a stable boy from the home farm had both collapsed at their work a few days later.

David Ainsley was forced to abandon the isolation of individuals. Andrew Mallard proved a staunch help. He and

David worked together to try to persuade all the people in both villages to remain within their own parishes. To achieve this, David set up a temporary hospital in the village itself. No Man's Barn had been taken over for the use of the desperately sick. His Lordship lent a horse and cart to transport the unfortunate patients. Thatcher Gibbs constructed a stretcher for the cart, to give greater comfort to the sufferers, during these dreadful journeys.

At the barn cots were set up, a rough curtain separating male from female. Great loads of logs were carted, for a fire to give warmth. The ancient hearth had been used only at harvest suppers and village events. Now the medieval chimney sent up a spiral of smoke day and night. The great hearth gave comfort and cheer to the patients, as they lay sick and lonely for their families, under the great timbered roof.

Behind Seckington Hall David set up his supply rooms. The old still room had four tables arranged down the centre. Here the maids sat each day cutting up clean linen and rolling bandages. In another room, an old kitchen, the girls worked in turn at the old coppers, filled with boiling water and suds, heated by fierce fires in the fire holes below, they steamed hour after hour. Sheets of linen, towels, night gowns, night shirts and contaminated clothing of every kind was sent from the barn to be boiled here. Constant clouds of steam escaped through the open doors and windows, which were not to be closed, on Dr. Ainsley's orders. All the soiled linen was handled with care. Sticks with hooks and dolly sticks were used. The laundry came by cart each day - picked up from the barn and the infected houses with pronged forks.

Each day the cart was disinfected. After boiling in the coppers, the linen, now no longer dangerous to handle, was hung in the air to dry. Charlotte Ainsley herself supervised the laundry under David's direction. She did much of the work herself.

In this wing of the Hall an ancient kitchen had been modernised nearly eighty years before. It had now become out of date and old fashioned. Nevertheless, it had two great ovens. Here all the staff of the Hall spent hours baking bread, cooking endless pots of broth and gruel and making great jugs of refreshing herb brew. This last involved chopping up piles of mint and thyme and other herbs. It was a recipe which Lady Isobel's Mother had come by many years before. It had always been useful for sickness and vomiting. Being a refreshing and pleasant drink, David had decided to try it for his patients. It was essential that those who were very ill, and particularly those with sores and open boils, should take plenty of liquids. David believed it washed the poison from their systems. Indeed, a great many who were not yet ill but who had been close coupled with the pestilence were drinking the herb brew as a safeguard. David was well pleased. The brew was boiled twice in its preparation. Failing red wine, it was a good drink for all, far better than the highly suspect well water.

In the Hall's old kitchen, Anne Barnes came daily and worked tirelessly in bread making, cooking, and chopping herbs for the brew. Helping as much as any kitchen maid. Beyond the orchard, Thatcher Gibbs and other Estate workers toiled away the hours, chopping up wood to feed all the hungry fires in the kitchens and No Man's Barn. They worked from first light until dusk. The mild weather continued but plague victims felt the cold even on warm days. Those in high fever shivered under three or four blankets. Two carts of logs were used in No Man's Barn daily. Great baskets of logs were carried into the kitchen and laundry rooms to feed the bread ovens and boil water in the coppers. Another cart took logs to the cottages where there was sickness.

In the house at Seckington Hall, Lord and Lady Ainsley managed with only the help of their youngest daughter, Esme, and Lady Isobel's maid, Jenny Bains. It was all these brave efforts which helped the ordinary folk to overcome their terror of the malignant death which threatened them all. They were upheld, every man, woman, and child by their ever growing faith in David Ainsley, he seemed never to rest, never to tire, never to lose heart, never to look anything but calm and cheerful.

David rode on Beauty about the parishes. None who asked his help were turned away. He was fearless, he tended cases where lesser men would have fled. He encouraged the sick, often giving comfort where there was none. He lanced swellings and carbuncles, when the stench of the poison within burst forth, causing even the closest and most loving relatives to withdraw.

And afterwards he himself cleaned up and disposed of the foul residue.

Within two days of Eliza Dale falling sick, her twins also became ill. Several days later Arthur Dale began to feel unwell one morning. Simon was showing the red ringed spots upon his body and was so sick that he could only lie groaning in his cot in the living room. Sailor was in high fever only four hours after his first feelings of shivering cold and sickness. On them both David found the dread 'Tokens' rash. It was on the day that he found them both almost certainly doomed, that he realised that he must have somewhere to take them. Some sort of hospital. While he was at Wood Cottage, Arthur was at last forced to admit to feeling ill himself. David settled him on the couch in the kitchen but it was not to be tolerated that he should lie there so close to his sons who were so much more sick than he.

David had been immensely cheered that day to find Eliza, upstairs still, past the worst of her suffering. She had had no token marks and only two minor swellings, which had both burst of their own accord. As yet, she was as weak as a kitten and would need care for sometime yet. It was impossible to let her be above the others to listen to the pitiful cries of her family.

Old Albert had so far remained in his usual rude health. His pipe was never out of his mouth. He puffed about the house all day, giving what help he could. Yet he could not be left to nurse four sick people, so David Ainsley was forced into his idea of a hospital ward. The old barn came to mind at once - it was big and airy, at the most central point possible for both Upper and Lower Telso and isolated from other dwellings.

David talked at once with his Father. It was only a matter of hours before a huge fire had been lit in the great hearth aperture below the chimney opening. Lord Ainsley's game keepers cleared and swept the building. A dozen beds were knocked together in the carpenter's shop at the Hall. Each was lined with strong hessian. Every spare blanket was hunted out of the cupboards at the Park and the Hall. Tables and chairs were sent in Lady Isobel's pony and trap.

By nightfall Sailor and Simon Dale were installed and lay side by side in the two beds nearest the fire. Their Father was in a bed a few beds away, in the hope that he might be less badly affected.

Old Albert was left at the cottage to tend Eliza and run the home. At Number five, the Row, Flossie was too ill to be moved. Ainsley went daily but the condition of the house itself was against Flossie Hastley's recovery. It was ill lit and dirty. Phoebe Hastley could not be persuaded to take proper care of her sister or her Father. Both became very ill, both developed terrible swellings. Old Ben became delirious in fever, during which he had to be tied down to prevent him from harming himself. He came out of his threshing violence only to drop into a deep comatose sleep. He lay for hours with his eyes open and his face expressionless, staring at the ceiling.

Flossie died very quickly. Her sister did nothing but sit rocking and weeping, her arms hugged across her chest, she was too fearful to help either her sister or her Father. David knew he couldn't save Old Ben but he had him moved to No Man's Barn in spite of it, feeling that the old fellow would be happier at the last in the company of men who had been his friends.

Tom Hart, the Sexton, began then to show the brave stuff he was made of. With great courage he took a horse and cart loaned by Andrew Mallard and, with a plain coffin, which he made himself in the Parsonage stables, he went along to number five, the Row. He manhandled Flossie Hastley's heavy body into the coffin, nailed it down and transported it to the grave in the Churchyard which he had dug out some hours before. Andrew Mallard came to him in the churchyard and said a few simple prayers over the open grave. There were none there save their two selves. Directly afterwards Andrew insisted that Tom went home and changed his clothes. Andrew Mallard watched the big man out of sight beneath the yew trees. Then he took up the spade and filled in the grave.

The next day Phoebe Hastley set out for No Man's Barn, loneliness overcame her and she went in search of Old Ben. She felt stiff and weary, finding difficulty in keeping a straight course along the path. Her neighbours, not daring to risk their children, retreated inside their cottage doors. Near the churchyard gate she paused, gazing across at the new turned earth near the wall, her vision blurred, and earth, grass and trees, swung dizzily in front of her. She stumbled on a few steps before she fell forwards on her face. There was no movement, the stuff of her worn dress blew and moved a little in the wind. The wood pigeons called in the yew trees, the lane was quiet and empty.

Raven Dyer saw the fluttering gown and the still form from her window at Lower House. She said nothing, the family had enough worry struggling to nurse Francis Trewis, who lay exhausted from vomiting for two days and nights without sleep. Raven ran across the stack yard and across Home Field to Dr. Ainsley in No Man's Barn. David went with the cart to fetch Phoebe. Although she was still alive and put into a warm bed and given every care in the hospital place, it was to no avail, she died three days later, a few minutes before her Father. That day proved to be one of David Ainsley's worst days. Simon Dale died during the afternoon, in an agony of sepsis from a burst carbuncle in his groin. All David had been able to do for the young, bright-haired fifteen year old, was to dope him with laudanum, to quiet his screams. The moment he was gone, gasping and fighting to the very last, David had to turn to his brother. Sailor, Simon's twin, gave up his slim grip on life and slipped into a deep sleep from which he did not waken. David kept him warm but made no attempt to rouse him. The boy had a great rash of 'Tokens' upon his back and thighs. When this dread sign appeared death was inevitable. David's blue eyes saddened as he covered their faces and sent word to Andrew at the Parsonage.

New graves in the churchyard seemed to be dug daily. Tom Hart refused to put a spade into the earth until Dr. Ainsley or Andrew Mallard had personally informed him of the latest death. It was as if the big Sexton would hold back with his own strength and determination the creeping and insidious progress of the plague. The Dale twins were laid side by side in a quiet green corner of the churchyard near the Lych gate. When Lord Ainsley's stable boy died a day later, Tom Hart dug his grave close against the twins. He clamped his mouth tight shut and determinedly refused to acknowledge the need to leave a space for Arthur Dale beside his sons. Even though Arthur lay in dreadful weakness on his canvas bed in the barn.

The next to fall ill was John Symes, Lord Ainsley's ploughman. It happened while he was at work. Lord Ainsley sent him straight to the barn, anxious for the man's wife, Cathy, and their three children in the Row. Four more beds were filled that day. Two men from the Park - a gardener and a stable boy. Then came an old woman from one of the Estate cottages. The other new patient was the cause for much anxiety. Jenny was a maid servant from the Hall. It was the closest the plague's seeking fingers had come to the great house itself. News of it lay like a black shadow in the minds of all the other servants there.

Charlotte and Esme were very brave. They worked on in the great kitchen and laundry, cheering the others with their prattle and jokes, while in their hearts they were as frightened as the rest. Lady Isobel Ainsley felt a deep pride in her daughters and her beloved Doctor son, but a little shame in herself. She went about her duties in her usual steady matter of fact fashion, underneath the calm, she longed to gather up her husband, her son and her two daughters and flee far away from the deadly death which seemed to lie in wait for them all.

Unknown to anyone David made a map of the two villages. On it he marked a cross beside each house where the plague had raised its ugly head. He tried, far into the night, to find rhyme or reason, some sort of pattern in it all. Two of the men who now lay sick had come from Upper Telso. Before that none had been afflicted in the top village. It seemed the plague could bare its fangs and bite deep anywhere. If so, then surely they themselves within the small community must put up some kind of barrier round the two villages. Andrew Mallard had said something about cutting themselves off from the outside, when they had talked at the Lower House gate a day or so back. David tossed and turned in his rough bed at the end of the barn, long after he had put his map away in the table drawer. They must try to close off the villages without delay. David dropped into fitful sleep.

Next day he faced the problem anew. Andrew Mallard had already closed the Church. Services brought people together, such contact was dangerous in these times. David had agreed with him, they had parted when David was on his way to see Cathy Symes, to tell her the news that her husband seemed a mite better today. David had gone on to see Francis Trewis, only to find that his son Albert was ailing now as well. He had urged Amanda

Trewis to let both men come to the barn, if only for the sake of the rest of the family. Amanda had tearfully agreed. Francis himself, weak and very sick, had already been urging her to do so. Now they were both installed in the barn near the warmth of the fire.

David was able that evening to spend an hour at Crab Tree. He made up his chart there and saw with horror that there had already been eleven deaths in the villages. In his mind he ran over the cases still alive, both those at home and those in the temporary hospital. At least five of those in the barn at the moment he held out no hope for. It was a dreadful payment for a Pedlar's careless greed for a few pence. It was time he went back to his patients. To be long away made him restless. He had spent every night in the barn since the first patient had come in. He washed and changed, enjoying the feel of a clean shirt and stock against his skin. The blue eyes in the mirror looked back at him from a hardened mouth and pale skinned face. It was the price he paid for loss of sleep and anxiety for the families of lost patients.

A few minutes later he left the haven of the house, his cast off garments flung beneath disinfectant water in the copper. Mabel Dunn would boil them for him the following day. He was on foot, he always walked, leaving Beauty in the freedom of the paddock. Tonight he went via Wood Cottage, he had not seen Eliza Dale since the night the second of her twin sons died. She had taken their loss with great courage. Still in bed herself, she had pinned her hopes on her husband's recovery. Today it looked as if he might have a chance. If his progress continued good, David planned to keep his bed away from the others in the barn until such time as he could go home to Eliza and Old Albert. There he would be a comfort to his wife and away from the lowering anguish of men and women dying all about him.

When David reached the cottage he stood a few minutes in the lane. It was a beautiful Spring evening. The birds sang for joy. Somewhere in the nearby woodland a song thrush trilled into the warm evening air. In the bank, a clump of primroses spilled scented pale gold blossoms above a patch of purple violets. By the gate a bullfinch swung to and fro on the catkins in the hazel nut bush. For the first time in days a great smile lit his face and shone from his eyes. The world was still beautiful. Sometime this would pass. There was room still for faith. There in the window of John and Betsy Price's cottage burned a small candle. Across the lane, from Eliza's window, came the answering glow of her shining flame. There was a valiant defiance about these small emblems which touched David's heart. He went up the path between the now fully opened snowdrops. "Where there is life," he said to himself. "Where there is life!"

It had been a disturbed night in No Man's Barn, in the curtained off women's area the old woman from Lord Ainsley's cottage had fought out her losing battle to beat the strangling death the plague exacted from so many of its victims. David Ainsley had had very little sleep. He had no regular help. The number of patients in the barn had risen rapidly during the past few days. There were now sixteen patients under this roof. Tom Hart, 'the giant', came whenever he could to help lift and carry heavy bins of soiled linen. To take away the dead and a dozen unpleasant jobs. Andrew Mallard came for an hour or two each day. His courage was never at fault, but though physically robust he was not a young man and this limited his ability to help with the heavy work of nursing the very sick. David knew that he must put a brake on himself soon. He would have to get some help, even for a few hours each day. Who? The difficulty was that he dreaded asking anyone with family ties to share with him the tightrope existence between life and death, that anyone long in this building faced.

He covered the limbs of the old woman, straightening the blankets to hide the ugliness of her death. Poor brave old soul - she had never given up - some were like that, age had nothing to do with the quality of a person's courage. As this thought went through his mind, he saw a shadow come in through the barn door beyond the curtain. The barn doors stood wide, as they did both day and night. Probably Andrew - it was early morning - his time - he often came across the field before breaking his fast. Andrew would move along the line of beds, saying a prayer over the newly dead, giving a kind word of comfort where it was needed. Andrew and David had come very close in friendship these last weeks.

David moved quietly down the row of cots to the small

section near the wide doors. It had been curtained off for his own use. A cot, a couple of chairs and a table for his equipment were the simple furnishings. He drew aside the curtain, a smile forming in greeting to his friend. He stopped in his tracks. Seated at the table, looking him full in the face was Rachel Bistock. David stood quite still, his blue eyes examining her upturned face with its halo of corn coloured hair. He found great pleasure in what he saw, she looked so young and fresh - untouched by the misery that haunted him day and night. Neither spoke, he had not seen her since Eliza Dale had been taken ill. Chalfont Farm in its high windswept isolated position had so far escaped the plague's clutches.

Rachel, who had planned and rehearsed what she would say to him, was tongue-tied. She had been so poised and confident. Her resolution went from her at the sight of him. She had long since faced the fact that what she felt when in the presence of this man must be hidden, almost even from herself. Her tongue ran over her dry lips as she looked at him. The eyes which reminded him of honey bees were very vulnerable at this moment. David recovered his composure and spoke first.

"This cannot be the place for Mistress Rachel." His voice was quite gentle.

"Looking at you, Sir - there is need for *someone* here. I never saw a man more drawn and weary." She began with trembling hands to remove her bonnet.

"You cannot mean to stay? I am a physician - it lies on me as my duty to be here, I have long been in grapple with this vile enemy. Indeed, I sometimes think we have so long been in conflict one with another that he bothers with me no longer!" A smile was in the blue eyes now, it was a sweet mockery and she warmed to it. Yet she hid her feelings.

"That is dangerous talk," she snapped at him quite crossly, "'Tis well known that plague throws his knife to strike where none expect it, as it has in our villages."

"I know it - no one takes more care than I, but Chalfont lies high - it has been free of infection; surely it is best that you keep away."

"I came to help. I mean to help. I have fought with my Father and Mother to come these last days. Must I also go to war

275

with you, even when you need another pair of hands so bad? Anne Barnes is working like any serving maid in the kitchen, your own sisters work at the Hall, helping with laundry and any other way they can. Am I to stand back while they take all the risks - perhaps even to die? Esme is younger than I." She paused for want of breath, her eager face flushed with the battle.

"That is at the Hall, there is some risk there, as there is everywhere - but here!" He waved his arm towards the long line of beds expressively. "Here there be more than a dozen people who," he lowered his voice lest any of his patients should hear, "who are mostly in desperate case. At least half - I have almost no hope of saving. The risk to you would be too great - I should not easily forgive myself ...." He left the sentence unfinished. The sadness and weariness in his voice when he spoke of those who would die, caught at Rachel's heart strings. It showed how over-strained and tired he was under his cheerful exterior. Her stubborn resolve was immediately strengthened.

"My parents were against my coming, but they accept my reasons for doing so".

"If you carry the pestilence to them - perhaps without warning, unwittingly - what then?'

"I have a valise," she pointed in the corner, "with my things - I wondered if I might ask the Rev. Mallard to give me houseroom, I understand that his children are away and that he and Mistress Mallard regularly visit amongst the sick houses, so they are at risk, in any case." Her red lips closed in a tight line. David looked at her, half in admiration, half in exasperation.

"Do you know what you undertake ? Nursing your Mother was one thing, this is no easy illness. Here there is suffering and sights I little like to think of you seeing. Dying of plague is ugly and terrible - there is no dignity. I doubt you could face some of the tasks that must be done."

"I beg you let me try, I am not squeamish, and I am strong and well used to hard work." As she spoke she laid down her bonnet and removed her cloak. Beneath, she wore a work dress and white apron.

"You disrobe as though you are determined to stay. If I so allow, you must promise me something." He frowned as he spoke, the dark brows drawn together.

"Yes, if it be fair and reasonable."

"That you will be guided by me in all things, especially your safety. Fresh air, rest, eating, drinking, changing your clothes, washing - all the things on which our lives depend. It is not easy - the disciplines of the pestilence - not even for me - and I have had much experience."

"I know that you have thought me self-willed and wayward, but I am not foolish - of course, I shall do as a good nurse should - work under the physician's instruction, I only hope I can be useful and not be faint at the first blood." Her hands locked, the fingers twisted together. Her cheeks grew red in her efforts to convince him.

He relented then, thinking how pleasant her company would be to him. Someone to share with him the sadness of the patients in his care. Someone who would laugh sometimes, perhaps. He lifted her cloak and bonnet and carried them outside.

"First bring your valise. I never leave any garment or anything I can help within the barn - I put them here instead." He led her to a small lean-to where some old nails in the wall served for hanging coats. A small table held bottles of red wine and glasses covered with a cloth. He hung her cloak and bonnet.

"When Andrew comes, he will carry your bag to the Parsonage. I make no doubt he will be glad to give you shelter there. Harriet will take pleasure in your company."

At that moment, Charlotte Ainsley arrived in the pony trap from the Hall. David went to meet her with a cheerful greeting.

"Well, Sister, and how does the Hall this morning?"

Charlotte, whose wide skirts were looped up, jumped drown from the trap and tied the pony's reins to an iron stave before replying. Rachel saw that her hair was tied up in a net away from her face. Stout buttoned boots showed beneath her riding outfit skirt. She looked dressed for the occasion and very workmanlike. In the trap, baskets of clean ironed linen were stacked two deep. David Ainsley rolled his sleeves and began to unload the baskets as they talked.

"All at the Hall are much as yesterday. We are becoming short of mint and other herbs for the brew - the gardener says he knows it be mild for March, but he complains that we do pluck the plants near to the ground and give them no time to grow. But with so many wanting the brew, 'tis hard to keep up with filling the jars."

"See if the Park can provide some. Lady Loundes will help all she can. I see you've brought a goodly basket of soft rag - that helps - we need so much."

"Does Mistress Rachel come to help you in the work? 'Tis brave. I dare not go in the barn." Charlotte smiled at Rachel.

"I have tried to dissuade her - I like not the risk." David frowned a little as he spoke, the line between his eyes deepening.

"Well - I'm glad - so will Mother be, for someone to help you, I mean. You risk yourself so many hours every day amongst the Death - and no respite. Our Mother will be deep relieved when I tell her." Charlotte gave her brother a severe look as she spoke.

"'Tis settled now - and I am glad to be able to do something of use. I have felt put to shame by you and your sister and Mistress Anne and the Doctor himself," said Rachel.

"And in truth, I shall be more than glad of the help." David lifted out the last basket as he spoke. Charlotte climbed back into the trap and her brother untied and handed her the reins.

"I'll get back. Is there ought you want?" She tilted her head to hear his reply.

"Only to tell Groves to send the dirty linen cart at about twelve. We'll make the heap here as usual, but I like not that it shall be about long," David reminded her.

"Twelve noon. I shall be sure to tell him. Good Day Mistress Rachel. I wish you well with your first day." She flicked the reins and drove away up the fields.

"Come - let us get started." David began to ferry the baskets into the barn. Rachel helped him. It was easy, they were no heavier than the poultry food buckets she was so used to at home. Before they were done, Andrew Mallard came across the field. He wore his long black vestment and carried a prayer book. He looked tranquil, his fine hair a little ruffled and his thin face curiously unlined for his forty-five years.

"Are you lucky enough to have gained an assistant at last, David?" he asked after greeting them both. David explained what had happened. Andrew Mallard at once said that the Parsonage House would be pleased to find Mistress Rachel a room and any other help she might need.

"Also, we have plenty of hot water! David makes us all wash umpteen times each day, you'll find. 'Tis much like being in the ranks of the King's Army, to be under Dr. Ainsley's charge." Andrew smiled drily. Rachel could see how deep was Andrew Mallard's affection for David, by the humorous tilt of his thin eyebrows as he made this utterance.

"Well - what do you have for me this morning, Doctor?" Andrew called.

"The old one - the very old woman is gone, she lies covered. All the others would like a word. A prayer, perhaps, for those that can appreciate it." David moved back into the barn and took a large pillbox from his table in the corner.

"Here - take one before you begin." He offered the box to Andrew.

Andrew took one - put it in his mouth and moved away towards the first bed.

"And we must each do the same. They are not unpleasant. Put it in the side of your mouth and keep it there while you are with the patients. It is part of our protection. Now, let me just explain the routine. Charlotte comes every morning with the fresh linen. We go to each bed, make changes of linen where needed, dress the blains, and some are foul and the stench is bad, I must warn you. We throw all soiled linen into these bins. I lance and clean and give medication as I go - it saves disturbing the very sick so many times. There are fifteen patients here. We had sixteen, an old woman died in the night. Rev. Mallard goes his round ahead of us. When we are done I roll the bins out and make a heap on the earth. We do not handle the dirty linen again. No one does. A cart will come with a couple of men with forks and hooks. It is carted away up to the laundry room at the Hall. Another cart will also come. Andrew will tell Tom Hart, the Sexton. He will dig a grave for the old one. It may appear like unseemly haste but it has to be. The sooner the dead are buried, the better and safer for those still alive." His eyes were very gentle as he explained to her. He went on speaking,

"It's better that you understand what has to be done. Remember, we are very few in numbers - we can only do our best. If you feel you may vomit or faint at any time, leave me and go into the fresh air. It will revive you. There are red wine and glasses in the lean-to - we must take at least four glasses each and every day. There is a rough privy behind the barn. It is long since I worked with a Lady. If you need to leave me for a few minutes - don't ask - just go - I shall do likewise - I dislike false modesty in these matters. I expect, as a farmer's daughter, you are the same?"

Her eyes came up to meet his. "Yes, it's true, I am the same. I thank you for making all so plain. I shall hope not to disgrace you in a faint on my first day."

"Very well - let us begin - 'Tis usually an hour and a half's work. Afterwards I've some visits in the village, to the plague houses, mostly."

As soon as they passed beyond the curtain, Rachel was aware of a different atmosphere. There was a feeling of expectation in the very air, yet it was not a happy expectation. It was compiled of several ingredients, predominant was the strange smell, a smell of disinfectant, sweat, human bodies and .... fear. It was dim and quiet here under the high hammer beam roof. The four window openings had never been glazed. This suited David. He had had netting hung inside. This let in air but kept out insects. Light came in but the thick walls created their own cool dimness. David Ainsley, or any other medical man, would have identified the smell here as a smell of death. Rachel had no experience of death. The smell gave her a feeling of tension and insecurity. The hard earth floor seemed suddenly not quite stable beneath her feet. She steadied herself with determination and went to the first bed with Dr. Ainsley. This was the women's section. In this bed lay the housemaid from the Hall. All her country girl bloom was gone, she had been in fever for three days and had lost a lot of flesh. Looking down at her, Rachel's fears evaporated in a wave of compassion.

"I expect you know Jenny from the Hall?" David said gently. "She has been most poorly, but is better today. Is it not so, my Dear?"

"Aye, Doctor - thank'ee." The voice was so thin and small that it startled Rachel. David turned back the covers and examined the girl.

After a moment he said, "There now - that's good. Now we

shall want a fresh bed gown and a length of linen to lay under her. If you would fetch them from the baskets?" Rachel went to do his bidding, when she returned she saw that he had gone to the end of the barn where the log fire burned in the open hearth. Here on a long table were earthenware bowls and squares of yellow soap on a tray. Over the fire, on two great hooks, hung two big iron kettles. Nearby a covered wooden barrel held cold water. David came back to Jane's bed with a dish of warm water. Rachel watched him wash the patient and change her gown and bed sheet. There was no feeling of false modesty. The girl was too ill and wasted, Ainsley too professional and neat. As he worked he made very little conversation and yet just enough to give comfort to his patient.

"The sun shines today, Jenny, we'll need to get you well soon, then you can have a week or two at home with your Mother, in the sunshine."

"Aye, Sur - t'would be nice that - real nice. Did ..... did the old lady die, Sur?"

"Yes - I'm afraid she did - she was very old, Jenny, she's at peace now."

"She were that kind to me - she was more worried that I get well than fer her sen." Tears pressed under the lashes onto the thin white cheeks. Rachel took a clean square of cloth and gently wiped them away. Then she bent to speak to the girl.

"There now - she'd not have had you crying over her. Keep brave - you are doing well." Rachel found the words of comfort came easily to her and that she had spoken them without thinking. She felt a little surprised at herself.

"That was kind - well done, Mistress Rachel," David approved her as they moved away. The next two beds were empty. Blankets and linen lay folded and ready. Patients were brought here at all times. Day and night. The next bed held the body of the old woman who had died. A linen cloth covered it completely, but could not hide the grim outline. Rachel forced her eyes to look and then she walked on. She felt David Ainsley's comforting hand under her elbow as he guided her beyond another bed length curtain into the men's section.

Here they spent what for Rachel, this first time, was an hour of horror, redeemed only by Dr. Ainsley's compassionate dealings with every patient. At each bed the routine was the same. Careful examination - treatments where needed. Washing the patient and changing the linen, then on to the next bed. Ainsley made no attempt to spare Rachel. She had never seen a man naked before. She saw many that morning. Two of them had septic swellings deep in the groin. Another had a similar swelling in his armpit. All three Ainsley skilfully opened. Laying cloths to catch the vile smelling blood and pus which came from them, he showed Rachel how to fold away these cloths, turning the edges quickly inwards, trapping and covering the discharge.

"We must not spill any of this evil matter - 'tis full of infection." David had a big deep bucket into which all such horrible debris was flung. Rachel fought valiantly against the sick repulsion which swept over her at these indescribable sights and smells.

She saw for the first time the round pus spots ringed with red which were the hallmark of Plague's beginnings. On some men she saw the under skin reddish-blue rash known as 'Tokens'. Ainsley pointed out these things and quietly showed her how to clean and dress a lanced wound. How to turn a heavy man over to slip clean sheeting beneath his body. How to slide her arm beneath a heavy patient to lift him up in bed to enable him to take a drink.

"This cordial is a herb drink - the more they can take the better. It washes through and cleanses the bloodstream."

At last the mornings round was finished. Together they cleared up. Dirty water was tipped into two buckets. Ainsley put a handful of grey powder into each. It gave off a strong acrid smell. Later he flung the water away in the grass, well away from the barn.

"Disinfectant - nothing else to be done with it. Expertly he trundled the two barrels of soiled linen outside, tipping them into a heap.

"Just a minute - one more thing." He came back and tipped the bucket with the vile residue from the wounds into the hot ash of the fire. It hissed and belched smoke for a moment. David laid more logs across and swept up the ash. Rachel thought how tidy it all looked after this dedicated man's hard work. Many of those in the beds still moaned and tossed in pain, but some seemed more rested. Some lay quiet. The most restless was Francis Trewis, he was hot and constantly shifting and moving.

"He has been days in fever - it wears a man out," David explained quietly. In the next bed lay Albert, Francis's eldest son, white and exhausted against his pillow. It was he who had had the great swelling in his armpit. David Ainsley paused by his bed, laying a hand on his shoulder. "Easier now, Albert?"

"Aye, Doctor - but it's tired me - I'm fairly done in."

"Rest now - it's the sepsis - it wearies the best of men."

"How does my Father?"

"We can't tell that until the fever breaks - I don't expect it to last much longer. You may comfort yourself - he doesn't feel much or know himself to be so restless."

"You be real good to us all."

"That's what I'm here for, my friend."

"Aye - but there ent many as ud do what you do - ent much cop for the young lady neither."

"We shall both do well enough. Rest now. I'll be back to see you later on." David piloted Rachel outside.

"Come into the fresh air. It gets putrid in here - however much we try to keep the air moving - you are not used to it either." As she came through the doors and into the green world of Springtime once more, Rachel was horrified to find herself becoming faint. She stumbled, feeling the ground beginning to tilt.

"So silly - when I thought I had been ...." David Ainsley caught her as she fell. When she came to herself she lay a little way from the barn, on the sweet grass of a bank. A wave of sickness followed which she could not control. She leaned over to vomit, and found his arm supporting her and her head gently held. When it was over she lay back exhausted but furious with herself.

"What a useless person I am - seemingly another patient - instead of a help to you," she gasped out.

"No! No! It was too much for your first time within that place - you did very well, indeed I blame myself for letting you stay in that bad air too long. Come along." Gently he helped her back to nearer the lean-to. He fetched a chair and pressed her into it.

"Now sit here in the sunshine while I get us both some wine." When he brought the glasses it sparkled and glowed red in the sunlight.

"I shall be sick again, if I touch it."

"No - on the contrary, it will settle your stomach. It is not sweet, but it is the best antidote to plague that I know. Come - drink up - then you have finished for your first day. Andrew has taken your bag to the Parsonage - you go along there. Remember to wash well and change your clothes. Put the used clothes out with Mistress Mallard's soiled wear. She will instruct you. Will you have enough clothing? You will find you need several changes - especially day gowns?"

"I have three more work dresses in my bag - shall I come this evening?"

"If you wish - but rest first and Mistress Mallard will see that you eat a good meal." He smiled to see her grimace at the mention of food.

"What about you, Doctor - I feel I do not help you much."

"You will soon learn - let us make haste slowly, Now run along. I don't want you to remain in that soiled gown." He watched her walk away across the field. In the sunshine her hair shone. She did not look back until she reached the gate. Then she turned, her cloak and bonnet dangled from one hand. She raised the other to wave to him. He gave an answering salute and then returned to his patients.

Ten minutes later, Tom Hart came with the dead cart to fetch the body of the old woman. Soon after that, Groves came with the dirty linen cart. Later again, Esme came from the Hall with the pony and trap. This time it was loaded with pans of broth and stone jars of cordial, a crock of fresh boiled milk and some linen parcels of fresh bread.

"How long, I wonder, until this desolate traffic may cease?" Ainsley mused to himself. It was a question to which he had no answer.

CHAPTER IX

CHAPTER IX

By the end of April twenty-three people had died in the two villages. Many were still very sick. Each cottage had become an isolated unit. All were in fear of human contact with their neighbours. There was still one small meeting point amongst the village folk. In the 'Dingle' beside the lane between Glebe Cottage and Wych Cottage Andrew held a short service each Sunday. It was a sheltered peaceful place. He would stand on a small mound in the bottom of the steep banked green dell. In his hand a bible and prayer book. The ever diminishing congregation would stand on the banks in small family groups, keeping apart from neighbours. Some, weak from nursing or recovering themselves from the dread illness, would sit in the short grass amongst the whin bushes. Andrew gave them no sermon. Prayers were said and a short piece read from the bible. Then Andrew would give them any Parish news and instructions for their health from Dr. Ainsley. It was a moving and tragic moment which then followed. David would step down beside Andrew Mallard and read out the list of names of those who had died since the previous Sunday. Often members of the families named would be present. They would move closer together, their sobs the only sound in the silence which followed the reading of their dear ones' names. Around them the scent of violets and primroses. The joyous singing of the birds. On one Sunday there came the first call of the cuckoo. Beneath their feet the perfumed carpet of flowers, above them the blue sky and sunshine. So much joy coupled with so much sorrow moved many to tears. The service ended with the reading of the twenty-third psalm. Then the people would slip away in their ones and twos to face the unknown perils of another lonely terrible week.

At nights now every window where life remained, burned its small candle. David Ainsley, often in the villages after dark - moved from tiny beacon to tiny beacon, a prayer on his lips at every garden gate.

The villages stood alone in their grief. The boundaries were now closed to all traffic. Andrew Mallard had persuaded his flock that, unless they so confine themselves, the pestilence would creep and spread to other villages round about. The two parishes were now within the circle of an imaginary cordon which included the valley and the hillside of Upper Telso. It was agreed that none must go beyond the edge of the moorland to the East and West. No one to pass beyond the banks of the Cliven above Higher Telso. The edge of the lane beyond Hill Farm which wound round the back of Seckington Hall formed the North Eastern boundary. This left Chalfont and Seckington village outside the limits. Both were so far free from plague. To the South the Mere and the Southern wall of the Quarry formed a natural boundary. It did not however succeed in confining the Romanies.

David Ainsley had formed the habit of walking a mile or so in the fresh air any evening when he could spare such precious time. Striding along Rock Bottom Lane he found solace in the peace of Low Wood and often stood a few minutes on Brays Bridge listening to the bird song and the sound of the Cliven as it trickled the stones. Beyond the bridge lay the open moor. Here rocks had been thrust into the road and against one a board planted in the earth. On it the great red painted cross. Below the words in rough painted letters 'Lord have mercy on us'. No other warning was needed to keep travellers away. Similar boards stood sentinel on every road to the villages. Since they were erected no one had come beyond their dire warning.

Now that the villages were closed, David Ainsley's medical supplies and all other goods from the outside world were deposited with Bernard Bistock at Chalfont. Twice each week all such items were loaded into his cart and taken to the footbridge at Chalfont Well and here left at the side of the track. Lord Ainsley sent Esme and Charlotte to collect the supplies with pony and trap. Everything was then distributed from the Hall. Money for goods was paid in coins. The coins were left in the low stone trough at Chalfont Well. Here ran the moving stream, cleaning and purifying the money. Bernard Bistock collected all such monies and paid those who supplied the goods. Before plague went from the villages it was not unusual to see basins of water by the cottage gates. Into these money given in payment was dropped for cleansing.

One evening David had walked to Brays Bridge, Andrew

Mallard had freed him by giving an hour's service in the barn. It being fine and dry and the air full of bird song, he decided to walk back through Quarry Bottom and across Potters Paddock. David had seen nothing of the Romanies since the plague had begun again in earnest: in February. When he reached the clearing at the bottom of the cliffs he pulled up short. The gypsy caravans were gone. No piebald ponies cropped the grass. Only the oblong bald patches in the grass where the vans had stood, and the blackened ash rings from fires long dead remained. He stood a moment astonished. As long as he could remember Black Dyer had held sway in the Quarry. In summer his sons might come and go, some of the vans travelling South for the fairs and the seasonal farm work. But always Dyer himself had stayed, laying his claim to this sheltered private camping ground, keeping the woods 'warm' for next winter's poaching.

They must have packed up and slipped away unnoticed under cover of darkness. He wondered when, no need now to try and impose any ban on Black Dyer's movements. They must have got wind of plague and fled.

"Rats from a sinking ship perhaps, or migrating birds? Depends how you rate it, I suppose," David murmured to himself.

He passed on through the deserted camp and climbed the stile to Potters Paddock. It grew dusk now. As he passed Church Cot and Thatchers Cot he saw the candles beginning to cast their glow across the window sills. Glebe Cottage stood in darkness. Empty since George Swift and Tom Cater had died, nor had Jack Acres escaped plague's evil touch. He had been brought to the barn ill and had fought hard for his life for over a week. In the end he had died from the poison of a great carbuncle which David had tried unsuccessfully to cut away.

Lower House Farm had endured more than its share of suffering. Francis Trewis, after a long period of fever, had broken out in 'tokens' and died quickly. His son Albert had followed him to the grave less than a week later. Francis's wife Amanda had never reached the shelter of the barn. Her daughter Velvet had found her lying dead against the cowshed wall one afternoon when she went to collect the eggs. Amanda had not been outside long enough to be missed, yet on her body Tom Hart and David Ainsley found patches of 'tokens'. She had complained of a headache and feeling tired - nothing more.

Lying in the barn near to where his Father and brother had so recently been, William Trewis had experienced sickness and fever and slipped into the deep sleep from which victims so rarely wakened. At the farm this left Johnny Trewis aged twenty-three and Armstrong, his sixteen year old brother, to run the farm where previously there had been three more men in the family. They had to cope with the same amount of work. Now there was no Mother at the helm in the house. Velvet stepped sadly into Amanda's shoes to run the house. In a few weeks she matured from carefree girlhood into a serious faced woman. All the maternal love in her nature rushed forth to wrap itself about young Arms and her baby sister Hannah.

Raven Dyer helped all she could. Johnny Trewis was now the head of the household. A quiet steady, slow to anger young man, responsibility settled upon him easily. His open face and shock of reddish curls, so unlike the usual dark Trewis men, endeared him to the whole village. He was naturally protective of his sisters. He made himself now a strong corner post for Velvet to lean upon during the time when in the secrecy of her bedroom she wept bitter tears of loneliness for the Mother taken from her so suddenly. Johnny saw the sweetness in Raven Dyer almost from the moment his Mother was laid in her grave near his Father. From that very evening she strove to give comfort to Velvet who could not keep back her tears. She would break down even as she tried to prepare a meal or carry out her ordinary duties. Always Raven's arms would come about her and would bring kind words to console her.

As the days passed Johnny found his thoughts resting more and more on Raven. In his work about the yards he would watch for her coming across the orchard with a basket of laundry, or taking pails of water to the hens. It happened very quickly for him, this falling deep in love with Raven.

One evening, two weeks after Amanda Trewis's death, David Ainsley came to see them. They were all in the house - their simple meal finished. Johnny saw Ainsley through the window as he came across the yard and knew by his face what he had come to say.

"'Tis Doctor comes across the yard. I'm afraid 'tis bad with William."

"Oh No!" Velvet's hand flew to her face, "Are none of us to live? Are we all to die - one by one?" Tears started again in her eyes as Dr. Ainsley knocked and entered. His sad face spoke his news before he even opened his mouth.

"Willie?" Velvet voiced the single word. Ainsley came to her and put his arm about her as he tried to comfort her.

"T'was no use, Lass - he had more of the rash than any I've seen."

"I don't know if I can bear it - are we all to die, Doctor? Some houses it .... it hasn't even touched." She burst into more desperate weeping.

Raven moved across the kitchen; she had not spoken, bending she picked up little Hannah from the child's chair. The little girl in her red smock dress and laced boots was almost in tears herself. The rounded lips trembled, upset and uncertain by her elder sister's weeping. Raven put the little one into Velvet's arms and guided them to the ingle seat against the fire.

"Sit with the bab, my dear. She do need 'ee so much now her Mam is gone. I'll see to the dishes - you rest whiles." Velvet still wept but she hugged the little girl to her. Hannah's chubby arms came round her sister's neck and the dimpled childish face was pushed tight against her sister's cheek.

Two days later Johnny Trewis went into the barn for a batten of straw after milking was done. Raven was up the stack collecting eggs from the rogue nests. She put her feet over the side of the straw pile and slithered to get down. Johnny stepped close and put out his arms. She had no choice but to land within them. He knew nothing of wooing - only the lonely expectancy of the ugly death which seemed to lie in wait for them all. Only how much he wanted her. His arms drew her tight against him. Her small breasts came each in turn under his hands. His mouth sought hers, found it and drew life from the warm fullness of her lips. She made no resistance. She had never given him a thought as a man or a lover, but at his first touch she woke to him. She had never loved, never been loved or wanted. Had she not been

291

waiting for this? She felt the fire in Johnny's body through her gown, and only wanted that it should burn more fierce. She was not afraid - her only fear was that he should let her out of his arms leaving unanswered the passion of her gypsy blood. Leave her to fall back into the dreary, dark, hopeless world in which they had all lived so much of late. He began to fumble with her gown, clumsy and inexperienced.

"Help me! I must have thee - I've wanted to - I've wanted." His hardness thrust vainly against her - entangled with the stuff of her dress.

"Come - come through t o the hay - 'tis dark there - none shall come to startle us." She pulled him after her through the narrow doorway to where the hay was stored. A moment later they lay in the soft sweet scents of dried grasses. Her skirts pulled up by her own hands, she gave him no delay. He fumbled with shaking hands at his breeches. It was she who unbuttoned them to free him. He arched his back and then with one deep downward thrust he was within her, giving a half gasp of joy and release. She felt one sharp stab of pain as her virgin's skin was ruptured. Then only warmth and joy in the quickening of their union. She cried out several times. When it was over he still held her as if he would never let her go.

"I can't be sorry - never sorry, little Raven - you knows that I has to have thee. Something warm that lives. Something so full of good. 'Tis to wed thee I wants - mek no mistake - always, always I wants you - since that very first day you come. We - we may die but none can tek this from us can they?"

"No. Oh no, never - but us shan't die. Us must promise that mustn't we?"

"Yes - yes, my love - but if it should befall - you will know - know how I do treasure thee." They kissed, gently rovingly and held each other very close amongst the soft hay.

CHAPTER X

CHAPTER X

The Park had remained almost untouched by plague. The household had known fear and sadness when David Oaks, the stable boy, and Andrew Tysen, the head gardener, had died. But they were not 'of the house'. Both had lived in the cottages along the lane near the Inn. The House had remained free, all the staff fit and well, due in part to Lady Loundes's fortitude and good sense. She kept her servants and family away from the villages and watched over the storing of food. The household staff all lived in and since the coming of the Death had not ventured outside the grounds.

After Jonathon's passing, Lady Jane Loundes had quietly moved back into the main house. The staff, especially Mason the butler and Mrs. Burns the Cook, had welcomed her Ladyship's coming with sighs of relief. Elizabeth Ainsley was still in a sorry state, she had become vague and withdrawn. Her beauty fading in her inward looking dreamlike behaviour. She seemed unable to take in even the ordinary domestic affairs which went on around her.

Lady Loundes slipped easily into the long familiar management of the household. Changes were at once in evidence. Boys whistled once more as they mucked out loose-boxes. Gardeners rested occasionally on their spades enjoying a pipe of baccy. Maids hummed tunes and flicked dusters in a new relaxed way. Flowers filled vases, spilling perfume into the lavender polished sitting rooms. Cook and Mistress met each day in the morning room in homely friendship to plan roasts and pies and syllabubs and tasty dishes to tempt Elizabeth. Lady Loundes sent many items of food to Lord Ainsley's kitchens to support the plague victims but her first concern was for her beloved daughter, restored to her in such poor health and spirits.

Elizabeth kept much to herself. None knew what she had suffered She never spoke of her marriage. Dr. Davis, the medic from Wesperton, who had come with the magistrates at the time of Jonathon's death had been much concerned at the young Widow's lost vitality and obvious ill health. He had called and made his addresses to Lady Loundes, offering his advice and services to help her bring about Elizabeth's recovery.

295

Since then he had called once or twice each week, running the gauntlet of crossing the 'closed road' from the mill bridge to the Park gates. At his instigation Lady Loundes had moved Elizabeth from the marriage bedroom back into the humbler, smaller room at the side of the house, which had been hers as a girl. It was a sunlit cheerful room and Elizabeth's health improved from the first night she slept there. Dr. Davis was a quiet man, he was square made, stocky, sharp eyed and sensible. His short curled hair was cut unfashionably short, showing well shaped ears. He had no fancy ideas, was against bleeding his patients and favoured nature's own remedies. He made no demands on Elizabeth at all. He strongly advised Lady Loundes to do the same. He advocated rest and quiet, fresh air and no ordered routine as the best possible medication.

Elizabeth, left thus to herself, began slowly to mend, she still experienced terrible nightmares, waking at times soaked in sweat, to see Jonathon with whip poised, towering over the bed. The image would at once fade, but it was no less terrifying for that. In spite of these continuing dreams, gradually the colour began to return to Elizabeth's cheeks and the hollows in her flesh to fill out once more. Cook and Mason discussed it in the kitchen.

"I reckon she do begin to mend at last." Cook's plump hand poured hot fat expertly over the two capons she was turning on the spit as she spoke.

"Aye. 'Tis slow, but us is lucky she has that Dr. Davis as is so quiet and nice with she. If she'd fallen in with some Quack as bled 'er every five minutes and poured they sick physics down she, then likely it 'ud be a different tale".

Mason stood with his thick legs apart, standing to warm his breeches at the heat of the fire. A knowing look upon his broad round face.

"I does quite like 'un - but 'twas Dr. Ainsley as I took to," said Cook firmly. "Handsome, he were, a real handsome Gentleman."

"That's natural - son of a Lord 'ee be - the quality, that's what. I don't reckon there'll ever be comings and goings 'atween Park and Hall agin in our times, Cook."

"They'll never come together agin, you means?"

'Tis over. That romance. It were in Dr. Ainsley's face - that day he come to young Ilsa."

"Maybe for best - change the name, they does say!" Cook pushed him away and shut the oven door with a slam of finality as she spoke.

"Dinner be up - you going to stand all day then, Mr. Mason, or be you gonna stir them fat legs and sound the gong?"

Mason, recognising female supremacy at once when he saw it, retreated to the outer hall.

By the middle of June it had become very warm. There had been very little rain that spring and early summer. Heat began to build up and the lanes and paths grew dusty. The barn, thick walled and shaded by the new thatched roof, only finished by Thatcher Gibbs a few months before, remained cool and comforting to those who lay sick.

David and Rachel now worked well together and a smooth running routine was established. The morning's work, with its often unpleasant jobs, now took them a little less time. Often Rachel would move on ahead amongst the beds, leaving David to lance a wound or cut a festering carbuncle. She could wash a patient, clean vile wounds without vomiting, apply dressings with neat fingers and manage alone. She had mastered the knack of turning a heavy patient over in bed, helping a man pass his water and many other often not very pleasant duties. The patients warmed to her - her low sweet voice and the soothing kindness of her hands gave comfort even to those most sick.

David Ainsley was secretly immensely proud of her. Only on one point was he adamant. He never let her touch the dead - it was a kind of fad with him. Nearly all who died had the death rash of 'Tokens', he dreaded her hand upon them. Because of it, Plague victims were not washed or 'laid out' in the normal decent Christian way. David recalled with horror scenes in London where human remains had been thrown in dreadful piles of unshrouded bodies into the pits. Here, at risk to himself and Tom Hart, he never allowed such burials to occur. It was his habit to remove and burn all septic dressings, straighten limbs and lay a clean length of sheeting over each body. When Tom Hart came with the dead cart the sheeting was used as a wrap around shroud and went with the corpse to the grave. This prohibited the risk involved in washing, touching and handling bodies more than was absolutely necessary. David changed his shirt, stock, breeches and hose at least twice daily. All his clothes and Rachel's were carried away to be washed and boiled in Charlotte's make-shift laundry, or the Parsonage House coppers. It was a necessary safeguard, to which Ainsley firmly believed they owed their lives.

It was not all gloom and death, however. David never quite knew when it was that he began to enjoy the evenings, he only knew that it came to him one day that he now looked forward to dusk falling upon No Man's Barn. It was their routine to finish the morning round by twelve noon. David then stayed to deal with the laundry and to help Tom Hart when it was necessary for a burial to take place. After that food would be brought from the Hall by Esme or Charlotte with the pony trap. David would carry food to all in the barn who were able to eat or drink. By then Andrew Mallard would come across the fields for his second visit of the day. Andrew would remain with the patients while David took a two hour break at Crab Tree. At home he would relax, wash, change, rest and take his main meal of the day.

During the afternoon Rachel would walk back from the Parsonage where she also had washed and changed her gown, enjoyed a meal with Harriet Mallard and rested in her room for an hour. From then on their routine varied, sometimes patients needed comfort, sometimes a herb drink, sometimes a new patient had to be brought in from the village and sometimes, sadly much less often, a patient had to be taken home to his family. These were the lucky few - over the worst of their illness, but weak and much in need of careful nursing.

When darkness began to fall the atmosphere in the barn changed. David was continually amazed at the courage of his patients. He had disciplined himself to accept that most of those who came to the barn would never return to their families. He railed against his lack of knowledge of his enemy, having to be content with the certainty that without his care even more would have died. Often members of a family coming to the barn saved from infection those left at home. The closed up houses of London had shown David proof of that. There a whole family often died, none left of ten or a dozen people.

Yet the men and women in the barn, many of whom were near to death, would still display courage and humour. At dusk they would light the candles. Eight candles burned through the night. Many were sent by Andrew Mallard, church candles paid for out of his own pocket. Lord Ainsley also supplied many of the candles used. Four were placed on four up-turned barrels down the barn centre - where all the sick could see them and draw comfort from the steady burning flames through the dark watches of the night. The other four candles Rachel placed on the wide sills; these could be seen by the villagers, from them every cottage and farmhouse could draw comfort and hope in the certainty that there was life in the barn and that their dear ones were being cared for.

David spent some time each evening writing up the day's log. It was a habit left from his Navy days. However bad the day had been, the written word left his mind uncluttered and clear, once it was writ neat in the log book. He would sit at his small table, the curtain drawn back, giving him a view of the whole length of the building. At the far end the crackling blaze of the log fire, only built up at night now, for then the great building grew cold. From where he sat, the fire was a cheering sight. Between, along either wall, the rows of beds, each with its shadowed form. Some lying still, some restless in fever. Rachel moved about a lot in the evenings, sponging faces, shaking pillows, giving words of comfort and sometimes singing. David found great strength and pleasure in seeing her so. It began when the first children came to the barn. After John Symes died, two of his children became ill. Cathy, John's wife, was still well, so was her son, the lad who had fetched David on the night Emmy Bones gave birth to her child. David persuaded Cathy to send the two little girls into his care. David had put them side by side in the women's area of the barn. In the evenings Rachel would sit by them, telling them stories and singing them songs. One evening she chose by chance Greensleeves. Its lovely haunting melody caught at more hearts than just the children's. Arthur Dale, after the fight of his life, was at last unbelievably on the mend. He spoke for all of them.

"Sing it agin', Mistress Rachel - does me good, does that." Rachel complied and as she sang walked up and down between the rows of beds. She had a lovely low voice warm as honey. David, like the rest, watched her and listened to every word. After that it became an every evening pleasure for them all. She sang the old country songs that had been sung on the farm all the seasons through for as long as any of them could remember. But their favourite was Greensleeves. In the candle-light her performance had a magic quality. In the daylight, under the summer sun, Rachel was a bonny, robust, pretty faced young woman. A country beauty of rich honey gold hair and warm brown eyes. In the candlelight she was beautiful, her hair turned to transparent silver her skin to cream. Her full breasts and hips, soft shadowed by the candlelight, matured her to womanhood. It brought out in her a quality in her which David likened to an angel an angel of mercy. In part it was the emotion roused by the singing, but there was in it also a motherliness - a tenderness which he had never noticed in her before.

As David listened he was suddenly caught in a great rush of feeling. He wanted to leap from his chair, run to her and grasp her in his arms, to carry her away - far away from the dangers of the faceless, fanged serpent which lurked under every blanket and on every poisoned body in this vile place. He felt sweat run down his face and back, he at last conquered the feeling, but could no longer keep his mind upon his writing. A few minutes later he got up and went out to the lean-to for her cloak. His eyes scanned the starlit sky. It was a dark blue velvet night. The vast heavens made no answer to his upturned questioning gaze. When his eyes came back to earth he knew himself to have fallen deep in love.

When he returned to the barn, she was in the women's area, bending low over the two little girls, they were both very sick but the youngest had been weakened more than her sister Kate. Neither yet showed 'tokens' but the tiny girl had had two nasty tumours which David had been forced to lance that morning. The child was only four. She had cried and screamed and struggled. Rachel had held her and helped to clean the septic matter away. Afterwards she had comforted the little one and many times during the day David had found her by the child's bed. He went now behind her and put his hand on her arm. "Time for you to get away to the Parsonage, I'll walk with you to the gate."

She turned and followed him out of the building, they set off across the turf towards the main path which led into Home Field. It was dark under the stars but a half moon gave some light from beyond the woodlands. Neither spoke until they reached the main path. The desire to protect her was still strong in him, but he knew her independent spirit.

"You seem a little tired today, Mistress Rachel." He still used the formal address, she never having encouraged otherwise - usually she addressed him simply as 'Doctor'. There was a frankness between them which was born of a shared contact with sickness and human bodies of both sexes. It would have been quite out of place in any other circumstances, it was responsible for her reply now.

"No, it's nothing, Doctor - just that I'm a little unwell, as a woman is at times."

"You should have told me - I would not have allowed you to come back this evening had I known."

"But you are just as weary. I did not wish to leave you to struggle alone. It's been so warm today, soon it will be July. Do you at times feel that these dreadful days will ..... will never end?" Her voice broke and he felt her to be more depressed than ever before.

"It's the children, is it not? The little girls? It's hard for a woman, suffering in the children." His voice held a great tenderness such as he had not shown her before.

"I would so love to save them. Is there nothing else we can do? They are so small - already so dear to me."

"My dear, I know - I could see it today, but we can only hope and pray, like with the rest."

"They have no 'Tokens'."

"No but 'tis early days yet. You must try to clear your mind when you leave the barn. Return to it fresh each day. Mind, I'm a good one for such speech - I feel I carry every one of those desperate souls with me for every step of every day. But for you - one day you will have sons and daughters - babies of your own. Pin your mind upon that. I think .... that you .... will make a wonderful Mother - as you are an excellent nurse."

He strove to keep his voice ordinary and steady. She blushed deep in the darkness and was unable to reply. They walked on in silence and reached the gate. It stood wide. With such constant trafficking to and fro from the barn, Johnny Trewis had taken the hay crop off Home Field but had not put any stock in since. In consequence the grass grew lush again. Rachel felt it wet with dew about her skirts. The gate stood open day and night for all the carts and traps to come and go freely. David felt a sudden reluctance to let her go from him.

"I'll bid you good night then, Doctor." Her voice was small, distancing her from him in its formality. She began to walk away from him in the direction of the Parsonage. The silver moonlight touched her light hair and illuminated the soft green of her cloak.

"Rachel!" It was spoken low but it was yet a command.

"Yes?" She turned, startled, he had never used her Christian name unprefixed before.

"Greensleeves. I was thinking of the song - and of your green cloak."

"Oh, I see." But she did not see.

"If we ..... if I should come out of this .... this bad time alive, would you consider being *my* Lady Greensleeves?"

"It grows late. I think - I think you tease me, Sir."

"You are indeed right. It does grow late. You are also wrong. I do not tease you or mock you." There was a sadness in his voice now. "I shall expect to see you in the morning. Good night, Rachel." He turned on his heel and strode back across the field.

Rachel ran on up the drive and into the security of the Parsonage House. Her head was filled with a tumult of thoughts. Her heart pounded, he could not have meant it. She went through to the back of the house, all was quiet. She carried with her the candle which Harriet always left lit on the hall table for her use if they had already retired. In the back kitchen a clean blue day gown hung from a peg by the door, a pair of slippers reposed beneath; she slipped out of her clothes and plunged them straight into the copper in the corner. The smell of disinfectant rose from the disturbed water. Andrew, Harriet and Rachel all used this method of protection. Rachel stood a moment and slipped on the day dress. There would be cold food set out in the dining room but she wanted nothing tonight.

A few minutes later, candle in hand, she slipped into the quiet of her room upstairs. She loved this room although it was not large. The window faced across Big Fields to Telso Woods. If she looked across to the left she could distinguish the outline of No Man's Barn, dim in the moonlight. In daytime she could also see the churchyard which nowadays made such a cheerless picture. At night the dark yews mercifully cast shadows which hid most of the new graves. Looking across the Glebe Land she could see the Lower House, it's high chimneys and steep roof, the low cow house and farm buildings. The long staircase window there glowed. The customary single candle gave out it's staunch message of hope.

Rachel drew away from the window and pulled the curtain across. On the washstand a jug of water stood ready and beside it a glass and a carafe of red wine, which was part of Dr. Ainsley's caring for her welfare. Rachel did not have much taste for wine but she poured a glass and downed it with a childlike grimace of distaste. She slipped out of the work dress and began to wash her body carefully. Her skin was clear and creamy, the breasts high and firm, fuller than was fashionable. Her body and legs were firm and strong. She was not tall but there was shapely sturdiness about her which was womanly and very much of the countryside from which she came. She always took pleasure in the cleanliness of her person. Tonight, as always after being in the barn, she felt soiled and sticky. This was accentuated by the cloth she must wear for her flux. It was past now and she dropped the soiled rag into the bucket beneath the washstand, feeling pleasure as women do in being without it. She tidied the washstand and brushed out her hair. Reaching for her nightgown she put it over her head. It was home-spun but had a little lace at the cuffs and neck. She looked very young and desirable; if he could have seen her, David Ainsley's vision of her as an angel would have been confirmed.

For a few minutes she knelt at the bedside, her prayers were childlike, spilling out according to her needs, mostly centred on her family at home at Chalfont, and those who lay in the barn, especially the little girls. Tonight she added a word about Dr. Ainsley.

"Oh Lord, let it be Thy will to keep my dear Doctor safe from the perils and dangers of this night. Let him think of me as I do of him - but if he does not - and will not - then let me not make myself foolish. Amen." This seemed to her muddled, perhaps the good Lord would unravel her meaning and be able to understand even if not to grant her wishes.

A few minutes later she lay under the covers, she tried to bring to mind all that David Ainsley had said to her but after a few minutes she became drowsy and quickly fell asleep.

July faded into August in a blaze of sunshine, across Big Fields, Long Fields and Gleaners Acre, the corn began to change colour. Bright patches of scarlet poppies swayed a little in the breeze. On some of the corn stalks fat harvest mice clung to the ears of corn, busy with sharp teeth nibbling to reach the sweet centre of the ripening grain.

The Cliven ran sluggish and slow, Old Albert Dale, fetching water in two buckets for Wood Cottage, had to scramble up stream for fifty yards to find pools deep enough to fill them to the brim. He did so with a good heart; in spite of everything he was a happy man, he thanked God humbly every day, that he, an old man of nearly eighty, should have been spared to care for Arthur and Eliza. Arthur was home again now - thin and gaunt - but alive! Both he and Eliza still needed care. Albert took great pride in being the one to give them that care. Pleasure in the cooking of simple meals and keeping the place clean, against the day when the plague would be over and done and the Babe could come home.

As he came back along the lane he stopped, set down the heavy buckets and peered over the hedge at Wych Cottage. A cheerful voice hailed him.

"Hello there then, Albert. I got him here, by the gate - you cum an' look." Albert picked up the buckets and advanced along the lane to the small wicket gate where he again came to a halt. His gaze went over the palings, his old eyes bright and expectant in his wrinkled brown face. Betsy Price stood there, round faced and cheerful, a chubby baby boy chuckled and wriggled up and down in her arms.

"'Ent 'ee lovely? Don't 'ee come on?"

"Aye, an he's a dead spit of his Mam. Does give me good heart to see un so bonny."

"Let's hope I can soon bring him home, Albert - not but John and I shall miss him when he do go - I'll tell 'ee that."

"You'm best keep him a bit whiles yet. Dr. Ainsley did say don'ee tek any risks, us at Wood shall abide by all he do say."

"Of course, Albert - the Death still keeps on dreadful, don't it? John has kip the Smithy open but he does all the shoeing outside in the open air. Not much work on, truly. With the village closed up, there's none comes in from Seckington way. Seems never ending, don' it?"

"Aye it does, and them two little gels, Cathy Symes's little uns, us heard as Dr. Ainsley do have they in the barn now."

"Please God - they be spared. Cathy have lost her man - some seems to be struck time and time agin. Like Lower House - three men there and then the Mother after."

"We bin lucky, when us looks at others. Even though our dear boys was took." Tears formed in the old man's eyes. Albert dashed them away with a gnarled old hand and bent to pick up his buckets.

"Best tek the water in and get them a bite to eat."

"How do they go on now, then?"

"They be comfort one to the other. Eliza do come on slow, she do grieve so for them dear boys. Arthur do begin to fill 'is clothes agin, I gets real pleasure seeing 'un eat up the grub I cooks."

"Surely! Surely - tell 'em how this boy does and give they our good wishes. I'll be goin' in now, Albert and get this little 'un in bed - only kep 'un out to see thee go by." Betsy turned and went up the cobbled path into her cottage. Albert watched her, the scent of the lavender bush lifting from her long skirt as she brushed past. Then he too turned away, going towards Wood Cottage, his back bent under the weight of the buckets.

Before the end of July Ainsley and Rachel faced some sad days in No Man's Barn. In the middle of the month four men died in the space of two days. One of them was Lord Ainsley's groom, James Painter. He was the father of young Matthew Painter, the Blacksmith's apprentice. A widower, he was a much respected man in the villages. He had been born in Seckington and no doubt would have wished to be buried there. As things were, he had to lie at rest in Lower Telso along with the other plague victims.

Two days later George Arms was taken sick at the Cross Keys Inn. He had closed the hostelry a month before. He and his wife having decided that it was wrong to encourage the villagers to come together. Esther, his wife, was determined to nurse him herself. There was no one else to consider. Their only son, Daniel, was away at sea in the Navy. He had not been seen in Telso for five years. They had no other family. George only survived the plague for three days. David Ainsley went to visit him each day, but although there was no rash on his body and he had no swellings, he became fearful. When the onset of fever came he was worn out by his own fear and horror at what had befallen him. He died gasping for breath in the height of his fever, unable to recognise either the Doctor or his wife as they struggled to hold him down forcibly in the bed. Ainsley felt no surprise when suddenly the Innkeeper fell back dead. He had seen it happen a hundred times before, but Esther was shocked beyond measure and herself collapsed a moment later.

It was night time and Ainsley when sent for had summoned Andrew Mallard to take a turn of duty in the barn during his absence. David was now faced with setting the corpse to rights after the fearful contortions of his violent death. Covering it with a sheet and reviving the widow. He also knew he must get back to the barn as soon as he could. He had twenty-five sick people there and no one but Andrew with them. This was one of the greatest difficulties that the Doctor worked under. Lack of help. In ordinary illness he could so easily have knocked up a neighbour to come in for the rest of the night to see after Mistress Arms. With plague, no one dare come and Ainsley dare not ask them in case plague should thus be carried to another house. In the end he gave Esther two glasses of wine from the Inn's own stock and left her by the kitchen fire. He laid on fresh peats before he left, and then locked the door of the bedroom on the corpse and went away with the key in his pocket.

The tale had a sad ending. Esther went out of her mind and wandered the village street for days looking for George, seeming unable to accept his passing. One sunlit morning, Zeb Mysen the Miller found her body floating face down in the mill pool. She had been dead for hours and must have wandered there the night before. Afterwards the Inn stood empty and silent it's windows blind and shuttered. No candle burned there at night to comfort the neighbouring cottagers.

When David heard of it he blamed himself for not staying with her on that first terrible night, but he could not have done so with so many lives dependent on him in the barn.

David was also deeply concerned for Rachel during those sunlit July days when nature's face was so beautiful with the promise of ripening harvest in every field. It was almost impossible to believe the misery that overshadowed the whole village, while the glory of the English countryside surrounded them.

Rachel had fought every step of the way to save the two little Symes girls, but little Mary slipped away very early one morning when the church clock had not long struck two. It is the hour at which all humanity lies at its lowest ebb. When death often reaches out to lift up the weak and the dying. David Ainsley, knowing this, had expected that it would be so. Rachel had stayed with the child until midnight when David had sent her home to rest. Unable to sleep, she had come back just after two o'clock only to find that Mary had died a few minutes before.

"If only I had not left her - if only I had stayed. I can't forgive myself! I shall never forgive myself." Tears ran down Rachel's cheeks.

"Shush. Shush. Little Kate sleeps - her fever has broken - don't wake her - come on - come along outside." David half carried her out of the building. Once outside, the last remnants of her self control went from her. All the bottled up emotions of weeks bubbled up to choke her. Tears for all the horror she had witnessed, for all those who had suffered and died, burst from her eyes, nose and mouth. She stood before him stripped of all steadiness and youthful maturity. She looked as a child looks who has been hurt beyond bearing. Her hands fumbled together, twisting in the stuff of her dress. Her shoulders heaved and she rocked to and fro in the misery of her grief. She had no handkerchief and the tears flowed unchecked.

"They all die! Every one of them! What's the use?" her voice rasped between the low painful sobs. "Why do you not die? Why do I not die? What have they - those little ones - done to deserve it? How can God be so cruel? He does not listen any more! He did not even let me be with her! Oh Mary! .... little Mary!"

It was then that David took her into his arms. He held her against his chest, his arm about her. With his other hand he began gently patting her back. Then she was on his knee as he sat down on a chair in the lean-to. Now his hand was on her head, stroking, smoothing and gentling through the curls. Gradually through her weeping she began to listen to his soothing words. "There, there, you're just a baby yourself, really - are you not? There, my little one. My own little brave Greensleeves. My Darling. My Darling girl. Little one - my own little one. Better in a minute. Just rest now. Little Mary has only gone home - gone to her Father - she was John's favourite you know. Now they are both at peace. You made her happy so many times. There's nothing to blame yourself for. Let her go now - there's a good girl. Here, let me dry your eyes, Sweetheart." She clung to him as he reached for a clean piece of linen. Gently he began to mop up her face.

"Don't let me go. Please hold me," she whispered but the great shaking sobs began to subside. He gathered her again in his arms and, lifting her, carried her away across the field. He scarcely knew her weight - he only knew the pleasure he felt in her need of him. At the Parsonage door he set her down but she clung to his hands, shaking at the prospect of being left alone.

"All right. All right. I only seek to open the door. You're my patient now - I always see my patients safe tucked up."

He opened the door and shepherded her in, lifting the low burned candle from the table to light their way. In her room he set it down on the bedside table.

"There now, a good cry is a release - a safety valve." As he talked he undid the buttons of her dress and pulled it over her head.

"Now your petticoat, Sweetheart" He turned back the covers and pushed her gently into bed.

"I have to put on my bed gown," she said, worried as a child might have been.

"You look very sweet in your shift, precious child - I shall take your dress and petticoat; they can go in the barn laundry tomorrow. Now sit up and take your wine like a good girl."

308

He fetched a cloth and sponged her face and hands then waited while she drank a glass of wine. Then he replaced the glass on the washstand and came to the bedside. She had slipped down beneath the covers, her lashes curled on the pale cheeks. The soft feathers below her, drawing her into the sleep which was nature's reaction to the spillage of so much pent up emotion. Her eyes opened and the candlelight threw mauve shadows beneath their dark circles. It was the face of a worn out child. It came to his mind that at this moment she did not look much older than the little girl Mary who lay beneath a sheet in the barn.

He bent and cupped her face with his hands, lifting it up to his own. He looked into her eyes for a full minute before he kissed her. He saw the spark, the expectancy, the joy dawn. Then his lips came upon hers and her eyelids flew down and shut him out. It was a child's mouth, untried, and he gave it only a brief tenderness.

"Good night .... my Lady Greensleeves." he said.

As soon as daylight, came David rose and left his patients for a few minutes and went to rouse Andrew Mallard and Tom Hart. Tom threw on his shirt and breeches, and without waiting to break his fast came into the lane with his spade. Andrew was always an early riser - he delayed only to snatch up his prayer book. The three men separated; Tom went to the churchyard to fashion out a small grave close beside John Symes's recent resting place. David and Andrew went to the barn and wrapped the pathetic small burden in a blanket. David carried her to the churchyard and laid her in the kindly earth. They said together the words of the Lord's Prayer. Andrew gave the blessing, then preacher and Doctor left Tom Hart to reunite the Father with his favourite small daughter.

When Rachel came, a while after, it was all over, Kate lay weak from fever but able to take the bread and milk which David was feeding her from a spoon. Rachel was pale but composed. She carried through the day's routine just as usual. All day David watched her out of the corner of his eye, but she kept brave and made no reference to the little girl's death.

When David went to tell Cathy Symes the sad news, he was

at least able also to impart the consolation of little Kate's improved condition.

On the last day of July a thunderstorm broke at sunset and deluged the dry valley. The Cliven filled and ran freely over the dry banks and shingles. The days that followed were cooler and easier to bear, for the sick and those who cared for them. The storm proved to be a flash-in-a-pan and the weather quickly settled down again. The rain had sweetened the soured grass and a fresh greensward sprung up for the cattle and sheep. In the corn fields the ears filled and swelled. As the sunshine came again in renewed strength the corn rapidly turned to golden bronze. Lord Ainsley began to prepare for harvest.

Normally a team of five and twenty men went forth to reap the corn. Since the coming of Plague, nine of these men had died, victims of a greater reaper's knife. Altogether, there were now over eighty new graves in the churchyard. Over half were men and women who had worked on Lord Ainsley's Estate. Lord Ainsley faced other difficulties; three of the best men he had for handling a scythe were gone. Jack Acres, George Swift and Tom Carter were all dead. All had been master craftsmen with the scythe, the axe and the plough, as well as the shepherd's crook. No men could be 'borrowed' from neighbouring villages to stand in for those lost. The 'closed' boundaries prohibited such risk. Lord Ainsley decided to begin reaping early with his limited labour force. A number of men, under no obligation to do so, rallied under his Lordship's banner. Leaving their other employment to do so. One of these was John Price. The huge blacksmith was as good a hand with a scythe as the next man, in spite of spending half a lifetime at the anvil fashioning crude iron. Tom Hart, the sexton, was another. Being older, he could no longer keep pace with the younger men, yet his help was still welcome.

On the fifteenth of August, sixteen men assembled in Big Fields at sun-up, with Martin Bones as their leader. A job inherited through the death of John Symes. David Ainsley and Rachel watched their progress with interest from the barn's entrance. For half an hour there came the unique sound of stone upon sickle blade as every man present sharpened and tempered their scythes. Then began the age old craft of the harvest. They ranged themselves along the hedge line of Big Fields. Martin Bones placed himself at the corner of the field under a great oak, laden now with smooth, knobbly cupped green acorns. Bones strode forward and swung out his scythe into the first swathe. Within seconds he had established the easy flowing movement of the experienced reaper. When he had gone a few yards in from the headland, Thatcher Gibbs, who had stood alongside him by the hedge bank, moved forward to take his turn. A tall man whose powerful shoulders looked built for work, the corn fell in a smooth silken golden ribbon before his blade. The next man followed, taking up the continuous rhythmic pattern. Then the next following on until all sixteen men were moving steadily across the field.

It was a joy to watch, a sight to gladden the eyes of any countryman. David Ainsley - long absent - felt tears rise in his throat at this well remembered scene. More particularly was there a vein of hope in the harvest. A living hope of better times to come. Early morning mist still clung near the woodland, but the risen sun's rays had fingered their way into every corner of Big Fields. Golden corn with patches of scarlet poppy and blue flax stood full fat before the diagonal line of men. Each man maintaining a steady even flow, keeping a few yards behind the man in front. Razor sharp knife blades could take a man's foot off, if the holder came too close behind a fellow reaper.

The corn fell with a steady swishing sound, much akin to rain falling upon water. It was a colourful scene. The sky a brilliant blue-violet. The woodland olive green, enhanced by the glowing patches where leaves began to turn yellow. The golden corn holding captive the patches of brilliant scarlet poppies, white moon daisies and blue flax. The men's shirts and kerchiefs bright against the backcloth of the harvest field.

Then came the women, white sunbonnets and full skirted work gowns of every hue. The skirts looped up to give freedom of movement. Their task was to gather up and heap the corn, tying it, with lengths of its own straw, into sheaves. These sheaves were set together in stooks of six or eight to catch the wind and the sun for drying.

David Ainsley was pleased to see Emmy Bones and Cathy

311

Symes amongst the women in the harvest field. They had been so much confined in their cottages of late. Emmy was now some months on with the carrying of her second child. Her first lay in a clothes basket under the hedge, while she worked amongst the fallen corn nearby. So far her little family had been spared the Death; she had been luckier than Cathy Symes whose husband and little girl now lay in the churchyard. Her young boy helped with other lads to heap the piles of corn for tying. All day long the reapers worked. Breaks were taken for thirst quenching, cider for the men and lemonade for the women and children. Usually tankards were sent with the barrels and shared. This year, with Plague a constant threat, they all brought their own drinking vessels. Dinner came in baskets brought by Charlotte and Esme in the pony trap. Pork pies, bread and cheese and pickles and huge apple duffs were shared out by the two girls. It was a happy time in spite of everything. Everyone kept a little away from one another. A restraint imposed by the pestilence. There was none of the kissing and tumbling amongst the sheaves, which usually went on at harvest time.

The fine weather and hot sunshine held. It took until the last day of August to finish the cutting. All sixteen men worked from first light until dusk. When the corn was cut behind Wood Cottage garden, Arthur and Eliza Dale were recovered enough to walk to the bottom of their orchard with old Albert to see the harvesters at work. Much friendly banter and news was exchanged over the fence.

In the evening, Anne Barnes and Ilsa Dale came down to the harvest fields and would join in the work until dusk. Another casual helper was Mathew Painter, the blacksmith's apprentice. Alone since his Father's death a month before, he found the cottage near the boarded up empty village Inn a lonely place at the end of his working day at the forge. He joined the harvesters for company most evenings. Ilsa Dale began to notice that Mathew was often at work stooking the sheaves alongside her own patch. She had always been shy and fearful of men. Since Jonathon Ainsley's vicious attack on her she had been unable to speak to any man. She never once looked at Mathew and clung tight to Anne Barnes' apron strings to avoid having to exchange a word with him. Mathew had never been much for girls, but Ilsa's shy avoidance of him caught his interest and forced him to make an effort. The other men, quick to see how things were, made fun of him.

"Now Lad, here's yer chance - you, with an empty cottage - you needs some'un to do for 'ee. You'm better look out for a likely lass, you 'ad."

"I seen one in a blue skirt tripping by, not long back. Did 'ee happen to see 'er, Thatcher Boy?" Thatcher Gibbs winked at Anne before he replied.

"I surely did - I got me eye fixed my sen - cut and carried by Michaelmas I be getting she. Keep me warm come winter - that's what I thinks."

"Gets very cold, do the bed - for a lone man comes winter nights."

"You think about it, young Mathew, you git that house a mite pretty, then ask she to share it with 'ee. Have to be a mite gormless lass to turn down a fine set young chap like you, her would."

"'Tis right, Lad. George be givin' you good sound advice - and if you needs any instruction .... in wooing she, or anything like that - I can easy give 'ee a hint or two that direction."

A burst of ribald laughter followed this remark. In spite of his red faced bashfulness, Mathew did not sleep easy in his bed at nights during the weeks of the harvest, nor could he keep away from Ilsa's side. He felt as drawn to her as a pin to a magnet. He became every day more conscious of her shape beneath her rough work dress. More aware of his own body needs increasing. All sorts of new feelings jostled with one another and eventually forced him to make his first move. His approach was very clumsy. One evening, at dusk, Anne slipped away from Ilsa and vanished into the next field, with Thatcher Gibbs arm about her waist. Finding herself alone, Ilsa crept away across the brook and over the footbridge, taking the path for the Hall, and the safety of the kitchens. Matthew, further up the field, saw her go. Seeing his chance, he splashed across the brook and pelted headlong through the undergrowth, hoping to cut her off on the path before she reached the Cliven. He was successful and blundered out onto the path in front of her, thrusting aside hazels and brambles as he did so. She was scuttling along like a scared rabbit in the dusky gloom of the overhanging trees. They both stopped dead in their tracks. Mathew's hands were scratched and bleeding. His clothes dishevelled from his recent scrambling through the thorns.

"You be goin' wrong route, you be." Her voice was sullen, her head bent, her eyes on the path in front of her.

"You won't speak to I - you doesn't give a chap a chance - I 'ent done aught to upset ' ee."

"What I does 'ent none of they business, Mathew Painter! Them men in the fields! They talks real dirty to you about me! I heard 'em at it agin today."

"I can't help wot they says. Don't matter two buggers what they says. 'Tis wot you says do matter to I."

"Well, I 'ent said nothing."

"That's just wot frets me - I don't know aught about .... about womanhood. I never even had a mam. Died, she done, afore I cud walk - How does I know wot to say to 'ee?" He sounded indignant, maltreated and misunderstood.

"Wot does you want to say to I?"

For the first time, she lifted her eyes to meet his. She saw nothing to frighten her, only a red faced, red headed young man whose normally laughing blue eyes looked ill at ease and unhappy beneath his thatch of untidy hair.

"Well .... " he said slowly, realising that at last he had her attention. "Well, I may as well come straight out with it. I wants you to come and be with me. I have got a nice little place - all me own since Dad's gone - God rest he. There's a good table and chairs, a bit o' fire in the hearth come winter nights, a few pots to cook a good dinner, nothing fancy like - but us cud likely get a bit of curtaining and mek a rag rug, I dare say. The men may be real rude times, but they be right. 'Tis no use me havin' a big bed o' feathers and lie in she on me lonesome. Mind, I should expect her as does come to be as I chooses. Warm and that .... with I. I'd like fine to kiss and cuddle at nights and tek my turn at makin' little 'uns. Needs little 'uns, does this village, with all they dead ones along there." He pointed towards the churchyard with a long thrusting forefinger. Then he fell silent. Glancing at her, well satisfied with his long speech, he waited for Ilsa's response.

"Does thee think I intends comin' along o' thee an warm thy

bed and let 'ee play the bull, when you 'ent courted I. Not one little bit you 'ent. I've better things t'do with my life than let you fill me belly and tek all thy pleasure - an us never been to church for no ring nor nothing! She ran out of breath, and tears of fury clung on her lashes.

"I had one man be dirty with me - I aint havin' it no more." Her eyes dropped before his startled glance and her cheeks grew scarlet in the gathering darkness.

"Ah!" His voice softened, "Does you think I'd tek thee unwed .... and me Dad so respected and only dead a month? That 'ent my plan - I wants you for wife - I wants us wed and all on a paper as be right! But no waiting, mind! Soon as Parson calls banns - you mun marry with I. I 'ent never wanted a Lass afore - but now I do and I wants thee, quick like. Is that agreeable to thee?" He looked anxious as his eyes rested on her face.

"In that case - I don' know - well maybe - yes - yes I'm agreeable to that."

"Now you're talking." His face lit up with a broad grin "Let's have a kiss on it - I'm that hungry for a kiss and a touch of thee." He took her in his arms and planted his warm lips on hers. At first it was a very nervous tentative embrace but his hands found her thighs and warming to his task his fingers moved enjoyably up to her breasts and down again. His kiss deepened and he felt her lips begin to respond. Then he let go of her so suddenly that she almost fell over.

"By Heaven! That was a real sweet sample - we shall be just the thing together, you and me - no mistake. 'Tis no wonder folks gets wed and them old men is forever on about it - so keen, I bin missing too much, I reckons. I shall see Parson right away, Lass. And come Sunday I fetch 'ee to see my little house and you'm can choose some bits to mek it homely like. Now turns us about and I'll see 'ee safe home - now us have it all settled." Hand in hand, they moved along towards the bridge. Both lapsed into silence. Neither were great talkers and so much conversation had left them exhausted for words.

CHAPTER XI

CHAPTER XI

By the end of August the number of names David Ainsley was forced to read out, at Andrew Mallard's Sabbath Day service in the Dingle, began to grow less. By other tiny signs David and Andrew began to believe that the end of the sickness was at last in sight. Some of these signs were so small, almost intangible, that the two men spoke of them to no one else save each other. They walked the tight rope, each in their own way. Andrew spent more time upon his knees, begging, entreating, praying for salvation for his beloved village. David became more watchful, took less sleep, less time for himself. Both waited with a tiny gleam of hope in their hearts.

The last week of August had been bad. Three Estate workers died, two of them gamekeepers, one of them a gardener from the Hall. Also, Mary Anne Sykes, wife of Evan Sykes the harness-maker, had been taken ill, to die a week later along with her first born baby, which she was still suckling. They had lived in a small lean-to cottage against the closed up Cross Keys Inn. David Ainsley suspected that they had caught the pestilence from the same source as George Arms, the Innkeeper.

In spite of these losses, David's patients in the barn began to grow fewer. On September the third he and Rachel carried little Kate Symes home to her Mother's arms. It was a moving reunion. Cathy Symes, who had kept so brave through John, her husband's, death and the tragic loss of little Mary, broke down and wept when she felt little Kate's arms about her neck. She was unable to speak. They left her with the little girl - very thin but happy to be home. Kate sat on her Mother's knee, the boy Peter, her brother, wasted no time in tears. He pranced up and down in delight, shouting his welcome to his little sister. "Cum on, Mam," he said, "us is a family agin, that's wot."

In the villages both David and Andrew noticed that there seemed at last to be a lightening of hearts, a feeling of hope amongst the people. David firmly believed that it had to do with the harvest. For in the gathering of the corn, the men and women had come together for the first time since February, overcoming to a great extent their fear of catching the Death one from another.

Betsy Price had taken Eliza Dale's little son Edward home to Wood Cottage. Eliza's faded cheeks had now begun to regain a touch of their former country-woman's bloom. Her joy lay in her firm belief that the baby had been sent to them late in life to make up in some measure for the loss of her beloved twins. Arthur Dale was back to work in Lord Ainsley's cowsheds. Ilsa's betrothal to Mathew Painter was another pointer to better times. Eliza and Arthur were glad for their daughter, having feared her to be marked for life against men since her time at the Park.

By the seventh of September, David Ainsley had only three patients left in the barn. Two of them were women. One was Lucy Fulton, the kindly woman who was Andrew and Harriet Mallard's devoted housekeeper. The other, greatly to David's grief, was his own housekeeper, Mabel Dunn. So near the end of the pestilence, the Plague had struck close to the Parsonage. It had not been seen there since the shepherds had died at Glebe Cot, in the previous autumn.

Just before the two women became sick, David Ainsley had sent Rachel home. Since the death of little Mary, she had been under strain and had looked withdrawn and sad. David had felt her to be greatly at risk. He had seen so often people who were low in spirits go down with the pestilence. David was less willing to admit to himself that his protective feelings for Rachel stemmed directly from the feelings within his heart. With so few in the barn now, and Andrew to give him a hand, he felt less anxious knowing Rachel to be back at Chalfont amongst her own people and near to the pure air of the moors, where she saw the larks rise and was removed from the dangers of the valley. But he missed her - he was too good a Doctor to let his feelings touch his work, but Andrew Mallard was very close to him now and sized up the situation at once.

"You know, David, I don't often talk to you like a preacher and I'm not going to now - but my advice to you as a man is, don't let that Lass slip through your fingers."

"What Lass?" David replied, somewhat dishonestly.

"Don't fence, David. Harriet tells me - and I'd have known it myself in any case, that Rachel is deep in love with you."

"She's just a child. T'was just calf love for an older man - and a medical man - that often happens."

"You should know, as a man of medicine, that female children turn quick into girls and girls into women at a man's whim. If you prove foolish enough not to make that sweet child into your wife before someone else snatches her up, then you are foolish indeed."

"While plague lives in this place, I cannot form even the vaguest attachment with any woman, Andrew - whatever my feelings."

"And what are your feelings?"

"Are you probing as a man or as a Parson?"

"As a man. You forget I'm married these twenty years and have two youngsters. I count myself lucky in my children having missed the scourge - but it is in my wife that lives my real joy. Ours has been a good union - and not least in the marriage bed."

"I'm a man as much as the next. My attachment to Elizabeth Loundes was a romantic dream - a young man's dream. If I am honest, I was more hurt in my pride than in my heart when it ended. Rachel is a different matter - she's made of strong stuff. There's passion, love, a woman in the making, a mother and a mistress there for some man to take to his heart for as long as life lasts."

"And are you going to be that man?"

"I think myself too old - there's too many years between us. I am nearing thirty - I haven't been a woman's man. I've had women, of course. The Navy breeds that hunger in a man. Rachel has an innocence - a youth that somehow I don't feel able to match." David's voice faded.

"Nonsense, man - you're tired and worn out with so much contact with the pestilence, and now, with Mabel Dunn and Lucy Fulton amongst your patients as well, 'tis almost too much to be shouldered by one man. The burden grows ever heavier. I ask you most earnestly to remember that Rachel came to you in the barn - at the risk of her life! Do you think she came because of dedication to plague's victims? A young woman like that! She came because she has given her heart to you. Don't let it go to waste - you sent her home because you feared for her safety. She will read into that, that you did not want her. Wait, if you must, until the plague is past - we both feel it must soon be over. God grant us with no more deaths. But when it is over - take the gift that this woman offers you. You know that you love her. God does not give us so many rare gifts that they may be thrown aside."

"You're a good friend to me, Andrew. I shall not forget it."

Andrew smiled very sweetly. "So long as you keep firm in your mind that Rachel is the only woman for you - with that I will be content."

The harvesters began to get the corn carted on September the fifth. The bulk of the sheaves were carried to Gleaner's Acre. It was fine and dry but much cooler. All day long the wagons, each pulled by two horses trundled to and fro. One gang of men in the field pitching the sheaves into the high wagons. A man was perched on top of each wagon, his task was to pack the sheaves in layers to form a tidy shaped load on the wagon, which would transport it safely to the rick without mishap. In Gleaner's Acre the round ricks rose like mushrooms. Here another gang of men unloaded the wagons and shaped the circular ricks, tight packed with sheaves against winter storms. Usually the sheaves were carted into the barns at Home Farm, Hill Farm, Chalfont and Lower House. Because of plague, it had been decided to make all the ricks outside in the open air. Thus, the men would not be in close contact during the carting period. Later Thatcher Gibbs would have the task of pegging a good thatch of straw on top of each rick. Then it would look as if a Celtic village of round houses had sprung up in Gleaner's Acre.

In the middle of the carting time, David Ainsley had cause for both joy and sorrow in his last struggles with the plague. The last man to be incarcerated in the barn was Keeper Anderson; he suffered both sickness and fever, having been brought from his work complaining of blindness and head pains. Fortunately, it had come on him suddenly while he was away from home. He lived in a cottage above Dumble Wood with his wife and six young children. Seeing him brought in so ill, David had visions of losing a whole family, all infected by the Father. It was not the case and nor did Anderson himself die; although he came in with the rash of blistered red ringed early plague spots, he never developed any of the dread 'Tokens'. In a few days he lost a great deal of weight as his body fought the violent fever. As suddenly as it began it ended, leaving him weak but alive. He was taken back to his family thin and pale but obviously mending. As the pony trap from the Hall transported him home across the fields, it passed near Gleaner's Acre. The men building the harvest ricks sent up a great cheer of encouragement. Anderson, weaker than he could have imagined, like a scarecrow, in his clothes for the first time since he fell sick, lifted his hand to them. He could not shout back, weak tears of joy filled his eyes as the trap bumped on across the field. Charlotte Ainsley, who held the reins, was a kind understanding girl; she kept her head averted until Keeper Anderson was master of his emotions once more.

David Ainsley was not so lucky with the sick women. Lucy Fulton refused to fight for her life and dropped into the deep sleep so common after fever. She never woke again. Dear old Mabel Dunn, who was far more sick, and showed 'tokens' upon her back and breast, fought every step of the way, refusing to give up, then one afternoon, while David sat at her bedside feeding her broth from a spoon, she suddenly pushed his hand away.

"A little sleep now, I think, Doctor," she said, then her head slumped forward and she was dead in the shelter of the arm he put about her shoulders. She was the last in the barn. He laid her down and set the bed to rights, covering her with a clean sheet. He looked down the line of tidy empty beds. All was quiet. He remembered so many things out of the weeks he had given to this wretched place. Most of all the evenings - and Rachel. Her singing .... to the children, the sick and the dying. Was it over at last? He went and sat at the small table and, taking up his pen and Log Book, made the simple entry: Mabel Dunn's name, age and the date and hour of her death. He sat then for a few minutes, feeling very tired, as though a great heavy weariness settled upon him. His mind filled with the faces of his patients, the dead mingling inextricably with those who had survived. Across the fields he could hear the shouts of the harvesters in Big Fields and Gleaner's Acre. Sometimes a burst of laughter. He was not a praying man, he had always been more a man for doing than for words, yet now an old verse long remembered came into his mind - a psalm was it? He couldn't be sure. He took up his pen and wrote out the words in his log.

323

"There shall no evil befall thee, neither shall any plague come nigh thy dwelling .... For He shall give His angels charge over thee, to keep thee in all thy ways." (Psalm 91).

Had he been thus guarded? - kept safe, perhaps, to help others? Had he helped others? So many had died. He had lost so many. No use to dwell upon it - perhaps at last it was over. He must seek out Tom Hart to dig a grave for Mabel Dunn. He rose to his feet, squared his shoulders, and after taking a glass of the ever protective red wine, he headed away towards the church. It was bright sunshine outside the barn, he was struck by the sudden sense of freedom leaving the barn gave him. The air was very pure. In spite of the autumn sunshine there was a sharpness in the air which might portend a frost after sunset. The late afternoon sky was mauve-blue. A crescent moon hung above Dumble, It was very still, the shouts of the harvesters and the clanking of the wagon wheels over the rough stubble, could still be heard across the fields. He turned and looked up across the now nearly empty corn fields towards Chalfont. He could see the roof of the house and the outline of the buildings against the purple moors. Below lay the track which wound amongst rocks above Chalfont Well. She was up there - Rachel - his own Rachel - thinking perhaps that he didn't want her. Could he go to her now? He was almost tempted to turn about and run to her. Run like a half-crazed schoolboy in the throws of calf love. No! No! Steady. With the plague still on him, in his clothes, his hair - perhaps upon his breath, but not in his soul - never in the depths of him. He pressed his lips firmly together and faced again towards the church.

Before he reached the Parsonage he heard a sound, a spade in the earth. He crossed the grassy lane and went in at the lych gate. The sound came from beyond the great yews, their branches brushed the turf like great sweeping skirts. He pushed them aside and stepped into the open area, now filled with so many graves that Andrew had spoken of consecrating an extension. It was Tom Hart; he was over to the right nearer the Parsonage House, he was digging. "Tom," he called quietly. Tom paused in his work and turned at the sound of a voice.

"Ah, 'tis you, Doctor. Terrible business, 'ent?"

"Dreadful - I thought we were done with it at last. How did

you know? It was not long since. She had been so brave - always makes it harder. Will you bring the cart? I shall wait until you come. Then I plan to close the barn. Seems strange after so long, but I begin to dare hope at last." David came up to the Sexton and looked down sadly at the half dug grave. Tom Hart rested his spade in the dug earth and put his scarred, work stained hand on the grass at the edge of the pit in which he stood.

"I scarce dare tell 'ee, Sur." His voice seemed very small for so huge a man. David's tired mind woke and grasped his meaning at once

"This grave is not for Mabel Dunn? I had just come to tell you. She died less than an hour since. Who then? Who is this for?"

"'Tis Mistress Mallard, Sur - the Reverend's good Lady."

"Oh no! But she had not been ailing - surely it cannot be?"

"He'd bin - the Reverend had been cleaning and making ready to open up the Church. Us have all been thinking the Plague nearly gone. He did tell me that he wanted all nice and ready against young Mathew Painter getting wed to Arthur Dale's lass. He were that pleased and she too - his Lady wife, that is. She'd gone into the garden to gather some blossoms for prettying the altar up a bit. When she were long in coming, he went seeking after she. He found her on the path. Terrible it were - all they blossoms scatterin' about her. But she were gone. T'was nothing to be done - Wonderful 'ee were - so quiet like - just told I .... " 'Tom, let us carry her inside - no wait - we must have a sheet about her - Dr. Ainsley, he'll be after us.' That's all he said - then after, well he told I to come and dig a place here for she, just to do it all quiet like - not to bring trouble to no other." Tom Hart was deeply affected as he spoke. David Ainsley's years of training came to his aid.

"Of course, Tom. You're a good man. What should we have done without you all these months? Keep up your courage, my friend. Where is Reverend Mallard now?

"He went back into the Church, Sur."

"All right, Tom - you carry on here. I'll go and see if he is all right."

David found Andrew Mallard seated in the church pew which his wife had always occupied. He sat very quiet. There was grief filled acceptance in his bent head and stooped shoulders. David, coming alongside, saw his friend's face; lines of suffering and shock about the mouth and eyes, told their own story. The thinning hair and narrow pale face all contributed to the sudden ageing caused by the shock he had just received. Tears ran unheeded down Andrew's cheeks, he brushed them away when he saw David.

"It is wrong of me to weep - just the shock. I had so hoped I might keep her by me a little longer - especially now - so near the end."

"Oh, Andrew - my dear friend - I am saddened for you - it is so damnably hard after all you've done. Both of you - visiting the sick, comforting my patients. Giving a helping hand to so many. Your kindness to the dying, and every one of those hundred and more souls whose remains lie out there. Not one was laid to rest without your prayers and blessing. No one was denied a decent burial. When I recall the ghastly endings of so many Christian people in London - and I realise the risks you have taken here to guard every member of this flock of yours. Both you and Harriet have written a story here which ranks with the bravest in England's history. A hundred years on - nay, three and four hundred years on, people will remember our village and marvel at what you have done here, in so confining the people of your flock as to keep the plague trapped within the Parish boundaries. That Harriet should be taken now. It is such a blow - I know not how to give comfort."

"If such a story is to stand in tomorrow's memory, your name must be writ high in the script, David - for you have done more than us. I tried, you know, to persuade Harriet to go to the children when it first began. She would not leave me." The tears had stopped. The voice was almost conversational.

"She loved you dearly, Andrew. Just as you loved her - it would not be her wish that you grieve now."

"I cannot help but grieve, but I must shut it deep in my heart like the rest have had to do here. Many have lost more than I, soon the children will be able to come home - we .... my wife and I .... spoke of it only this morning." His voice failed.

"Shall we go together to the house? Tom is almost ready, I think." David laid a gentle hand on his friend's arm. Andrew

Mallard rose to his feet. When he spoke he was quite calm.

"That would be kind - it is best to be quick - until the burial there is so much risk to all concerned."

"Would you like Tom to fashion a coffin? It would not take long," David offered.

"Oh, no," said Andrew decidedly. "She would have wished to be just the same as all the others - I have laid her in a sheet already. If you could help me .... I .... we put her in the outhouse. She would not have wanted to risk the house - the children coming home, you see."

"Of course, that was thoughtful." David kept his tone matter of fact.

On the way to the Parsonage he told Andrew of Mabel Dunn's death. Tom had already begun the second grave when they reached the churchyard.

By the time the Church clock struck the hour of six, and the harvesters laid down their forks and unharnessed the horses for the night, both women were at rest in the quiet earth. The two graves were side by side, close under the Parsonage wall. Andrew had gathered up the blooms which had been Harriet's last offering to the church. He laid half of the flowers upon each of the two graves. Taking three spades, they shared the labour of filling in the graves. Tom fetched a rake and they left him to finish tidying up his work.

David and Andrew parted at the Parsonage gate. Neither man spoke but they clasped hands and stood thus for a moment.

"Another day, David, we'll talk another day." Andrew turned and went up the drive beneath the trees. A lonely rather bent figure. David sighed, squared his shoulders and went back to No Man's Barn. Here he slammed shut the doors and dropped the iron closure bar into its slots for the first time in weeks. Time enough to burn the grim reminders within and disinfect the place. Give it a few days yet, leave the beds ready - an insurance against others needing to use them.

He turned his face for Crab Tree, carrying only his Log Book. There would be another entry - Harriet's death must have its place in his records. The fields were quiet now - the workers gone home. The sun almost set. Only the crescent moon hung in the sky. A few stars began to twinkle above him. At the orchard

orchard gate at Crab Tree, Beauty gave him her whinny of welcome. "Well, Lass - God be praised - I think I've come home."

Harriet Mallard was the last to die in the dreadful scourge which had lain like a great black shadow over the villages for so long. The plague had lasted from the autumn of 1665 until the autumn of 1666. Six months of that time, the villages had isolated themselves to prevent it's spread. Over a hundred lives had been lost in a population of under a hundred and eighty people. Very few households remained untouched. The pestilence left many scars. Yet villages are like families, they close ranks. When someone dies the others move in closer to knit together the gaps and fill the empty chairs. So it was in Upper and Lower Telso.

Autumn 1666 was to prove a rare one for weddings, beddings and baby getting. The doors of No Man's Barn were scarcely slammed shut after clearing and disinfecting within, before Mathew Painter was waiting at the altar steps within the Church for his Ilsa. She came to him in a simple country-maid's gown of pink wool. Her cheeks flushed and a posy of wild flowers in her hand. He waited for her, scrubbed and clean - his thick red curls tied at the nape with a dark ribbon. His Sunday best breeches, though patched and darned were spotless, as was his white shirt. The church doors stood wide open, the brass and woodwork shone, where every village woman's hand had rubbed and polished the day before. In the churchyard outside Lord Ainsley had supplied green turf enough to cover and soften the scars of the graves.

After Andrew had joined them as man and wife, they came out into the open to sunshine and a crowd of villagers wishing them well. Little Kate Symes ran excitedly up the path to meet them, and flung her bowl of wheat over their heads. It scattered their hair and clothes. A roar of laughter went up.

There was no money for feasting, instead Ilsa made her curtsey and Mathew his clumsy bow to Andrew Mallard, then they took hands and ran away across the fields to their new home in Upper Telso. The children chased them over every stile along the way, but Mathew was young and strong, he jumped his bride over every railing and outran them all. Bride and Groom reached their cottage door out of breath and full of laughter. He whisked her over the step, banged the door shut and drove home the bolt. Then he pulled the red curtains at the front window.

Ilsa had only been here once before, since which Mathew had been hard at work preparing for her coming. A fire was laid in the old hearth, a rag rug in front and two country chairs one either side. The old table was covered with a good red cloth, given by John and Betsy Price. It was loaded with simple gifts from well-wishers. Everyone had wanted to give to the young couple. This wedding was shared by every villager. It was not only the closing of a door on the bad times, but a long awaited beginning of renewed happiness and normal life. This loaded table was the evidence of that hoped for beginning. There was a pork pie from Lower House, eggs from Hill Farm, an iron cooking pot from the Smithy. John Price had fashioned it with his own hands. From Chalfont a cheese had come, round and fulsome in its cloth. Honey was here from old Albert's bees at Wood Cottage. Two thick wool blankets lay folded in cosy newness from Seckington Hall. A basket of blackberries and another of cob nuts from Cathy Symes and Emmy Bones. Lady Loundes had sent a new dress for the bride and her staff had sent a pair of boots for Mathew.

Ilsa stood, round eyed and speechless with admiration, "Tis beautiful - we be that lucky."

"You mun come and see t'other room," said Mathew proudly pushing her towards the ancient wall ladder which led upwards through a hole in the ceiling. She scrambled up in front of him and found herself in a low sloping room under the roof. There was a tiny dormer window in the end wall, hung with a handkerchief size curtain. A large wooden box, a rag rug and a great iron bedstead completed the simple furnishings. The bed had a big soft feather mattress. Thicker and deeper than any she had ever seen. Folded on it lay a folded patchwork quilt which had been Eliza Dale's. Two knobbly flock pillows and a couple of much patched but clean lengths of sheeting.

"Now, what does thee think of that? I've left that for 'ee. I'll carry up they two blankets as his Lordship has gifted to us - an you can mek that bed real cosy for us - do you not think?"

"'Tis the thickest mattress I ever did see." She fingered it wonderingly.

"Surely it is. Now us is going down to light that bit o' kindling. Then us eats a bite of summat nice and sits a bit by our own fireside. Then us'll begin our married life and try out that bed. Is thee agreeable to that, Mistress Painter?"

"Aye, I'm agreeable to that," she replied.

Came the Monday morning, Mathew emerged somewhat sheepishly from his cottage door. The village had tired of trying to catch a glimpse of the newlyweds. No one had seen hide nor hair of them. Now no one was about. Mathew paused, tightened the belt of his old cord breeches, assumed a slight swagger and set off for the Smithy. John Price was there before him. He was stoking the fire, with his jacket off and his sleeves rolled above his elbows. He looked up from his work.

"Ah! And how does the bridegroom, then? I hope thee finds enough strength left to help I with Gaffer Bistock's plough-shares." John Price uttered a great loud laugh, showing huge white teeth within a gaping red mouth. He began to work the bellows, vigorously forcing life into the Smithy fire.

Mathew was not to be drawn - he threw off his jacket and fetched his harness from the work bench. John Price tried again., "And how be Mistress Painter - be she expectin' to enjoy married life along o' thee?" A slow grin spread over Mathew's face. He brought the hammer down on a bar of iron with a resounding clang before answering.

"If she 'en' expectin', it aint my bloody fault!" Up went the hammer again and the mighty crash it made on impact drowned his tormentor's comment, to Mathew's complete satisfaction.

At the Lower House another wedding was in the offing. Johnny Trewis had taken over the master's chair at the head of the kitchen table. Round it at meal times sat his younger brother, Arms, and his sisters, Velvet and Hannah. Hannah had now begun to use a kitchen chair instead of her former baby chair. Beyond her sat Raven Dyer. They were at their Sunday dinner, when the last morsel was cleared from the plates, Johnny banged his knife on the table for quiet.

"Seems now, at last, that our village is cleared of sickness. I have spoke with Doctor and he says, being as nights begin to come frosty and none have died these twenty-eight days, we can begin to breathe free again. For which we all do thank Almighty God. Even if we be still in sorrow over those gone from us." He paused and looked round the table; catching Velvet's nod of approval and Hannah's round attentive eyes, he continued.

"But us may grieve and, no doubt, shall do these many days. Same time, us has to keep place going and go on with the job of living. Seems I am to be Farmer here now, and I have asked Raven to come to me as wife. I hopes you all is pleased in this. 'Tis a great source of joy in me and I hope in her as well. I think the house stands very empty with so many gone. 'Tis our hope - God being willing, that is, that we shall be blessed as soon as may be with some childer. I have spoke with Parson, and us goes to Church when the Hunter's moon comes full. Of course, I want Arms and our Velvet and little Hannah to make their home and lives along of us as always. That's all I was minded to say - so now us better have a drop of cider to wish us all luck in this house."

CHAPTER XII

CHAPTER XII

The roads and lanes leading into the villages were open once more. The rocks rolled away and the plague notices up rooted and burned. Traffic moved freely once more along the grassy byways. The road which led through Seckington to Wesperton was a rough one. The autumn rains had begun. There were potholes full of muddy water. Autumn leaves mingled with the mud and laid hazard in the way of travellers.

One wild windy day in October a young man came striding through the puddles towards the villages. He passed over the Cliven, pausing on the bridge to look about him. Hill Farm cottage stood empty on his right, beyond it he could see Hill Farm house and buildings. In front of him the valley spread wide and beautiful in all the splendid colours of autumn. In Big Fields two ploughmen with a team of horses each, were turning the old stubble. The sunlight caught the gleam of metal on the great cart horses' harness. Behind them the backs of the two men were bent over, as they leant into the reins and gripped the plough handles, intent upon their work and the even lie of the fresh turned earth behind them. The rich bands of new ploughed land made pleasing contrast with the stubble and the green grass of the meadows nearby. Around the ploughmen, flocks of noisy seagulls swooped and dived after worms and insects in the fresh earth. Far from their native shores, they yet made a living moving contribution to the scene before the stranger who watched.

"Bloomin' Seagulls! Thought I'd left 'em far behind." A grin spread across the broad tanned face. He was a short, sturdy built young man with a seaman's air in his walk and stance. His hair was close cropped and curly. His clothes were well made but of common stuff. His gaiters dirtied with the mud of much walking. He carried a leather pack slung across his broad back. From its strap hung a metal drinking cup.

He saw no one about at Hill Farm, had he but known it - they were all down at the Church, for today was Johnny Trewis's wedding day. The next habitation was the Smithy - here was more life. John Price and Mathew Painter were hard at work. The sounds of their hammers drew him into the Smithy. There a great fire burned, in which a circular iron band of massive size grew molten hot ready for clamping round the wood spoked wagon wheel which John was bent over as he prepared and cleaned off its mud-caked hub. John looked up as the young man entered.

"Good Day, Stranger - what brings you in these parts?"

"I don't count myself a stranger - I think you have forgotten me. I'm Daniel, son of George Arms, used to be host at the Cross Keys Inn yonder. Five years I've bin gone - nay, 'tis nearer six - as I come to think - I've come by coach from Liverpool, far as Banbury - Shank's pony since then."

John Price frowned - hesitating before he spoke again.

"We have just come through bad times - have you heard of it?" he asked tentatively.

"Aye, I knew the Death had taken many - and my old folks amongst 'em. His Lordship was kind enough to see that I had word of it. T'was he suggested I come back and take the reins at Cross Keys. He did say as the heart is dead in the villages with the old Inn closed up and empty. So here I am - my time's done in the Service, in any case. Right glad I am to be here - a man gets homesick after five years at sea. 'Tis long enough for any man."

"Well, I wouldn't have known you - I recall you as a whey-faced lad with no meat on his bones. Being a sailor has built you up brave, I reckon." John Price was feeling relief that he hadn't to break the news of the boy's parents being dead.

"You'll be wanting the keys, young fellow - hang there, they do - on that hook." John Price pointed to the wall beyond Mathew's shoulder. Mathew laid down his hammer and reached a blackened hand for the keys. He gave them to Daniel Arms with a smile.

"You'm gonna be my near neighbour, then. I lives along of my young missus in the next cot along from here. My name's Painter - Mathew Painter. My Father be gone, too. Lord Ainsley's head groom he were, but the plague took 'ee. There's few round here as didna' lose someone. So we're in good company. I wish you good luck in your venture down-along."

"Well, I best be getting settled in. Thank you for the keys." He shouldered his pack once more and walked away towards the Inn. The old door creaked as he swung it back on its hinges. A draught of musty air issued forth. Everywhere was dark and dusty. The bar stood neglected and empty. Daniel flung down his pack and went to the windows.

"Down with the old boarding. Let in the sunlight. First things first," he said to himself, and energetically set to work.

And so it was that new blood came to the villages. Old blood also returned. David Ainsley had been living quietly for some weeks. He was quite alone, having not replaced Mabel Dunn. He had determined not to go to Chalfont until he was sure plague was truly ended. He wanted time to think and recover his peace of mind. He had spent his time out of doors; sometimes on Beauty's back - sometimes walking. He began to feel better in spirit and fitness.

It was a bright day that he chose to walk through the Quarry and so to the Parsonage to see Andrew Mallard. He took the footpath through the woods, over his ankles in dried leaves now, with the onset of autumn. He paused for a few minutes beside the bridge, leaning on the parapet. He had spent a half hour with his Father that morning. Two topics had been discussed. First, Lord Ainsley had told him news of London.

"There comes news of a great fire, David. It has burned for four days and taken the greater part of the city. Saint Paul's is gone, Parliament house and vast numbers of dwellings. Lord Ransome writes me that it has been a great purging of the dank putrid parts of the city and taken everything in its wake, almost no loss of life, he tells me."

"Perhaps it has taken Plague's seeds with it. If so, it is for good in some measure, I have no news of Vincent Fallon yet - I would dearly like to know he's safe. Still - there's something else I wish to speak of with you, Father - a more personal matter." David hesitated.

"Ah! - Is it Mistress Bistock?" His Lordship's eyes twinkled.

"How the Devil did you know, Sir?"

"Oh, Charlotte and Esme have both confided that they think her deep in love with you since the days of the hospital in No Man's."

"'Tis well I think it is but calf love - I'm too old for her. But if, well, if it should come to anything, would you .... would you and Mother ...." David became tongue-tied.

"I have talked with your Mother - just in case." Again the kindly eyes twinkled "We are both of the same mind. Families like ours, David - need sometimes new blood - marrying into the high rankers too many times can bring trouble. Jonathon may have been a product of your Mother's and my blame. We were, as you know, second cousins. If you can find happiness with Rachel Bistock, we shall give you our blessings. I long to see an heir - to see children to gladden your Mother's heart, David, after so much sadness." He smiled deep into David's eyes as he spoke.

Standing on the bridge, David remembered his words, but what ought he to do. Rachel was so young. Still he was unable to make up his mind. Turning from the bridge, he climbed a fence, crossed Rock Bottom Lane and went into Quarry Bottom. As he rounded the bend in the path, he saw that Black Dyer had returned, three caravans were parked in their usual places, and two piebald ponies grazed nearby. There seemed to be no one about, it was not until David had almost reached the stile into Potter's Paddock that a voice hailed him.

"Oh, the good medic - and how does the good Doctor?" David turned and saw Black Dyer climbing up the bank from the Cliven. There was no doubt as to what he had been doing. In his hand he held two fat brown trout. He was unchanged, still the dominant colourful old tyrant David remembered.

"I'm well enough, and how are you?"

"Just as ever, that is, in my health - going up in the world as to my station, it seems!" A broad grin cracked across the seamed face.

David looked at him nonplussed.

"'Tis my little Raven's done the trick - marrying she is in a few days. Mr. Johnny Trewis - he's the lucky bridegroom. Yeoman farmer he is - in the holding of Lower House Farm. Us haven't bin bid to the feast but 'tis still mighty pleasin' to know that brats born in Lower House from now on'll be my grandchildren."

"Well, that shows your good sense in letting Raven go there in the first place, does it not?"

"Well, of course, t'was her welfare I had in mind at the time, doin' the best I cud for 'er - like I allus done." The gross untruth, spoken in such an oily voice, caused David to bring forth a shout of laughter. He turned away and began to climb the stile.

"Anyway, it's nice to see you back, Dyer, in your accustomed place."

"Back? What the hell you mean - back? Us have allus bin here. Dyer's land this be - allus was - allus will be!"

"I'm sure you're right, Dyer!" David threw the last remark over his shoulder at the old rogue standing looking after him. Nonetheless, David had found pleasure in his encounter with the Romany leader. The Dyers were as much a part of the valley as the old Church or the beech trees in Dumble.

Andrew Mallard was in his small study talking to Cathy Symes.

"Come in - come in, David," Andrew called to him. "You can hear my two lots of good news."

David entered and smiled a greeting to Cathy and her two children. Kate was growing bonny again now. The boy, serious eyed now and grown in height, was the lad who had summoned him on the night of Emmy Bones's childbed. They were all dressed in their Sunday clothes, looking rather uncomfortable in their unaccustomed neatness. After greetings were exchanged Andrew turned to Cathy.

"Now, Cathy, suppose you go and bring us a glass of wine and let the children explore the kitchens."

"Yes, Sur - and we gives thee thanks, Sur. Us shall do our best to come worthy of your trust, Sur." She curtsied and shepherded the children towards the kitchen.

Andrew turned to David, a gentle smile lighting up his thin face.

"I had the idea this very morning, David, and lost no time in putting it into practice. Cathy Symes, having lost her man and still living in that undesirable cottage, I myself in need of a housekeeper, well, they are to come into the Parsonage. They will live in Parson's Cot - but for now, here in the house. Tom Hart is cleaning out Parson's Cot and lime-washing - after Mabel Dunn, you know. When it is ready, I shall move them in there. Then they will come to me in the daytime. The little girl will be with her Mother during the working day. Young Peter is young yet but he'll be nine next month. He's to help Tom Hart about the Churchyard and Parsonage garden. As you know, I've just returned from a few days in Banbury with the children. They are to come for all Luke's holidays - he began at the day school in September. Maisy is become quite a young lady. Her Aunt is teaching her more than I can here at home. They are to come for a while at Christmas and again at Eastertide and the Summertime holiday. I fear I was in danger of demanding them home, just for my own company. Now I see that it would be wrong. Little Kate running through the house will bring it to life again. Cathy is a good woman, clean in her ways and a fair cook and so kindly with it. Do you not think it a most fortunate arrangement?"

"I do indeed - especially as I heard from my Father yesterday that Martin Bones and Emmy are to move up to Hill Farm Cottage next week, to be installed there before the second child comes. My Father settled it with Tarant Barnes last week. Barnes doesn't want the cottage until Arthur marries, and the lad does not as yet go courting and seems disinclined to do so. Anne Barnes, when she marries Thatcher Gibbs, has shown a preference for Thatcher's Cot along the lane here. My Father intends to level the rest of the Row to the ground and not rebuild on that low lying area again."

"Anne Barnes and Thatcher are to come to church next week, and already I have joined Johnny Trewis in matrimony with your little gypsy, Raven Dyer. That will be three weddings in almost as many weeks. It will bring the villages new hope, David. It has lifted my heart to see the old Church put to such happy purpose again."

Cathy brought their wine and then returned to her new duties. David resumed the conversation. "You do not carry all the news, Andrew. I have some also. Black Dyer is back in his old lair. Slipped back under cover of darkness, no doubt. Also, I had a meeting with John Price yesterday and he tells me that young Daniel Arms has been to the forge for the keys of the Inn. Seems the lad has come home from the sea to take up his parents trade at the Cross Keys. It will bring back some life to the hill top, no doubt. Going across the fields and into the lane, and then to come face to face with the boarded up windows at the Inn, has depressed me since George and Esther Arms died. I believe my Father has had a hand in finding young Daniel."

"I agree - 'tis very good to see life come back into the

340

villages. But what of yourself, David, you have no housekeeper yet?"

"No - but then I've not sought one."

"You know well enough my views, David."

"And you know mine. If you are hinting towards Rachel. Well, Rachel is only sixteen. It's full young to pile on her the burden of being a middle-aged Doctor's wife."

"Rubbish, man! If you don't want her, then say so, and there's an end to it. But don't try to pretend to yourself that you make a sacrifice by keeping her from you because she is too young! All you in fact are doing, is making her pine and breaking her heart." Andrew's voice was sharper than David ever remembered hearing it.

"How can you possibly know that?" he asked mildly.

"I do know it. Mistress Bistock sent for me yesterday. They are anxious concerning Rachel's good health and sought my advice. She has been moping and full of tears these last weeks. Rachel has said nothing but her Mother has decided to send her away for a few months. They believe that her contact with the plague has upset her greatly and that a change is the only thing."

"When do they plan to send her, and where is the destination?"

"I think she is to travel on Monday's coach from Wesperton. I believe Bernard Bistock's brother lives at Aylesbury - they have a fish business there. The purpose being that she may meet some young persons. A young man, perhaps. Mistress Bistock told me, in a private moment we had together, that she thinks all these weddings .... especially Anne Barnes's happy union next week, have upset Rachel greatly." Andrew's face remained bland as he rambled on. The look of consternation on David Ainsley's face was comical, to say the least.

"But that is preposterous! Rachel is far more beautiful and desirable than Anne Barnes! Is she to be married off to some young popinjay she happens to bump into in a fish shop!"

"Why don't you call and see them - perhaps the girl is ill? Perhaps what they need is a Doctor!"

Ainsley threw his friend a sharp glance - was he being mocked? Andrew's face remained impassive.

"I may just decide to do that. I find it monstrous foolish that a sixteen year old must be rushed so hasty into marriage just because a few young ones hereabouts are marrying and settling down after the plague has at last ended. Anyway, I must be on my way. Beauty needs some exercise - it's three days since I had her in the bridle." He took his leave and left, a thunderous frown between his dark brows.

David passed a sleepless night. Only in the early morning did restless dozing come to him. Then dreams came and went in crazy muddled pattern. He woke to recall the last of these fantasies in which he had seen Rachel stepping down from a crowded coach into the arms of a stout young man in a blue and white fishmonger's apron. He had felt himself enmeshed in string nets, struggling to get to Rachel. Free at last, he had run sweating and gasping towards her, tripping, in his haste, into the mud of the gutter. As he rose up he found himself gazing into Black Dyer's mocking face and feeling the wet slap of live trout against his flesh. Dyer's mouth hung wide, shouting at him: "Too Late! Too Late! She's wed the fishmonger yesternight! You lost her, Ainsley - You lost her." Dyer ended in a high laugh which exposed his blackened teeth close up to David's face. David woke in a sweat and climbed immediately out of bed.

The four visits to patients which he had to make that morning seemed to pass by at a snail's pace. The last was to a wealthy merchant in Seckington who was recovering from shingles. Here he was delayed by the courtesy of the man's wife, who plied him with wine and sweetmeats and much conversation. At last he managed to escape.

He put Beauty into an easy gallop once he was clear of Seckington village. It was a bright breezy day and the air was pleasant in his face as he turned the horse off the main way into the lane which led to Chalfont Farm. Bernard Bistock was in the yard and came to greet him like an old friend.

"Good Day then, Doctor. 'Tis good of you to call, we did mention to the Reverend how concerned we be over Rachel. He said he would ask you to call by. Go along into the house, her Mother's there - she understands these things better than I. All I want is for Daughter to perk up and turn back into our lively maid again. Well, well - Mother will talk it over with you - I make no doubt. I must get on, time is money, as they say." Bistock backed away and vanished from sight within the barn doors, shouting to his sons as he went.

A moment or two later, David was in the kitchen with Jane Bistock, she had filled out a little since he had last seen her. She wore a grey gown, plain, with just a little lace at the neck. Her face held a calm quiet sweetness; he could see where much of Rachel's charm had come from. He realised suddenly how long it was since he had been here. Chalfont, so high up, near the moorland, had escaped the ugliness and danger of Plague. The family had helped all they could, carting supplies for the stricken villages from Wesperton. Allowing Rachel to take the enormous risk of helping him nurse those in the barn. This woman must have disliked that very much. She must have worried, every hour of every day. An anxiety to be borne bravely, silently, perhaps, in front of husband and sons. Probably with much secret suffering. None of it showed in the calm face before him. He found himself with a great respect for Mistress Bistock. He pulled himself up - realising that she was speaking to him.

"I'm glad you've come, Doctor - let us sit down." She took a chair at the table - her skirts spread about her - her hands resting in her lap. He took a chair opposite to her and waited for her to speak.

"May I speak freely, about our girl, I mean?" -

"Please do. Is Mistress Rachel in ill health?" She looked at him a moment, a little uncertain, then she began to speak.

"Rachel, you see - Rachel has always been a very determined headstrong girl. When the plague came, she nagged and nagged at her Father and me because she wanted to help. If she'd been older, we wouldn't have stood out against it so much, but she is only sixteen and our only daughter. In the end .... she wasn't sleeping - she was so wretched - we gave way. We knew you would give her every care you could. At the time .... you'll forgive me saying - it was little comfort to me, knowing she was in your care, I mean. It was so bad, so many dying - it seemed all would die. Still that's past and gone now. Then when you sent her home and we all knew that the plague was almost over - we were glad we'd let her go. She was so happy you see. She was tired - well naturally - but she was so full of joy. We could see

343

that she felt a pride in herself that she had done something worthwhile. It had made her grow up such a lot, she was singing at her work - well, she was like a maid in love. We wondered if she'd fallen in love - with one of the patients perhaps? But then everything began to change."

"How did it change?" David asked quietly.

"Well, first we heard that the Plague was over and the roads open again. Of course, we were all deeply thankful. But from that day - every day, every week that passed, Rachel became more and more upset. When young Mathew Painter married Ilsa from Wood Cottage, we were so glad, you know, like a new beginning for the villages after such bad times. But then Rachel burst out weeping. Since then it gets worse every day. And now Rachel's friend, Anne Barnes, is to be wed, well, our girl seems to be going to nothing. She doesn't eat her food - she doesn't sleep. I hear her in her room at night weeping, she just goes up on the moor for hours then, when she comes back, she is so pale. She scarcely speaks. It makes me afraid, Doctor - afraid of her going up there alone on the moors. We talked it over, Doctor, and we feel it's best if she goes to Bernard's brother. Away from here for a while." She paused, clasping her hands together and leaning across towards him.

"D'you know what I believe? I believe she fell deep in love with one of the patients. One who died - perhaps he died after she came home, or perhaps he was married and that's why she does not confide in us."

"I don't think he was married, Mistress Bistock, and I don't think he died. I think he was a fool, a blind fool - who should have had more sense." David Ainsley smiled at her, his eyes very blue and sparkling, as he rose to his feet.

"Do you think it's for the best - for her to go away?" Jane Bistock's voice was questioning.

"I would like to think that won't be necessary. Where is Mistress Rachel now?"

"Up on the top - up there." Jane Bistock pointed through the open window, up the track which led through the bracken to the open moor. "She went an hour ago - worries us so, Doctor, with her being so unhappy."

"Let me go and find her - perhaps, if I talk with her -

perhaps, we may even see her happy again soon, Mistress Bistock."

Up on the moor it was another world, a world of rocks and heather, high winds and gorse bushes. Small, fast running tumbling streams pelted down over the stones. Here was a hunting ground for the fox. A haunt for wild creatures under the vast sky, where sparrow hawks hovered, seeking their prey amongst the gorse and heather far below. It was years since David had been up here, not since when, as a child, he had played hide and seek with Elizabeth and his brother. From here he could look down on both villages. Higher and Lower Telso became clusters of roofs in a tapestry of fields. To the North he could see the Church of Seckington and the hamlet itself in it's woodland setting. Beyond was Wesperton Castle on it's high hill with the town spread-eagled below, clinging to the willow clad banks of the River Avon.

At the crown of the hill he paused. Here there was a circle of ancient upright stones. Reputed locally to be haunted, they were symbols of worship for a people lost hundreds of years back in history. Of Rachel there was no sign. He cupped his hands and called her name again and again. He heard no answering cry. It was no use to stand here; he chose a direction at random and went East towards where the moor swung in a gigantic half circle above Home Farm and Seckington Hall and on down, skirting Dumble and Rock Bottom. Suddenly he saw her, she was sitting in a small hollow dell, a rocky bluff at her back. But it was her attitude that caught and held his attention. Her knees were drawn up and her arms clasped about them. Her head was down, resting upon her knees, it was an attitude of pathetic dejection. He felt a rush of tenderness, then he moved very quietly over the hundred yards of rough slope that separated them. When he was close beside her and she had not moved, he was sure that she was unaware of his presence.

"Rachel." He spoke softly. Slowly she lifted her head, her face was pale and tear-stained, the wide honey-brown eyes dazed with surprise. The tumbled hair was lovely as ever, warm golden brown mixed and blown by the wind. Her eyes met his and held them but she did not speak. Again he said her name, "Rachel -

my Dear, I heard you were unwell - I came to see you - to see if I could help?"

Her eyes never wavered but they became wary, like some small animal fearing itself to be trapped. He saw that he must move slowly. He sat down beside her and took her two hands in his own, he felt a small shiver of response. So far so good. What step should he take next? Into the deep water, perhaps?

"Rachel, are you not going to speak to me? I thought us better friends than that. Well then, perhaps I must talk to you. The village is a happy place again now, Rachel - I can't have you up here every day - all alone - crying and lonely. There are happy times in the days to come. Our people are beginning again, Rachel - some are getting married. Your friend Anne Barnes has been called in Church." He felt the small hands try to wriggle free but he held them fast.

"What about you, Rachel - when are you going to marry the man who holds your heart in his hands?

"No one .... no one wants to marry me - no one holds my heart." She spoke so low that he had to strain to catch the words, her head turned away from him.

"How can you be so sure - perhaps he thinks you too young - or perhaps that he is too old."

"The man the man I thought ... Oh, it's no use."

"Look at me, Rachel - come on - look at me." He released one of her hands and, leaning close, put his hand under her chin and lifted it so that he could look into her face. What he saw shocked him, all the childishness was gone, the mouth was mobile and quivering, the nostrils a little flared, eyes were tight shut, long lashes sweeping onto the white cheeks. There was suffering in the lines at the corners of her eyes and in the blue shadows below them. He felt her quiver and shake at his touch and as he watched her, new tears pushed from beneath her lids and rolled down her cheeks to fall onto his hand. He put his arm around her back and pulled her very close.

"And what if you are wrong and this man loves you so much that he wants you for his own, as wife or sweetheart or mistress .... now this very day?" David's voice was low and held a tender note of teasing.

"Ainsleys .... Ainsleys don't marry with farmer's daughters, they marry women .... women like .... like Elizabeth."

He brought his mouth down upon hers, silencing the end of her sentence. She felt his embrace tighten and his hand move down until it cupped her breast. He felt her heart thump beneath his caress. Her eyes flew open, to find them locked by the blue ones which held a look she had despaired to see in them since the night he had taken her home to the Parsonage.

"Just in case you thought that I was treating you like a child, little Greensleeves" He kissed her again and drew back a little so that she lay in the cradle of his arm.

"There are things I want to say to you, Rachel - I have wanted to say them these many weeks, when you were singing in the barn, when little Mary died. But then I might have been infected with the pestilence myself. When I sent you home, it was because - I loved you - because I wanted you so much, *not* because I didn't want you at all. Do you understand that now?" He shook her a little within his arm.

"Yes." The long lashes were lowered, the mouth tremulous.

"It's hard to know how to woo a maid that is half a little girl - half a woman grown, Rachel." He took her hand again, stroking the fingers. "I like the little girl in the maid well enough, but when a man looks for a wife, he looks for more than a girl with sweet ways. He wants a woman to share his bed and bear his children. A lover - a mistress and a wife all within the same woman. Will you be all that to me, Rachel?" Again she did not answer and more tears began to fall.

"There seems little hope, if all I can do is make you weep, little Lass."

"'Tis only that I'm so happy, I have missed you so much - I thought you didn't want me. It has been so long."

"You haven't answered my question. Are you to be my wife, Rachel? A man does not like to be kept waiting." His eyes twinkled a little.

Suddenly he saw a glimpse of the old independent Rachel, she looked him full in the face, tears and laughter mingling in her bright eyes.

"Perhaps if you were to kiss me again, - t'would help me to make up my mind." He reached for her and clasped her so close that it took her breath.

"For that, mistress, I'll kiss you until you cry for mercy!" It was a long time before either of them spoke again. At last he released her.

"I think we should make way down to the farm and let your Mother know that the Doctor has managed to find a cure for her ailing daughter," David said as he rose to his feet. Rachel brushed the moss and grass from her skirts and gave him a saucy smile.

"Of course, 'tis likely I may have a relapse unless we can be married very soon."

"In that case, we both sit astride my mare and go to the Parson as soon as we have your parents' blessing. He's been chivvying me for weeks lest I let you slip through my fingers." David laughed as he spoke. A look of surprise crossed Rachel's face.

"Well, I always did think Reverend Andrew Mallard was a most discerning man." She fluttered her lashes at David and put her small hand into his as she spoke.

There was no mistaking the pleasure and pride their news brought to Bernard and Jane Bistock, a glass of wine was drunk in the Chalfont parlour before the young folk set off for the Parsonage.

An hour later they rode on Beauty's back across the field track down towards Lower Telso Parsonage. David took Rachel up in front of him and rode with his arm close about her waist. She snuggled back to be near him and her hair blew against his lips and nostrils. It smelt of heather and the lavender water she used. Life, he felt, was going to be very good from now on.

'Tis a nice way to travel, Sir," she teased him.

"That is why I urge the mare so little - that the journey may be as much prolonged as possible."

"The village will talk of nothing else if we are seen, David." His name came very shy off her tongue.

"Then their wagging tongues will no doubt leave someone else alone," he replied. Then reining Beauty to a halt, he turned Rachel about and planted a laughing kiss full upon her lips.

"Oh, David - Oh, David," she whispered.

In the garden of Wood Cottage old Albert Dale came out of

the privy with the baby Edward in his arms. He had just been to hold the child out on the small wooden seat, to oblige Eliza. The old eyes, still keen and sharp, saw the riders coming across the field. The dark hat of the man and the billowing blue stuff of the woman's dress caught his attention. The old man chuckled to the child in his arms, "Danged if it 'ent another pair of they at it. Never did see the like - back end o' the year. 'Tis supposed to be Springtime when young wenches gets bedded. Seems they'm in such a bustin' hurry as they can't wait. Still, all them babbies 'll have summer days waiting when they'm getting born; now, who be they two, I wonders?". His eyes strained to see across the fields. "When they be past Up Tops stile I reckon us'll see they then. By God - By Golly - 'tis Doctor's mare - Doctor himself and, if that lass b'aint young Missy Rachel Bistock, I'll eat this 'ere cap, young Edward. By Gum - us must tell our Eliza this tit bit, an Ainsley with a farmer's daughter - that be summat, that be. This plague have driven everybody clean barmy, I reckons .... Eliza! Eliza! Are you goin' deaf, woman?" His voice raised to a shout as he trundled along the path, rolling from side to side on the uneven bricks. Little Edward jerking to and fro in his arms.

"Mind that child, you old fool! You'll drop him. Give 'im here and quit yer silly yelling. I can't hear a word you says, you stupid old goat!" Eliza snatched the child from his arms. Albert thrust his wrinkled old face up to hers.

"Wot I says was - Doctor Ainsley be up along Big Fields on that mare o' his, and he's got young Rachel Bistock in front of the saddle, and they'm kissing for all to see!"

"Best thing that cud happen!" snapped Eliza crushingly as she hugged Edward to her.

"Here take him, Grandad! I best pop across Wychwood and tell Betsy."

"Women!" said Albert, spitting in expert fashion across the cabbage patch. "Women allus gets last word."